Praise for Cat

Night Bird Calling

"Gripping. . . . Gohlke creates a cast readers will love, and the strong themes of the bonds of family forged outside one's kin resonate."

PUBLISHERS WEEKLY

"*Night Bird Calling* interlaces themes of redemption, friendship, and grace, and its depiction of a small southern town is reminiscent of writings by Lisa Wingate."

BOOKLIST

"Engrossing. . . . A sumptuous, textured ode to small-town relationships."

FOREWORD REVIEWS

"In *Night Bird Calling*, Cathy Gohlke mines the national spirit on the cusp of WWII and successfully illuminates how communal change can manifest through unconditional love."

SARAH McCOY, *New York Times, USA Today,* and internationally bestselling author of *Marilla of Green Gables*

"With her signature gift for delving into topics and truths as relevant to us today as they are to the characters found within these pages, Cathy Gohlke delivers a poignant story rich with vibrant characters, woven with spiritual depth, and bound together by hope."

AMANDA BARRATT, author of *The White Rose Resists* and *My Dearest Dietrich*

"*Night Bird Calling* inspired a whole range of emotions. It made me smile, then cry. I became angry at the villains, then rejoiced because of the bravery of the characters. I kept turning pages because I had to know what would happen next. One of the best books I've read all year!"

VANESSA MILLER PIERCE, bestselling author of the Loving You series

"*Night Bird Calling* will break your heart before it fills it up again with hope. Lilliana has endured what no person ever should—abuse in the name of religion. . . . I applaud Gohlke for vulnerably sharing this story of messy redemption. Read Lilliana's story, but then please share it with someone who is also desperate for the freedom Christ offers."

LUCINDA SECREST McDOWELL, author of *Soul Strong* and *Life-Giving Choices*

"*Night Bird Calling* is a spellbinding story about the evils of racism and abuse but also the transformative power of forgiveness. With her signature style of elegance and grace, Cathy Gohlke has created another beautiful, poignant novel that stirred something deep within me. This is a gift for all those who love to read redemptive fiction."

MELANIE DOBSON, award-winning author of *The Curator's Daughter* and *Memories of Glass*

"Sight and sound, feeling and scent permeate *Night Bird Calling*, Cathy Gohlke's sensate and gripping new release. Deft with description and tact, Gohlke handles unfortunately timeless issues sensitively and with hope."

JANE RUBIETTA, speaker and author of *The Forgotten Life of Evelyn Lewis* and *Brilliance: Finding Light in Dark Places*

"Cathy Gohlke tells a stirring story that touches on challenging life events—abuse, racial tensions, and injustice—through the eyes of a woman seeking sanctuary and a precocious preteen trying to make sense of life events beyond her maturity. Beautifully written, this novel is a powerful, poignant, and sensitive portrayal of imperfect people struggling through their frailties and learning how choosing grace, mercy, and love can heal many wounds."

MICHELLE ULE, author of *Mrs. Oswald Chambers: The Woman behind the World's Bestselling Devotional*

The Medallion

"A riveting read from cover to cover, *The Medallion* is one of those extraordinary novels that will linger in the mind and memory long after the book itself is finished."

MIDWEST BOOK REVIEWS

"This is a thought-provoking novel of courage, survival, and unselfish assistance during the Holocaust."

HISTORICAL NOVEL SOCIETY

"Cathy Gohlke skillfully weaves true stories of heroism and sacrifice into her novel to create a realistic portrayal of Poland during WWII. *The Medallion* is a stunning story of impossible choices and the enduring power of faith and love."

LYNN AUSTIN, author of *If I Were You*

"A master storyteller, Cathy Gohlke has created unforgettable characters in unthinkable circumstances. This story completely undid me, then stitched me back together with hope. A novel that has grabbed my heart—and won't let go—for what I'm sure will be a very long time."

HEIDI CHIAVAROLI, Carol Award–winning author of *The Hidden Side*

"*The Medallion* is a beautifully written story with a riveting plot, realistic characters, and moving themes of sacrificial love, redemption, and forgiveness. Highly recommended for readers who are willing to stay up late, because they won't be able to put this book down!"

CARRIE TURANSKY, award-winning author of *No Ocean Too Wide* and *Across the Blue*

Until We Find Home

"Gohlke's powerful historical novel features a suspenseful and heart-wrenching plot and unforgettable characters."

LIBRARY JOURNAL, starred review

"Gohlke's latest takes place in England's lush Lake District during the early days of World War II. Readers will likely smile at appearances from various literary icons, such as Beatrix Potter and C. S. Lewis, among others. The story is well researched and well written."

ROMANTIC TIMES

"Splendid at every turn! *Until We Find Home* is a lushly penned novel about a courageous young woman whose definition of love—and trust—is challenged in every way. A must for fans of WWII and British front history. Not to be missed!"

TAMERA ALEXANDER, *USA Today* bestselling author of *To Whisper Her Name* and *A Note Yet Unsung*

"*Until We Find Home* is a deeply moving war story. . . . Gohlke's well-developed characters, vivid descriptions, and lush setting details immerse readers into the story. All the way to the very last page, readers will be rooting for the unlikely family forged through the hardships of war."

JODY HEDLUND, Christy Award–winning author of *Luther and Katharina*

Secrets She Kept

"Cathy Gohlke's *Secrets She Kept* is a page-turner with great pacing and style. She's a terrific writer."

FRANCINE RIVERS, *New York Times* bestselling author

"This well-researched epic depicts life under the Nazi regime with passionate attention. While the Sterling family story serves as a warning about digging into the past, it is also a touching example of the healing power of forgiveness and the rejuvenating power of faith."

"Gohlke takes the reader on a compelling journey, complete with mystery and drama. She weaves in real stories from Ravensbrück, making this drama one that will be difficult to forget. It is well researched, and the multilayered characters demonstrate the power of love and sacrifice."

"Gripping . . . emotional . . . masterfully told, this is an unforgettable tale of finding family, faith, and love."

Saving Amelie

"Moving. . . . At times both emotional and suspenseful, this is a fantastic novel for those who love both historical fiction and human-interest stories."

"In this compelling and tense novel, Gohlke tells a haunting story of the courageous few who worked tirelessly and at great risk to themselves to save people they did not know. . . . Reminiscent of Tatiana de Rosnay's stirring stories of human compassion and hope, this should appeal to fans of both authors as well as to historical fiction readers."

"Definitely worth the read. Cathy Gohlke is a very talented author, and . . . I recommend *Saving Amelie* for everyone who likes World War II . . . fiction with inspirational tones."

FRESH FICTION

A Hundred Crickets Singing

Also by Cathy Gohlke

a

Hundred Crickets Singing

CATHY GOHLKE

Tyndale House Publishers
Carol Stream, Illinois

Visit Tyndale online at tyndale.com.

Visit Cathy Gohlke's website at cathygohlke.com.

Tyndale and Tyndale's quill logo are registered trademarks of Tyndale House Ministries.

A Hundred Crickets Singing

Edited by Sarah Mason Rische

Designed by Lindsey Bergsma

Published in association with the literary agency of Natasha Kern Literary Agency, Inc., P.O. Box 1069, White Salmon, WA 98672.

Scripture quotations are taken from the *Holy Bible*, King James Version.

A Hundred Crickets Singing is a work of fiction. Where real people, events, establishments, organizations, or locales appear, they are used fictitiously. All other elements of the novel are drawn from the author's imagination.

For information about special discounts for bulk purchases, please contact Tyndale House Publishers at csresponse@tyndale.com, or call 1-855-277-9400.

Library of Congress Cataloging-in-Publication Data

A catalog record for this book is available from the Library of Congress.

ISBN 978-1-4964-5348-8 (HC)
ISBN 978-1-4964-5349-5 (SC)

Printed in the United States of America

28	27	26	25	24	23	22
7	6	5	4	3	2	1

For Dan Lounsbury
Amazing brother, encourager, lifelong friend and ally,
lover of words, stories, adventures and cohort in their discovery
With love and thanks for everything

Acknowledgments

No book is created in a vacuum, certainly not one that encompasses the voices of different eras, generations, and races. Definitely not this book.

I am gratefully indebted to my brother, Dan Lounsbury, and to family members from earlier generations for their research and provision of Goforth family history, especially the archives of Samuel Smith Goforth, who inspired parts of the story of Elliott Belvidere, including his loyalty to the Constitution, service in the NC militia, trial before Jefferson Davis for treason and the unusual provisions made by Major Sloane, who saved his life through noncombatant service in the Confederacy.

Thank you to my literary agent and dear friend, Natasha Kern, for championing this book and for walking with me through the challenges it presented in our current national discussions on race.

Thank you, Stephanie Broene and Sarah Rische, gifted editors, for your insightful questions and edits that have so improved this book; Lindsey Bergsma, for this tremendous book cover; Andrea Garcia, for marketing; Katie Dodillet, for publicity; and to all my publishing team at Tyndale House Publishers. You are the best team an author could imagine, and I am so grateful for all you have done in helping to bring this book to life and to readers.

Thank you, Tina-Marie Cornelius, friend and correspondent, for the title of this book. In a wonderful letter early in our correspondence you mentioned, in relation to something else entirely, "a choir of a hundred crickets singing." I knew right away that was the perfect title for this book.

Thank you, Robert Whitlow, inspiring author and attorney-at-law, for generously helping me understand the moral questions, legalities, and ramifications of deeds destroyed, and for brainstorming possibilities to escape "deep legal waters" in this work of fiction. I'm so grateful. Any mistakes are mine.

Thank you, Elisabeth Gardiner, precious daughter, for reading an early version of this manuscript and for sharing your insights. I love sharing reading/writing ventures with you.

Thank you, Joe Garofalo, longtime neighbor and family friend, for teaching me how to make red gravy and multiple forms of pasta, the recipe passed through generations of your Rossetti and Garofalo families. Any mistakes in my story's explanation of this art are mine.

Thank you, dear family, friends, and readers, for your enthusiasm, encouragement, and prayers for the writing of this book and its journey into the world. I pray that the Lord will bless our joint efforts to bring glory to Him and hope and healing to those in need.

Thank you, Uncle Wilbur Goforth, for reminding me that our service to our Lord is daily, wherever we are, whatever we're doing. When torn between two career paths for the second half of my life's journey, you reminded me that a sure way to know I am working in the will of God is to ask, "Do I have joy? Is this yoke easy? Is this burden light?" The answer is still yes—writing gives me great joy, the weight of this yoke is easy, and this burden shines as light in my heart.

Beyond all measure I thank my heavenly Father and Lord Jesus Christ for gifts of hope, life, love, family, this season of writing, and for eternal unmerited salvation. In Your daily presence is fullness of joy.

May this book serve as a bridge to understanding the past, as an instrument of peace in the present, and as hope for future transformation of hearts in our world. May it point only to You, heavenly Father, for You are the hope we crave, and You are the healing and salvation we all so desperately need.

Prologue

A thousand cannon burst at once and lightning split the sky,
exploding gnarled branches of Garden's Gate's two-hundred-year-
old oak, planted before the Revolution was a glint in Patriots' eyes.
Surely that storm was God speaking—shouting judgment—across
No Creek and the world in a tornado of fire and wind and rain.

By His mercy, sheets of pelting rain quenched the flames that
shot up in the tree before the house caught fire. But it never kept
that oak from crashing through the attic roof to slam open a door
into a world none of us knew, one that would forever change
our lives and what we'd long believed true about No Creek, the
Belvideres, and ourselves. I reckon a violent, sudden storm can
do that—rattle old bones and raise ghosts from the dead.

FROM THE DIARY OF CELIA PERCY
NO CREEK, NORTH CAROLINA

Chapter One

MARCH 1944
NO CREEK, NORTH CAROLINA

Despite the raging midnight storm soaking her to the skin, fourteen-year-old Celia Percy helped Chester, her eleven-year-old brother, drag a heavy tarp from the barn, through the house, and up the attic stairs, doing their best to shield nearly two hundred years of Belvidere ghosts and treasures from pelting ice and rain.

But it wasn't until the stark light of day that the attic gave up its secrets. Even then, in the streaming late-winter sun, Celia wasn't sure she could believe her eyes.

"It's a room—a whole room under the eaves been sealed off somehow." She whistled, gooseflesh creeping up her pink arms.

"You reckon Miz Hyacinth ever knew about this place? Or Miss Lill?" Chester, brown eyes wide, pulled the rain-soaked tarp from some small and ancient chests in the middle of the narrow room, barely twelve by three feet, set against the stone chimney.

"Never said—at least not to me. Don't know how they could have known. There's no door." Celia could hardly believe such a mystery room existed. They'd been living at Garden's Gate with Miss Lill for over three years and never heard of such a thing.

"Look here—there's a door. Been sealed off, is all." Chester, with skinny, winter-pale arms, pulled aside a rotted ceiling-to-floor drapery to reveal a door in the wall. "Locked." He jiggled the knob. "Been plastered over from the other side."

"Why would anybody do that?" Celia couldn't fathom.

Chester raised his eyebrows, pushing dark-brown hair from his forehead. "It's a mystery."

Celia caught her breath, thrilled to her core. "Sure enough."

"Let's see what's in those trunks."

There was nothing Celia wanted more than to rummage through those trunks, but it was up to her to see that she and Chester got to school on time. *Mama'll have my head if she learns we skipped—even for this.* "After school. We have to wait till after school."

"We can't leave with this hole in the roof."

"Doesn't look like rain today. Let's cover this stuff up best we can. We'll need Olney Tate to help with the roof anyway. I'll leave word with Pearl Mae at the store, ask him to stop by after school."

"But, Celia—"

"Don't 'but Celia' me. You know that's what Mama'd say. I don't want Pearl phoning her up tellin' tales, worrying her. Mama's got enough on her plate, what with Daddy in the hospital all banged up. So be sure to wear your jacket this morning. Pearl Mae will be watching the bus stop from the store and report every word to her mama and ours. Besides, no point catching your death."

Chester grimaced. "I guess."

"If Mama thinks we're not doing right, she'll get the next train out of Norfolk, and then where will Daddy be?"

Their mama had feared leaving them alone, what with Miss Lill in England and Ida Mae away at her sister's in New York. But their daddy's only chance of getting his job back in the shipyard was if he made a clean recovery.

"He needs you, Mama, he does," Celia had assured her. "We'll be all right. What can go wrong in a week or two?"

Celia had every intention of walking the straight and narrow while her mama and Miss Lill were away. *Can I help it if trouble trails me?* It was not a new lament.

. . .

Nobody'd expected such a storm in the middle of March—not snow, but freezing rain in torrents and wind to rival twisters.

"Mmm, mmm. Ides of March, that's what they call it," Olney Tate, longtime handyman for Garden's Gate and anyone else who needed him, mused when he stopped by after Celia and Chester had returned from school. "Winter's last hurrah before the spring thaw. Usually means snow in these hills."

"Snow would have been better," Chester conceded.

"Not that much snow." Olney shook his head.

"It was the lightning split the tree in two. We saw it out the back kitchen window, plain as day. Like an act of God." Celia thrilled to the drama of it all.

"Good thing you and Chester hadn't gone upstairs to bed. A tree that size, you never know—could have gone through to the second floor."

Celia shuddered, not wanting to think on that. "We can't leave this hole in the roof."

"Or that tree in the attic," Chester worried.

"Reckon not," Olney sighed, pushing his billed cap back on his head. "Let's take a look at that attic, see what needs doing." He climbed the stairs and walked the length of the room, a good portion of which was cut off by the giant tree. Turning from side to side, he took its measure. "Let me talk with the brothers down to Saints Delight. We'll get two or three come up here and pull those limbs out, cut up that trunk, get a tarp on the roof till I can mend it. What's left in the yard can wait a day or so. You two stay out of this mess till we get things secure. Don't want any limbs fallin' and crackin' your skulls."

"But we were gonna—" Chester began but Celia elbowed him. "Ow! What'd you do that for?"

Celia drew in a sharp breath. *Little brothers are impossible.*

"You were gonna what?" Olney asked, fixing his best eye on Chester.

"Nothing," Celia intervened, stepping between Olney and Chester.

"Celia Percy." Olney's graying brows rose. "Don't you be messin' with me. Your ears turn pink when you don't tell straight, you know that."

Celia grimaced. "We just want to investigate."

"Investigate what?" Olney looked as if he didn't trust either of the two before him.

"The room!" Chester piped up, unable to keep quiet. "There's a secret room—trunks and everything. Come see!"

Now that the cat was out of the bag, Celia couldn't contain herself. She worked with Chester, pulling aside the heavy tarp to reveal the narrow hallway down the far end of the attic, its front wall made to look like the end of the room.

"Well, I never," Olney wondered aloud, reverence in his whisper.

"No telling how long this has been here—built with the house, I guess." Celia'd been wondering, thinking on it all day. "And these old trunks—we haven't even looked in them yet. Why would all this stuff be here? Why would they seal it off so nobody'd see?"

"Just that reason. So nobody'd see, nobody'd know. I swan. I never really believed my daddy or his, God rest their souls." Olney shook his head, running his hand down the grayed stubble on his brown chin. "Been hidden . . . must be more'n eighty years. I vowed it couldn't be so, knowing old man Belvidere ran the Klan here. What a torn-apart family."

"What couldn't be so?" Chester pushed.

"What you're lookin' at is a hidey-hole—a room in a safe house, a place where those on the run could hide till it was safe to move on."

"Run from what? Safe from what?" Chester demanded, but Celia felt the knowing grow.

"Slavery." Olney nearly spat the word. "Slavery, and slave catchers."

Chapter Two

NO CREEK, NORTH CAROLINA

The stories that Rosalee told me after her escape from Millpond—
a slave-owning farm not three miles east—liked to curdle my blood.
Brutal whippings across her back with a cat-o'-nine-tails from the time
she was thirteen, iron contraptions beaten into spiked collars forced on
her mother, and metal bits shoved into the mouth as punishment for
sassing—crueler by far than any we'd force upon an unbroken horse.

I did not doubt the veracity of her tales. Her back displayed a criss-
cross of fresh welts and old scars—a vile, wicked testimony. The sight
of those scars on so slight a girl, a girl younger than my nineteen years,
nearly made me vomit. How weak a woman I'd become. I'd never been
beaten, never so much as threatened, white as I was, and yet I near
fainted.

I recorded Rosalee's every word in my diary as Mother carefully
washed and dressed her back, peeling shreds of her torn dress from
bloodied wounds cut deep into her flesh.

"One day soon, Minnie," Mother vowed, her eyes filled with tears she wouldn't shed, "it will be your turn to dress the wounds and your daughter's turn to record the stories, unless our government frees these dear people." She swallowed painfully. Even in the dark of the attic and with the pale light of one candle, I saw her grimace—something more than the heartbreak she nursed before her. She'd been weary for days, and I'd seen her growing weaker with the passing of each sun.

Not many runaways passed through our house, and I didn't have a daughter, wasn't even married, but Mother's hope for our Union was not idle. News from Washington City—reports of the deep divisions between our states over the issues of slavery and territory and the rights of states to pursue their own destiny—poured through our small foot-hills town of No Creek, isolated as we believed ourselves to be.

North Carolina had already voted to stand with the Union, and we in Wilkes County were determined to remain steadfast, at least many of us. But with South Carolina and now Virginia, our neighbor north, seceding two days past, what choice did we have?

At least that's what Grayson, my younger brother, insisted. Father and Elliott, the oldest of my siblings, were determined that we remain loyal to the Constitution, insisting that secession was not an option for the old North State. At any rate it was no option in Belvidere Hall. But I wondered at every turn, *How can we fight this tide?*

"No battle is lost until it's over," Mother constantly reminded me. "Our business is to do what we need to do, what God has equipped us for, what He expects of us."

"To stand for those oppressed, to clothe the naked and feed the hungry, to take in the foreigner . . ." I quoted themes from Scripture I'd learned at Mother's knee, ones Father read each morning from the Bible as our reason for being, our cause for wealth and stature within the community—to give home and succor to those in need.

In early days, Belvidere Hall had hidden and helped runaway inden-tured servants who'd been severely mistreated or patriots who'd escaped the king's prison guards. In more recent years, that meant slaves escaped from the coffle marches south or those like Rosalee and her baby who'd run from cruel owners . . . her baby sired by her former master's raping, so sickly as likely not to live.

The runaways who came through our home we hid in our barn loft or in the attic safe room until they could run or be moved to the next safe house. Most were young men, strong and strapping, who'd been bred and fed for hard labor in their masters' fields. Knowledgeable about the boundaries of their owners' land and resourceful enough to make their way, they found opportunity to slip out under cover of darkness.

But it was the few runaway women and children who stole my heart. Determined women, but rarely strong enough for the grueling trek, and children unable to keep up, often going without food and with little water for days, owners and slave hunters and pattyrollers at their back. Babies couldn't be made to keep quiet, unless they'd been fed a bit of laudanum, which wore off eventually. Sometimes their mothers were so weary they could not raise needed milk and that set the little ones to howling, which in turn meant discovery—beatings or maiming or death for all.

But freedom—the very hope of it—was everything, and those who ran vowed they'd run or die trying. Some did both.

. . .

Three days after Rosalee arrived, she fell ill with fever; we buried her baby in our back orchard. Ten days later, Father found means to smuggle her to Petersburg in a false-bottom wagon, then send her north by train—weak, but with fever subsided and her wounds sufficiently healed to wear clothing. Though risky, we garbed her in widow's weeds with a black veil so long and thick you couldn't see her face, and black gloves and stockings to cover every inch of her coffee-colored skin. Rosalee rode first class with my brother Elliott as his aged aunt, grieving her husband. It wasn't too much for Rosalee to pretend age and grief; she'd borne enough in her lifetime for a woman three times her age. Elliott said all she need do was remember. Memory bent her back but steeled her will.

When Elliott returned, he said he'd seen her cross into New York and connect with those who would aid her. He knew she would one day soon make her way across the border and shake the Lion's paw, free from slavery under Canada's British rule. It was a time of quiet rejoicing in our house, even as Elliott's wife, sickly from the start of her third pregnancy and with no living children, entered her confinement.

Less than two weeks later Mother died, further weakened from her bout with scarlet fever—scarlet fever, Grayson swore, that had come from Rosalee and her dead baby.

• • •

Though Grayson was only fifteen and the youngest among us, he carried on as if he were master of Belvidere Hall. I didn't know how much more of his tirade Father could take, especially with Mother barely cold in her grave.

"You killed her—as good as pushed a knife in her breast—both of you!" Nearly as tall as Father, Grayson bellowed louder. "She'd never have been infected if you hadn't taken in that slave and her baby. And for what? Breaking the law—that's what you're doing—and you dragged Mother into it. You're the devil incarnate, both of you!" he all but spat at Father and Elliott.

Father paled at the accusation, as if the blow were physical. I steadied him, horrified and frightened all at once.

"Enough, Grayson! Father had nothing to do with taking in Rosalee and her baby. It was Mother's decision. You know that. You know she would make the same decision again." Elliott, Father's firstborn and strongest advocate, placed a firm hand on Grayson's shoulder. "If anything, Mother's example—"

"In breaking the law—egged on by you and Father. You've even got Minnie involved, teaching slaves to read! You want to see our sister swing from a tree? You'll all hang sooner or later. You know that, don't you? Once we join Virginia and—"

"Enough, Grayson." Father spoke quietly.

"I won't be part of it anymore, I tell you. You'll all be sorry when North Carolina secedes, when the noose tightens, when you're found out. What will you do then?" Grayson jerked from Elliott's grasp, tearing from the room.

"Grayson!" Horrified at such anger, such disrespect, I meant to go after him.

"Let him go, Minnie," Father sighed.

"But, Father, he's—"

"He's a hothead, and bound to cause trouble, to shoot off his mouth." Elliott slapped his hand against his thigh.

"He's hurting, grieving over your mother's death, like the rest of us." Father still spoke quietly, still deathly pale.

But I knew my brother's fury wasn't only over Mother's death.

Grayson was furious that Father had allowed Obadiah, a Negro, to help carry Mother's coffin to the grave site, included as a pallbearer for the family. But that was just it: Obadiah *was* family—had been like a brother to us, a son to Mother and Father, for as long as I could remember. Obadiah, older than Elliott by less than a year, grew up with him. He genuinely loved Mother and always treated her with the greatest of respect, was always there to help her accomplish everything she wished. The same could not be said of Grayson. From childhood he was spoiled, the last of Mother's babies that lived past a year.

Beyond doting on her children, Mother's strongest desire was to help those in bondage escape the shackles placed on them—those that bound their wrists and feet, and those that bound their hearts and minds. All my life, I stood in awe of her . . . love made manifest.

From the time I turned ten it was my job to record the names of those who passed through our home and to teach those who stayed awhile to read, to count money, to speak with the best English they had time to learn so they could get on in the North. I loved doing those things. To see the light in a man or woman's eyes, to see the brightness that reading brought a child . . . It was a gift.

Elliott helped those who could travel on to the next stop, and Father supplied them with safe haven, coin and food, better clothes and shoes. Obadiah and our house slaves were as much employed in supplying those needs—sewing, cobbling, laundry, cooking, teaching a trade— whatever it took to help those passing through prepare for their new lives.

Mother had always coddled Grayson, letting him run and play while the rest of us worked—spoiling him, yes, but with greater purpose.

Mother and Father knew that the only way to keep the attic room secret and maintain our safe house was to keep up the semblance of a wealthy Southern home, a home that owned slaves and participated in and supported the community. Grayson was so much younger and such a talker that things were often kept from him for the sake of those we helped. Did he feel excluded, pushed aside? Our house was filled with secrets, and secrets come with a cost.

Father said that's why he hadn't freed our twenty-five slaves and why he'd never sell one—we were a large family intent on helping those in need. I never heard complaint, but I wondered how our slaves felt about that decision being made for them.

Father trusted Elliott to free our slaves after his death if the government didn't do it before. He thought, more likely, that slavery would die a natural death, left on its own. Until then, he intended we prepare them to step into that new world, to own and work land he meant to settle on those who stayed, and to help us get the others north to freedom.

I understood Father's reasoning but believed he should free our people now, not risk waiting longer. With war on our threshold, anything could happen. The door to choosing their freedom might close forever should the Confederacy prevail.

Little did my voice matter in our house.

Chapter Three

Celia didn't want to wait to explore the attic but knew she had no choice, at least not for the moment. Olney'd promised to return within the hour, to get the worst of the tree out before dark.

True to his word, Olney brought two men from Saints Delight Church, Deacon Barlow and his oldest son, Jay, all three carrying axes. Chester made a fourth. Together they chopped and hefted and pushed until the top of the tree no longer rested on the roof or in the attic. Celia pulled out long, skinny pine branches, handing them up to Jay, who'd climbed to the roof to throw them out.

Pulling out those limbs, working with Jay, reminded Celia of Marshall, Olney's nephew, who'd helped to restore Garden's Gate a few years before. But Marshall couldn't stay. A colored teenager with ambitions to better himself, maybe even study to be a doctor, found no place in No Creek at the time. The Klan saw to that.

Celia didn't miss Marshall for the hard work he could do. She missed his friendship. But friendships between young colored men and white girls were forbidden in No Creek—a thing Marshall had nearly lost his

13

life learning. Now Marshall, like so many young men Celia knew who'd gone to war, was stationed far away. She only hoped that one day he'd return, that he'd be able to return.

They secured the tree just as the sun fell behind the mountain.

"Let's get these tarps tacked in place for the night, keep out what we can till I get some lumber ordered for these rafters, see what we can do about patchin' that roof." Olney scratched his head. "Miz Lill—Miz Willard—might want to replace the whole thing while we're at it—'bout time, anyhow. Tomorrow I'll come back, take some measurements, and see what Pearl Mae can order on credit before her mama gets home."

"Thank you all for doin' this, Olney, Deacon Barlow, Jay. I know Miss Lill will make it right. I'd no idea what or how to do." Celia meant it.

"You two did fine haulin' in that tarp. Best you could do in the middle of the storm. Keep your front room fire goin' tonight. There's gonna be a draft through the house, but you're safe enough."

"We can go in that room now, can't we?" Chester wiped the sweat from his brow.

Celia frowned. She'd had no intention of asking permission of Olney or anybody else and every intention to explore the minute the men cleared out.

Olney looked at Celia. "I don't suppose it's worth my breath to say otherwise. It's safe enough now, I reckon, but those trunks and whatnot belong to Miz Willard. You ought to let her go through them first. She's the last of the Belvideres, so whatever there is and what's done with it is up to her. Y'all keep that in mind."

He looked over at Deacon Barlow and his son. "Deacon, reckon you and Jay can keep this room under your hat for now? There's reason I'd like to talk it over with Miz Willard before folks get wind."

Deacon Barlow nodded. "I understand that good reason, Brother Tate. You have our word."

Jay, wide-eyed, nodded.

Olney looked at Celia and Chester, brows raised.

"Yes, sir," Chester vowed.

Celia smiled. If he thought she'd agreed, well, that was on him.

. . .

The men hadn't been gone two minutes before Celia raced back up the attic stairs, a screwdriver in one hand and a flashlight in the other. "Bring that crowbar!" she called to Chester.

"Celia! You heard what Olney said. We ought—"

"I never agreed not to look!" Celia flicked on her flashlight and gingerly climbed over the broken wall, careful not to tear her dungarees. Her mama'd not stand for that.

"This place is creepy in the dark," Chester whispered, crowbar in hand, not three feet behind.

"Dark enough to raise ghosts," Celia quipped, deliciously scared. "Come help me with the lock on this trunk. Hold the flashlight. I'll try the screwdriver."

Chester frowned. "I don't relish explainin' to Olney that we busted locks."

"I'm not trying to bust them, but they're not Olney's trunks," Celia retorted.

"So they're ours?"

"Just hold the flashlight, will you?" Celia wiggled the screwdriver in the keyhole. Nothing happened.

"Lift the latch on that end," Chester ordered. "Maybe it's not really locked."

Celia raised the other latch, but the lid didn't budge. She pried the middle of the lid, just above the keyhole, until the wood gave way.

Chester lifted the lid.

"Whoa! What's all this?"

"Looks like old clothes and papers and stuff. From what Olney said I thought there'd be slave shackles or something," Chester lamented.

Celia gave her brother a withering look. "They'd have gotten rid of all that before they ran away. Nobody could run in shackles. Anyway, I don't think they used those all the time."

"How do you know?"

"I don't. Let's just see what this is." She pulled yellowed muslin from the top layer. Beneath was a wealth of black bombazine fabric—yards and yards of gathered bombazine skirt sewn to a bodice with a line of tiny buttons and edged in black tatted trim. "Wow." Celia could hardly form the word. "It's clothes from the war period—the War between the States, I'm sure. This is a mourning dress, and a veil—like the ones women wore when they had war dead."

"A dress. It's just a dress." Chester moaned. "What else?" He pulled aside what looked like petticoats and things ladies wore underneath.

"Books. More books—look! There's two piles of books here almost alike—looks like *Les Misérables* divided up into shorter books."

"Why wouldn't they have kept these in the library downstairs?"

Thumbing through the pages, Celia didn't know the answer. Bookplates in the front all bore the same name: *Minerva Belvidere*. She checked the copyright dates. "They're from before the war. *Uncle Tom's Cabin*, 1852. Here's a newspaper, *The Liberator*, 1854. *North Star*, *Freedom's Journal*." Chills inched up her spine. She sat back on her heels. "It's all . . ."

"All what?" Chester wanted to know.

"Abolitionist stuff—writings from the North about freeing slaves. Which makes no sense." Celia pondered. "Mama said that old Mr. Belvidere was head of the Klan here, that his family owned slaves before the war. They even owned the Tate family once upon a time."

"Nobody owns Olney Tate," Chester argued with finality.

"His ancestors. I don't get it. What's this room here for if they owned slaves?"

"Maybe they kept them prisoner up here," Chester whispered.

"That's not what Olney said. He called this a safe house. I read about that in one of Miz Hyacinth's books. Said it was part of an Underground Railroad—escape routes for runaway slaves."

"My teacher said that whole thing's made up, that nobody in the South would do such a thing—hide slaves and help them run away from their masters. She said it wasn't Christian." Chester crossed his arms.

"Shows what she knows. Let's see what else is here."

They pried open the lids of the other two trunks. One held ledgers listing what looked like everything the Belvideres had ever owned or bought, right down to silver teaspoons and homespun for slave clothes, and deeds to what looked to be the lands and boundaries of Garden's Gate, only it wasn't called Garden's Gate. "Belvidere Hall," Celia read.

"That's what Miz Hyacinth said it used to be called," Chester remembered.

They spent an hour combing the contents of all the chests and trunks. The most exciting finds were old coins, Confederate scrip, and a saber with a note about some battle in the Revolutionary War.

"Guess that's it. History stuff," Chester pronounced. "Reckon it'll mean something to Miss Lill."

"Reckon it will." Celia sat back, still excited and intrigued, but a tad disappointed.

. . .

Celia lay in bed that night, wishing Miss Lill was home to Garden's Gate, wishing she could ask the hundred and one questions running through her mind.

But Miss Lill, recently turned Mrs. Willard—owner of Garden's Gate since her great-aunt, Hyacinth Belvidere, had passed—was away in England, looking after her injured husband, having left the estate in the Percy family's care. The Reverend Jesse Willard had been gone into service as a chaplain major a good two years when he received his first leave home from the war—long enough to get down on one knee and place a ring on Miss Lill's finger. They wed in the flurry of his two-week pass. At the end of that leave, he'd left her starry-eyed and miserable, bound again for the war to ease the minds and pour God's courage into the hearts of the men he ministered to.

Six weeks later, Miss Lill received one of those telegrams nobody wants—saying he'd been wounded, sent to a hospital in Britain. Despite the war and perils of crossing the Atlantic, Miss Lill had finagled and paid, finding a way to get herself shipped to England, leaving the charge of Garden's Gate to Celia and Chester's mama.

Miss Lill had been nothing but good to them ever since she'd come to No Creek, letting them live and work with her and Miz Hyacinth at

Garden's Gate while their daddy was serving time for running moonshine and later as he worked at the shipyard in Norfolk, Virginia.

But the idea of waiting for Miss Lill to return to untangle the mystery of the attic room was intolerable—a new word Celia was using every chance she got.

Nearly asleep, Celia stared at stars through her window—ones that shone brightest in the clear March night—when the thought came to her about what Miss Lill had found in her grandaunt Hyacinth's hope chest, after she'd passed. Lots of stuff—a wedding dress and veil, books and letters and news clippings and poems. But in the bottom, in the far back corner, there was a little finger hole. When Miss Lill stuck her finger in that hole and lifted the panel, a whole new level had come to light—a Ku Klux Klan robe and hood, full regalia, and with it some crazy stories from the Belvidere family's past.

Celia sat up in bed and threw off the covers, the thrill of inspiration burning inside her. She pulled her robe over her pajamas and tiptoed, barefoot, up the attic stairs. Flicking on her flashlight, she climbed over the broken wall, careful not to step on tree splinters and wood shavings. She lifted the lid of the wooden chest—the one that held the copies of *Les Miserables*. She pulled out the dress, the books and newspapers, every little thing until she reached the bottom of the chest and ran the beam of light over the bottom, around the inside perimeter. There, in the back corner, the very same as in Miz Hyacinth's chest, was a pinky-size hole. Celia stuck her little finger inside and lifted the edge of the wooden panel.

Chapter Four

MAY 20, 1861

Mother's lily of the valley had bloomed that first week in May while she still drew breath. White, delicate, and pure on sturdy slim stalks, filled with a perfume so sweet it made the birds sing, it had long spread each year around the perimeter of Belvidere Hall. I thought of it as Mother's flower, the one that most reminded me of her. I was glad to offer her those small bouquets before she left us.

I knew I should wait for autumn to dig the roots, but as soon as the blooms began to fade, I thrust in my spade. I transplanted a little patch upon her grave and across the graves of the three babies she'd lost, buried in a row at her feet. Next spring those graves would bloom in profusion, at least I hoped they would, gathered together at last. It was a small thing, but a means of paying Mother tribute, a step in moving my broken heart forward.

I'd walked home and scrubbed the dirt from my hands at the pump in the yard, watching the water rush over my chafed skin till it was near raw in the cool spring air. That pain helped me draw the ache from my heart, helped push aside, if only for a moment, the forever loss of my mother.

I wondered how the world could go on breathing, how the coming seasons would turn over on themselves, how a person might place one foot in front of the other when weighed down by such a grief. Perhaps that's why I didn't hear Grayson enter the garden, didn't realize he was there until he stood in front of me. Startled, I straightened.

The flush on my brother's face meant there was news.

"North Carolina's seceded!"

"You're sure?" It was a stupid question, but my heart raced. *Surely, dear Lord, war is a mistake.*

"It's all over the county." The more Grayson talked, the brighter his face glowed. "You should see No Creek, Minnie! Men cheering, throwing caps into the air, ladies waving handkerchiefs and storming the general store, getting ready to pack hampers for their men to go enlist. They vow we'll whip those Yankees by Christmas! Elliott—"

"Is deputy sheriff and captain of his militia, loyal to the Union." I cut Grayson off.

"There is no more Union in North Carolina. We're at war—our second war for independence! Every Belvidere must fight, just as we fought in the Revolution!"

I turned away to hide my frustration. "You're too young. Father will never permit it."

"Boys my age are going, some younger yet to sign up for drum corps." He grabbed my arm, nearly pleading. "But I'm willing to wait—a little while. I'm going as a soldier."

I shook my head. "Father will never—"

"Soon I'll be old enough he'll have no choice, no say. Elliott must go."

"He won't."

"There'll be conscription, even if he doesn't volunteer. If he goes now, he goes as an officer."

"He's already captain of his regiment," I repeated. "That's service enough."

"That's the local militia, formed under a Union state. We're part of the Confederate States of America now." Grayson's shoulders squared, as if it had anything to do with him.

I groaned inwardly. We were a house divided and had been for too long, but it had all been talk. Now there was war—actual war! *What will that mean to Elliott, to his men who've sworn oaths to the Constitution? What will that mean to our Union-loyal friends and their families—to Tom, who's all but asked to court me?* I stopped drying my hands on my skirt. *What will it mean to us, to our slaves? Oh, dear Lord, what will it mean to them and their hope of freedom?*

Elliott's wife, Emma, though mistress of Belvidere Hall since Mother's passing, was indisposed in her confinement. I was the last Belvidere woman by blood. *Oh, Mother, I need your wisdom now!*

· · ·

A week passed before I ventured into town, my heart still raw. I was not ready to endure talk, even sympathetic, over Mother's passing, let alone questions regarding my family's political stance. So many had pledged loyalty to the Union weeks before, but now that we were at war . . .

No Creek, so named because there was no creek for baptisms by the church the first Belvidere built, boasted only a general store with post office, a law office, Dr. Hendrix's home, from which he operated his surgery, a saloon which we were not the better for, the jailhouse, where Elliott served as deputy sheriff, and a two-room schoolhouse. Closer to Belvidere Hall stood Shady Grove church and cemetery, the church my family founded and built for the community before the Revolution. Twice that clapboard church had burned. Twice it had been rebuilt by our slaves and the men of the church.

I hoped with all my heart that my family's long standing as founders and pillars of No Creek, along with Elliott's public service and Mother's years of charitable works toward so many families, would stand us in good stead, despite the charged political climate.

As I neared the store, groups of men in twos and threes or more stood, some in earnest conversation and others slapping one another on the back in boyhood style, giving me little hope that war fever had abated.

Just inside the store two women—Mildred Honeycutt and Eudora Newberry, women I'd known all my life and gone to school with as girls—turned their backs and leaned toward Tom Chatsworth, Elliott's good friend and the young man who'd walked me home from church socials for the last year, whispering as if what they said was confidential. Tom caught my eye but looked away, his cheeks crimson. My mouth ran dry to realize that Mildred and Eudora's news trumped his manners, and possibly his affection for me.

Chatter in the store stilled. Cordova Mae, wife of Gordon Mae, who owned the store, pasted a smile so unnatural on her face that I might have laughed if the room had not reeked of rancor. "And how may I help you today, Miss Belvidere?"

Not *Minerva*. Not *Minnie*, as she she'd called me since childhood. Not "and how are you faring? We desperately miss your dear mother." I swallowed what felt like lumps of red Carolina clay in my throat.

"I've come for the mail and a few things on my list."

Cordova did not speak but tilted her head.

I wondered if the tension in the room made her reconsider waiting on me. "If you're busy, I can leave my list and come by later . . . or send Martha to pick up my parcels."

Cordova straightened. "That won't be necessary, although I do believe we are experiencing a few shortages, even in these early days of the war." She emphasized *the war*.

The shelves looked fully stocked to me. I knew for a fact that Cordova had ordered extra supplies as talk of secession had flourished. I wondered if every family might experience tightened rations at the store or if that honor was saved for Conservatives, households of Union persuasion. I didn't ask.

Cordova sighed and turned to gather our mail and the items on my list. I noticed she cut the muslin I'd indicated nearly a quarter yard short, but I didn't say a word. The coffee beans she measured bore disadvantage when her finger tipped the scale. She looked at me, lifting her chin, daring me to object. When my order was complete, I lifted the packages, placing them in the basket over my arm, and whispered across the counter, "I thought we were friends, Cordova. Our families—longtime friends."

She reddened but cast a nervous glance at Tom, who was nearly to the door now, and the other women, still standing silent on the far side of the store, watching our exchange. Cordova drew in her chin. "We were. We can be again, once your family stands on the side of right."

So that was that, portent of things to come. I pressed my lips together, willing them not to betray me. The lump in my throat refused to go down, but I kept my composure until I reached the door, when Mildred stopped me.

"I reckon we'll be without a deputy sheriff soon."

"I don't see why." I feigned ignorance.

"Surely Elliott will go to the county seat and enlist in the regular army, now that war's declared. Every able-bodied man is. My Richard's already gone."

She waited for me to speak. How could I? What could I say? "I pray he'll come home safely."

"Richard will do his duty, as all our men must."

I said nothing but walked through the door, down the steps, and began my trek up the hill, keeping my chin from crumpling until I'd passed the churchyard.

"Minnie!" It was Tom calling from behind me.

I pretended not to hear. I would not let him see me cry.

"Minnie! Minerva, please wait." His boots crunched on the dirt road behind me.

I could not outrun him, so I stopped, swiping at my tears before he reached my side.

"Minnie, I'm sorry."

I shook my head, as if I didn't care, as if I hadn't noticed a thing. "Whatever for?"

"For the way Cordova Mae treated you, for Eudora and Mildred . . . that I didn't stand up for you—or for Elliott. I'm sorry. It was wrong of me."

"Yes, I think it was. You needn't concern yourself now."

He took my hands in his. "But I do."

I pulled away. "Tom, please. You forget yourself."

"I do, and I'm sorry again. No, that's not right. I'm not sorry for taking your hands. I need to ask you something, Minnie, and I want you to tell me straight, no matter the answer."

It was not what I'd expected, if I'd expected anything at all. "I always speak truthfully. You know that."

"You speak straight. I'm not sure any of you Belvideres speak altogether truthfully." He only half smiled.

I squared my shoulders. I would not be chafed in the middle of the street by Tom or anyone else.

"Don't get your dander up. It's just that I've never been surprised by the number of darkies that enter your home and don't seem to come out."

I held my breath.

"Don't fret. I've no truck with those who beat slaves, and there's a part of me that admires what you're doing—though it's against the law and dangerous, now more than ever. The danger for you is what worries me."

Still, I said nothing. Tom would know if I lied.

"You know what I think of Elliott. We've been best friends since we were in knee britches. I don't know a better man. I'd be proud to serve with him."

"You're going to the Union?" Elliott had spoken of men slipping off in the dark of night, heading over the mountains, then north, willing to walk hundreds of miles to Union lines to enlist.

"No." He shook his head. "North Carolina is my home. I've already enlisted, Minnie."

"Tom, you swore an oath!"

"That was before Lincoln called for troops—75,000 troops to fire on Virginians and South Carolinians and now us. He's getting ready for a war of aggression. I can't stand by and see my people slaughtered."

I turned away. The loss of another lifelong friend to this confounded Confederacy felt too much.

"My mother's here, Minnie."

"You don't owe me explanations."

"No, but I care about you and I want you to understand. I'll defend my mother and our home with my last breath. I'll defend you and your home with my every breath. No matter what others say. And they will say, they will talk—you know that. I just worry they'll do more than talk or turn their backs once our boys start dying. You need to talk with Elliott. Convince him—"

"You of all people should know that Elliott does not listen to me, does not listen to anyone other than—" I stopped. I wouldn't give Tom fodder to later turn on my brother. "Elliott will do what he must, what he believes is right in God's eyes."

Tom's mouth flattened. "I worry for him. I don't want to meet him on a battlefield."

My heart thudded in my chest. The idea that two people I loved might charge one another with guns was preposterous, horrific.

"Minnie, I don't know where they'll send me or how long I'll be gone. May I—will you write to me?"

"What?" I gasped. The change in direction came too abrupt.

"This war's gonna draw lines between families and friends. I don't want that to happen to us."

"My family is loyal to the Constitution. Father will always be a Union man, and you've just told me that you've enlisted with the Confederacy."

"That's right, and I'm asking you to write to me, to allow me to write to you. This war can't last forever. They're saying it'll be over by Christmas, and then things will settle down. I'll be back, and I hope . . . I hope we can take up where we left off."

Father would be furious if I even entertained such a thought—*correspond with a Confederate soldier?* But this was Tom—our Tom, and the closest thing to a beau I'd ever known. Did I want to turn him away forever because of this stupid, stupid war?

"Please, Minnie."

"I don't see how." The hurt in Tom's eyes showed me that he didn't understand. "I mean only that I can't be sure they'd be delivered to me, or how I could write to you without—without . . ." I couldn't finish. I couldn't be openly disloyal to Father.

"Mother. You can send your letters through my mother, and I'll write to you through her. Surely your father will allow you to visit my mother . . . a widow. You have before and your mother did—many times. Please, Minnie. Don't let this war that will be over in a few months come between us for the rest of our lives. I won't ask you to wait for me, only to consider me. To pray for me."

"I will pray for you, Tom Chatsworth, every night."

The relief and joy that washed through Tom's eyes eased the pain in my heart. How could I do less for my friend?

"You'll write? Allow me to write you?"

"Through your mother. Yes, but please, don't—"

"Not another soul will know, for your sake."

Chapter Five

Back in her room, Celia pored over the diary she'd discovered beneath the trunk's false bottom. She read until the fine script turned muddy so she couldn't see the letters and the book fell from her hands.

Celia dreamed of slaves running and cannon bursting and swords thrusting into the bellies of soldiers in blue and gray and butternut. She dreamed that a woman, a few years older than herself, stood in her room at the foot of her bed.

It was the last part of that dream, the woman's eyes penetrating Celia's, that made her sit up in bed with a start, gasping for breath. It took Celia a moment to remember it was 1944 and that a different war raged across the world.

Looking round her room, she wondered if it had been Minerva's—Minnie, as she'd read in the diary. Celia wondered if the young woman in her dream was Minnie and, if she'd stayed asleep longer, whether the woman would have spoken to her. Celia wondered what Minnie would think about her diary being discovered and read by another girl all these long years since.

Celia lay with her eyes closed, trying to fill the rooms of Garden's Gate—of Belvidere Hall, as it had been called then—with the Belvideres and their slave staff who'd lived and worked the estate. Third-floor rooms would have been quarters for the house slaves that peopled Minnie's diary. The second floor, where the family slept, and the first floor, would've been laid out as they'd been in Miz Hyacinth's day, though it sounded as if there had once been a summer kitchen out of doors.

In Miz Hyacinth's time, the original pantry had been opened to enlarge the winter kitchen, and the two rooms created Garden's Gate's roomy and only kitchen. Now the first floor, except for the kitchen and dining room, had been turned mostly into a lending library that Miss Lill and Miz Hyacinth had opened to the community at Celia's suggestion. Even the parlors and hallways held books for locals as well as family. Colored and white came on separate days, a division they'd learned the hard way to keep.

Celia thought of Mama's favorite saying: "I don't understand all I know." There were lots of things Celia knew but didn't understand about separating people based on how dark their skin was—*segregation*, they called it.

She also knew that in No Creek, there were things you just didn't ask, opinions you dared not give voice to, unless you were sure of the person.

Celia picked up the diary again and pulled the quilt up to her chin. With Chester to cook for and their chores to do and school and the bus to catch down to the general store, she hadn't much minded her mama being gone during the week. But Saturdays, when their mama generally made pancakes and Celia scrambled eggs fresh from the hens, were different. The house seemed colder, empty. Even with Minnie's diary to keep her company, Celia felt the chill from the drafty attic sweep through the house.

Knock. Knock. "Celia?"

Chester's banging on her bedroom door made her jump. She pushed the diary beneath her covers and slid the portfolio of documents she'd found in the trunk's hidden compartment under the bed.

"Yeah?" Celia groaned, doing her best to sound sleepy and frustrated at being wakened.

"You ever gonna get up?"

"What time is it?" Celia faked sounding sleepier yet.

"Past ten. I milked and ate and ran down to the store for mail, but I'm not collectin' eggs. That's your job. Hay-Hay's in a temper." Chester hated Hay-Hay, their Rhode Island Red. For whatever reason, she couldn't abide men and tended to scratch their arms to bits if they dared ply her nest for eggs. But Chester'd milked the cow, and that was the job Celia liked least. She was grateful.

"Okay, okay. Feet on the floor." She picked up slippers and dropped them, hoping he'd leave her alone.

"Can't fool me, but what do I care if you sleep till noon? Got a letter from Giuseppe in my pocket. Don't guess you care about that, either." He laughed and took off like his shoes were set afire.

Celia shot out of bed, not bothering with robe or slippers or to comb the knots from her hair. "Chester, get back here! Give me that! It's my letter!" But bellowing did no good.

Chester laughed, hale and hearty, all the while he tore down the stairs.

"Chester!" Celia yelled again, tripping into the hallway until she slapped the newel post on the bannister, as if that might show him.

There was nothing for it but to dress and track him down. She'd probably have to bribe him with something baked or do some irksome chore of his to get her letter—the letter she'd waited two weeks for from her military beau across the sea. At least she pretended he was her beau when no one else was around. When they were, she was just doing her patriotic duty, writing to a lonely soldier from up north who missed American hearth and home—a friend Marshall had introduced her to by mail. Besides, Giuseppe's letters almost always included one from Marshall, and Marshall would be very interested in everything she'd found in the attic.

· · ·

Dressed at last, Celia found Chester in the kitchen with Olney Tate leaning forward, intent and worried-looking. They glanced up like they'd stolen catfish, fried them in cornmeal and lard, and swallowed them whole.

Celia looked down, making sure all her buttons were buttoned and her dungarees zipped. Unless her brown hair had sprouted green, their conspiracy ranked a puzzlement. "What? You two look like you're up to no good. What is it?"

"Olney come by," Chester spoke up, "thinkin' maybe we ought to see what's in those trunks and chests in the attic." He had the decency to blush.

Olney's brows rose.

"Me and Celia . . . we opened them already," Chester confessed.

"It was too hard to wait." Celia spread her hands. "We didn't mess up anything—not a bit."

Olney nodded. He'd surely expected as much. He'd known them all their lives. "Mind tellin' me what you found?"

"Just books and clothes and ledgers and stuff. But there was a sword from the Revolution!" Chester warmed. "At least we think it was from the Revolution."

Olney waited. "That's it? That all?" he said at last.

Celia hadn't told Chester about the false bottom of the chest. She didn't want to share the contents with anybody until she'd read Minnie's diary through, until she'd read through all the papers inside the portfolio. "Were you thinking there might be somethin' more?" she asked, innocently as she could.

Olney looked away and heaved a sigh. "You opened all the trunks? Every chest? Each one?"

"We did," Chester was quick to answer, clearly sorry to disappoint their friend.

"No legal papers? No documents?"

"Not one," Chester vowed, looking to Celia for confirmation.

But Chester didn't know what she knew, and Celia didn't want to say. Besides, she didn't really know what was in the portfolio. She hadn't studied it out yet. "What did you think might be there?"

Olney shook his head. "Can't rightly say. A dream, I guess, like somebody walkin' over my daddy and granddaddy's grave. Nothin' but old men's dreams." He pushed his hat back onto his graying head and walked out the door.

"You dreamed there'd be something?" Chester walked after him, leaving Giuseppe's letter on the table.

Celia grabbed the letter and held it to her heart, glad Chester'd been distracted. But she stopped short. After lying to Olney, or as good as, her glitter had lost its shine.

. . .

Celia lit the stove and set the teakettle on to boil, then sat down to the table to read Giuseppe's letter, negotiating all the while with her conscience. *Is it really so wrong to want to hold on to something for a time? I want to savor this find, just for a spell. I won't keep quiet forever.*

What is it Olney hoped we'd find, anyway? But Celia pushed those questions away. She'd think about them later. Now she had a letter to read.

Giuseppe's letter was short and to the point. There was nothing from Marshall.

Dear Celia,

Thanks for your letter and for letting me know about M's mom. I've been worried that I haven't heard from him, even though I write every week, but that probably explains it. Her death must have hit him really hard. That he hasn't answered my letters makes me worry a little about what kind of comfort he might reach for.

There's all kinds of sharks in the water—male and female— and they're not all from No Creek.

Before we'd enlisted, when we were both in our colleges, M told me what happened to him and his uncle in No Creek. Italians have it plenty hard back home, but not like that—not for just talking to or working with some girl. At least I haven't run into the KKK. I can hardly believe he hopes to go back there after the war, after med school, to practice.

M needs friends from home, people who know him, know what happened back there and what he should look out for now. It's too easy to fall into the wrong kind of company when you're far from home and hurting. I know this from experience. Write him, Celia. Don't say anything to his uncle or aunt. No point worrying them. But maybe remind him he needs to be careful, keep his life on track.

Send the letter to me and I'll get it to him.

Yours truly,
Giuseppe

Celia set the letter down. *What in the world does that mean?*

Chapter Six

MARCH 1944

Giuseppe Alonzo Rossetti straightened his tie and the crease in his uniform trousers as he stepped out of Charing Cross Station. It was his first two-day pass in more than a month, and he was set to meet his friend Marshall Raymond and see the sights in London—at least the ones that hadn't been closed or bombed out.

Marshall had written, urging him to get a two-day pass and meet him at Trafalgar Square. It was rotten luck the powers that be hadn't allowed them to sign up in the same unit—both wanted to be trained and serve as medics, but different skin colors slammed that door. At least that's what they'd said at the recruiting office.

Basic training had made it crystal clear. Giuseppe, growing up in an Italian neighborhood in Philly, hadn't known many colored fellas before Marshall, but he'd never seen why the shade of a guy's skin should matter. It sure mattered in the South, where they'd been sent to separate camps for basic and then on for medical training.

Their bases weren't far apart, but they'd learned in a split second that it wasn't safe for them to meet in town for a drink or a coffee or an ice cream soda. There wasn't even a café or diner that would allow them both in. Giuseppe had never seen anything like it, but Marshall had, and the things that had happened to his father in Georgia and to him and his uncle's family in No Creek, North Carolina, raised the hairs on Giuseppe's arms.

But now they were in England. Jolly old England, where the locals treated colored American soldiers pretty well—sometimes better than their brash white counterparts. That didn't include Giuseppe, but he was used to the slurs—*Mussolini papist* along with the supposition that his mother wasn't married to his father being the most common. He didn't care too much. He'd heard worse back home from the Irish neighborhood gangs. Still, the vitriol had convinced him to adopt the American form of his name—Joe, Joe Rossetti. GI Joe, to anybody who asked.

He'd even taken to filling out forms and signing his name as Joe, each time praying his grandmother would never find out. He was Joe now to everybody else except Celia Percy, who he only knew through letters. Celia thought Giuseppe "a most romantic name." His grandmother would agree.

Those letters had started out as covers for correspondence between Celia and Marshall, who they always referred to as M, contact between colored fellas and white girls being forbidden in No Creek. Giuseppe—Joe—had gotten a kick out of being the liaison between the two unlikely friends back home. But once they'd enlisted, Joe had decided to write Celia, too. He'd asked, and she'd agreed, saying their teacher had encouraged all the kids to write to American soldiers, it being their patriotic duty.

Joe's grin spread wider. It was Celia who'd urged him to read up on England and see all the sights while there—something she'd sworn she'd "simply die to do." Through Dickens, she'd introduced him to the Victorian slums of London and issues of social justice, things the author wrote about with a passion. She was crazy about Victor Hugo and *Les Misérables*. The idea that Jean Valjean had been sentenced to twenty years for stealing a loaf of bread to feed a starving child incensed her. The girl was on fire for reading and championing the underdog. Justice and mercy were her causes, reading and writing her weapons of choice.

Joe couldn't get enough of Hugo's characters or their desperate plights. He wanted to shake Javert for his relentless persecution of a man who'd changed—or more likely returned to his core—and lived to protect and help the downtrodden in his path.

He wondered if Dickens and Hugo had been friends or maybe rivals for readers. Once he'd read both authors, something fierce and personal rose inside Joe until he, too, railed against the injustice of the times—then and now—and the powers that kept people of other races and the poor under their heel.

Celia'd brought all of that to him through her letters. And after all, there wasn't much to do in barracks at night besides read . . . unless you wrote letters or wanted to join one of the ongoing craps games. Joe wasn't about to do that. He was saving every penny for medical school when he got out of this stinking war. It was a pact he and Marshall had made. They'd do their service for their country, get all the medical training the Army provided, then apply to medical school the minute they returned Stateside.

Joe checked his watch—3:30. He needed to find the pub near Trafalgar Square where Marshall'd said they could meet, where he wanted to introduce someone special to Joe.

Joe had figured it must be a girl keeping Marshall busy and distracted, though he didn't know of any colored American women stationed in the UK. He'd seen guys in his unit, one after another, fall like dominoes for the pretty English girls ready and willing for a good time from the "rich Americans."

Well, what could anybody expect? England had been at war over four years already—a war that sure hadn't gone well for them, even on the home front. American soldiers swaggered in strong, healthy, with good supplies and plenty of cash compared to the few Tommies home on leave. "Overpaid, overdressed, oversexed, and over here"—that was the phrase he'd heard so many times he wanted to puke. Not a good beginning to community relations. He couldn't blame the British soldiers for their resentment.

He just hoped Marshall wasn't in over his head, whoever she was. He had years of medical school ahead and didn't need to be distracted on missions. Having somebody to love sounded great. Having somebody to worry about could make for a deadly mistake on the battlefield, cause a fella not to pay attention. At least that's what Joe told himself when he was lonely, which he was, more and more. *Remember the goal* had become his motto, and he was sticking to it. He'd make sure Marshall did the same.

• • •

Joe glimpsed Marshall before he reached Nelson's column. He'd be hard to miss, crowded as the square was. Six feet three and the only dark face in the crowd at the moment, with a smile that spread from Dover to Calais.

Joe knew his own smile was just as wide. Not given to reservation, Joe crunched Marshall in a bear hug, slapping his buddy on the back. "Good to see you, man! You look great!"

"You, too, Joe! What'd you do? Gain ten pounds in muscle since we hit England?"

"Must be all that great Army food!" Joe laughed. He'd needed to put on some muscle and weight, which pleased him no end, but he'd never gain Marshall's height.

Marshall stood back, scanned the crowd, checked his watch, and scanned the crowd again.

"Are we being stood up?" Joe half joked. "Long bus ride, maybe?"

"No, Ivy lives not far from here. She'll be along."

"Ivy?"

"You're gonna love her, Joe. She's the greatest woman on two feet." His grin spread even wider if that was possible. "There she is now!"

It hadn't crossed Joe's mind that Marshall might try to fix him up with a girl. And yet, across the square walked the prettiest chestnut-haired girl with blue eyes and a laughing mouth—a girl with creamy skin and rosy cheeks, a girl any guy would be proud to walk out with. Still, they'd made a pact, and he had to say it, even if it was half-hearted. "You promised never to set me up, Marshall. What'd ya do that for?"

Marshall nearly split his side. The closer Ivy came, the harder he laughed.

"What's so funny? What'd I say that's so funny?"

"You better believe I'm not settin' you up, Joe." Marshall took the smiling Ivy in his arms and kissed her soundly on the lips, right there in Trafalgar Square in front of God and everybody. "Joe Rossetti, I want you to meet my fiancée, Ivy Greenfield."

Joe knew if a Hawker Hurricane buzzed through, strafing the streets of London at that moment, he'd never make it to cover. He wanted to say, *Marshall, she's white or didn't you notice? Are you crazy? Your CO'll never let you marry a white woman!* But all he could say was, "Your fiancée?"

The two smiles in front of him confirmed it.

"We're getting married—today. I couldn't write it in a letter, but I wanted you to be here, to stand with me—best man."

Joe couldn't coordinate his mouth with his brain, so Marshall continued.

"I got a weekend pass, had to buy it off a lieutenant."

Ivy stuck out her hand. "I'm so glad to meet you, Joe. Marshall talks about you all the time—'Joe and I did this' and 'Joe and I did that.'"

But Joe couldn't seem to close his mouth. When he did, he couldn't unstick his teeth. He wanted to be civil, welcoming. He wanted it all to be a joke Marshall was playing on him. But the longer the two in front of him talked, the more he saw that they were honest-to-goodness in love. "For real?"

Ivy tilted her head, but Marshall seemed to understand.

"For real, Joe."

Joe couldn't speak.

"You look a little pale in that white skin, man. Let's go down to the pub and get a table. Talk."

Joe nodded, a reflex action. He followed Marshall and Ivy, trying to pull the scenario together. He and Marshall had only been stationed in the UK since November. Where could Marshall have met Ivy in that time? How could he get enough leave to get to know her, to go out with her, let alone propose marriage?

The bell over the pub door jingled when they stepped through, a welcome Joe always appreciated. Not so much like bars back home, pubs were more community centers with drinks. Guys played darts, gossiped like old women, sometimes played cards. Even some respectable women came in with their husbands or boyfriends.

Marshall led them to a table near the back. Eyes followed the colored soldier and white girl, some curious, some with a grimace. Joe wondered that neither Marshall nor Ivy seemed to notice, or care.

"Three teas, please, ma'am," Marshall said to the barmaid who'd shown up even before they were seated.

She smiled at Marshall's use of "ma'am" and responded, "My pleasure, soldier." Probably not what she'd been called by anybody else, Joe figured. English women liked the manners of the colored American soldiers and how they didn't look down their noses at working-class Brits, not like some of the white soldiers.

Marshall and Ivy snuggled on one side of the table while Joe watched from the other. Tea was fine for now, but he figured he might need something stronger before this day was out.

"Surprised?" Marshall couldn't stop grinning.

"You never said." Joe tried to steady his hands, fingers laced, set on the table before him. He tried to return Ivy's persistent smile, but he knew it was pasted on. "I thought you wanted to see the London sights. Your letter said—"

Marshall sat back.

"I can see you gents have some catching up to do. I'll just go powder my nose. Keep my tea warm when it comes." Ivy stood, squeezing Marshall's forearm.

He covered her fingers with his own. "Don't be long."

"Never." She smiled at Marshall, gave Joe a wink, and was gone.

Joe took a deep breath but couldn't look at Marshall.

"You okay, Joe?" Marshall turned serious, as serious as a man head over heels and planning to say *I do* within hours could.

Joe shook his head. "Okay? No, man, I'm not okay." He pushed back from the table. "You get me up here under false pretenses—made it seem like we're in for a weekend of sightseeing and catching up, and—"

"I told you I had someone special I wanted you to meet."

"When I saw her walking toward us, I thought you'd set me up!"

"We promised never to do that."

"We promised lots of things—like staying focused in the Army, getting through, going to medical school. How's any of that gonna happen if you get married?"

"We fell in love. I've never been in love before, didn't see it coming." Marshall spread his hands.

Joe leaned forward, whispering across the table. "She's white, Marshall! Did you forget what happened back home when you got involved with some white girl? You got amnesia?"

"I was never involved with Ruby Lynne. She helped me with my reading. That's all it ever was."

"They nearly hanged you! What you think they're gonna do the minute they catch you in bed with your wife? You know the Army's rules!"

"They're not gonna know."

"What are you sayin'? You gotta get permission from your CO to marry."

"I talked to him. I did."

"And what did he say?"

Marshall looked Joe in the eyes. "He said no. He said just what you said . . . only he said what they'd do if they caught me."

Joe waited.

"Said more than half the states in the US wouldn't recognize our marriage as legal—don't allow 'miscegenation.' I'd be brought up on charges of rape. Grounds for court-martial . . . and hanging."

Joe sat back, the heart in his chest hammering.

Marshall leaned forward, his hands spread wider yet on the table, as if that might help Joe to see, to understand. "That's why we're doing this on the quiet."

Joe turned away, helpless fury and fear growing inside his aching head.

"We got a British license—they don't segregate here."

"You're not a British citizen, in case you forgot."

"I didn't forget. I know it's a stretch—it just means we have to be careful, not tell anybody till after the war, till I'm out of the Army and I can work things out."

"How you gonna get her to the US? Or is everything we ever planned off now?" Joe pulled out every stop he knew. Somehow, he needed to knock sense into Marshall.

"Nothing's off, Joe. We'll still do everything we ever said—finish college, medical school, practice."

"How's that gonna work with a wife in tow—a white wife—and maybe a kid or two? You'll be in debt and diapers before you know it. And where you gonna live? You always said you wanted to go back home to practice. Mixed-race marriage in North Carolina? I don't think so. You're beggin' for trouble—real trouble."

"Calm down, Joe. This is my decision—mine and Ivy's. We love each other. Nobody's ever loved me like she does. I've never felt this way about anybody. Can you try to understand?"

"I'm scared stiff for you—and for her. How'd you meet her? Do her parents know? Did they agree?"

Marshall sat back, shoving his hands in his pockets. "A flyer was posted in the mess hall, inviting whoever wanted to go to a church in the village. It's a white church, but they welcomed all us colored fellas like we were family. Told every soldier keen for a Sunday dinner to put their names in a box. Families drew names and invited us home on the spot. A real nice older couple invited me and another fella, then invited their neighbors and a couple of girls on their block, figuring it would be nice for us to meet some local folks."

"They did that out near our base, too," Joe remembered.

"You go?"

Joe sighed. "Tried. Once they drew an Italian name, they put it back in the box. Somebody'd written *No Mussolinis wanted* on the back of mine. Afterward the vicar, sorry for us, pulled out all the names left and invited the rejects home."

"I'm sorry, man."

Joe shrugged. "It's nothin' I've not heard before. Nothin' you've not heard before."

Marshall leaned forward again. "That's just it. Nobody ever treated me like this—like I'm same as them, like the color of my skin doesn't matter."

"What about her parents?"

"Nice enough when their daughter went to meet a soldier at the neighbors' table. But the minute they heard Ivy and I hit it off special, that she was stepping out with a colored . . . they refused to meet me. Didn't even want to know my name, just told Ivy she couldn't come home till she was done with me." He shook his head. "I'm good enough to take Sunday dinner with their daughter, but not good enough to marry her. Ivy pretended she broke it off with me, just never said anything more. She lives with some other girls now. They don't know, either."

Joe shook his head and pulled back. He'd never been in love himself, but he recognized the signs and knew better than to try to talk sense to somebody who was. "Why'd you get me out here, Marshall? You know if I'm part of this and they call you in, I'll be in trouble, too."

"You're all the family I've got here, Joe—my brother. I wanted you to meet Ivy, be glad for me. I want you to stand up with me at our wedding. Best man and all that. We always said we would."

Joe sighed—nearly snorted—in frustration. It was true. Marshall was the brother he'd never had. Every hard thing had bonded them from the moment they'd met that first semester in college—their commitment to medicine, the tragic losses of their parents, the prejudice they'd encountered, their determination to ace every class, to climb out of poverty and to make a difference by helping the most vulnerable who needed medical care. And then there was their ability to laugh together when there was absolutely nothing to laugh about. They'd made a pact to be there for each other no matter what—through good times and bad, like blood brothers. "If I do this, if I sign your death warrant—"

"It won't be that way. We'll be careful. I swear."

Joe closed his eyes, but at last he nodded. He couldn't say no.

"There's one more thing."

"She's not pr—"

"No, nothing like that. You know me better." Now Marshall sounded truly offended.

"Sorry . . . What is it?"

Marshall hesitated. Joe saw the Adam's apple go up and down his friend's throat. "I wouldn't ask, but we have to be really careful here."

"What? What else can there be?"

"Our honeymoon. There won't be much of one. I could only get a two-day pass and there's not many places we can go—petrol rationing and trains not reliable. Not much money."

"So?"

"So, Ivy found a little hotel about five miles out in the countryside. She's rented a room there in her name. The thing is, if I go out there on my own, the landlady may not rent to me. But if we go out together and you sign, there should be no problem."

"You want me to go with you on your honeymoon?"

Now Marshall pushed long fingers through his hair. "I want you to rent room for the two of us, after Ivy's gone in a while. Then when things get quiet, I'll go to Ivy's room, or you'll swap with her—whichever has nobody near. You'll get a good night's sleep in a decent bed and a good English breakfast—all on me."

"You've got to be kidding."

"And Ivy and I'll be forever grateful."

Joe might have laughed at the craziness of it all if it hadn't been so serious. "And if we're caught?"

"We won't be. My name won't be there and there's no reason you can't stay anywhere you want."

Joe shook his head. Marshall was using him. Ivy was using him, and he didn't like it. "No 'good English breakfast' these days is worth that. You can't wait till this stinkin' war is over?"

"Which of us knows if we'll come out on the other side? We're gearing up for invasion. You've seen the influx of American troops. It can't be long now."

"And what if you don't come back? Ivy's gonna be a war widow."

Joe hadn't realized that Ivy had returned behind him, but she'd clearly heard. She sat heavily beside Marshall, taking his arm in her own.

"As will thousands of other British women. No matter what happens, Marshall and I will have had our time together, and I won't trade that for anything in this world. But I don't believe that's going to happen, Joe.

We're going to build a future—eventually in America. We know it will take time, but we're getting married today, with you or without you. I know Marshall would like it to be with you. It's up to you."

Joe felt his face flame. He'd gone too far. It was one thing to be straight with his best friend—even insult him if it might help knock some sense into him—but he didn't want a war with Ivy. Turning his best friend's new wife against him was the last thing Joe wanted, the one thing that might cut in two the best friendship he'd ever known. And it was clear Ivy loved Marshall.

It was the kind of thing Joe wanted one day, if he ever found someone to love him like that. He knew that neither hell nor high water would keep him from claiming the love and potential family he might someday find, and like Marshall'd said, who knew if any of them would make it out of this war alive. No, he wasn't about to mess this up for his friend; he had no right and no desire. Joe gritted his teeth and pulled in a deep breath. Point of no return.

He pulled his wallet from his pocket. "So, my friends—old and new—this fancy tea party's on me. Consider it the only bachelor party you're likely to get, Marshall. Ivy, pretend you've got bridesmaids running all over the place. Think we should pick up some flowers? What time's the wedding?"

Chapter Seven

MAY 1861

Elliott returned home late the next evening and found me filling Father's pipe with fresh tobacco. When he stepped into the library, his angular face shone pale in the lamplight, as haggard and drawn as Father's. Unshaven, his uniform askew, unlike the professional and conservative Elliott we both knew. Still, seeing his son brought light to Father's eyes and a lift to my heart.

"Son." Father clasped his hands around Elliott's. Elliott returned the grasp and sank to the chair beside him.

"Have you eaten?" It was not the question I most wished to ask.

He shook his head. "Emma. How is she?"

I hated to tell him, to heap more worries on his head. Emma had already lost two children before their birth. "She's had some bleeding. Dr. Hendrix was here this morning."

Elliott's eyes registered alarm, then resignation. "I must go to her." Wearily, he pulled himself to his feet.

"What will you do, Son?" Father's even tone belied his anxiety.

"See to my wife."

"About the Confeder—"

He glared. "What I've always done: drill the militia formed under our governor, protect our homes."

"But it's all changed now, Elliott," I burst in. "It's—"

"Nothing's changed, Minnie. Not for me. I accepted Governor Ellis's commission when he reorganized our militias in anticipation of this war. I swore an oath to our country, to the Constitution. I'll take no part in destroying it. You should know that."

It was all I'd ever known of my brother, but before this week his words had rung with truth and honor and instilled great pride in my bosom. They still sang true, and still I was proud of him, but now that North Carolina had seceded from the Union, his actions clanged dangerously of treason in this world turned upside down.

I turned away, knowing I possessed as little means to persuade Elliott as to reason with Grayson. A sister caught between meant nothing to either of them. I shook Father's stray tobacco leaves from my apron into the fire with worry and a vengeance.

Tom was right about one thing. President Lincoln's April call for troops to suppress the rebellion was a death knell to our state's loyalty. I'd seen it in the burning eyes of the men in town, in the set jaws of the women. Didn't Elliott understand that North Carolinians would never fire on their brethren or neighbors, that such a belligerent demand would mark the state's turning point? Our neighbors north and south had already seceded. As Grayson had said, *What choice do we have?*

Such views would smack of heresy to Father, to Elliott, even to Mother, God rest her soul. But how could we fight a tide as relentless as the sea? Wouldn't we all be swallowed up and drowned?

· · ·

In the days that followed, Grayson took to staying out late. I knew he was up to no good, carousing with men half again his age, men afire for war, swearing they'd be "free or die." Sober, they weren't much threat, not yet. Drunk, they terrorized every soul out after dark. The saloon in town was bad enough, but every holler and nearly every home produced its own brand of moonshine. There was no trouble finding it, even for a boy.

Father didn't confront him. Still grief-stricken, he hardly distinguished day from night but spent hours in the darkened library poring over account books, land deeds, and I didn't know what all. I hoped for good reason but feared for his mind.

Elliott ignored Grayson, staying away with his militia more than he used to after Emma lost their third child, the baby we'd all so hoped would be born alive. I was unsure if he and Emma planned that for her recovery's sake or if Elliott was planning insurrection. From all I heard through Obadiah, whom I prodded daily for information, Elliott continued to drill his men, just as he'd vowed. He sparked no feuds with local Confederate recruits, but how long could he continue without rousing the powers that be?

I understood Elliott, more than he knew. We Belvideres were proud of our service to our country, of our patriotism in the Revolution, of our fight for freedom. To turn on the country we helped to birth was unthinkable.

But I understood Grayson, too—at least in his claim that we were doing nothing more than fighting a second war of independence, that we couldn't allow anyone to dictate our way of life or invade our country, our state. And I understood Tom, determined to protect the home and families he loved. *I wonder if he truly loves me . . . and I wonder what I feel about that, how I feel about him. They can't all be right, can they?*

I knew so little of the world beyond No Creek, but I read the newspaper and listened to the talk. What would the North do without the South's cotton and tobacco and rice? What would we do without the manufacturers of the North? There was talk in the newspaper of ports being seized and fear of trade with England coming to a standstill. What then? How could we get the goods we needed when trade with the North stopped?

I cared about our economy and the right to govern ourselves, but wasn't the conflict over slavery the core issue, the thing that drove men gathered in Washington City from the many states to throw down the gauntlet?

Contrary to Father's belief, I saw no sign that slavery would die a natural death—not when girls like Rosalee were raped and beaten by their owners and when men as strong as Obadiah were brought to their knees in fields by the horsewhipping of overseers. Not when children could still be yanked from their mothers and sold away as chattel at a master's whim. Owning land, casting a vote into the say of their government or their lives here in the South was a dream no slave spoke of. But to own themselves, to live and breathe free—I saw that desire in the eyes of every man and woman who labored in the house or fields of Belvidere Hall, and I was too often ashamed to meet those brave eyes.

The war I saw brewing in my own home was a small picture compared to the storm raging in the outside world. Both, I feared, could only end in blood.

I knew that I should not fear, for Father God was at the helm, but we were so cruel to one another. Sometimes I wondered why He left us to our own devices, and more, why He loved us at all.

. . .

Months passed, and by the summer of 1862, more than a year into the war, we began to feel the pinch of supply. Most of our needs we grew in our own fields and gardens. In a weaving house set behind the barn we spun wool from our own sheep. One of No Creek's few freedmen ran a tannery close to the Yadkin River, and it wasn't until the Confederates took it over that we feared want of shoe leather.

Confederate foragers roamed the hills and hollows, sometimes offering bare-bones prices for bushels of corn or livestock. If farmers refused, the foragers took them anyway or scattered good corn across the ground, promising someone would follow to reimburse with a lower price yet. They rarely did.

Because of the size of our estate and the hope that our crops could continue to supply the army throughout the war, we were generally better treated by the Confederates, as long as Father met their demands. Little did they know how much we held back, how much was hidden away in burrows beneath the ground, how often we fed deserters and supplied their families against starvation.

So many secrets, each one dangerous for someone. I limited my trips to the store and post office, fearful something might show in my eyes, that some slip of my tongue might bring disaster—to Father, to Elliott, to our slaves, to the men and women we clandestinely aided.

Sometimes, before I fell asleep at night, I recounted who knew what and who must never know, praying that would keep me sharp, discerning. Conflicting images haunted my dreams—Confederate cavalry brandishing swords and riding crops, Rosalee's baby dying in our attic safe room, Elliott and Emma torn from the child they never bore and, it seemed, never would.

It was in late September, after just such a night of mixed-up dreams, that I woke near dawn, heard Elliott's footsteps pad the hallway, heard him set his boots outside his and Emma's door, heard the door open and close. Snoring came through the wall in minutes. I knew he'd sleep till noon. If I got to the kitchen early, I could ask Martha to save back some biscuits and gravy for him. Anytime, that was Elliott's favorite meal.

Half an hour before breakfast I found Obadiah in the outdoor kitchen with Martha—nuzzling her neck behind the half-closed cupboard door. So entrenched were they in each other's arms they never noticed me, so I quietly stepped back outside and sneezed as loudly as I could before entering the room and chattering away, "Martha, I hope you're planning biscuits and gravy this morning. Elliott's home just now and likely to be starving."

The two sprang apart like quail at the blast of musket shot. It was all I could do to keep laughter from my lips. I did not succeed with my eyes.

"Miss Minnie!" Martha, a little breathless, half admonished, half scolded.

Obadiah grinned, not sorry in the least.

"Caught in the act," I chided. "Whenever are you two going to stop this nonsense and tie the knot?" I couldn't help but prod, desirous as I was for their happiness.

"Just as soon as we get those freedom papers in hand, Miss Minnie." Obadiah sobered, his grin gone.

My smile fell with my heart. "Obadiah. I've begged Father. He—"

"I know what he says, Miss Minnie."

"Then why wait? You two clearly—"

"I won't have our babies owned by another man. I won't have Martha or our children sold away."

"Father would never do that. You know he wouldn't."

"Massa Horace won't live forever. No tellin' what happens then."

It wasn't my place or privilege to tell him. I'd been admonished by Father that I was not to share his plans to have Elliott free our slaves at his death, either with them or anyone else. Such talk ran more dangerous now than ever before. Few in our end of the county owned slaves, rarely more than two or three. But those that did feared uprisings in ways they never had before, and that too often resulted in crueler treatment.

"*Where there's possibility there's temptation,*" Father'd said. Such talk infuriated me. As if any of our people would harm a hair on his aged head.

"Since the battle at Sharpsburg there's talk that President Lincoln might issue emancipation . . ." It was all I could freely say, but my words cut short as Obadiah shook his head, leveling me with his eye.

"Talk—they's lots of talk from lots of folks. None of it matters unless bluecoats win this war."

"When they suppress this rebellion," I countered. It could be no other way. "The idea of the South winning the war and continuing slavery forever is inconceivable."

"Inconceivable, maybe," Martha whispered. "Not impossible. Time goes by, then where will we be?" She nodded beyond the door where we saw Grayson jump from his mount, toss the reins of his stallion to Rex, our blacksmith, and without a word stomp toward the house, acting every bit the master of a great plantation.

Hairs prickled on the back of my neck. For the first time I realized the possibility, far-fetched though I prayed it was, that both Father and Elliott might die before this war's end. The image of Grayson as master of Belvidere Hall loomed very much like a nightmare.

Chapter Eight

Two hours after their tea, a radiant Ivy, wearing a navy suit and pale-blue ribbon corsage, stood happily beside Marshall, who was decked out in full dress uniform—so nervous his hands shook. Joe stood beside his friend, holding the slim gold band entrusted to his care. All three faced the vicar, who looked as if he was late for his evening tea and would just as soon be anywhere else.

"You're quite certain, Ivy?" the vicar asked.

"I am, Reverend Sloane."

"Your parents—"

"Are not the ones I'm marrying. If you won't do this, we'll go to the Presbyterians, though you know I'd much rather you marry us. After all, you baptized me, and this church is my home." Ivy's emotional ploy impressed Joe. The girl had nerve, he'd give her that.

The vicar pressed his mouth into a firm line. "Let me see the license." He knew he was being manipulated, as sure as Joe knew he'd been manipulated. Somehow that made Joe feel a little better—not the only one under fire. The man took his time reading the fine print of the license, as if he hadn't seen dozens in his time. How Ivy'd gotten the license or if the names on it were theirs or if it was legal without approval from the US Army, Joe couldn't guess and didn't want to know.

The vicar opened his black prayer book and intoned, "Dearly beloved, we are gathered . . ." as if the church were full and not just the three of them plus the vicar's wife as witness.

It was over in five minutes—ten at a stretch, Joe figured, and no wedding cake, not even the cardboard-covered wartime kind. But Marshall and Ivy had eyes only for each other and seemed perfectly happy with the outcome. And somehow, that made it all right. They'd have to be careful, and who knew what the road ahead might hold, but Joe figured they'd be okay . . . as long as they could get through the guesthouse business tonight.

He hoped Marshall would never ask anything so daring of their friendship again. But, who knew, maybe there'd come a day Joe could collect on this debt. He relished the thought.

• • •

Joe had underestimated Ivy's and Marshall's abilities. Ivy had arranged her guesthouse reservation the week before. Marshall'd been ordered to pick up a load of medical supplies as part of his swap to get a vehicle for the weekend. The three of them piled into the front seat of the truck, Ivy in the middle, snuggled up to Marshall at the wheel. Joe wished he could drive through the gloaming, less than an hour before blackout, sure Marshall wasn't keeping his eyes on the road.

But they made it to the bus stop, just as the last bus of the day pulled away. Ivy hopped out, overnight case in hand. She kissed Marshall roundly on the lips and waved. "See you soon, Husband!" And off she marched.

"Where's she going?" Joe didn't like seeing her walk off into the growing dark alone.

"The guesthouse is less than a quarter of a mile down that lane." Marshall pointed to a side lane Joe hadn't noticed. "She'll get her room, get settled. We'll wait forty minutes or so, then drive in, so they won't know we came out together." Marshall turned the truck around, drove a half mile back the way they'd come, and pulled off into a darkened lane.

Joe frowned. It wasn't like Marshall to be so deceptive and it didn't sit right. Marshall'd always been a by-the-book Christian, something Joe wasn't but still respected about his friend. He understood the injustice that made Marshall and Ivy plan and connive and slip around, but it was still illegal. Thinking about a potential court-martial and the death of all their dreams for medical school tightened the knot in Joe's stomach.

"Look, Joe, I know this isn't where you want to be. It's not how I wanted my wedding night to play out, either. We just couldn't think of another way."

"I get that. I do. It's just . . . all this sneaking around."

Marshall's mouth straightened into a line. Moments passed. "If it was you marrying Ivy, there'd be no sneaking around. Your CO would have interviewed you both, interviewed her parents, done whatever they do in those examinations, and you'd be guaranteed your bride would be sent back to the US after the war, no charge, no sweat. None of that happens for me and we both know why."

Joe nearly swore. "That's not fair."

"No. So we couldn't see any other way around this."

Joe sighed. It was just the kind of thing Celia'd get her back up about—a modern-day Dickens wrong to be righted. Only Joe didn't know how to right it, so he'd play along. He figured if he was any kind of friend, he'd wish Marshall and Ivy all the joy in the world and watch their backs.

• • •

An hour later Joe marched through the guesthouse door. "Got a room with two beds for a couple of weary medics, ma'am?" Joe turned on every ounce of Italian charm, entirely lost on the landlady but not on the young protégé standing with her at the desk.

"Of course, Corporal. Always glad to accommodate our 'visiting American servicemen.' Where's your friend?"

No doubt about it. The Brits were the real soldiers in the minds of locals. The Americans were lowly would-be helpers and annoying tourists. Joe didn't mind the snub. "He'll be along. Just securing our truck—sorry, our lorry. Says out front the room comes with a real English breakfast. Looking forward to that. Home-cooked meals are hard to come by these days."

Joe signed the registry for both of them. No need to leave a paper trail for Marshall. "Nice place you have here, ma'am."

The woman turned the registry book back to read Joe's signature. "Corporal Rossetti. Italian?" The smile was gone from her face.

Joe shrugged. "Second-generation American all the way, here to help you folks out the best I can." He tipped his cap to her. "Room number?"

She hesitated. "Room six, second floor, end of the hallway. There's no house breakfast on Sundays."

Marshall came through the door then, his duffel slung over his shoulder.

The woman's brows rose, and her young assistant's eyes nearly bugged out of her head. The landlady's shoulders squared as she addressed Marshall. "We're full at the moment, soldier. No vacancies."

Marshall set his duffel on the floor.

"It's okay, ma'am. He's with me. Room six. Sorry to hear about that breakfast. We were really looking forward to it. Ma'am." Joe didn't give the woman a second to reply but tipped his hat, hefted his duffel, and strode toward the stairs, knowing Marshall matched his steps.

The younger woman stifled a giggle—a giggle the older woman shushed.

At that moment Ivy came down the stairs. Joe did all he could to look away, but she was so pretty, so young and alive. The woman at the desk shifted uncomfortably. "Can I help you, Miss Greenfield?"

"Please, ma'am. It's so cold in my room. I wonder if I could trouble you for another eiderdown or maybe a hot-water bottle."

"Edna will bring a heated brick straightaway."

"Thank you, that will be lovely." Ivy smiled. "Room four."

"Yes, of course, I know." The woman sounded irritated but whispered, loud enough to be heard across a stage and not missed by Joe or Marshall, "Lock your door, miss. We've a full house tonight." She nodded toward Marshall and Joe, who pretended not to notice or be offended as they started up the stairs.

"Man, what luck—right next door," Marshall whispered as Joe turned the key in the lock.

"Shut up! You want they should hear you?" If Joe was going to play resistance, he was in all the way and not about to get caught.

Joe took the bed near the window. It wouldn't matter to Marshall. After the long and crazy day, it felt good to take his shoes off, loosen his tie, and lie back on the single bed, arms locked behind his head. It was all he could do not to laugh at his friend, who sat on the edge of the other bed, all pins and needles, still holding his duffel. "Better relax, man. You know you can't go over there till lights-out."

Marshall nodded. "Right. I know." He pushed his duffel aside, got up, and paced across the room, back and forth.

"You're gonna wear that carpet out, then we'll have to pay Atilla double."

Marshall stopped. "Oh, man. Just nervous, I guess."

"Better leave your stuff here, in case there's a room check—you know, like at camp or something?" Now that his part of the bluff was past, Joe could enjoy his friend's misery.

"Right. Right." Marshall didn't catch the joke. Joe realized he'd probably never been to any kind of camp outside the Army.

A *tap, tap, tap* came at the door down the hallway. A door opened. "Your brick, miss." It was the young woman from the desk, maybe the landlady's daughter.

"Thank you so much." It was Ivy's voice. "I'm sure this will do the trick. I'm sorry to keep you up so late."

"It's all right. We're off to bed now. Blackout anyway. Mum turned back the vacancy sign. She's worried about those soldiers—right next door to you. Doesn't want her other customers seeing Yanks or Italians or Negroes here, you know. Bad for business—even if they are devilishly handsome. Straight out of Hollywood, if you ask me. Mum said to keep your door locked. Said you never know about them. *Overpaid, oversexed, over here.*"

Joe looked at Marshall and Marshall looked at Joe. It was all they could do not to burst out laughing.

Once the girl had gone, a few minutes passed before a note was slipped under the door. Marshall picked it up, read it, and folded it, placing it in his breast pocket.

Joe figured it was Ivy, saying it was time. "Her room or ours?"

"Hers. You're good where you are." Marshall pulled a Bible from his duffel bag.

"I don't think you'll need that tonight, my friend."

"I need it every night. We're gonna start this off right. This night is the beginning of the rest of our lives together and we aim to keep God first."

Joe sobered. He didn't know if he believed in God or not, but he sure wouldn't be thinking about Him on his wedding night. That Marshall did reminded Joe of his friend's consistency, his constancy. He was a good man and deserved every good thing. "Getting married shouldn't be this hard, Marshall. I'm sorry that it is for you and Ivy. I wish you both the best in everything."

Marshall smiled. "Thanks, Joe . . . for everything."

With that, Marshall was gone on cat's feet, slipping silently through their door and down the hallway. Joe didn't hear Ivy's door open, but he heard the soft click as it closed. He flicked off the light, rolled over, and determined to hear nothing more till morning. He just hoped nobody else would, either.

• • •

Ten hours later a subdued Joe and Marshall, who couldn't seem to keep his grin in check, descended the guesthouse stairs.

The younger miss manned the desk. "Have a good night, fellas?"

"The best," Marshall answered.

Joe grunted. "Better than the barracks, ma'am, that's for sure."

The young woman smiled, all but batting her eyelashes at Joe. "You come back anytime."

Joe sniffed the air. "That sausage I smell?"

"Blood pudding." The girl looked uncomfortable now.

"I thought there was no Sunday breakfast. Your mum change her mind?" Joe was hungry and wouldn't mind pushing.

"No, her mum didn't change her mind, not where the two of you are concerned." The landlady walked up to the desk, holding out her hand. "I'll take my room key, if you please. Next time you're in the area, find another guesthouse . . . if you can."

Joe slapped the key onto the desk. "Appreciate your hospitality, ma'am." He deliberately winked at the woman's daughter, who blushed with pleasure.

"Let's go, Joe." Marshall was all business now. "We've gotta get those supplies to base."

Joe wanted to say more, to spew a little venom, but he felt Marshall pushing him toward the door.

They threw their duffels in the back of the truck and got in the front.

"What about Ivy?" Joe hated leaving her there.

"She's gonna enjoy that 'good English breakfast,' then meet us at the bus stop in an hour. We'll drive into town, find some breakfast until then." Marshall kept his eyes ahead and shifted the truck into gear.

They'd driven five minutes in silence before Joe spoke. "How do you stand it, man?"

Marshall grunted.

"I've been called Mussolini more times than Mussolini. Not serving either of us breakfast, treating us like second-class citizens even though we're in uniform—over here, helping them out."

"She let you in, Joe. She took your money, gave you a room."

"Yeah, well, I guess money has no color bar."

"That's right. It's green. Unless it comes from me or somebody like me. Then it's tainted, black, like me." The grin had gone from Marshall's face. Joe saw his friend's knuckles tighten as he gripped the gear change and steering wheel.

"What are we fightin' the Germans for if not to end this?" Joe swore beneath his breath and determined in that moment that he'd help Marshall and Ivy in any way he could, that nobody'd stop him, and that he'd do all in his power to help his friend get his bride home to the US after the war.

Chapter Nine

MARCH 1944

A week had passed since the storm. It was late Friday night when Chester finally went to bed and Celia snuggled beneath her quilt with a flashlight, the portfolio of documents, and Minnie's diary. Opening the book, Celia stepped again into Minnie's world.

January 1863

> *This morning I met Tom's mother on the road to church. She clasped my hands in greeting, slipping me a letter, dirt-smeared and, if I am not mistaken, bloodstained. I hid it in my pocket, beneath my cloak, though I fear Grayson may have seen the exchange.*
>
> *Despite our town's and my family's many differences, we still worship together on Sundays. Reverend Snow does his best to keep war outside our church's doors and preach compassion for all those who suffer. How he's done this going on these two years when anger runs white hot and the blood of too many of our young men has*

run red is something I've marveled over and greatly admire. I pray God will bless him for this.

The new year began in such high hopes among our slaves. President Lincoln issued an emancipation proclamation for all enslaved in states of rebellion. The joyous weeping within our walls and outbursts of thankful praise liked to break my heart.

Obadiah and Martha and all our slaves gathered with Father, Elliott, Emma, and me in our parlor for watch night and to pray in the new year. Only Grayson was absent—the first watch night we did not meet as a family entire.

We beseeched God for Union victory that will bring emancipation truly throughout the South. Spirituals sprang from every throat, black and brown and white. In those voices there was among us joyful harmony, a common and precious life cause. Surely the Lord received this as an offering of praise.

Why Father does not himself give papers to our slaves now of all times I cannot understand. The government—the government he is loyal to—is willing. Why is he not? Despite President Lincoln's proclamation, Father still insists it is best and safest for our slaves this way, while the war lasts.

But what if the Union should fail? General Lee's recent victory in Fredericksburg marked a turning point Father and Elliott cannot ignore. If the Confederacy prevails, President Lincoln's proclamation will carry no weight here, and how do we know new laws won't prohibit freedom papers? This concern agitates me more each day, and yet I continue to pray for Tom and his safety. So many concerns. I cannot discern the way of the Lord in this.

Celia closed the diary. So many voices, so many views. *Tom.* She'd seen that name somewhere else. Where? Tom—she remembered now—was the name, part of the inscription, in one of the books Celia had found in the attic trunk. *Why did Minnie save two copies of the same book, hidden away?* Celia hoped Minnie's diary would say.

Of more immediate concern were the documents in the black leather portfolio. Celia had puzzled over them, and if she understood what she was reading, then bringing them to light was like to set No Creek on fire . . . or lead to a string of lynchings. The family at Garden's Gate had fought the Klan once and survived. Even Miz Hyacinth, God rest her soul, had fought that battle against her own daddy in his day. But this . . . this would rip wide open a wound that had festered since slavery days.

There was too much at stake to go to Olney Tate yet, even though he and his family would want to know what she'd found, had every right to know. Celia couldn't go to the Maes for help. They were good people as far as No Creek went, but blind members of the Klan, Celia'd bet her eyeteeth. Reverend Willard or Miss Lill would be ideal, but he lay in a hospital bed across the world in England and she wasn't about to leave him.

That left old Doc Vishy—Dr. Vishnevsky, who was Jewish and from New York City, and years before that from war-torn Europe. Nobody in No Creek would expect him to know or pay heed to anything about slavery or land rights or papers from before an eighty-year-old American war. They hardly listened to him about doctoring unless they were desperate for a cure beyond their kitchen and herb gardens. Still, he was the wisest man Celia knew, and he'd certainly experienced injustice and suffering. He'd give her sound advice.

The next morning, she waited until Chester had gone off to Red Tuttle's house to play stickball, then packed up the black leather portfolio, hiding it beneath her jacket, and made her way through the woods to the doc's cabin.

· · ·

Doc Vishy's door swung open before Celia could raise her hand to knock. Little Cecilly McHone, not much past toddle days, grinned from ear to ear and threw herself, bouncing yellow curls and all, into Celia's arms. "Celia! Celia!"

"Hey, Cecilly!" Celia swung the little girl, her namesake, into her arms and up toward the ceiling while she squealed.

"Cecilly McHone, you're gonna break Celia's eardrums!" Charlene

McHone, the little girl's mother, laughed. "Celia, it's good to see you. Come on in."

Celia stepped in gladly, drawn by the smell of fresh bread or something just as delectable baking in the doc's cast-iron oven.

"I'm just about to take up apple dumplings—molasses, sorry to say, not sugar. Stop and have one with a cup of tea?"

"Nothing I'd like better!" Celia meant it, though she knew it was a squander of the McHones' resources. She missed her mama's cooking with a vengeance and had surely dropped three pounds since she'd been gone.

"Then set yourself down in my kitchen while I pull them from the oven and add a little cream."

It really had become Charlene's kitchen—a far cry from the spare kitchen Doc Vishy'd kept before the homeless McHones had moved in with him over two years before on Christmas Eve, the very night baby Cecilly was born in a shed behind Shady Grove church.

Celia had been supplying the couple with food and blankets, but it was Doc Vishy who'd delivered the baby by lantern light during the unusual church Christmas play Celia had directed in Ida Mae's absence, and who'd taken the threesome into his home and heart.

Clay, Charlene's husband, worked anywhere and everywhere he could, helping farmers with crops or repairing machinery or construction—he'd done most of the rebuilding of the barn at Garden's Gate after the Klan had burned it down. Charlene cooked and kept house for them all, and little Cecilly made everyone's life bright—especially Doc Vishy's.

Charlene swiped a flour mark from her forehead, leaving another in her honey-blonde hair. "What brings you by? Lookin' for the doc?" She poured a steaming cup of tea and ladled an apple dumpling into a bowl set before Celia.

"Whoa, Charlene—heaven!"

Charlene grinned, pulling Cecilly into her lap just as the little girl reached for Celia's spoon. "Uh-uh—that's Miss Celia's. Share Mama's, darlin'."

Cecilly did.

"I am lookin' for the doc." Celia pulled the black portfolio from inside her jacket and set it on the table.

"Mmm. Looks official." Charlene raised her eyebrows. "What you got there?"

"Not exactly sure. That's why I need to talk to him."

"Joe Earl, drunk as a skunk, went and pulled the tail on Hector Baldwin's mule. Gave him a kick in the thigh Joe won't soon forget."

"That's gotta hurt."

"I reckon. Doc went over to set his leg early this morning but should have been back before now." Charlene looked at the kitchen wall clock and straightened her mouth.

"What?"

Charlene shook her head, hugged Cecilly, and stood up to pound the yeast dough she'd been kneading. "I'll bet anything he's gone over to the post office. He does that every day now and if the mail's not in, he sits and waits for it."

"Looking for a letter from Marshall?" Celia knew two things worried the doc no end—his longtime friends in Europe suffering under Nazi persecution, and Marshall, who he'd taken in after the Klan had beaten and nearly hanged him.

It was only now, as Celia had grown older and understood more of what Hitler was doing to the Jewish people of Europe, that she realized the risk the doc, Jewish himself, had taken in marching into those woods to save Marshall. If it hadn't been for Reverend Willard coming too, Celia sometimes wondered if the Klan would have hanged them both. She shuddered at the thought.

"Or from Europe. I'm not sure if he's more feared of what he'll hear or what he won't. Marshall used to write every week, sure as the calendar turns. He hasn't heard from him in weeks, not since the doc wrote him of his ma's passing."

Celia sighed. She couldn't imagine what it would mean to lose her mother, let alone what it would mean if she was stuck in some faraway country on the other side of the world. Giuseppe had understood that.

"I don't know why he enlisted. Schooling and doctoring was all he ever wanted, according to Doc, and he was doing so well in that Pennsylvania college."

"He'd've probably been drafted if he hadn't."

"Maybe. But the doc's been nearly beside himself for three weeks, not hearing anything from Marshall, frettin' that he should never have told him about his ma dying. I worry for him, Celia. He's aged like I never saw before. He needs to slow down. The doc's too old to be traipsin' over the countryside all hours. He needs help."

"Doc's claimed Marshall as family, same as you and Cecilly and Clay." Celia knew, because Doc Vishy had claimed Chester and her as family, too. "He's scared he'll lose him in this god-awful war, just like he lost his own family during the Great War." It was the first real thing Celia had learned about Doc Vishy when he'd moved to No Creek, how he'd watched his family die before his very eyes and not been able to stop the carnage. Celia shuddered to remember. "Reckon I'll go along and see if I can't meet up with him."

Charlene gently pushed Cecilly from her lap. "Wrap up warm." She wrapped another dumpling in wax paper. "For Chester. Mind you don't eat it."

Celia grinned. Charlene knew her too well.

• • •

Celia called twice before Doc Vishy saw her trudging toward him, pre-occupied as he was.

"Celia!" He spoke as if surprised to find her on the road. "Have you heard from your beau?"

She felt her face warm. "Giuseppe—Joe, he generally goes by Joe now—is just a friend, Doc, but I did get a letter from him just the other day. He's still in England, near as I can tell, though he's not allowed to say much."

"And Marshall?"

Celia shook her head. "Nothing. Sorry." She felt she needed to apologize for Marshall and Giuseppe both, but she had to keep faith with Giuseppe's request for secrecy. "I'm sure he would have said something if Marshall'd been sick or—or anything."

Doc Vishy's eyes bore into Celia's, taking her measure, surely wondering if she believed that to be true or if she was trying to comfort him. At last, he nodded. "Yes, he is Marshall's good friend. I just don't understand why—"

"Maybe he's just busy—training and stuff." Celia knew that was lame. Marshall was never too busy to write Doc Vishy, the man who had sponsored him through school and into college—the man who'd connected him with doctors and professors of medicine to help him find placement in a college that accepted Negroes. Doc Vishy was as much family to Marshall as blood.

Doc Vishy shook his head again. "I should never have written him about his mother's death. It was not my place."

"Olney asked you to do it. You had to, and Marshall had a right to know. A letter was the only way."

"Knowing—and deciding what to do with such awful knowledge— are different things." He looked so stooped and gray in ways Celia had never noticed. She wondered just how old the doc was. He'd seemed ageless to her, at least before this year.

Charlene was right. The doc needed help for his rounds. He needed Marshall and a place they could both practice medicine, a place where people would mostly come to them instead of the doc running all over this end of the county to folks' homes.

"Marshall said his battalion's treated better in England than here. At least you know he's okay." All Celia's sentences swung up at the end in hope.

"Yes, he wrote that—treated better by the British civilians—but not treated better by the American Army," Doc Vishy nearly spat.

Celia had no answer for that. It boiled her blood that men like Marshall were prepared to fight and die to keep Germans from killing Jewish people and political prisoners and Poles and whoever Hitler didn't cotton to, but the US Army treated its own colored troops like bugs squashed down in the dirt. It wasn't just Marshall, who'd written Celia stories of rotten things that had happened since he'd enlisted. She'd heard the same from Giuseppe. It was hard for him, too, being from an Italian family, but not so bad as it was for Marshall.

"Go home, Celia. It's cold out." Doc Vishy pulled his coat collar up around his neck and walked on.

"Doc Vishy, wait! I came round to see you. Can I talk with you?"

"You are ill? Or Chester?"

"We're fine, but I found something—something I need to know what to do with, and I don't know who else to ask. Please. I'm near desperate to talk." She waited but could see that Doc Vishy was trying to muster strength. "It might even have something to do with Marshall—something really good could come of this for him."

Doc Vishy's eyes lit.

"But I'm not sure." Celia squirmed. She shouldn't mislead him or take advantage of his worry, but it really could, in a roundabout way, connect to Marshall. His mother had been a Tate—Olney's older sister. "Can you come to Garden's Gate? Now? I don't think I should let anybody else know about this until I know what it is, what to do."

"Celia Percy, you intrigue me."

"That's not a bad thing, is it?"

He chuckled, at last. "No, Celia, not a bad thing at all. Lead on."

. . .

On the way to Garden's Gate, Celia filled the doc in on the tree from the storm and the secret room they'd discovered. Each revelation fired Doc Vishy's curiosity, lightened and quickened his steps. Especially when she told him of Minnie's diary written during the Civil War and the documents she'd found.

Chester was still out when the doc and Celia reached Garden's Gate. She let them in through the back kitchen door, flicked the electric light, and spread the contents of the leather portfolio across the table. The doc sat down and polished his glasses.

"I'll make us some tea." Celia lit the fire under the kettle, but the doc didn't take notice.

"Mmm" was the only sound she heard. And then, "Hmm," and then "Hmm," again.

Pins and needles crept up Celia's spine as she waited, patiently as she could. The kettle boiled. She spooned tea leaves into the pot and poured hot water over them, stirring the loose tea, then wrapped the pot with a clean dishtowel while it brewed.

Still he studied the documents, one by one, turning over the fragile sheets of paper, squinting at their faded ink.

Celia cut a slice of bread—she was pretty good at baking bread—and buttered it, spreading it thick with her mama's raspberry jam. She cut it into little triangles to make it look fancy and set it before the doc. She poured the tea, set the cup and saucer near his hand and the bowl of rationed sugar beside. Still, he took no notice. The clock in the front parlor bonged the late-afternoon hour.

At last, he sighed and pushed back from the table. His tea had surely chilled, but he sipped it anyway.

Celia couldn't wait any longer. "What do you think?"

He looked at her, as if across a century. She understood that. "You've not shown this to anyone else?"

"Not a living soul."

He sipped the tea again, staring into space, and set his cup in the saucer. "Do you know much about the days of slavery in this country, Celia?"

"A little. Miz Hyacinth said it was a shameful time and good riddance to the past."

Doc Vishy nodded. "Sit down."

Celia did, hadn't even realized she'd been standing over him all that time.

"I am not an expert on American history, but my understanding is this. Before the War between the States, the Union and Confederacy, slavery was legal in this country, at least in the Southern states. Men, women, even children were bought and sold. They had no rights, not even to live together as husband and wife, not even to keep their own children."

Celia had heard this, read some of it, but even in the Garden's Gate library, extensive as it was, there wasn't much to explain slavery beyond *Uncle Tom's Cabin* by Harriet Beecher Stowe, a book Miss Lill had insisted on adding a few years before. That was horror enough.

"In order to become free of such bondage, a person had to receive manumission papers from his or her owner." Doc set his glasses on the table and rubbed his eyes. "If I understand all that I've read, these are the original manumission papers for a man named Obadiah Tate, his wife, Martha, and someone named Alma, apparently the sister to Martha."

"Alma was Granny Chree's name. Could that be her? And Tate? Olney's family?"

"I believe so. They are dated before the war ended, signed and stamped with a family seal by the owner. My understanding from Olney is that his enslaved family wasn't freed until after the Confederacy lost the war, forcing Southern owners to free their slaves. If that is so, then the Tates were held in captivity long after they were actually freed."

"I don't understand."

"Nor do I. Did you read the signatures on the document?"

"I tried, but it was such curlicue handwriting."

"There are two signatures. Horace and Elliott Belvidere."

"Belvidere—that's Miz Hyacinth's family!"

"Olney Tate told me once that his grandparents were owned by the Belvideres."

"I heard Miz Hyacinth say that Granny Chree was her nanny when she was young. If Martha and Obadiah married, that meant they were Olney Tate's grandparents, and Marshall's great-grandparents. And if that was so, it means that Alma—Granny Chree, Martha's sister, was blood relation to Olney—a great-aunt or something." *No wonder Granny Chree gave Marshall her life's savings when she died.* Figuring that out made Celia's head hurt. But she couldn't be sure of the relationships until she read more of Minnie's diary. She hoped it would make it all plain.

"There is more."

"Worse than that?" Celia held her breath.

"Or better. There is a deed, signed and sealed by the same men, for land awarded to Obadiah Tate. If I understand correctly, it is acreage that adjoins land the Willards hold and the plot of prime land Miss Hyacinth willed to the Tates, but this larger tract of land is not owned by either of them. It is owned, I believe, by—"

The front door burst open then, jingling the bell over the library entrance. Chester and Red thundered through the hallway. Celia knew they were on their way into the kitchen.

Before she could speak, Doc Vishy swept the papers into the black portfolio and beneath his cup and saucer.

The boys burst into the kitchen. "Hi, Doc Vishy! What brings you here? What's for supper, Celia? Can Red stay?"

Supper? The litany of questions confused Celia. She hadn't thought of anything beyond Doc Vishy and the documents.

Doc Vishy stood, tucking the portfolio beneath his arm. "Good to see you, Chester, Red. I need to be going, Celia. Let me know if you hear from our friends."

"Sure, sure I will." But she wanted to stop him, to ask him more questions.

Chester and Red raided the cookie jar, which contained precious little, as Doc Vishy walked out the door with the portfolio. She hadn't expected any of that, and the portfolio, walking out into the March dusk and wind, felt like a sudden loss.

Chapter Ten

SUMMER 1863

"Miz Minnie, Miz Chatsworth passed me this parcel on her way to the general store, asked me to place it in your hands and none other." It was Martha's sister, Alma, who often ran errands to town for me now that she wasn't tending Emma. Alma helped Martha in the kitchen but was also our own midwife and herb doctor. There was none who knew better what herbs to grow, dry, grind, or brew for a headache or the ague, whether in teas or a poultice or salve. Though young, she'd delivered more babies than I could count for the slave women at Belvidere Hall and surrounding farms.

"Thank you, Alma." My heart raced. It was a surprise from Tom, surely. "How is Mrs. Chatsworth today?"

"Reckon she's fine, Miz Minnie. Sportin' a new bonnet with real feathers. Can't say where that handsome scarlet ribbon on it come from, though I did see some stowed behind Miz Mae's counter." It was a sly observation. Tom's mother was known to consort with Cordova Mae, who received stacks of fabric and yards of ribbon and laces from a man in the flatlands who traded on the coast with blockade runners. You'd think blockade-run goods would never reach the Piedmont, but they extended even into the mountains. *Everything for a price.*

"Nor should we say." I smiled.

Alma smiled in return. She knew Cordova Mae and her secrets ran in many directions. "You reckon some of that scarlet ribbon made its way into your parcel?"

We all longed for a bit of color and joy these days. It was telling that a swath of ribbon we'd once so taken for granted could now be the cause of speculation and hope. "I sincerely doubt it. But you might want to check the bonnet I left on the hat tree downstairs—the one with pink rosettes and ribbons. I'm thinking that perhaps I've outgrown it—that my head's gotten too big."

"Don't reckon that's likely to happen." Alma looked skeptical, but I pressed on.

"Do you know anyone it might fit? Someone about your size, about your height, someone with your lovely brown eyes?"

Alma's tempered grin broadened into a smile that filled her face. "I might."

"Then I hope you'll take it along and give it to her."

"Yes, ma'am!" Alma was halfway out the door.

"And Alma."

"Yes, Miz Minnie?"

"Please don't mention this parcel to anyone."

"Yes, ma'am." Alma hesitated, her hand on the doorframe. "You don't need to give me that bonnet to keep me quiet. I won't run my mouth, won't tell Massa Horace or Massa Elliott. I know it's a gift from your Tom."

"I know that you'd never do anything to hurt me, Alma. I'm sorry it came out that way. It was wrong of me to frame it so. I only meant that I know you love pretty things—like I do, like we all do—and I want you to have it. I was teasing, but I should have made it clear that the two things are not related."

Alma nodded.

"Please . . . a gift from me, if you want it."

"Thank you, Miz Minnie. I'll consider it."

I nodded, wondering again if I'd treated Alma differently than I would treat any friend, sad in the realization that I had, and sorry for it. For all I intended to treat the slaves I lived and worked with as equals, as Mother had taught me, I realized again that I had so much to learn—so much to unlearn and do better.

When Alma had left, I slowly tore back the brown paper on my parcel.

I'd not expected anything. Yet I found a book—five books. *Tom knows I love books. We always shared books from our libraries.* When I turned them over I laughed, delighted. *Les Misérables.*

The group was an inferior edition to the one I already owned and had read, books Elliott had ordered from New York for my birthday and had smuggled behind enemy lines through friends in Philadelphia—the set I treasured beyond any gift or book I'd ever read, save Scripture.

It delighted me to know that the two men who loved me most and knew me best had selected exactly the same—just what they knew I would treasure. That the story meant so much to each of them thrilled me. More than that, it gave me hope for Tom's change of heart for the enslaved. Tom's family didn't beat their slaves, but he considered owning them his God-given right and responsibility. Victor Hugo made his love of freedom and detestation of human bondage strong in the story. Only one in full sympathy could rejoice in its publication and popularity.

Tucked inside the first book was a note in Tom's hand.

My dearest Minnie,

   I hope this gift finds you well and enjoying peace in our No Creek these late-summer days. I imagine the fragrance of peaches, ripe and sweet in your orchard, and that the apples are turning shades of red. I miss sunsets over the mountain and walking home with you from services. I miss you, Minnie, and long for home.

   I don't write today of sad things, battles or encampments or any of the things that so cruelly separate us. Today I write, my dear friend—a fine moniker, but one I hope will soon be replaced by terms of greater endearment—of books.

Do you remember those long winter evenings by the fire in your library when your father read aloud, and we'd discourse the merits of books and authors? I remember seeing your eyes light when a new thought came to you or when you embraced a cause from our readings.

I treasure those memories and even now, on cold nights as I watch the stars crawl across the heavens, I recount those discussions—some more lively than others—by the fire, or on those Saturday afternoon rambles through the orchard back of Belvidere Hall, or rocking on my mother's porch after a full Sunday dinner.

Stories—parables—that offer lessons and insights we are unable to convey in conversation have long proven a thread between us, and for that I am grateful. Never do I fear that we'll run short of books or ideas to enliven our discussions as we age. Your mind is as keen as mine, Minnie, and I long to share that, my heart, and all that I am with you.

You will find sentiments in these books by Mister Hugo that I have longed to speak but have not found the words for—sentiments that I believe we share. The esteemed author expresses himself more eloquently than I can ever hope to do. He writes of the tyranny of despots, of the oppression of a people longing to live free, to rule their own destiny.

My breath caught. At last Tom understood the longing of slaves to live unfettered, to own themselves as all men and women are meant to. That he had made this leap, even if he still wore the hated uniform, softened my heart, made me long for him.

We have been too long divided over circumstances beyond our control, Minnie. I hope these books will help to mend that, to bring us closer together in our appreciation for all that surrounds us in this broken world.

They are so popular among my men who, unfamiliar with the French, have taken to calling themselves "Lee's Miserables." Many are indeed miserable in poverty and near starvation, in their

longing for home and freedom. To see the bare and blistered feet
they march upon would break your heart, dearest Minnie, as it
wears on mine.

I know you will be moved as you read. When you've finished,
write to me. Tell me what you think, let me know that you
understand the gravity of all we fight for. Share my hopes for a
time when we, like those battling from the barricade, will end
this war, victorious and free to make our own laws and establish
forever the rights we deem ours in a country of our own.

It will not surprise you that I end with hopes of seeing you
again soon and that I declare my love for you,

Your Tom

My fingers trembled and my heart sank. I opened the cover of the
first book. Sheepskin. Printed by West & Johnson in Richmond, 1863,
with low-quality paper and ink. That would not matter to me, but the
publisher's preface to Victor Hugo's undoubtedly pirated masterpiece
was chilling:

It is proper to state here, that whilst every chapter and
paragraph in any way connected with the story has been
scrupulously preserved, several long, and it must be confessed,
rather rambling disquisitions on political and other matters
of a purely local character, of no interest whatever on this
side of the Atlantic, and exclusively intended for the
French readers of the book, have not been included in this
reprint. A few scattered sentences reflecting on slavery—
which the author, with strange inconsistency, has thought
fit to introduce into a work written mainly to denounce the
European systems of labor as gigantic instruments of tyranny
and oppression—it has also been deemed advisable to strike
out. With those exceptions—and they are after all but few
and unimportant—the original work is here given entire.
The extraneous matter emitted has not the remotest
connection with the characters or the incidents of the novel,

and the absence of a few anti-slavery paragraphs will hardly be complained of by Southern readers.—A. F.

Tom had not read with the same eyes, the same heart, as I. He'd not even read the same words. I closed my eyes to keep back wells that threatened to spill. Tom's belief that this beloved book would bring us closer marked but one more barrier between us.

Chapter Eleven

March had turned to April. Back in his barracks, Joe took out pen and paper, knowing he couldn't put off writing to Celia any longer.

> *Dear Celia,*
>
> *I hope you're keeping well . . .*

He'd started the letter a half hour past and gotten no further. Usually he'd be full of news, especially if he'd gotten off base. Celia loved to hear about England and everything Joe encountered. Now he couldn't think of anything but Marshall and Ivy but wasn't at liberty to tell Celia—or anybody else—a thing. He wrote, *Our friend's okay, no need to worry. Sorry I said anything.*

What Joe really wanted to write was something so scathing about the Army's segregation policy that it'd make the staff sergeant's eyes burn and ignite his conscience. Celia would love that but it would be censored, get Joe KP or worse, and in the end accomplish nothing.

When I visited M we didn't get to see as many of the sights as I'd imagined—lots of things closed off since the bombings, and some of the buildings took hits in the blitz. St. Paul's is in good shape, and Westminster Abbey and the Tower of London and London Bridge still stand. Wish you could have been with us. We could have tracked down some of Dickens's old buildings, or what's left of them—all those places his books bring to life.

The British like their old stuff, so maybe, someday, if you make it this side of the Big Pond, it will still be here.

Joe hesitated. Was that something the censors might strike? They'd likely black out everything he'd said about London.

Shortly after he'd returned to base, trips to London were discouraged. All nonessential civilian travel to the south of England had been stopped. More ships and supplies poured into British ports by the week. Training, staged in places that closely resembled the beaches of Normandy—at least that was the rumor—ramped up, and leave, even for the day, was hard to get. Nobody needed to spell out what was coming.

The long-term goal had always been to invade France and push the Germans back. It wouldn't be long now, but Joe couldn't breathe a word, surely couldn't write that to Celia.

• • •

When the call came from Joe's CO to report to his office, Joe's stomach clenched. He couldn't think of any infraction he'd committed. It was like being called to the principal's office when you were a kid—knots in the stomach and mentally running through the catalog of what you'd done or thought of doing that could get you in trouble.

But the CO didn't look mad when Joe stepped into the room and saluted.

"At ease, Rossetti." He pulled a paper from a stack on his desk and tapped it against the fingers of his other hand. "There's no good time for things like this, Corporal Rossetti, but this has to be the worst. I thought of holding this for you until after . . . until after the invasion, but that's not right. I'm sorry we can't give you leave to go home now. I know you were close to your grandmother."

Joe's stomach sank to his feet, followed by lead pushing down his heart. He didn't want to look at the paper the CO held out to him, wondered briefly if he didn't take it, refused to accept it, if he could make time go backward, make it stop.

But his hand took the paper. He wouldn't read it, not in front of the CO. He saluted, waited for the return, and turned on his heel. *Hold it together. Hold it together. Step back. Don't internalize.* Those were the methods he'd used to make it through every training and combat session dressing wounds and stitching up guys that he'd encountered. It would serve him now. It had to.

He made it outside, made it back to the barracks, but couldn't go in, not now. It was pouring rain and the air was pea-soup thick with fog. *Nonni. Nonni's gone.* He tried to hold himself steady. He was a soldier, a medic in the US Army about to invade France. He couldn't fall apart. Too many people relied on him, relied on every man to be his best, do his part.

Still, he needed space—a little space, a little quiet.

Except for Marshall and Ivy's wedding, Joe hadn't been to church since that day the vicar took pity on him and invited him home to dinner. He had only gone because he'd been lonely. Now, with tensions ramping up, with word going round that they could be sent to France any day, lots of guys were going to church, stopping by the chaplain's office, writing letters home, and smoking like chimneys or shooting craps to get their minds off what lay ahead.

There was a little chapel on base. Joe figured it might be empty, or at least not packed this time of day. He headed there now, not minding the rain that beat against his chest, poured down his neck. Maybe it would cover tears, if he shed them. If he could.

Nonni was the only blood family Joe had, the only family he'd had since he was six years old. That's what made Marshall such a miracle . . . a brother for the first time in his life. And Celia—writing to Celia had seemed like having a kid sister or a cousin.

Joe wasn't what he knew Celia would call a "believer," at least not like her. He'd been raised in the Catholic Church by his Nonni—no better woman on the face of God's green earth, Joe was sure. He'd gone to church all his years at home and eaten fish every Friday to please her. He'd have hung the moon and swiped the stars for her if she'd asked. He wished she'd ask him now—anything.

But the night his parents died, Joe had stopped believing God cared, or that He was powerful enough to do anything even if He did care.

Joe had been six years old when he'd stood outside their two-story apartment building on the back streets of Philadelphia, crying, screaming for his mom and pop. A firefighter had pulled Joe out of the building when he found him crawling along a hallway, doing his best not to inhale smoke. It was something he'd learned in fire safety lessons at school. But his mom and pop had been asleep in their beds.

Too short, too scrawny, Joe had beaten on the firefighter's back, yelled at the top of his lungs to go get them, but the man didn't hear or didn't listen. He'd slung Joe over his shoulder, barreled down the exit stairs, stumbled out the front door, and fallen to the ground, exhausted and overcome by the smoke, while the building burst into flames.

Joe had scrambled free, tried to run back toward the building, but somebody bigger and stronger had yanked him back and thrown him to the ground, yelling, "Stay back, kid! The place is gonna blow!"

And it did—a giant explosion—the furnace in the basement, they later said. Joe was knocked ten feet back, and still he prayed and cried to God, "Save them! Save them, please, God, please!"

But God hadn't saved them. He hadn't saved eighteen of the sixty-two people who'd lived in the apartment building. Joe had decided then and there that he'd never believe again. He went to church when Nonni took him. He genuflected and went to confession, offering up what he figured the priest wanted to hear. He even took the sacraments, but in his mind, he'd closed the door. Strange now that the only place to find a little peace was a chapel.

Inside the chapel were a few guys, sitting in chairs in the makeshift aisles, heads bowed, hands clasped. Joe knew they were praying, asking God for protection or maybe to look after their families—Joe didn't know what. All he wanted to do was scream at God. *Why her? Why Nonni? Why now?*

When he'd thought of home, it was always of Nonni. Nonni, who'd shown her love through food, who'd taught him to make linguini, spaghetti, ravioli, red gravy, lasagna, biscotti. Nonni, who, no matter how poor they were, had managed to join with a neighbor or two and create the Feast of the Seven Fishes on Christmas Eve, who'd trudged through snow in her old-fashioned boots to attend midnight Mass. Most of all he remembered her smile. He could see it now—wrinkles gathered into an upturned wreath around her face, eyes warm and brown, her arms, still strong from years of kneading bread and pasta, ready to embrace him.

The day Joe brought Marshall home for dinner, she'd embraced him, too, adopted the big guy like another grandson, sent them both care packages at college. The night before they were shipped off to basic, she'd commissioned them to look after each other like brothers all their lives long. Had she known then that she wasn't long for this world? It would be just like her.

Joe found a seat in the back of the chapel and swiped hot tears from his eyes, tears he never meant to shed. He pulled out the letter from Mrs. DiSantis, their longtime neighbor. She'd sent a message from Nonni's doctor, old Doc Mason. *Tell Giuseppe that his nonna's heart gave out. She died peacefully, in her sleep, with a half-smile on her face.* Mrs. DiSantis wrote that she must have been dreaming of her grandson and imagining their reunion in heaven.

That did it—the tears gushed, and Joe couldn't stop them. He stuffed his handkerchief into his mouth to keep from crying out, from mourning so loud he'd draw attention.

How long he sat there, head in his hands, he didn't know. But at some point, a hand rested on his shoulder and another body sat in the seat beside him. Joe couldn't look up, couldn't acknowledge who it was. A hand picked up the paper Joe had dropped on the floor.

"Ahh. I am sorry, my son."

Nobody'd called Joe "my son" for years. It nearly sent him over the edge.

"You were close, your *nonna* and you."

Now Joe nodded. He'd testify to that.

"A sorrow and a gift."

Joe lifted his head and swiped the last of his tears. He wouldn't cry in front of this man, this chaplain or whoever he was. "Sorry, Padre, I'm not seeing any gift here." If he sounded defensive, angry, well, he was.

"She passed from this life peacefully, in her sleep."

Joe's throat knotted.

"You're Joe, aren't you? Medic, I remember."

Joe didn't deny it.

"How many of us would like to leave the carnage of this war and go like that, without pain, at home in our own beds? I would. Dreaming of my loved ones."

Joe hadn't thought of it that way. He'd worried, when he'd enlisted, about Nonni being left alone at home. She'd seemed fine but he'd known from the doc that her heart wasn't strong. And she was old, after all. He'd worried that she might collapse sometime while out to the butcher's or the deli on the corner or walking home from Mass. Who'd help her then? He'd made her promise to get the kid next door to run her errands, to walk to and from Mass with Mrs. DiSantis. She'd promised, but she'd laughed at him for such worry. Nonni had the greatest laugh. He could hear it now and it stabbed like a bayonet in his heart.

"Do you have other family? Is there someone I could reach for you?"

Joe shook his head. No one. No one in this world . . . except Marshall and Celia, and now maybe Ivy. But real, blood family? No. There was nobody.

The chaplain was speaking again, but this time not to Joe.

"Father God, we come before You with sorrow in our hearts for the loss of Joe's beloved *nonna*. You know what she meant to him, what she means to him even now, especially now. Bless every memory Joe has of her and of their life together. Everything she taught Joe, Lord, let him take with him from this moment. Every encouragement and affirmation she gave him, let those sink into his innermost being. Comfort him, Lord, help him through the grief of this great loss.

"Joe needs You, Father. He needs You now. He has a lot ahead of him and, by Your grace, a long and productive life. He's pledged to help those in need, and there are many who need him now and will need him even more in the days ahead. Help him pour into those around him the love he learned and felt from this fine woman, this daughter whom You've taken home and given rest. Thank You for her life, for her peaceful passing, and for the life You've given Joe. May both bring You glory. Through Jesus Christ, our Lord, amen."

Joe nodded, his heart too full to say anything, but he meant to thank the chaplain. Somehow, the prayer had brought him comfort. The things the chaplain had said were true, after all. Nonni was special—everything to Joe—and her life had been a glory to God and to everyone who knew her. He didn't know if his could be, but he knew it was true that he'd be needed in the days just ahead. That was something.

"God bless you, Joe. If you need to talk, to pray—anything—I'm here."

Joe nodded again. He figured the chaplain would understand. It wasn't until the man stood, squeezed Joe's shoulder, and walked away that Joe realized the chaplain's gait was a little off. His pants hung askew on one leg. The man stopped, lifted and straightened his pants leg. In that moment Joe saw it was a wooden leg—a prosthesis. He'd never have gotten into the Army with that. It must have happened in the midst of combat.

Joe winced. *Why is he still here? Surely, they'd let him go home.* But Joe knew. The chaplain's job, as he saw it, kept him here . . . giving comfort, helping shore up the hearts of men about to faint from fear or loss or grief or going crazy from the noise of combat or homesickness . . . or the worst news from home.

If he made it back from Normandy, Joe would thank the man with words. If he didn't, well, he figured the chaplain would understand that, too.

Hours later, as he lay in his bunk, listening to guys around him snore or whisper rosaries or just too quiet to really be asleep, Joe wondered. Marshall'd told him more times than he could count that there were no atheists in foxholes.

Joe flopped on his back. The chances of digging into a foxhole on the beaches of France were zilch. They'd be lucky to make it off Higgins boats and onto the beach without being blown to pieces by the Germans. If that happened, maybe he'd see Nonni sooner than he thought . . . if he believed. Did he?

Joe knew his unit would likely be part of the second wave, and the first three medics always went in the early stages to set up the first aid station. Not that there'd be much of a station—no time for as much as a tent, but the safest spot they could find, a place to offer triage and wrap wounds or tourniquet limbs. More serious wounds would be addressed later by doctors onshore or aboard the ships that had dropped troops, quickly turned into hospital ships bound again for England. Guys deemed out of the war would be shipped back home to the US.

Joe turned over. He wished he were home now, in Nonni's kitchen, chowing down on risotto and home-baked bread, torn to shreds and dipped in olive oil and herbs. But that wasn't going to happen. Not now, not ever. If he had any hope of reliving those memories it would have to be Joe doing the cooking and the baking, the kneading of bread or rolling macaroni over Nonni's *chitarra*. He closed his eyes, mentally forcing himself back to the work at hand.

There'd been a briefing late that afternoon, after he had returned from the chapel. Each medic would be assigned two medical kits instead of the standard one. The goal was to get ashore and help whoever needed it. They'd each been assigned a group of men, but once in the chaos of combat, you helped whoever needed it, whoever you got to first.

He wondered how Marshall was doing. Part of the colored balloon brigade, he'd be in the thick of things early once they got to France, treating wounded while the men in his unit launched balloons intended to keep German planes from flying low enough to strafe men storming the beaches.

Please, God, keep him safe. Bring him home to Ivy—don't let . . . But Joe couldn't go on. He realized he was praying. If he didn't believe, what right did he have to pray, to beg?

There are no atheists in foxholes. Marshall's words came to him again. Maybe he was right. Something about the praying made Joe feel not so alone. *Marshall and Ivy had the right idea. No telling who of us will come out alive, or whole.*

CATHY GOHLKE

There were no girls he knew well enough or thought enough of to court, let alone ask to spend a lifetime with him. The only girl he wrote to was Celia Percy. He'd never actually met her and she was only fourteen going on fifteen—still a kid, and he kept that in mind each time he wrote.

He'd told her about Nonni, about growing up in an Italian neighborhood in Philadelphia. He'd never told her about his parents' deaths, just that he'd been raised by his grandmother and every other grandmother on the street. That's how it was in Italian neighborhoods. But now he needed to tell somebody about Nonni—somebody who mattered—before he maybe couldn't.

Joe pulled a flashlight from beneath his mattress and a pen and some paper from a notebook he kept there. He wasn't sure what he'd write, but he needed to tell someone what Nonni meant to him, who she was so she wasn't forgotten.

He sat up against the wall, used his pillow to shield the light, and began to write a new letter, an honest one.

Dear Celia . . .

Chapter Twelve

Despite all that lay between us, I prayed daily for Tom's safety, longed for his companionship as in days of old, and was dreaming of him when Alma woke me before dawn.

"It's a message come from Miz Chatsworth," Alma whispered. "She begs you come, quick as you can."

My heart gripped. She'd not send a slave runner out before daylight when there were curfews and pattyrollers unless urgent. *Tom.*

"Her girl, Shelby, is waitin' in the yard. What you want me to tell her?" Alma twisted her night shift in her hands.

"That I'll be there soon as I can dress." My feet already searched the floor for slippers, my heart sick in my stomach.

"What you want me tell Massa Horace when you not down to breakfast?"

"That I've gone on an errand, tending one of Mother's friends."

Since Mother had passed, I'd done my best to continue her kindness in the community—not an easy task since loyalties were at odds and everyone knew my family's position, divided though it may be. We were not trusted by either side.

But there were now many poor among us and many needs among those who were poor. Even the once wealthy were poor in spirit.

Raiders and bands of deserters hiding in the Piedmont and the mountains increasingly stole at night or took openly with no recompense. Anyone refusing to sell to army foragers was guaranteed their livestock or crops would be taken anyway, their barns or fences often destroyed in the process.

So I took what I could from our kitchen, what Martha said we might spare. My first visit was always to Tom's mother. If I'd allowed my heart to bend, she could so easily have become a second mother to me.

I cared for Tom, surely, but in his letters he as much as begged for so much more from me . . . a promise for a future that would push all thought of this bloody war to the far reaches.

I'd not written him since sending a short and rather formal reply for the gift of books he'd sent. How could I encourage him when our thinking stood so far apart? I longed for home and family, too, and I imagined, in another time and place, wanting them with Tom, that I might grow to love him.

I pulled a dress over my gown and hastily, with fumbling fingers, fastened the line of buttons down the front.

If the South should win . . . The thought of Tom's position regarding the enslaved was too horrible. I could not become mistress of Chatsworth Lodge and own slaves. I would not.

All these things ran through my mind as I pulled and pinned my hair into a loose knot, not bothering to comb it out. Tugging on my boots, my heart gripped.

Before long Elliott will surely be arrested and Grayson conscripted. Father is failing, and Emma's strength is small. I could lose my entire family before this hellish war is done. The thought so terrified me that sometimes I woke sweating and tangled in my bedcovers from nightmares those imaginings produced.

I vowed, pulling on my riding gloves, that if I was the last Belvidere standing, I would free our slaves. I'd write their papers the day I buried my last family member that might oppose me.

Obadiah stood, waiting in the yard, holding Tammer, our oldest and most gentle horse, hitched to the buggy. "You want me to go with you, Miss Minnie? You ought not travel alone before daylight."

It was a bold offer and one I wished I could have accepted given the predawn hour, before curfew had ended. Knowing he realized the risk of his offer made me love Obadiah all the more. He was in so many ways more brother to me than my own brothers. "No, I can manage. It's best this way. But thank you."

He grimaced, knowing I was right, knowing that it was wrong for a man, colored or white, not to protect his family and those he cared for. But being out during curfew hours with a white woman could mean his death to a drunken or vengeful pattyroller, no matter what either of us said. He helped me up, handing me the reins. "You be careful now."

"I will." I tried to smile, to look brave, though I trembled inside.

The three miles to Chatsworth Lodge seemed to take forever, no matter that I urged Tammer forward, pressing the old mare as hard as I dared.

Nearing the big house, I saw a single lamp burning on the second floor and the shadow of a woman at the window, holding back the drape as if waiting for me. The drapery dropped. My throat tightened. *Please God, not Tom. Even if we're not meant for one another, please spare him for his mother's sake, for his own.*

A Negro I didn't know stepped from the drive, grabbing hold of Tammer's bridle and steadying her. I nodded, thrusting him the reins, unable to speak without tears, and ran up the steps. The door opened before me and a dark young woman pointed me toward the staircase. "They waitin' upstairs, ma'am."

I took the steps more slowly, summoning every reserve. A door at the top opened a few inches to Mrs. Chatsworth's broad smile and worried brow—a mixture I didn't understand. "Come in, my dear. Quickly."

I slipped through the barely open door. There stood Tom, in gray uniform, his right arm in a sling, but otherwise in perfect health. "Tom!" Relief and love I didn't know I possessed washed through me.

Before I knew it, I was in his arms—his arm—pressed against his chest. Confused, for I was the one who'd rushed to him, I stepped back, flustered, uncertain. There was nothing uncertain in his eyes, in the light of his smile. "Minnie." He breathed my name as if it was sacred to him.

"I was frightened, so frightened for you. But you're—"

"Only a flesh wound. Nothing that won't heal—in fact, is already healed. Afraid I've made more of it than needs be so I could get home to see you—and Mother."

In that moment I became aware again of his mother. She flushed and beamed, then discreetly stepped from the room. The realization that I was alone with Tom in his bedchamber made me pull back. "It's barely daylight." Confusion muddled my brain.

"And my attaché will be here within the hour. I'm sorry for sending for you so early, but it was the only way I could safely warn you."

"Warn me?"

"To warn Elliott. A detachment is on its way to round up deserters and to arrest him. He's disregarded every Confederate order wired to him. General Lee is frantic with the number of desertions from the Army of Northern Virginia."

"Elliott's not a deserter."

"He's not arresting deserters, though he's been ordered to. He's known to consort with them, to entertain them in your home. He's drilling a regiment that won't fight. Minnie—" he pressed my arm with his good hand—"you've got to understand. They'll try him and, in the end, they'll shoot him as a traitor."

My lungs couldn't draw air. "Is that why you're here? To arrest my brother?"

Tom looked away. "I asked to be assigned so I could see you, so you can get word to Elliott. He's hidden men by the dozens in the mountains. Surely he knows somewhere he can—"

"Elliott won't turn them in, and he won't run. He's made his choice. He took a stand to remain loyal to Governor Ellis and the Constitution— from which he has never wavered." I looked Tom in the eye and spoke quietly. "We've all made our choices, Tom."

"North Carolina seceded before Governor Ellis died, Minnie! Governor Vance supported the Confederacy before he ever stepped into office. Elliott cannot believe that Governor Ellis's orders for his regiment still stand." He spread his hands, appealing to me. "I'm here as a friend to Elliott—a friend to you, and more, I hope. If you warn Elliott now, he can change his tactics, help us track down those deserters . . . or if he won't, he can run. There may still be time for that."

I stepped farther back, seeing Tom standing there, seeing the room, seeing my life and Elliott's and Tom's more clearly. It was as if all the years of our lives passed before me and brought us to this place, this moment in time . . . perspective that I'd not captured before.

"Minnie? I've risked my rank and my life to tell you this. I love you, Minnie. I don't want this to come between us."

"The death of my brother not come between us?"

"Minnie." He reached for me, his eyes filled with longing.

But I couldn't look at him, and I couldn't stay. "Thank you for the warning." I hesitated, but there was no more to say. "Goodbye, Tom." I turned and pulled open the door, taking the stairs as quickly as I dared, long skirts in hand.

"Minnie!" He called after me, but I didn't answer him.

. . .

Warning Elliott did no good, as I knew it wouldn't.

"I won't run, and I won't turn in those who refuse to fight our Union. I stand by my allegiance to the Constitution. If they arrest me, that's what I'll tell them." Elliott had barely looked up from his breakfast. When he was finished, he stood, kissed Emma goodbye, and saddled his horse to go and drill his regiment, as if it were any other day.

The hours were a living hell for Emma and for me. We started at every sound, ran to the window each time we heard the hoofbeats of horses on the road. But evening came and went and there were no visits from Tom or any of his detail. Elliott returned for supper.

I fell into bed, exhausted, glad to hear the relief in Emma's voice in the room next to mine as she and Elliott talked. I couldn't make out their words and didn't want to but was thankful for their happiness, however long or short it might prove.

Whispers and even occasional laughter from Elliott and Emma's room hushed and the library clock bonged twelve before I finally fell asleep, believing—hoping—praying that Tom had somehow changed his plans or received new orders to leave Elliott alone, that we were safe in our beds for another night.

It was the crunch of frosted grass beneath the feet of a dozen men outside my window that woke me from a light sleep. I didn't breathe.

The sudden pounding on the front door downstairs made me jump and started my heart hammering in my chest. The pounding came again, louder this time, as if the butt of a rifle aided the call. I heard Elliott and Emma's door open, then heard Father sleepily call, "What is it?" from his room at the far end of the hallway.

I shoved my feet into slippers and pushed my arms through a wrapper, cinching it at the waist. Though terrified to open my door, I dared not wait. If it was violence for my family, I'd face it with them.

Emma shivered in her nightdress and shawl outside their bedroom. I joined her, wrapping my arm tight around her slim waist. We crept to the newel post and peered from the top of the staircase. Elliott, fully dressed as if in expectation, lit the lamp in the downstairs hallway. Even so, the banging on the front verandah door commenced louder than before. Father joined us at the top of the staircase, pistol in hand.

"Father, no—please," I begged, doing my best to pull the revolver from his hand. Whatever was about to happen, I trusted that Tom had no intention of shooting Elliott or any of us, but Father, in his rage and growing dementia, could initiate an all-out war on our doorstep.

He jerked the gun from me and took the stairs as quickly as his stumbling feet could descend, "See to yourself, Daughter! Stand back with Emma."

"Elliott!" I hissed. "Father!"

But Elliott's hand was already on the door handle, pulling it open, when he turned to see Father brandishing his weapon. "That's it, Father, thank you! Let me have the gun. You've done well." Elliott met Father's raised gun and pointed it toward the ceiling just as three Confederate soldiers burst into the entryway.

"Lower your weapon!" It was Tom who gave the order, sharper than I was prepared for.

But it was too late, and in Elliott's struggle to relieve Father of the gun, it went off, shooting a hole clear through the ceiling. The gunshot drew the weapons of every Confederate soldier in our home and evidently some unknown number surrounding it. I heard pistols and rifles cock and feet rush to the front of the house. The back door crashed open, shattering the window glass. Two more soldiers stomped through the downstairs hallway. It seemed the whole Confederate army might converge in our parlor.

"Tom! It's Father, he's not himself. Elliott's not armed!"

But Tom ignored me. "Hands in the air!"

Elliott flinched in the face of his friend but did as he was told. Father, too, as if the order were given to him.

"Tom? Tom Chatsworth?" Father's eyes narrowed. "Wearing a Confederate uniform?"

I groaned inwardly. Father knew this, had known it since the start of the war. Was his mind truly that far gone or was he initiating a feud—one that would certainly not help Elliott?

"Mr. Belvidere." Tom nodded, polite as ever. "I'm sorry to visit your home under these circumstances."

It seemed that Tom's acknowledgement of Father as the head of Belvidere Hall drew from Father some semblance of proprietorship. "Why are you here? Why bring this riffraff into Belvidere Hall?"

But this Tom ignored, except for a curt nod to Father. Turning to Elliott, he became all military. "Captain Elliott Belvidere, you are under arrest. You are to come with me to answer charges made against you by the Confederate States of America."

"On what charges do you arrest my son?" Father pushed between them.

"Minnie," Elliott spoke quietly, "could you please come down here?"

It was the last thing I wanted to do, parade myself in my nightdress and wrapper before Tom and a handful of leering soldiers. But I knew Elliott needed me to take hold of Father, and there was nothing in this world I wouldn't do for my brother. I squeezed Emma's hand for strength and stepped quickly down the stairs to entwine my arm through Father's, urging him to step back, doing my best not to look into Tom's eyes. "Father, please. Emma and I need you now more than ever."

The lieutenant behind Tom stepped out, ready to handcuff Elliott at the same moment Obadiah walked in through the back door.

"I don't believe that will be necessary, will it, Captain Belvidere?" I heard the pain in Tom's voice and looked up, witnessed what it cost him to arrest his friend.

A gasp of pity for them both escaped my throat. Tom's eyes met mine, longing and desire and sorrow filling them for a moment; then a blink, and a squaring of the shoulders to do his duty. How was it my heart could break for the man who arrested my brother?

"Minnie, take care of Father. Take care of Emma . . . please. Obadiah, take—" Elliott's plea, spoken so softly, came thick in his throat.

"Don't need to say nothin' more." Obadiah stood behind me.

"I will," I promised.

"I'm ready, Tom." Elliott did not acknowledge Tom's rank, only that they'd known each other all their lives.

Tom's jaw tightened. He nodded to the man beside him, who clearly had no compunction about arresting Elliott.

"Get along, traitor," mumbled the man, shoving his gun into Elliott's side.

"Lieutenant," Tom admonished the younger officer. He turned to Father, gave a stiff but respectful nod, and looked me full in the eyes. "Miss Belvidere." He nodded again, this time with sadness, tipped his hat, then turned on his heel and left us standing in the middle of the foyer. Emma's door closed at the top of the stairs. Her weeping followed.

Father clutched his brow with both his hands. "What are we to do, Florence? They've taken our boy!"

It was the first time Father had cried out for Mother since her passing, at least the first I knew. I wasn't sure if he'd confused me with Mother or simply cried out for her, knowing she wasn't there. Either way, I needed to get him calmed and to bed. "Obadiah?"

"Let's get you up to your room, Massa Horace." Obadiah wrapped his strong arm around Father and half carried, half guided him up the stairs.

"You're here. Oh, thank God you're here, Obadiah. They've taken Elliott. I don't know where. I don't know what we'll do without Elliott."

The panic in Father's voice tore at my heart. Had he never understood where this would lead?

"I know, Massa Horace, but it's gonna be all right now. You know Elliott; he'll get through by and by. He's a quick one with his words and he's got right on his side. Don't you fret."

"That's right. You're right, my boy. Where's my faith?" Father held tight to Obadiah's arm all the way up the stairs.

"He's not right in his mind." Martha, having slipped into the room after the soldiers left, shook her head. "And he's gettin' worse near every day."

I pushed my tangle of hair from my temples. "I know. But I don't know what to do about it. He loaded his pistol. When Elliott tried to get it away from him it went off—shot a hole right through the ceiling." I looked up at the round hole in the plaster. There was little evidence on the floor.

Martha closed her eyes. "My, oh, my. What next?"

I must have swayed because Martha was behind me with a steadying hand. "What you reckon they'll do to Mr. Elliott?"

"I don't know. Tom thinks they'll try him as a traitor, then court-martial him . . . at least."

"Hang him?" she whispered, wide-eyed.

"Hang him? Shoot him? I don't know. Dear Father in heaven, I hope not. I pray he can make them see, make them understand the path he's chosen. He hasn't hurt anyone."

"Not how they see it, I reckon."

We heard Father's door close.

I don't know what made me look up the stairs then, but looking down at us, Grayson stood grim and, I hated to think it, with a look of satisfaction in his eyes.

"Grayson?" I needed to know I was wrong.

He didn't answer but turned and walked down the hallway toward his room.

"Grayson!" I took the stairs as quickly as I could in my long night-dress. By the time I reached the second floor, the door to his room had closed. I turned the knob, but it was locked. "Grayson!" I called, but he did not answer.

Chapter Thirteen

LATE APRIL 1944

Doc Vishy had returned the portfolio to Celia two days before, saying that she needed to contact Miss Lill, that it appeared something good for the Tates might come from the land deed she'd found, but he couldn't be certain. "Mrs. Willard will know. If not, she is the only one in a position to find out. You've done well, Celia, but for the good of all, do not share this information until everything is made clear."

The doc had left her with such hope Celia could think of little else. But before she could write Miss Lill, a letter came that whisked everything else from her mind. Celia waited while Ida Mae, postmistress and proprietress of the general store, finally returned to No Creek, held the envelope up to the light behind the counter, as if that would enable her to read the contents.

"England. Doesn't look like this one came through the armed forces. Nothin' but bad news comes these days from far away. Did you hear Rhoan Wishon got one of those telegrams the other day? His little brother, Troy, was killed in action, somewhere in France or Belgium or some such place. It's a shame, though I have to say that boy was nothin' but trouble. Still, I'd never wish that on a living soul. Hope your letter's got better news."

"I did hear about Troy—you told me yesterday." Celia figured that was about the most polite thing she could say about Troy Wishon, dead or alive. It might not be Christian to breathe a sigh of relief over somebody's passing, but she did anyway.

"Didn't you get a letter day before yesterday from that Giuseppe fella? Now this one from England and a woman—at least it looks like a woman's handwriting. Well, I declare. Maybe that Italian fella you're pen pals with's got friends. Can't say who it is."

Celia reached for her letter. "It's for me, that's what." But she was puzzled by the return address. *Ivy*, with no last name. Nobody she knew. A sudden lump grew in Celia's throat. *What if something's happened to Marshall or Joe? What if Joe's met some British girl named Ivy and she wants me to quit writing him?* The thought made her sick.

Celia slit the seams of the airmail letter, careful not to tear any of the words written in its crunched space. Letters were costly to post, and every word counted.

Dear Celia,

If you open this letter while still at the post office, walk out the door. Don't say a word—not to anybody.

Celia stopped dead in the middle of the store, aware of Ida Mae's brows raised nearly to her hairline. She turned away but felt those gray eyes following her through the back of her head. She swallowed, stuffed the letter in her pocket, and walked toward the door as nonchalantly as she could.

"Well, aren't you going to read it? Tell us what's going on? That's from a stranger, near as I can tell. England, of all places." Ida Mae spoke as if she had every right to her mail, which Celia reckoned she believed she did.

"Sorry, Ida Mae. Got to go. Need to get my chores done before dark."

"What's so important that you got to run off like—"

But Celia tuned her out and was through the door in a flash, the bell over the door jingling like Christmas. She held her breath as she half ran up the hill toward home, conjuring a million scenarios in her mind as to why Marshall'd written that. It wasn't until she was out of sight of the store and neared Shady Grove church that she slowed, pulled the letter from her pocket, and began to read.

I've asked Ivy to address this letter. I can only write this once— there's no time to write three times, so please let Uncle Olney and Dr. Vishnevsky read it. And don't any of you write me back about this. You'll understand why as I explain.

When we first shipped to England last November, I didn't know what to expect . . . more Jim Crow, I figured. We all did— just more Army and civilians spitting on us colored boys like we were dirt. But the Brits treat us better than any of us have ever been treated. They're grateful the US sent over soldiers to help fight Hitler, and for the most part they don't mind colored. They've been at war a long time and lost a lot of men and boys. They're living with tight rationing, but most still no worse off than what Mama and I lived on in Georgia.

White families here have taken any number of us into their homes for tea (tea here means tea AND food) and conversation and what they call sing-songs around their pianos or to the tune of a fiddle or a mouth organ. They invite us to their churches on Sundays to sit with them in their pews and home for meals afterward. One family had a neighbor by the name of Ivy they invited to the Sunday meal, thinking it would be nice for me to meet someone near my age.

Ivy's like no girl I ever met. She's kind and funny and strong. She works at the telephone station down in the town and volunteers in the evenings, staying with little kids while their mothers work night shifts or volunteer in the hospital. She loves God, no doubt about it. I see it in all she does. And she's beautiful—chestnut brown hair and eyes the color of Aunt Mercy's blue cornflowers, and a smile that lights up the world—it sure lights mine. She's helped me through these days after Mama's passing. I can hardly wait for you to meet her.

Her parents were none too happy about her walking out with colored, soldier or not. They threw her out. Truth is, we haven't told them what I'm about to tell you. We're married. We were married in a church in London last week. We see each other when I get a pass and Ivy can get somebody to cover for her down at the telephone exchange.

The military won't allow colored soldiers to marry white girls. They say there's still more than thirty states back home where mixed marriages aren't legal, so they won't allow it either. They say that if a colored marries a white, they'll bring him up on charges of rape, and you know what that means—court-martial and hanging.

I know this could bring trouble for you in No Creek, Uncle Olney, and I won't risk that for you and Aunt Mercy or any of the children. I don't know what we'll do after the war, where we'll live, what I'll do to earn my living, but I'll figure it out. I love my wife. Despite all the complications and the big hole of losing Mama, I never knew I could love like I love Ivy, never knew anybody could love me like this. Every morning I wake up grateful.

Should anything happen to me before this war is over, please be good to my wife. I know you will accept her as family.

Please don't write me about this. Every word is read for censorship and I reckon you understand what that means. Ivy's going to mail this, but don't write her about it, either. She's just moved back in with her parents. She told them she married an American serviceman. She just didn't tell them that serviceman was me. The time hasn't been right—not yet. I just wanted you to know.

Stay safe, stay well, and know that I'm praying for you. Please pray for us.

M

Chapter Fourteen

AUTUMN 1863

October had always been my favorite month, when the sun drenched the hills around us and blue-ridged mountains in the distance flamed in vibrant golds and burnt orange, when the maples outside my window took on scarlet and crimson gowns, when the air grew crisp and skies burst their bluest, when the ground carpeted itself in diamonds, glistening in first frosts.

But in that year of 1863, I seldom noticed the autumn wonder, and those few moments I did left me sick with guilt for loving life when my brother, full of his principles, might be facing a hangman's noose or a firing squad.

Emma had grown pale and wan, haunting the post office each day for word that did not come. Did they even allow prisoners to write home? I didn't know but urged her to remain at home, to save her strength.

Yet I was just as haunted and made a point to see Tom's mother whenever I could, in case there was any news.

November, with its leaf showers and somber skies, had arrived when Obadiah sent for me through Martha. I found him in the barn, hitching

Tammer to the buggy. "Met Miz Chatsworth on the road just now. Said she'd like a visit with you soon as you're able."

My hands fairly trembled. "I'll go now."

"I pray it's good news." Obadiah's eyes didn't hold the hope of his prayers. He helped me up and handed me the reins. "Careful now. You wanna get there in one piece." He stepped back. "Let me know?" Worry lines creased his forehead. I loved him for the love he held for my brother, for all of us.

"As soon as I learn a thing."

Obadiah stepped back, nodding. I flicked the reins and Tammer left the yard at a trot.

It was midafternoon. I had no expectations of meeting a soul on the road. If I did, well, I was out to pay a call. I tucked my hair into its snood with one hand, hoping to look presentable. This was the first time I'd gone to Chatsworth Lodge empty-handed since the morning I met Tom there, not so much as a jar of jelly to offer, but I couldn't wait. That she'd sent for me surely meant there was some word from Tom.

No one was out front to meet me this time, so I tied Tammer to the hitching post beside the drive and did my best to walk up the steps without running. Before I raised my fist to knock on the door, it opened and Mrs. Chatsworth met me, a thing never done by the lady of a grand house and one that raised the hairs on my arms.

She said not a word but pulled me into the front parlor and closed the door. "I've a letter from Tom." She led me to the settee. I needed to be led. She pulled a letter from her dress pocket, perused it quickly, and handed me one sheet of the writing paper. "This is what you'll want to know."

My eyes scanned the lines quickly and then again, more deliberately.

We accompanied our bound prisoners from No Creek to Camp Vance, where they've been placed under the jurisdiction of Captain James McRae's battalion of North Carolina Cavalry, authorized to serve as enforcer of the Confederate Conscription Acts for western North Carolina. From there some of the prisoners were to be escorted to Salisbury, though I believe that ultimately, they will be

*sent to Raleigh for trial, likely before the end of the month. I know
a man in McRae's battalion, James Edwards—you may remember
that he visited us once during the summer season. He's promised to
make me aware of any prisoner transport intended.*

The page ended there. My eyes met the eyes of Tom's mother.

"That's all there was. The letter was dated October 14."

"Salisbury. Raleigh. No telling where he is now."

"I'm sure Tom will write as soon as he knows more. He loves you,
my dear. He'll do all in his power to help Elliott."

"I know he will." Still, Tom wore a Confederate uniform. He'd
not held his vow as Elliott had. If it came to doing his duty to the
Confederacy or helping Elliott, I knew which Tom would choose. I read
the letter again. It was my only link and I must remember everything
to share with Emma. "He speaks of prisoners, as if there are more than
Elliott."

"I don't know how many. I rather think deserters . . . and some from
Elliott's regiment. John Robins was one, that I do know. His wife is beside
herself with worry. Her third child is due anytime. To be alone now . . ."

"I'll look in on her."

Mrs. Chatsworth pressed my fingers. "I knew you would. You understand that being Tom's mother, I cannot . . ."

"Yes. And I know he can't write to me directly—for his sake or mine.
I'm grateful you share his letters with me. It's the only news we've had."

She looked as if she was considering something.

"What is it?"

"I don't know that Tom would want me to say this, but I must. There
is more to his letter. He loves you, Minnie. He hopes for a future with
you. I believe you know that."

My eyes studied the hands in my lap. I couldn't look at her.

"He'll do all he can for Elliott."

"I hope for that."

"All that is in his power. But you must realize he cannot stop the
wheels of military law from turning. He cannot control the outcome of
Elliott's trial, or those of the other men."

Please stop. Don't say another word. I can't—

"He fears that this will come between you."

It already has! I wanted to scream those words but didn't dare. Mrs. Chatsworth waited, but I could not reassure her in the way she wanted.

"A word from you, some sign of—"

"I must get back now and share this news with Emma. She's desperate to know what's become of her husband. At least we know that when Tom wrote, Elliott was still alive. It will mean everything to her."

"Yes, of course."

It was not the answer she'd wanted. She'd been so kind. Could I offer her nothing? "I'll look in on Mrs. Robins and let her know about John."

"Best not to say how you know. I don't want Tom's helping to land him in trouble."

"No." I clenched my teeth but smiled. "No, of course not." I stood to go. "You'll let me know anything you hear—even the smallest thing."

"You know I will, Minnie." She stood beside me and drew me into her embrace. "Go with God, my dear, and may this war soon be over. May our loved ones all come home."

I choked back tears and nearly melted in her arms, so good it felt to have them around me, a reminder of my own mother's arms. But I could return only a quick embrace, conflicted as I was.

Chapter Fifteen

Celia kept Marshall's letter in her pocket for two days, trying to gather the gumption to go to Doc Vishy or Olney Tate.

She hardly knew whom to visit first. She knew it would break the doc's heart—all his dreams of Marshall going to medical school and becoming a doctor, coming back one day to join his practice. The doc had even said maybe between them they'd someday cross the color bar in No Creek and he wouldn't need to keep quiet about all his house calls to the folks of Saints Delight.

Celia didn't know if she believed that, but she had believed in the possibility of more doctors in No Creek, and maybe a medical clinic of some kind. She'd even hoped that maybe if his family owned that land described in the deed she'd found, he'd consider setting up a clinic there. Now that he was married and couldn't bring his wife to No Creek, he might need to sell that land and move far away, somewhere it was safe for colored and white people to marry.

She wasn't sure Ida Mae or Joe Earl or Rhoan Wishon or any of the rest of that crowd were ready for a clinic that served everybody in No

Creek anyway or that they'd let it come, even if the law allowed. But Marshall was needed, no doubt about it. Doc Vishy was getting on and near run off his feet. He never turned a soul away, no matter their color or religion or lack of hope or money. This news was gonna kill him.

Worse, Celia dreaded telling Olney and Mercy Tate. They had children of their own, but Olney'd always hoped Marshall would settle nearby. They would grieve something fierce over the terrible risk Marshall took in marrying a white girl, let alone the impossibility of bringing her home.

Pure irony that Marshall was nearly hanged once for false accusation of raping a white girl. Now he's gone and married one.

A few years back, Ruby Lynne Wishon had offered to teach Marshall to read right there in the kitchen of Garden's Gate. No more than that, but when Ruby Lynne got pregnant, her daddy, Rhoan Wishon, had been so sure it was Marshall and had accused Miss Lill of running a courting school between white girls and colored boys. But there was no truth in that lie. It was Rhoan's own younger brother, Troy—Ruby Lynne's uncle—who'd raped and beaten her.

Ruby Lynne was so afraid to tell her daddy the truth that the Klan, egged on by Troy, had nearly hanged Marshall—would have hanged him right there in the woods if it hadn't been for Reverend Willard and Doc Vishy stopping it. Once Celia had discovered the truth, the grown-ups confronted Troy and marched him to the enlistment office. Right away he was sent off to boot camp and made to swear never to set his foot in No Creek again. And now he was dead.

Celia knew if the truth of Marshall's marriage came out, it would mean arrest, unless the Klan got hold of him first, which pretty much included any No Creek lawmen anyway. In that case Celia didn't think even the doc or Reverend Willard could stop it.

Thinking about the doc and Olney and Mercy and the danger of Marshall married and Giuseppe grieving all alone far away made Celia's head hurt. It was like something she'd read in Minnie's diary:

The persistent, conflicting voices of all those I love, spoken and not, are deafening—a hundred crickets shouting, screeching in my brain. The mounting tension is intolerable. Help us, Lord!

Marshall didn't want anyone to write him about his marriage and he wouldn't be coming home till the war was over. Not telling the doc, who was so weighed down and worried already, seemed kinder. Not telling Olney and Mercy when she knew they'd do nothing but grieve in fear for Marshall seemed a mercy of its own.

Celia didn't figure God was going to give her the go-ahead either way, so she didn't ask Him, which she knew might be a mistake. She decided to keep the letter to herself a while longer, just till she could figure out what to do. Right or wrong, good decision or bad, that's what she chose.

What she didn't know was what to do about Giuseppe's letter. Raw, a primal cry of pain and loss of dearly loved family from a soldier facing battle. It stole her breath and set her heart to beating like a caged bird.

All this time she'd pretended, even if just in her mind, that Giuseppe was her beau. But, in truth, he was her friend—a friend in deep need, a soldier facing battle with a grieving heart. He'd turned to her, and he'd signed his letter Joe—not Giuseppe. What did that mean? He'd written once that only his *nonni* still called him Giuseppe, before Celia. To Celia it meant the pulling down of romantic notions, maybe saving his Italian name for his noni's memory. She didn't know but she'd take his cue and call him Joe.

Celia didn't feel up to the task of being what he needed now, but she feared for him. There was only One who could help him in the way he needed.

Please, God. Help Giuseppe—Joe. Help him turn to You in his need. Be his comfort and shield against this awful pain. Help him see in Marshall and me, in the doc and the Tates—and now maybe even Ivy—his family . . . a family that loves and cares about him. Be the father to him he needs, and the mother and grandmother and whatever else he needs. Watch over all three of them, Lord, and bring them home. Please, God.

Chapter Sixteen

Confederates constantly searched the hills and hollows, barns and corn-cribs for deserters as well as foraging every mile of the Piedmont for hidden stashes of grain and livestock. General Lee was on the warpath, not only with the Yankees, but to reclaim deserters from his own army.

Tom lamented the state of affairs in a letter to his mother:

Morale is low among the men. Some of our troops, ill clad and near starving, march barefoot. They battle frostbite and dysentery, but the fiercest war wages in their hearts and minds. Letters from home eat at their souls—mothers and wives desperate in their own need for food and cash and medical care, desperate for seed and help to plow and plant and manpower to harvest crops. Women plead, fearful of marauders and deserters, raiders and even our own and despicable Yankee troops foraging for supplies and things no woman should be subjected to, certain their children will die if the men do not return home to help.

I'd be a hard soul indeed if I did not pity them. But we're at a turning point in the war, Mother. Without troops, we cannot fight, and so I must deny leave, all the while knowing I'm cutting the heart and soul out of men as good and better than myself.

How I will look in the mirror by war's end, I do not know, only that I must do my duty now.

Tom wrote nothing of Elliott and I didn't really expect him to. He was a Confederate officer, after all, and my brother was a prisoner.

We'd heard nothing of Elliott from anyone for the longest time, and then in late November Emma received a letter in his own hand, sent from a hospital in Raleigh earlier that month.

My Darling Emma,

I have no idea if or when this letter will reach you, my wife. A nurse here has been so kind as to offer me pen and paper to write you and has promised to mail it for me.

Since leaving you I've been shuffled from place to place and told that ultimately, I am to stand before Old Jeff himself. But time has stood still while I was taken with measles and sent to this hospital in Raleigh. They plan on releasing me from medical care tomorrow, but what that means or where I'll be sent, I do not know.

I don't expect justice in these times or before this tribunal, only in heaven. Whether I see you soon, my beloved Emma, or first meet our Lord is up to Him. Each day I do my best to rest in His will, and I pray you do the same.

I am sorry most of all that I was not able to give you our child to raise, to provide companionship for you now and to care for you in years to come.

I know that Minnie and Father—as best he can—will stand beside you. I pray for Grayson, that he will become the man you all need at home if I am not there to care and provide.

One last request, my beloved. Urge Father to free our slaves now and not to trust that this task will be accomplished upon his demise. Before my arrest we had begun to map out plots for the

portioning of land to be awarded after his passing and upon their
freedom. He must not wait. Father will need help to complete
that task. I know you are capable, dear wife. Trust Minnie and
Obadiah to help you. Their hearts are true, and they are able.

Give my love to the family and our people. Let them know that
I think of each by day and pray for them in the night watches, as
I do for you, my dearest wife. I do not know if or when I will be
permitted to write more. If we are not to meet again in this life,
we will have a joyous reunion in heaven.

My love forever,
Elliott

To say that Elliott's letter was a comfort might be too much, but word in his own handwriting was a relief and gift beyond measure to Emma's broken heart. Knowing he was alive and being cared for in a Raleigh hospital—not far away in Richmond or somewhere impossibly deep in the South—meant everything.

Despite the gravity of his words, his request gave Emma resolve and a purpose—one she set about with a vengeance.

Father, on the other hand, proved more difficult.

Things came to a head in mid-December, just as we prepared for our first Christmas without Elliott.

Martha and I were draping the parlor mantel in vibrant green monkey grass that Alma and I had pulled from the woods nearby that morning.

"Let's double the strands—make it thick as thieves." I loved Christmas and though we were shrouded in sadness, I was not going to let the season slip by unnoticed.

"Obadiah picked me a bright bouquet of bittersweet—berries red as that velvet bonnet you wore last Sunday. What do you say we tuck some in here and there?"

Martha's generosity overwhelmed me. "Won't Obadiah wonder when his bouquet's gone missing?" I teased.

"That handsome man will just have to pick me some more. I reckon that won't test him too bad." She winked.

Our girlish laughter felt good and clean but was suddenly interrupted by Father's tirade from the library.

"I tell you no! I won't do it! You can't make me!"

Martha's brows rose, surely as high as my own. *"Miss Emma?"* she mouthed.

I figured she must be the cause. Ever since Elliott's letter came, she'd dogged Father with the issue of freeing the slaves—her own personal mission, which I applauded and one I knew was dear to Martha's heart.

But it wasn't Emma who shouted back. It was Grayson.

I pulled Martha closer, listening.

"Father, you must hear me. Elliott's not here to advise you and I am. I spend time in town and have been to the county seat. The war is not going in our favor. If you're going to reap any reward at all—if you want to save Belvidere Hall for our family—we're going to have to turn a profit. The crop hasn't brought what it should, and foragers have stripped us nearly clean. I'm not sure we have enough to pay the taxes, let alone feed our people. Now is the time to sell, I tell you.

"I met a trader over in North Wilksboro. He'll take three strong bucks and a woman—a good breeder."

Martha's eyes went wide, and my mouth went dry.

"If we sign the contract before Christmas, he'll wait until the new year—give 'em their Christmas week first."

"I've never sold a slave in my life, Grayson. I can't begin now. You must understand . . . ," Father pleaded, as if weakening.

"You've no choice, Father. If we don't raise the funds, the house, the land, and all those slaves will be taken from us and sold who knows where. You—"

I didn't know the truth of our finances, but I couldn't let Father be bullied. Just before I stepped from the parlor, Emma's voice came cold and fierce from up the staircase.

"That's not true, Father Belvidere. Grayson, you know that is not true."

Emma's steel gave me courage. Knowing her presence would only inflame Grayson, I urged Martha to return to the kitchen and joined the battle. "We've never sold slaves, Grayson; you know that. Mother would turn over in her grave at such a thought."

"I thought you believed Mother in heaven." He smirked.

Horror at his sacrilege caught me off guard. I wanted to slap him. Father wilted a bit more, but Emma took up the sword. "I never took you for a bully, Grayson, or a bearer of untrue tales."

Grayson's color rose to crimson, fury filling his eyes. "This has nothing to do with you, Emma."

"It has everything to do with me. You know the wishes of your parents—the determination of your mother before she passed. You know Elliott's expectations as heir of Belvidere—"

"Elliott is not here, and though it pains me to say so, Sister-in-law, is not likely to return. That leaves me as Father's adviser."

"Elliott is firstborn, heir to Belvidere Hall, and has committed his wishes in writing. You have no right to—"

"Stop! Stop this at once!" Father bellowed, covering his ears. For all his sudden rage he looked a broken old man, pale and bent under the strain of family feud.

I took him in my arms and led him back to his chair by the fire. "A brandy. Emma, get him a brandy."

"You can't mollycoddle him out of taking action, Minnie. You've seen the stores in our pantry and barns. You know—"

"I know we'll make do, Grayson," I whispered, massaging the rigid muscles of Father's neck as he all but whimpered. "Just as everyone is making do."

"We can come out of this war with our home and land intact or we can—"

"Lose ourselves and our vow before God! We are Belvideres, Grayson. Have you forgotten?" I tempered my urgency, hoping he'd listen. "We founded this land on principles of freedom."

"We are slavers, like everybody else."

"And we shouldn't be. Father has always claimed it is only to maintain a standing in this community so we can help those who run, give them sanctuary and help them to freedom."

"Well, they don't need that anymore, do they? There's freedom for any slave reaching Federal lines—contraband of war, or haven't you heard?"

"Then Emma and Elliott are right. Now is the time to free the men and women loyal to us all these years—long past time."

"Free them! And leave us paupers!" Grayson fumed. "It won't be done. Father's no longer fit and Elliott's not here. It's up to me now and I—"

"Not while I draw breath."

We turned as one to the voice embodied by the near specter framed in the library doorway. Filthy, missing one shoe, skin and bones clad in little more than rags, we didn't immediately recognize him. But Emma did.

"Elliott? Elliott!" She flew into his arms, catching him as he collapsed.

To Grayson's credit he was there in a moment, lifting our brother to the settee.

"Water! Get him water," Emma ordered, stroking the face she loved, then stroking his arms and legs as if making certain they were all of a piece.

I raced to the kitchen. Martha met me with a pitcher. She'd heard everything.

"Towels. A basin," I gasped, my eyes filled with tears of gratitude.

"Anything you need," Martha swore and pressed my arm. "Tell him, when he's able to hear, that we're mighty glad he's home."

By the time I returned to the library, Father was by Elliott's side, on his knees, stroking his son's matted hair. "My son, my son. You've come home. Home at last."

"How?" Grayson's voice cut the tender moment. "Have you run?"

"Not now, Grayson," I insisted. "There'll be time later."

Emma took charge. "Grayson, help me get him upstairs. Minnie, call Obadiah from the barn and have him carry up the washtub. Get Martha to boil water—pots and pots. There are lice and who knows what. We must get my husband clean and comfortable. Father, you'll be able to visit all you want once we get him into bed."

That was the Emma I'd known before the loss of so many children, the strong and resourceful woman Elliott married. She was the true mistress of Belvidere Hall.

Grayson's eyes smoldered. He grimaced as he pulled our brother to his feet, wrapped his arm around Elliott's rib cage and half carried him up the stairs. I prayed that Emma and Elliott would take charge and step into their roles before it was too late . . . for all of us.

Chapter Seventeen

JUNE 6, 1944

The call came at 0530. Joe trooped into the mess hall with every man from his barracks fifteen minutes later. They were served up a gigantic breakfast of sausage, eggs, toast—a breakfast each one wolfed down, or pretended to.

The weather was foul. Invasion had already been delayed because of it, but word came down that they'd go that day, come hell or high water. If not, there was no telling when it might take place.

Every man was weighed down with packed gear, fastened to his body—medical supplies for the first aid station, two medic bags, personal gear, weapon, gas mask. Joe tossed his mask aside, figuring he'd never be able to wear or see through it while rescuing men from bullets and explosive shells. Some men already looked like they'd stagger down the pier; how they'd manage if they needed to wade through water was anybody's guess.

They got off on time, but the waves and rain and fog spit and swelled the boats until they stopped offshore by ten miles or more. Breakfast didn't seem like such a good idea then. It was worse the moment men climbed down into Higgins boats. Waves tossed the small craft, despite sailors doing their best to keep them tight against the ships, holding the rope ladders steady as men climbed down and jumped into the boat.

Joe had never been much of a seagoing fellow, one of the reasons he'd joined the Army and not the Navy. Now he remembered every reason he'd not wanted to spend his service on the waves.

The minute the Higgins boat pulled from the ship, the ocean took over like it was demon possessed, throwing the front up in the air and slamming it down against the swells. Whitecaps formed in the wake of the boat's forward thrust. It was impossible to see what lay ahead. Men were crowded into the boat so close they could only stand, but that didn't keep breakfast from being shared among them—again and again. Every man, including Joe, puked while the wind whipped vomit across uniforms, whether his own or from the man beside.

Halfway back in the boat, Joe couldn't see the shore, but as they neared, he saw the balloons in the air—the ones with explosives and long wires tethered to the shore, meant to deter German planes from strafing soldiers storming the beach. He knew that Marshall was out there somewhere with his men of the 320th. *Keep him safe, Lord.* This praying thing, Joe realized, was getting to be a habit, a lifeline. *However short that life might be.*

The Higgins boat jerked sideways, and every man fell against the next one, nearly crushing the two on the far side. The sailor must have seen another mine planted by the Germans. The engineers were supposed to have gone in first, cleared the way. But as they passed dead body after dead body in the water, some hung up on barbed wire revealed when the tide went out, Joe knew they'd likely never accomplished their mission. That meant the water was an unknown enemy, an uncharted maze of mines ready to explode the minute their ramp went down. Getting to shore suddenly seemed a much bigger challenge than Germans raining machine-gun fire down on them.

The plan had been to land within a few feet of shore, but between land mines and sandbars that wasn't going to happen. The first two rows of men disappeared down the ramp and into the water. The rest surged after, every man doing his best to keep his rifle above water.

Medical kits were secured at the waist. The minute Joe stepped off the ramp, he knew that everything in both kits was soaked. He'd not expected that—wet bandages, wet supplies, everything down to the skin soaked in salt water.

Still, there was no time to think about that. Who to help first? Men screamed as bullets and fragments of shells found their mark. Marshall would have called it a turkey shoot.

Joe rolled over the first man he came to in the surf. Dead. He crawled, half swam toward the next. The guy was breathing, but half his arm was torn off. Joe pulled a tourniquet from his pack and tightened it around the man's upper arm, just above the elbow, and helped him to shore. Together they ran, stumbling to the closest rock. No point in dodging bullets. They beat down like hailstones.

"Stay low. We'll get you more help." And back Joe went.

Joe trusted the first medics off the Higgins to set up the first aid station if they could. His job was to pull men from the water, keep them from drowning.

He pulled man after man to the shore, at least those that breathed. There was no way to think about what he was doing, to answer the pleas in the soldiers' eyes. It was always the same question—*Will I live?*

Joe couldn't say, but what he said, nearly every time, was, "You're gonna be okay." It was what every soldier needed to hear, what every medic needed to say, whether he believed it or not. He had to remain detached enough to do his job, to help the next guy, and there were hundreds. Some of the wounds were clean. Those guys, the walking wounded, would be all right. Some were explosions to the chest or stomach, to the head or eye. Those were a different story, one Joe dared not think about. *Do your job, give them the immediate help they need, get them to the next station where they'll get more help, then back to work, on to the next man.*

Minutes or hours passed. Joe didn't know. He just kept running from man to man until something tore through his left shirtsleeve, ripping flesh. *Keep going. It's not that bad. You'll live. Next man.* A moment later something bigger, uglier, hit his foot, then a stab to his gut, knocking him off his feet. Joe landed in the crush of pebbles that made up Omaha Beach, nothing like the soft sand of the Jersey Shore back home.

He tried to get to his feet, but the mangled one wouldn't support him. The ripped arm kept him from army-crawling forward. The best he could do was push forward with his one good foot, pull with his one good arm, all the while machine gun fire exploded pebbles around him into fragments.

Mercifully, somebody—must have been one of the other medics—grabbed Joe beneath the arms and pulled him roughly up the beach to the back of a concrete slab. "Where you hit?"

"Left arm, left foot. Maybe . . . more." Exhausted, Joe fought to keep awake. *How much pain can you suffer and still stay conscious?* It was a crazy question, one that didn't matter, and Joe knew it. He didn't know if he'd been hit elsewhere. He couldn't tell anymore. He couldn't tell anything.

Chapter Eighteen

The days passed and Christmas neared. Elliott had been furloughed while still awaiting trial. Confederates were camped in winter quarters, as were the Federals, both with little action, if the newspapers were to be believed. The Confederates weren't in a position to play nursemaid to sick prisoners if they didn't need to.

With Emma's doting care and Martha's good cooking, Elliott slowly healed, though he did not come close to filling out his civilian clothes or regaining his sense of humor. He and Emma spent long hours alone, talking and doing what, I supposed, all married couples did. They developed a closeness, a oneness I'd never witnessed, though I'd never thought of them as anything less.

Father strengthened somewhat. His eyes lit each time Elliott entered a room or sat down to the dinner table. His mind gained moments of clarity, and in those moments he and Elliott finalized drawings, maps detailing acreage to be distributed among the slaves along with their freedom. It was a hopeful time. Father no longer spoke of waiting until his death to free our slaves but insisted on keeping plans secret, even from

Obadiah, and on waiting for the new year, saying only that everything must be set in place for Twelfth Night—a real Epiphany for all.

We were longtime Baptists but had always celebrated Twelfth Night—a holdover from our ancestors. I could see why Father thought it a fitting time, but I just wanted it to be done. I didn't understand the delay.

I knew we'd have trouble with neighbors' wagging tongues once they heard—anger, shunning, possibly violence, though I prayed not.

Grayson ranted daily, adamantly opposed to freeing slaves that he could sell to save Belvidere Hall. The longer Elliott was home, the more time Grayson spent in town, drinking and—I feared—gambling, mounting debts he surely could not pay. He stumbled in late at night, half intoxicated, oblivious to the groans of those he woke.

One morning shortly after the year turned over to 1864, I found Elliott alone in Father's library and stepped in, quietly closing the door behind me. "Elliott, is it true what Grayson says, that we're insolvent and likely to lose Belvidere Hall?"

"Lose our home?" He huffed. "No, not unless Grayson gambles it away." He set down the book he'd been reading. "You mustn't worry, Minnie. We have stability Grayson knows nothing of, and there are matters he doesn't understand."

"What does that mean?"

"It means you must trust me. Leave these things to Father and me. We've not let you down so far, have we, Sister?"

It was kindly said, but he treated me like a child. Did Elliott mean there was money or assets of some kind hidden away somewhere that Grayson had not been apprised of? Did he mean that Grayson simply did not understand the worth of decency, of integrity, and our promise never to sell a human being? I didn't know and resented that Elliott did not speak plainly, that he depended on me to help him accomplish his tasks one minute—work as important as writing out freedom papers for each of our slaves—and treated me as a child the next. I turned on my heel to leave him to his book.

"One thing, Minnie." He spoke quietly.

I stopped but didn't turn to face him.

"If anything should happen to me, finish the work Father and Mother began. You'll do that, won't you?"

Without turning, without showing the conflicting emotions I held toward my elder brother, I swore, "I will. On my life, I will."

Alone in my room I thanked God that it was only three days until the freedom papers would be issued, and I poured my heart into my diary. I believed Elliott when he said he'd been furloughed until mid-January, but I wanted everything out in the open and settled before he returned to custody. Grayson whispered that it was all a lie and that Elliott had surely run and would be tracked down before long, that I shouldn't get used to having our big brother around.

So I slept as if on eggshells, starting each time an unknown horse or rider entered the drive. Even so, I was not prepared when, on Sunday night, two nights before the freedom party we'd planned, a detail of Confederate soldiers thundered down our lane and banged on our door. Why they came in the dead of night I didn't know, unless it was to terrorize us. If that was their purpose, it worked famously.

This time it roused everyone, bringing to the front yard both household members and slaves from their quarters.

Tom was not among the intruding party. The captain in charge was not civil to Father or polite to Emma or me. This time one of the men clearly nodded toward Grayson, alerting me to the fact that my younger brother was the only one not surprised by their sudden appearance, and the only one still fully dressed. That cut me to the quick.

Elliott made no move to oppose them but was roughly handcuffed, pushed outside, and tied by the waist to walk behind the captain's horse.

Emma, her wrapper tight around her and her hair a cascade knotted from sleep, stumbled down the steps to the yard. She ran to the captain's horse and grabbed its bridle. "Captain, I beg you—allow me a moment to say goodbye to my husband."

But the captain sneered. "Your *husband* lost those rights and privileges when he turned traitor, ma'am. Reckon that means you, too . . . Next time, watch who you take to your bed." He turned and spurred his horse, forcing Elliott to stumble after him through the dark or be dragged down the road.

. . .

Emma kept her composure until she reached her room. Once the door closed behind her she released a wail, a keening so primitive it might have reverberated from generations past—a Scots-Irish keening my mother had described in such detail I knew it in a moment.

Father, still in his nightshirt, crumpled on the verandah. Obadiah lifted Father and helped me get him back in the house and up to bed, though I knew there'd be precious little sleep for him or any of us that night. Grayson had disappeared. When we finally got Father settled, I felt near collapse myself. Our world, which had felt so complete and hopeful the day before, was once again upended.

"You gonna be all right, Miss Minnie. You the strong one here, and you gonna be all right. You must take hold." Obadiah's reassuring words belied the fact that Elliott was gone, perhaps for good this time, and with him all our hopes. Obadiah's and Martha's and the hopes of every slave of Belvidere Hall had been championed by Elliott and his good effect on Father. Now what?

I couldn't answer Obadiah. It wasn't a question, after all.

Sleep was beyond me. I closed the door to my room and sat in the small rocker beside my window for the remainder of the night, determined to watch for the dawn.

. . .

The morning chill woke me before the black of night began to gray. I was surprised, even guilty, to realize that I'd slept at all. The house, shrouded in misery and uncertainty, lay quiet. No sound came from Emma's room. No light shone beneath her door. I prayed she slept. It might be the only mercy she could obtain after last night, and I knew how needed and rare sleep could be to a tortured soul.

I tiptoed to Father's room and peeked in. He slept soundly, so I stirred and built up the fire, then quietly closed his door, hoping he would sleep a long while yet. I was nearly back to my room when I heard stirrings belowstairs and realized a pale light shone from Father's library.

I could not imagine that even Martha would be up at such an hour. Tiptoeing down the staircase, I felt heat from the library before I entered the room. The fire, which should have gone out overnight, was bright, crumpled paper setting the blaze higher and higher. "What in the world?" I spoke before I saw Grayson standing beside Father's desk, pulling papers from an open drawer.

He started at my exclamation. "What are you doing here?"

"I ask you the same. In Father's library at this hour? Going through his papers?" Even as I asked, I saw. The drawer he'd opened and pilfered—and it had either required taking the key Father kept in his vest pocket or forcing the drawer—contained the manumission papers I'd so painstakingly written out for Father, the ones Elliott had dictated and that he and Father had both signed and sealed. The lump in my throat hardened. "Grayson!" I could barely speak his name but stumbled toward him.

Before I reached him, he tore in half the folded map Elliott and Father had labored long over—the surveys of plots of land to be distributed to our freed slaves—and threw it into the fire.

"Grayson!" I screamed this time. "No!" I ran toward the fire, intent on pulling it from the hungry flames, but Grayson yanked me back.

"Let it go! You'll be burned, Sister."

"What have you done? How could you? How *could* you?" I cried. It was destruction of all the work Elliott had given himself to, all the dreams Mother and I and even Father had conceived. "You have no right!"

"I have every right. With Elliott gone I will become master of Belvidere Hall. I'm simply protecting what's mine . . . what is ours. Someone must."

"But we promised—we've vowed to free our people and provide them with land. Martha, Obadiah—all of them! Mother and Father always planned to. You've gone too far—stealing what's not yours. You have no right!" In my helpless rage and tears, I tried to grasp his hands, make him see.

He pushed me to the floor. "We have debts to pay, debts you know nothing of, and no other way to raise funds. You don't understand."

"Debts from your gambling?" I clenched my fists, forcing myself to stand, and swiped the hated tears from my eyes. "You are weak, Grayson, and foolish. These people are not yours to sell—"

"They soon will be. Elliott's gone—probably to the firing squad he's earned—and you saw Father tonight. His mind is—I could have him declared incompetent in any court of law."

"How dare you?" I saw my younger brother as I'd never seen him before. "You're not even of age!"

Grayson brushed his hands down the front of his vest, as if relieving himself of something distasteful. "Someday you'll thank me. You don't know it now, but you will."

I turned away in disgust and despair. Twenty-five sets of manumission papers and twenty-five copies, signed and sealed and ready to be awarded to those who'd served our family faithfully—most from years before I was born—and who'd worked with us to help others to freedom all while they were still enslaved. The party was set for the next day, and though it was intended to be a surprise celebration, no doubt word had traveled through the quarters and barn and all of Belvidere Hall. I'd seen it in Martha's smiles as we'd baked Twelfth Night cakes together, in the knowing light in Obadiah's eyes, in the tenderness between them as they surely planned their marriage. How could we face them now? How could I?

But there is still time—not to redraw the maps, for I've taken no part in that and don't know Father's and Elliott's plans—but to pen the manumission papers and have Father sign them. It will take two days at least, perhaps the nights. Copies are important—

"If you're considering writing up new papers, forget it. Father made Elliott his power of attorney last month. If Father signs even one, I will take him to court and have him declared incompetent. Not a judge within a hundred miles would question my testimony against the competency of a Southern slaveholder who suddenly decides to free his slaves in the midst of this war, especially one who already knew he needed help making his legal decisions.

"Our men are dying to preserve our way of life. Father could not endure the trial—you know it—and that would be on your head. Go back to your needlepoint, Minnie, and leave Belvidere Hall to me." And then he marched from the library, leaving me aghast and alone, my family's dream and the dreams of twenty-five souls in smoke and ashes.

. . .

With Elliott gone and Grayson striding over our acreage as if he already owned all of Belvidere Hall and its lands, we walked as if in a bad dream—family and slaves alike. If the slaves ever knew they'd been within two days of freedom that was cruelly snatched away, they didn't say . . . though I could tell from the crease in Martha's forehead and the light gone from Obadiah's eyes that they knew so much more than I'd shared.

I did not expect it to be Emma who saw beyond Grayson's bullying and took the reins of clear thinking. I'd waited until the day we were to celebrate before going to her room, where she'd sequestered herself since Elliott's arrest. Despite her grieving, I told her all that had happened, all that Grayson had done. She pulled her dressing gown tighter, gritted her teeth, and steeled her spine. "He will not get away with this and he will not be heir of Belvidere Hall."

I wanted to believe her, but with Elliott gone . . .

"I'll help you. We'll prepare the papers, omitting the dates, and we'll find a way to get Father Belvidere to sign them without Grayson knowing. We'll get the papers to Elliott as well. I don't know how yet, but we will. They'll only be legal now if Elliott signs them too."

"Even if we could do that—and we don't know where he's gone, where they've taken him—who can we get to witness his signature in a Confederate prison? It's true what Grayson said—who in the Confederacy would sign papers to free slaves now? And what if he takes Father to court? Father couldn't bear it." Sickness bubbled inside me and despair weighed my heart from the horror of it all, and from the loss of both my brothers in a single night.

"Stop it, Minnie. You've got to be stronger than this, stronger than Grayson."

"I don't know how. I'm tired, Emma—tired of being the strong one."

She sat beside me on the bed and pulled me into her arms. "I've let you carry this burden too long, ever since Mother Belvidere died. Well, no more. You're not alone now. We'll fight this together. We know the wishes of your parents, their lifetime pledge. We can't let Grayson change that now. And we cannot count on the South losing this war."

She was right. We dared not depend on President Lincoln's Emancipation Proclamation for slaves in the states of rebellion, not when it meant the lives of Martha and Obadiah and Alma and all those I loved. Yet I couldn't depend on this high-handed moment of Emma's, much as I loved her for it. I didn't want to say it to her now, but with Elliott gone, if he was executed for treason or killed in battle, she would lose her standing as mistress of Belvidere Hall and would become completely dependent on Grayson's generosity for so much as a humble home—a home not likely to be Belvidere Hall.

I was thinking this when Emma clapped a hand over her mouth, turned nearly green, and dropped to the floor, pulling the chamber pot from beneath the bed. She gagged and vomited into the pot before I could even drop beside her. She reached out her hand, motioning toward the washstand, keeping her head over the bowl. "A towel—please!"

It was in her hand and I was on the floor beside her before I had time to think. "Emma, you're ill! I should never have told you all this. I'm so sorry—"

She heaved again and all I could do was hold the towel for her and gently rub her back. "Water? Do you want some water?"

She shook her head. "Not now." Finally, she sat back on her heels and breathed, then breathed deeply again, wiped her mouth, and slowly smiled.

"What is it? What can possibly be funny?" I could not imagine.

"You must say nothing until we know for certain, until all danger of loss is past . . . but I don't believe that Grayson will ever become heir of Belvidere Hall."

Chapter Nineteen

JUNE 1944

When Joe woke, the guns had stopped. The explosions of shellfire, the *rat-a-tat-tat* of machine guns was gone. The quiet made Joe wonder if he might be dead . . . except for the wince of pain when he breathed and the stink of engine oil, the rumble of a ship's bowels beneath him.

"Awake at last, Corporal." Somebody Joe couldn't see for the light in his eyes spoke. "Though I imagine after all you've been through, that ranking will improve."

"Doc?" Joe blinked, doing his best to focus on the white coat above him. He must have been carried to one of the LCTs—the large landing craft that had carried soldiers to the Normandy beaches, then been used as a seagoing stretcher bearer to carry the wounded back to England. He'd known that was the plan. He just hadn't imagined he'd be hitching a ride on one of them.

"That's right. Got yourself shot up pretty good, medic."

"Never meant to be on this end of the equation."

"Nobody ever does. Rest easy. You're going home." And the doc was gone.

Going home. For two seconds a long-nurtured hope rose in Joe's chest before it plummeted. *Nonni's gone. There's no home to go to—nothing, no one there.* Joe swallowed, only the lump in his throat wouldn't go down. It tasted like gas fumes and engine oil and blood and sweat and the stench of gangrene.

"Wasn't sure you were gonna make it, soldier." The voice came from the next stretcher over. "Glad to see you showed us what you're made of."

Joe couldn't look, couldn't have turned his head if he'd wanted to. "Thanks." It was the civil thing to say. Joe wasn't so sure he was glad he'd made it. But he was a medic. Rescuing people, that's what he did. "Can't turn my head just yet, soldier. How are you doin'?"

There was a moment of silence before the reply came in what sounded, even then, too bright a voice. "Guess I'll be sportin' wooden legs, but I'm alive. I'm goin' home."

Joe sucked in his breath. *Both legs gone. Going home half of what he came over as. Does he have somebody to go home to? How's that gonna be for him? For them?* But he said what he knew the man needed to hear, what Joe himself needed to hear. "I'm sorry. You're gonna be all right, soldier. You did good. You did your duty, made a difference for every-body back home."

"Yeah." The reply came a little softer, less bright.

God, help this guy. Please.

• • •

The ship docked at Weymouth and loaded the wounded into ambu-lances bound for the 50th Field Hospital.

Inside an operating-room tent Joe was moved to a table, where he sensed them cleaning him up.

Joe knew he must have been given more morphine. Later he couldn't remember the doc digging out bullets or shrapnel or stitching him up or setting his arm or leg. He couldn't keep his eyes open but realized just enough to know that was probably a very good thing.

He felt himself wake as he was lifted from the table to a stretcher and carried to a bed in a ward tent. He figured he must weigh a ton the way it pained him, every step a jolt to his nervous system.

There was nothing more to do but sleep. So Joe slept, the only relief he could find in mind or body.

It was early morning, just as dawn was breaking, when he woke, stiff and every inch in pain. It was still quiet in the ward tent, except for the involuntary moans of men in their sleep, men trying to turn over in broken bodies that wouldn't turn.

That's when Joe thought of Marshall, wondering if he'd made it, if he was wounded, or if he was still over there, picking up men, applying tourniquets, cleaning wounds, getting men ready for the stretcher bearers to get to ships. Every job a medic did made him a target for German artillery, but Marshall, with the height and shoulder width Joe had always envied, made a prime target. Joe swallowed, and he prayed, again, *Please, God. Not Marshall. Ivy needs him. I need him. He's a good guy. He's Your guy.*

By the time hospital staff brought food, most of the ward tent was awake and talking back and forth, some more than others, but everybody subdued. Joe figured they were all thinking of their buddies back on the beaches, wondering how it was going, wondering who'd made it through and who hadn't, wondering when they'd know. And underneath, though Joe wouldn't say it aloud, he wondered if it was worth it—all this death and carnage and broken bodies and lives.

What we're doin' here better make this world different, a better place, 'cause it sure cost us.

• • •

Joe had no idea of the time when they loaded him on the train to Cheltenham. Time didn't matter much at that point. Bound for the 110th General Hospital, a large Army-manned facility set up around an older English hospital, the train jerked and lurched and bumped through every kilometer. Joe felt each and every shock shudder through his body. By the moans and groans of men around him, so did they.

How many days passed before they stopped giving him morphine,

Joe didn't know. He'd been glad to give in to the drowsiness, to sleep through the pain and the worry for his men and Marshall and his grief over Nonni. He was glad she couldn't see him like this, didn't know how shot up he was.

Truth be told, Joe figured he was doing better than most. He wasn't a doctor but knew enough by now to recognize the stages of healing and realized he stood a good chance of full recovery, given enough time and the right kinds of exercises to strengthen his limbs. His arm was healing nicely. The doctor had set his foot straight. He might end up with a permanent limp, but not if he could help it. Joe knew the importance of physical therapy and determined to help himself. It was the blow to his belly that gave him the most trouble, the one slowest healing.

Even the doctor was surprised when he checked Joe out. "You must come from strong stock, Rossetti."

"I do, Doc, thanks. But there's something I need. I hope you can help me, Doc."

The doctor raised his eyebrows. "I thought I was helping you."

"Not me. My buddy. Another medic—in the 320th Barrage Balloon Corps. I need to know that he made it, that he's okay."

"The Negro battalion."

"Yes, sir. Corporal Marshall Raymond—great medic, my best friend."

"I'm not sure—"

"There must be casualty lists, sir. I just need to know he's not on them."

"Soldier, we're in the middle of an almighty mess here. You were there. You saw what those beaches looked like. We don't know who's alive and who's dead right now. We're just patching you boys up as fast as we can, as fast as you come in. I can't help you find your friend."

"I understand, sir." But Joe didn't want to understand; he wanted to know.

"Think you're ready to go home, soldier? You've done your duty here and in case nobody told you, you've been promoted to sergeant. You're stable enough to move."

Joe swallowed. If he spoke his mind now, he couldn't take it back.

But if he didn't, things would be set in motion that he couldn't change. Still, the fact remained, there was nothing to go home to, and there was lots he could do here. "I appreciate the promotion, but I'm thinking I'm not done with this war, Doc. I'm thinking I can heal up and still make a difference. Don't send me home. Not yet. Please."

"Sergeant—"

But Joe cut him off. "Medics are needed. You know we don't have enough."

"They'll never send you back into combat, son. Even if you heal up nearly good as new, that foot will give you trouble—trouble that no one can risk in combat."

"I understand. But there's other work—work in the field hospitals here in England."

"There's a troop ship sailing tomorrow. I'd planned to put you on it. The war can be over for you."

"I want to stay, sir." With every word, every plea, Joe knew it was exactly what he wanted. He needed to be needed and knew he could still help save lives, if they'd let him.

The doctor studied Joe and Joe studied him back, never blinking. "All right. I'll give you another month here to make sure that stomach wound is healing properly. If it does, and if there's no infection, I'll send you for physical therapy. No leg work till then, understood?"

"Yes, sir."

"You can start hand exercises as long as you don't use those torso muscles for now." He stepped back. "But when the time comes, if they deem you need to go home, there's nothing I can do."

"Understood, Doc. Thank you. I mean it." Joe shook the doc's hand with his one good one.

"I know you do, soldier. You keep an eye on that wound as well."

"Yes, sir. I will, sir."

The doc hesitated before leaving Joe's bedside. "You know, when all of this is over, you ought to consider medical school. I hear you saved a lot of lives on that beach."

"I will, sir." Joe grinned for the first time in a long while. "First thing after this war."

Chapter Twenty

Emma and I wrote the manumission papers for each and every slave. We penned a second copy of each one, determined to hide them in separate places—places Grayson could not find. Over the weeks, while Grayson was out of the house, we urged Father to sign them as he was able, and we bided our time, trusting that either Elliott would return or we'd find out where he'd gone and by some miracle get them to him to sign as well.

Winter passed. Spring swept in on heavy frost and fierce March winds, then crept out on lambs' feet to welcome the greening of the mountain. April spun tiny purple violets, yellow daffodils, and crimson tulips to fill every room of Belvidere Hall by day. Purple, lavender, and white lilacs perfumed the night. Dogwoods blossomed in all their glory—pink and white. Butter-yellow roses began to bloom in May, covering the picket fence bordering our front garden. Mother's favorite, lily of the valley, covered her grave and those of the lost children and formed a carpet for the perimeter of Belvidere Hall.

Once Emma saw the delicate ivory carpet on the graves in the churchyard, she asked me to plant the same for her lost babies.

I wondered if ever I'd bear—or bury—children of my own but pushed those thoughts away. There was too much at stake for too many to indulge thoughts of my future.

I began to think that things could work out, that Elliott might return home, that our slaves might gain their freedom, that this hateful war might soon end. Spring has its way of lifting spirits.

But the months of summer languished into dog days, hot, humid, and lazy, and still we received no word of Elliott's whereabouts.

September dawned, at last, as a hint of breeze swept down the mountain.

Emma carried their child, but we—slaves and Emma and I—had done our best to keep her secret from Father and Grayson. From Father in case the baby did not live; from Grayson because not one of us trusted him, and because Father had no strength to oppose him. Neither Emma nor I could be certain he'd not been responsible in some way for Elliott's early and harsh arrest or what Grayson might not do to assure his inheritance of Belvidere Hall.

Emma had entered close confinement, even within the walls of Belvidere Hall, in June. No one outside our small circle knew of her impending joy, we hoped.

When Grayson was home or Father downstairs, Emma kept to her room. As the months passed, Father, in his declining state, seldom remembered Emma lived there at all.

By all accounts the baby should come mid to late September.

As the time neared, no clothing could hide her treasure or keep the smiling hope from her eyes. Several times, most frequently when I saw him for the midday meal, Grayson asked about her, sometimes petulantly demanding to know why she did not join us for meals.

Finally, I unleashed the storm he'd earned. "How can you ask why she avoids you? Why she cannot stand to remain in the same room with you? You treated Elliott abominably the entire time he was here. You cheated our slaves—our friends—out of the freedom and land Mother and Father both vowed to give them." The longer I spoke, the more my fury rose. I could not abide sitting across from him, so I stood, throwing my napkin to the table. "None of us will have peace until we know what has become of Elliott. And I have to ask you, Brother, do you know where they took him?"

Grayson shrugged but didn't look me in the eye. "How would I know such a thing?"

"What part can you claim in his arrest? He was furloughed until mid-January and yet they arrested him like a criminal beforehand."

"He is a criminal!" Grayson mumbled. "He got what he deserved."

"You knew the captain."

"I may have met him in town when he was on leave. Soldiers like to find a drink now and then, gamble a bit."

"And exactly what did you gamble, Grayson?"

His color rose, as if I'd hit the mark, but still he did not meet my eye. "You're not the master of me, Minnie. Leave me alone." Now Grayson shoved back from the table, stood, and stomped from the room.

I wanted to tear my hair out in frustration. Grayson was a boy in men's shoes determined to confront the world head-on, to charge ahead with bluster and thunder and demand that others concede he was right—as long as there was no danger to him. He wanted to force others—even Emma and me—to think well of him. When we did not, he grew sullen and angrier still. I could not anticipate what form Grayson's retaliation might take.

. . .

We tried every way possible to obtain news of Elliott. We heard at last, through a family in the valley whose son had been released from Salisbury, that Elliott was there, alive and tolerably well for a man despised by his guards and cast into prison. He'd been hustled from garrison to garrison and forced to stand before multiple inquiries. We hoped that his sterling record before conscription or perhaps his family name and our family's long history of service might help him, or that God might intervene in a way we could not imagine.

The early September air, with the occasional breeze, refreshed me, though air in the upper rooms of the house still stifled. I was massaging Emma's swollen feet in her bedchamber when a timid knock came at the door.

"Miz Emma? Miz Minnie?" The voice came barely a whisper.

"Alma? Come in," I called, hoping she'd brought us a tray of lemonade and some of those ginger cookies Martha had baked that morning even before the sun rose.

But Alma slipped through the door and closed it quietly behind her, clandestine as a thief.

"Alma?" Emma sat up.

Alma pulled an envelope from her skirt pocket and placed it in my hands. "Saw Miz Chatsworth's girl, Shelby, over to the store this morning and she said Miz Chatsworth wanted Obadiah to come fetch somethin' for you."

"Obadiah went to Chatsworth Lodge?" I knew that was a bad idea.

"I couldn't let him do it, Miz Minnie, not with the way Massa Grayson keeps an eye on him. He'd get that whip out sure enough if he left the fields for anything."

I gritted my teeth. The fact that he'd forced Obadiah from the stable to the fields was bad enough. That he'd taken a whip to him every chance he got, despite my pleas and threats, went beyond the pale. "You went alone?" I feared for Alma, too, though I knew she'd do anything in the world for her sister's Obadiah.

"No other way."

"You could have called me. I would have gone."

"Too risky." Alma shook her head, handing me a small, folded paper. "This what she sent. Said to burn it once you've read it."

With trembling fingers, I unfolded the letter.

My dearest,

It is with a heavy heart that I write that our mutual friend has been charged with treason and sent to Richmond to stand trial before President Jefferson Davis on August 25. I can hold but little hope for the outcome.

I send you my love and sorrow, and remain forever yours,

T

I felt the blood drain from my face and my mouth go dry. My heart hammered in my chest. *No, Elliott, my brother! Dear God, please!* I dared not show the note to Emma, not in her fragile state. I could not look her in the eye.

Beyond the horror, beyond the fear and anguish for my brother's life, I had never shared with Emma that Tom and I had exchanged letters, and certainly not that he, a Confederate officer, the man who'd first arrested our beloved Elliott, still held futile hopes for a future with me. Only Martha and Obadiah knew of my meetings with Mrs. Chatsworth. How could I tell Emma now that she was so close to bearing her and Elliott's child that he might be shot and killed—before he even knew he was going to be a father? What would that do to her? To their baby?

"Minnie? What is it?" Emma pulled her foot from my lap.

Can I lie to her? Should I? Does her right to know, her need to know, outweigh the danger for her and her baby? I crumpled the paper and shoved it into my pocket. I stood, pushing Emma's foot aside, not knowing what to say. My breath came in a gasp, as if my brain had disconnected from my mouth.

"Is it her son? Mrs. Chatsworth's Tom? I know he was a lifelong friend of yours and Elliott's. I don't hold him responsible for Elliott. Is he—"

"He's not dead. He's not." I knew she meant Tom but I spoke for Elliott. He couldn't be dead; I couldn't bear the thought, although the date of the letter was weeks past. August 25, the date of the trial itself, was nearly two weeks gone. *Confound the slowness of our mail!* The room's heat overwhelmed me. "I need air."

Emma shifted her weight, trying to stand.

"No, please, Emma. I need to be alone."

She sat back. "I'm here if you want me. Anything, Minnie. Anything I can do for you, you know I want to."

Through gathering tears, I smiled at my dear sister-in-law as best I could. "I know. Rest, Emma. That's all you must do now. That's all we need for you to do."

I wished I could keep the relief in her eyes there always. But I could not. I had to learn the outcome of the trial—before I told her what I knew.

I motioned to Alma to follow me from the room and down the stairs. I couldn't risk anyone hearing, and if I'd learned anything in all my years growing up in Belvidere Hall, it was that the walls had ears and there was bound to be a human set round every corner.

"Walk with me in the garden." It was all I could say.

"Is it Mr. Elliott?" she whispered, unable to keep her curiosity at bay.

I squeezed her hand, insisting on silence until we reached the sundial in the back garden. "Let's gather mint as we talk."

Alma bent with me, keeping our backs to the house, where I hoped Grayson might still be lingering over a late lunch. I passed her the note. Alma scanned the words and her sharp intake of breath settled my mind that she knew what the trial meant, what the outcome might well have been. "Can't be. Just can't be."

"What 'can't be'? What are you two up to?" Grayson stood over us, a suspicious apparition that I'd never heard or seen approach.

I stood before him, shielding Alma, with my hand behind my back, wriggling my fingers, begging her to give me the note. "We're gathering mint to brew tea and chill it. Refreshing in this heat. Do you want some?" I hoped he thought me as innocent as I intended. I hoped he would go away.

"I meant what written secrets are you two sharing? What's that in your hand?" He pulled me aside, attempting to grab my hand and whatever it held, all the while ogling Alma. "And where were you this morning, Alma? I sent Martha looking for you but you did not come, naughty girl."

Before Alma could answer I jerked away from Grayson and pushed in front of her again. "I sent her on an errand—something I am free to do. If you have questions for Martha or Alma, you may ask them of me as long as Emma is indisposed."

Grayson smirked and pulled me aside once again, nearly knocking me off balance. "I believe Alma's a grown-enough woman to answer for herself, aren't you now?" I hated the way he looked at her, and the widening of Alma's eyes told me she knew and feared that look as well. Had my brother approached her before? I had no knowledge of it. The thought sickened me.

"Grayson, you're out of line." He was still my younger brother and I wasn't about to lose my backbone with him. I stood as mistress of the house in Emma's absence.

Now his attention turned from Alma. Storm clouds entered his eyes. He grabbed my arm and pulled me aside by several feet, though to any passerby he might have been escorting me round the garden in a firm lead. "Never, ever, speak to me that way in front of a slave again, do you hear me?" He towered over me, threatening in his nearness and anger and strength.

"Let go of me!" I jerked back, but his grip clamped all the tighter, till I knew his fingers would mark my arm for weeks.

"Grayson, take your hands off your sister!"

Stunned, we turned as one to see Father, supported by Obadiah on one side and his cane on the other, standing on the back porch. It was the first time we'd seen Father on his feet and out of doors since Elliott was arrested. Grayson dropped my arm as if it burned him.

I grabbed Alma's hand and quickly walked toward the house and Father, shoving the damning letter deep into my pocket. Fire burned in Obadiah's eyes and I wondered if he had sought Father as protection for Alma.

"Come here, Grayson." Father's voice, though frail, was clear and firm. "You ladies go on in the house. There will be no more trouble."

We did as we were told, as Grayson walked slowly, perhaps reluctantly, toward the porch. He was still Father's youngest son and I thanked God that some part of him still craved Father's approval. Father and Obadiah remained on the porch, which gave them both the advantage of height. Alma and I slipped inside, where Martha waited, her eyes round and her breath taut. We three kept the door ajar, determined to hear what might be said.

"Never let me see you manhandle your sister or any woman beneath this roof again. You are not to touch my slaves—not those in the house or the fields or the barn. We have an overseer for the fields and Emma is mistress of the house."

"Father, Emma has not performed her duties since Elliott was arrested."

Even I could hear Father's breathing become labored at the mention of Elliott's arrest.

"Miss Minnie doin' a fine job in the house these days," Obadiah interjected—a thing I knew would send Grayson very near the edge.

"This is not your affair, Obadiah. What are you doing here anyway? I told you to get to the fields."

That riled Father. "Obadiah is no field hand. He is my groomsman. He's taken care of Belvidere Hall's horses since he was a boy and is to remain in that position without interference. Is that clear?"

"Praise God!" Martha whispered, squeezing my hand.

"I said, is that clear, Grayson?" Father's spine was in every word.

"Yes, sir." Grayson sounded as if he were biting nails.

"There's news you'll want to hear. Come into the parlor. Obadiah, help me inside, then call the ladies to join us."

"Is it Elliott?" Grayson had the decency to ask respectfully, though I sensed he knew more.

Father paused. "Yes, it's news of Elliott. Join me."

"Oh, dear God in heaven!" It was a prayer that came in gasps from my lips. *Give us strength! Sustain us. Sustain Emma!*

"You best go prepare Miz Emma." Martha pressed my arm in support.

"I don't think I—"

"Yes, you can, and so can she. She got a right to hear. You're strong, Minnie. Be strong for all of us. Make your mama proud. Alma, go with her. I'll bring tea to the parlor."

"You best be bringin' somethin' stronger than tea," Alma countered, taking my arm. "Come on, Miz Minnie. We need to help Miz Emma down the stairs."

Each step felt like I was pulling a ball and chain up those stairs. I didn't even think to knock on Emma's door. She was lying on the bed, resting. What she saw in my face, I didn't know, but she sat up.

"Minnie? What is it? Is it Tom after all?" Her eyes filled with sympathy.

Oh, Emma!

"Massa Horace wants you ladies to join him and Massa Grayson in the parlor, ma'am. He wants you all to come right away. Miz Minnie and I's here to help you down the stairs."

"Grayson? I don't want to see Grayson now. I'm big as Father's barn. He'll know right away—"

"Emma! Minnie!" Father bellowed from belowstairs. "Are you coming? You need to hear this!"

Alma's eyes widened. "He ain't gonna brook no argument."

I drew as deep a breath as I could muster. "No, he won't. We can't send him into an apoplexy. Emma, let me help you."

She stood, looking from me to Alma and back again. "Minnie?" Blood drained from her face.

I knew what she was asking but, coward that I was, I feigned ignorance. "I don't know. Truly."

We got Emma dressed and her hair pulled back into a loose chignon. Obadiah met us outside her door and helped her down the stairs. There was no hiding her pregnancy now.

I walked in front of her into the parlor. Obadiah and Alma helped Emma to a chair behind me, but it was no use. Grayson's brows rose and his mouth straightened into a line. Father, sitting in his great chair and breathing hard, didn't seem to notice.

"Well, well, well. When is—"

But Father cut Grayson off. "Silence! I've received news this morning that will make all our hearts glad. A letter from Elliott, in his own hand."

Emma gasped. "Thank You, God!"

But I held my breath, wondering about the date of the letter, wondering what news it held, wondering why they'd let a prisoner write home now. I exchanged glances with Alma.

"Alma, you may go," Father began. "This is a family matter."

Grayson, leaning against a bookcase, straightened. "Obadiah, you heard Father."

"Obadiah stays." Father's eyes leveled Grayson's.

"You said this is a family ma—"

"Obadiah is family . . . as good and loyal as family."

Grayson's eyes smoldered, but he looked away.

Father handed Obadiah the letter. "Open it for me, then give it to Minnie to read."

Obadiah ripped open the envelope and crossed the room toward me while my heart ripped in two. *Elliott's final letter, surely.*

"Minnie," Father admonished, waiting. They all waited.

My throat went dry as the fishpond beyond No Creek in the height of summer. I moistened my lips, but it did no good.

My beloved Emma, dear Father, Minnie, and Grayson,

There is only time to write one letter to you all before I am transferred. Forgive the impersonal nature of all I will say, but I want you to know that I am well. Even now, I cannot comprehend the Providence of my circumstances.

Since I was with you at the turn of the year, I have been transferred from prison to prison, stood before tribunal after tribunal, until August 25 when I finally stood before Jefferson Davis in Richmond, brought up on charges of treason.

I was ordered to a cell in Castle Thunder and on the 25th brought before his one eye. Davis had the charges read aloud and asked me if they were true. I replied they were true in part and were in part false. He asked me which were true.

I told him that as a commissioned officer of the 92nd Regiment of North Carolina Militia, I drilled my company as usual until I was arrested, but that they lacked all of being a Tory company, as accused. We protected our people as we'd always done. That did not require us to fight for the Confederacy. Much as I may have wished it, we were never recognized by the Union. Of course, I did not say that last to Davis.

He asked me if I did not know that was treason against the Confederate government.

I told him no, that I did not, and that if he was going to try me for treason that I demand the protection of the Federal government.

There was silence in the room for the space of about ten minutes. He said he would answer me at one o'clock.

I was taken under guard back to my cell to await judgment. At the hour appointed I was taken under guard again, back to face Davis, and was condemned for treason against the Confederate States, the penalty being death. The sentence sounded out said that I would be sent to the 33rd Regiment of North Carolina Infantry and there be executed by being shot on the first day of September 1864.

Emma gasped. I dropped the letter, unable to continue. September first was past. I could not look at Emma or any of my family. I found a glass of water before my lips, offered by Obadiah's strong hand.

"Please, please . . ." I could only beg in the terrible silence of the room.

Emma pushed herself up, snatched the letter from my hand, and continued reading.

Even now, I cannot express my thoughts upon this sentencing. It was as if I'd come to the end of a long road.

I was sent off that evening handcuffed under a strong guard, bound for the regiment, which we found late at night in line of battle in the breastworks. Relegated to what they called the dungeon—a hole in the ground covered with logs and dust, where two soldiers armed with muskets stood guard.

And here stands the point of Providence: J. A. Gilmore is colonel of that regiment, but was home on furlough, having received a wound in his thigh at the fight at the Second Battle at Deep Bottom. Major Slone was in command.

Very early next morning, before sunrise, Major Slone, himself a fellow citizen of North Carolina, came to the dungeon and called me out, saying he wanted to see me. He asked to see the charges levelled against me, so I showed him, and gave him as well the copy of my commission under Governor Ellis. He looked over first one, then the other for some time. I told him that I'd drilled my company as usual, and that's what they called treason.

He asked me what I thought about being shot, and this is what I told him, what I write now for you to tell anyone who asks.

"As I have soon to die, I will tell you the truth and it is this: I have ever been opposed to this horrible war, and I shall die opposed to it, for it is unjust and uncalled for, gotten up by a few hotheaded secesh for the purpose of destroying the peace and power of the government."

Further, I said, "When you shoot me, I want you to say in your heart, 'I know I have shot a permanent 76 Whig, a man ever loyal to the Constitution of the Federal Government, that died for his principles.' And wherever you put my body say, 'There I have laid a 76 Whig.' And if ever you pass the spot say, 'There lies the dust of a 76 Whig,' and when you see the blood run from my body say in your heart, 'There runs the blood of the grandson of the Revolutionary father unstained or tainted with anything but the immortal Washington liberty won by the blood of his grandfather with thousands of others as good as him.' If there is any treason it is on the part of Old Jeff and them that coagitate with him."

The major was shedding tears by then and vowed I would not be shot if he could prevent it. He left, determined to stop the execution, though I couldn't see how. Still, while we live, we hope.

Major Slone returned later, saying that if I would agree to go into ranks with a gun, he was pretty sure he could get a reprieve for me.

There is no doubt I wanted a reprieve, but I told him that I'd made a vow to Almighty God that I will never fire a gun in this rebellion. I don't intend to break that vow.

He left me and I imagined all was lost. I sat in that hole, preparing to die, wishing only that I could see your dear faces again, hold you, my beloved wife, in my arms once more.

Finally, on the 28th, Major Slone returned again, saying that the only chance for a reprieve was for me to take a gun and go into ranks. He said that if I would agree to that, he'd make certain

I will never have to carry that gun. He vowed that before I was forced, he would take my place, if there was any honor or truth in him.

How he could manage such a thing for me I didn't know, but I told him that if he could procure my pardon with such an agreement, and if I truly should never have to carry that gun, then of course, on those grounds I would agree.

The next evening a courier came with papers of one sort and another. Among them was the order for my release from the sentence of death. Emma, if you could but know my relief.

But in that moment Emma knew. I could see it from her laughing tears and felt it in her heaving gasps.

"He's alive! He's alive!" she cried.

All I could do was hold her. I could not speak, my heart was so full. Across the room I heard Father weeping, "My boy, my son!"

I glimpsed Grayson and saw the conflict in his face, the welling in his eyes. Tears flowed freely down Obadiah's face. I took the letter from Emma and continued.

I told the major that I could never compensate him for the kindness he'd done me.

He told me to only stand by him and he would do all he'd promised. The case is under his control now. He said that my statements regarding my principles expressed his own and that he'd determined by the aid of Divine Power to see me released or to die with me.

At last, family, a like mind, and in such a place, at such a time. You cannot know my thanksgiving to our Father in heaven.

Major Slone discharged his cook and gave me his place. Martha will laugh at the notion that I'm now cooking. I'm in dire need of her recipes—if only we could get the ingredients—and afraid that until I learn to do better, the major is bound to suffer some amount of indigestion. But he has not complained, not once.

This is long and I must close now and prepare for duty—duty

*I am hourly grateful to execute—for now I bear hope in my heart
that I shall see you all again and hold you in my arms, dearest
Emma. Give my best to Obadiah and all our friends there. I
rejoice to know that they are free at last, one and all, and working
their own land along with ours.*

*You are ever in my thoughts and prayers, as I beg to remain in
yours.*

With all my love and hope,
Elliott

Every smile paused. Every wet eye turned toward Grayson, still leaning against the bookcase, his arms tight across his chest, his face flushed.
He met our eyes, briefly, landing on Obadiah's. What he saw there,
I could not tell from my vantage point, but Grayson's gray irises burned
until they cooled, an icy steel. In the moment before he straightened,
I saw grim determination in his mouth and the flex of his jaw. He walked
from the room without a word. Despite the joy of Elliott's letter, a chill
ran up my spine.

Chapter Twenty-One

DECEMBER 1944

After six months of recovery, Joe discarded his cane and limped through the hospital door to pick up files from the same doctor who'd given him leave to stay in Cheltenham. He'd have preferred to be working on men just off the stretcher-bearer ships in Weymouth or better yet in a field hospital in France, but a desk job in the Army was better than being sent home. At least for now.

"How's that foot, Rossetti?" The major had become Joe's friend, but that didn't keep him from being his doctor.

"Nearly good as new, Major." Joe grinned, determined to seem right as rain, though he was a good way from it.

"*Hmmf.*" The major knew better than to believe Joe, and Joe knew it. *Can't fool a surgeon.* "Get these files over to HQ, will you? Next list for those returning to the States. Could have been you celebrating Christmas at home. Regrets?"

"No, sir. Not a one." It wasn't exactly true, especially on cold, rainy December days—and every day in England now ran cold and rainy—but still, he wasn't sorry. It was better to be busy, needed, and paid in the Army than to be back home, broke, jobless, and without Nonni.

He was nearly out the door when the major spoke again. "Oh, Rossetti, I got something for you. You asked me about your friend— a medic in the 320th."

"Yes, sir. You said you couldn't help me."

"I couldn't help you then, but I wrote his name down and put in a request for information. Finally came through—Army lightning speed."

Joe held his breath.

"Private Marshall Raymond was shipped back to the US after D-Day."

"Private? Wounded?"

"The memo I received said demoted and held on charges for disorderly conduct, pending trial."

"What? That can't be. Marshall's an A-1 medic. He's a corporal. He's—"

"Says right here. Read it yourself." The major handed Joe the memo. "You don't need friends like that."

But Joe knew he did. "Where is he now, sir?"

"Stateside. Don't know where. But a little advice, Rossetti: keep your nose clean. You've got a bright future if you don't screw it up. Watch the company you keep."

Joe saluted and walked out. *There has to be some mistake. There has to! Marshall, brother, where are you?*

• • •

There was a letter waiting on Joe's bunk when, finally off duty, he was ready to drop then and there, still in his uniform. His foot and leg ached from too many hours on his feet. The hunger grip in his stomach from no time for mess hall didn't help. *But a letter! Celia?* Joe hadn't had a letter from Celia for weeks. Not surprising, considering he hadn't written one since being transferred back from Cheltenham, lousy friend that he was. She'd have no idea where he was stationed now, but the Army could surely find him if they tried hard enough . . . and it appeared they had. Maybe she'd heard from Marshall.

Hoping, he turned over the envelope. *Not Celia's writing.* He didn't recognize the penmanship, but he knew the name in the top left corner. *Ivy.*

Joe ripped open the letter, careful not to tear the return address so he could write back.

Dear Joe,

I've written you three times, but you've never answered. I don't know if my letters reached you or not. I hope with all my heart that this letter finds you and finds you well.

I'm writing because I'm desperate, desperate to know what's happened to our M. The last I heard from him was a letter sent the third of June. He knew he was going away—surely to France— though he couldn't say. I've not heard from him since and the Army won't give me any information except to say that he's not listed as KIA. I can't bring myself to spell out those words.

Please, Joe, if this reaches you, help me. I'm pregnant. The baby's due near the new year and M doesn't even know he's going to be a father. My parents took me in once I told them I'd married an American soldier. They believed I'd stopped seeing M. But when our baby's born and they see—I don't know what they'll do.

Do you have any idea where he is, why he hasn't written?

It's almost Christmas. I never imagined this Christmas without him, or at least without knowing if he's alive. M would tell me to trust God, and I want to . . . but it's hard. Please, Joe, write to me. I'm scared, really scared.

God bless you, wherever you are,

Ivy

Joe set the letter down, folding it so no one would see, even though there was no one *to* see. *A father. Marshall's gonna be a father. That makes me practically an uncle.* He tried to take that in.

Ivy's alone. Once her parents see the baby—she's right, from everything

Marshall said about them. Joe ran his fingers through his hair, rubbed the stubble shadowing his cheeks and chin. *Marshall, you've gotta be okay, gotta get whatever mess you're in straightened out and get back here. You've got a kid on the way, and soon.*

He turned Ivy's envelope over. The address was in London—Ivy's parents, he figured. In the Army it was easy to lose track of the days, but Joe knew it was less than two weeks before Christmas. He hadn't asked for leave, hadn't asked for so much as an evening off in months. There was no point. He'd had nowhere to go. But now he did. He couldn't stand in for Marshall, but he could be a friend to Ivy. Her parents didn't know how lucky they were to have a daughter—and a grandchild on the way. Marshall's child.

Joe would give anything for that much family. Maybe he could help them see that—the importance, the amazing gift of blood relatives, the need of family. *Ivy said she was the only child left, that her brother had been killed at Dunkirk, never made it off the beach. Surely, they won't turn her and the baby out.* But Joe had seen what Ivy and Marshall had to go through to be together, and Ivy's parents had turned her out once before, when they knew she was just dating Marshall, had called her a disgrace to her brother's memory.

Joe pulled off his shoes, rubbed the aches in his feet, fell back against his pillow, still rubbing the worst one. *Due near the new year—that's less than three weeks away. No way can a letter reach the US, let alone find Marshall before then. I'll put in for leave tomorrow, speak to her parents for Marshall—something. I'll write to Ivy and Celia and send queries—somewhere.*

But the weariness of the past twenty hours on duty pulled and pulled until Joe let go of the foot he rubbed, the one that ached, the one that had been pieced back together. He let go of all the plans. All his good intentions were put on hold.

· · ·

Joe never opened his eyes until reveille blew outside his window. He was still in his uniform, still clutching Ivy's letter. He felt like he'd been driven over by one of Rommel's Panzer tanks, like it had rumbled through his throat, set it on fire, then ground to a halt and parked on his chest. His head pounded. When he tried to sit up, the room swam, so he gripped the sides of his bunk to steady himself.

"Hey, Rossetti," the voice came from the bunk beside him. "You don't look so good. You sick or something?"

"Naw—I'm never sick." But he was. Joe tried to stand up but didn't make it to his feet before the room went dark.

. . .

When he woke, the first thing Joe realized was that the room had stopped spinning. His head still throbbed, and Rommel's Panzer still sat on his chest. He still felt the ache in his foot, but it was no worse than the smoldering ache that traveled his torso, his arms and legs, or left his throat raw. He could live with all of it; he just couldn't sit up. But he tried.

"Rest easy, there, soldier." The voice was feminine and sweet—something Joe hadn't heard in a while. The smile sweeter still. It stole some of the ache away.

"Where am I?"

"Hospital—where you belong."

"Why? How long?" There was something niggling at the back of Joe's brain, something he needed to do, that he couldn't grasp through the fog.

"Influenza, dehydration, exhaustion. Sound about right?"

Joe dropped his head back on his pillow.

"Well, now you're in for a rest. Major's orders."

That reminded Joe. *Marshall. Ivy. The baby.* "I gotta get out of here. I got things to do, people I gotta see." Joe's heart beat faster. *Family. I gotta help family.*

It didn't take much for the nurse to push him back to the pillow. "Easy, soldier. You've got five days here. More if you don't cooperate."

That wasn't news to Joe. He'd be lucky to be on his feet in five days. "What's today?"

"December 23. You've slept three days. Guess you needed it."

Joe closed his eyes. Ivy could have her baby before he got out, before he even wrote her back or found Marshall or wrote Celia or any of it. The nurse shoved a thermometer into his mouth and Joe did his best not to chomp on it. She took his pulse. Her touch sped it up, he was sure. She grinned and flashed him a smile—a smile he couldn't altogether resist.

"Looks like you'll be with us for Christmas. Any special requests? Turkey and all the trimmings?"

Did she flirt with all the soldiers like this or was he lucky? "Pen and some letter-writing paper. Can you get that for me? I need to write a few people."

She tucked her head to one side. "Your sweetheart?"

Joe nearly snorted. "I need to find a friend who . . . who's missing."

She sobered. "Hard to track people down these days."

"He's gonna be a father and he doesn't even know it."

"Ouch. A lot of that going around. Will that be good news?"

The room started spinning again. Joe closed his eyes, imagining for a moment what it would be like to learn he was going to be a father, that there was someone waiting for him, someone wanting him, and that soon there would be two. "The best news."

• • •

It took Joe five days to work through the fever and chills, to get the tank off his chest and the fire from his throat. By then Christmas had come and gone. He'd written to Ivy the day before, and to Celia. The nurse was impressed at such industry for friends and had promised to post his letters before she came on duty again.

By the time he was discharged and given the okay to return to barracks and partial duty, it was December 30. He'd put in for a two-day weekend pass, determined to see Ivy, meet her parents, and work as much magic on behalf of Marshall's coming baby as he could. It had been a long time since Joe had pulled out his Italian charm, but that didn't mean it was gone. He'd do what he could for his friends. Getting past the Mussolini slur was the hardest part. He hoped that wouldn't be a big issue with Ivy's parents, but given their treatment of Marshall, he couldn't count on it.

The London train took him to Waterloo Station. He'd no idea how far it was to Ivy's house from there, but a boy hawking papers said he'd be walking right by the address Joe showed him, if he wanted to wait a half hour and give him half a crown. Joe didn't feel he had a half hour to lose, and yet another part of him wasn't in a hurry to step into whatever mess might await him or try to find his way with street signs down. He bought tea and a biscuit off a railway vendor and took a load off his feet, parking on his bag, not far from the newsie.

"Got any gum, chum?" The newsie broke into Joe's worry, and he struggled to his feet.

It was the classic request. All American military were expected to stand loaded with gum and chocolate.

Joe pulled a pack from his pocket. "Have the lot."

"Thanks, mate! You're all right." The boy walked faster than Joe found comfortable, given his lingering limp. The boy seemed to notice and slowed a little, mighty little. "Got yourself banged up, did ya?"

"Some. But I'm still here."

"France? Africa?"

"Omaha Beach."

"Blimey. That was a bad one. Papers were full of it."

Joe didn't answer. It was bad—the worst Joe had ever seen, but he knew men who had seen that and gone on to see more—across France, Belgium, Germany. He figured he hadn't had it so bad after all.

They'd gone about as far as Joe believed his leg would carry him when the boy stopped. "Let me see your address again. What number?"

Joe showed him, but he didn't see street signs or house numbers anywhere on the depressed block.

"That one." The boy pointed to a gray stonework building, what looked like an old house converted into a group of flats. The front garden gate leaned off its hinge. The place looked inhabited, but worse for wear.

Still, Joe saw no number. "How can you tell?"

"Just know, that's all. All the street signs and numbers were taken down long already. Don't want the Jerries to know where they're goin' when they land, do we?"

"If they land."

"Right-o. Where's my half-crown?"

Joe stood, undecided. As near as he could tell he was standing in the middle of London in some backwater street, as lost as a man could be. He should have paid better attention to the route they'd taken from Waterloo. Joe knew he was tired and off his game, but he didn't want to be left stranded.

"Ya promised, mate." The boy grew testy.

"Let me see if this is the place. Then I'll give you the money."

"You trying to fox me?"

"No. Just make sure you've not foxed me." Joe took the steps to the front door and lifted the knocker. It fell but wasn't loud. He tried again. The boy shifted from foot to foot, anxious to be on his way. Joe was about to knock a third time when the door swung open.

"Here, what's this ruckus? Who are you, soldier? What do ya want?"

Joe removed his cap. "Joe Ro—Joe. I'm here to see Ivy. Is she home?"

The woman blinked and stepped back. "Joe? Ha! Well, I never. Wasn't a made-up story after all, was it?"

"Ma'am? Do I have the right house? Does Ivy live here?"

"Next door. Ivy and a half, I'd say. Thought she made up that story about a husband gone missing. Well, I'm not one to say I can't be wrong."

The boy peddling papers no longer seemed in a hurry to go anywhere but stood grinning at Joe with new admiration. "So, soldier, ya—"

But Joe wasn't about to find out just what the boy might say. He flipped him half a crown and a "Thanks, I appreciate the guide."

The boy caught the coin midair, still grinning. "Any time, mate!" He was gone, off the stoop and still chuckling, while Joe tried to pull himself together.

"Come to see the little lady, I suppose," the woman standing in the doorway countered.

"Yes, please, ma'am." Joe wasn't enjoying her smirk.

"Well, you're just in time and a tad late."

"Ma'am?" Joe's head was beginning to hurt.

"Off to the hospital, she is, with her mum. Dad's at work but I 'spect he'll stop to see her and the little one, once he's off, if it's still visitin' hours."

"Ivy's at the hospital?"

"Since early this mornin'. Bad time of it, from what I heard—such screamin' and cryin' and carryin' on. Breech birth, the midwife said— used my phone to call the ambulance. Theirs was out of order."

Joe swallowed. "What hospital? Do you know?"

"Royal Waterloo, I 'spect. Closest one."

"Do you know where I can get a bus or a taxi?"

"A taxi? You are a toff, I reckon." But she looked more amused than offended, maybe even a little impressed. "Three blocks that way and two blocks east should put you on the main road. See what you can find there." She pointed, then closed the door, chuckling. "A taxi to the hospital—mind that! A toff and no mistake. Wait till I tell Lu!"

Chapter Twenty-Two

Emma's labor began mildly before we left the library—brief spasms at first, or so it seemed to me. Obadiah carried her upstairs even as I called for Alma. For the first few hours the contractions came far apart, and in between Emma laughed, joyful that at last her hopes would be fulfilled.

"We'll have a baby before sundown, I know it. If I am not able, you must write Elliott for me—right away."

"That's something you'll want to do for yourself, darling Emma." I smoothed the damp hair from her brow. "No." She shook her head, groaning with another contraction. "He must know right away. Learning he's a father will give him such joy, such hope, such determination to come home alive and well to me—to us! *Aagh!*"

The contractions came closer together, then slowed, then seemed to stop for a long while. I didn't know what to think, but Alma, used to delivering babies, said that sometimes happened, especially after an upset.

"Best keep her feet up. Best keep to her bed. It won't be long now."

Emma was adamant that all would be well, that the baby be named

159

Elliott Jr., and that I sew him a christening gown soon as he was born. But we were Baptists and didn't christen babies.

"It doesn't matter. I want a special gown for him."

I agreed to anything and everything she wanted, certain that we'd be able to talk things through after the birth, after her burgeoning emotions stabilized.

Twice I teased that she'd best share with us the girl's name she'd chosen, just in case, but Emma had declared that there was no need. She was birthing the heir of Belvidere Hall and the baby must be a boy. "Father Belvidere has always insisted he will leave Belvidere Hall to a male heir to carry on the family name, so a grandson I shall give him. God will make my baby a boy to make him the heir."

She spoke in near delirium about the changes her baby would make once the slaves were set free, once Elliott returned, and by the way, where was Elliott now?

I couldn't keep up with her mental gyrations.

"Best just keep her calm, Miz Minnie. No need to make sense of all she says."

I thanked God again and again for Alma. Martha peeked in on us from time to time, bringing plates of food and pots of tea, refreshed basins of water and clean linens.

The hours turned to night and day and night again. As Emma labored, she weakened. Alma and I took turns sitting with her, cooling her brow with damp compresses, rubbing her back and shoulders, massaging her feet, helping her walk across the floor when she could no longer lie in bed.

By the second sunset Alma knew that Emma and the baby were in trouble. "Best send for the doctor. This more than I know how to do."

We sent Obadiah for Dr. Hendrix. Hours passed and he did not come. Whether he was away tending other patients or he delayed because of our known Union sympathies, I didn't know. Midnight came and there was no progress with the birth. I sent Obadiah to search for the doctor again.

Emma's strength waned. Twice I surrendered her and the baby to God, praying only that her horrendous pain would stop, that at least she would live.

Finally, in the predawn hours of the third day, a squalling baby girl slid into the world in a sea of blood. Dr. Hendrix still had not come. Nothing Alma or I did could stanch the flow. As we laid her precious daughter in her arms, Emma closed her eyes and whispered, "Tell Elliott we have a son. They'll all be safe now. They'll all be free." She'd barely said the words when she slipped away.

"Oh, dear Lord Almighty." Alma, covered in Emma's blood, sank, weeping, to the floor by the side of the bed.

"No. No." I couldn't move, couldn't grasp that she was gone, that life had gone from her body, that God had not granted my plea—for Emma, for this child, for Elliott, for us all. Numb and cold. That's what I felt. Emma's fevered hand cooled in mine.

I don't know what time passed—it could only have been minutes, surely—before I saw the screaming, linen-wrapped infant as a person. A tiny life in desperate need. Gingerly, awkwardly, I lifted Emma's child from her bosom. So small. So incredibly small.

Alma was beside me, taking the baby, washing her with a cloth from a basin of clean water we'd kept aside for that purpose. I heard Alma weeping, praying, weeping more. But no tears came for me, only disbelief.

If ever a child came into this world on a dark day, it was this one, this little girl with no name.

Chapter Twenty-Three

DECEMBER 1944

Hospital. Baby on way. More than I bargained for. Hope I'm not too late. Dear God, help her. Help Ivy now. Joe hadn't prayed much since his recovery, and now, as he hustled the best his lame foot would carry him in the direction the woman had said, he wondered why not. He'd found comfort and peace before, maybe even something more. Why had he left off? God hadn't answered his prayers in just the way he'd wanted, but something had saved him back on Omaha Beach. Apparently, something or Someone had saved Marshall, at least then. Now there was Ivy—Ivy and their baby.

Joe didn't know much about breech births except that sometimes the baby could be turned and all would be well, if extremely painful for the mother. Sometimes mothers died. Sometimes babies died. *Please, God.* He hustled faster.

Joe had to stop and ask his way to the hospital half a dozen times. It was nearly four o'clock by the time he limped through the front door and stood before the matron at the front desk.

The woman took her time, finishing a notation, before she looked up at Joe and raised her brows. Joe realized he must look half frozen and unkempt.

"Are you all right, soldier? You don't look very well."

Joe wanted to scream. "I'm fine. Fine. I'm here to see Ivy Raymond—she might be registered as Ivy Greenfield. She's having a baby. The landlady said she was brought in this morning—breech birth."

The woman actually smiled. "Of course, you want the Mothers Department. The girl said she was married."

"Of course she's married." Joe was insulted for Ivy's sake, for Marshall's sake.

"Nurse Clemmons will show you the way. I'm not certain what her status is now, but you will be able to wait on the floor if the birth is not yet complete."

Joe nodded, twisting his cap in his hands, and followed Nurse Clemmons.

"Can you manage the stairs, Sergeant?" Nurse Clemmons took in Joe's limp.

"Yes, of course I can manage stairs." Joe had had enough of nurses and their pity. But the woman looked chagrined. "I'm sorry, ma'am. I'm just a little tired—and nervous." What did it hurt to confess?

"That's quite all right. I understand." She smiled. "First time?"

"First time?"

"First child—first baby. It's always that way with new fathers."

"Oh, I'm not—"

"I have to say I'd love to see Matron's face when you walk in. She never believed Mrs. Raymond was married to an American soldier. We get so many who aren't these days—married, I mean."

Joe meant to correct her, but his head was swimming, and just then Nurse Clemmons pushed through a door and he found himself in a room with twelve other people—all men and women who looked up, like they were waiting on tenterhooks for medical reports. Joe recognized the signs of stress, and tired as he was, his first instinct was to help. That's what he'd been trained to do.

"Here we are, Sergeant Raymond. This is where immediate family waits. I'll let the doctor know you're here. I believe Mrs. Raymond's parents are just at the end of this row."

"I'm not—"

She pointed, and there, not ten feet away, a woman who could be Ivy twenty years from now rose from her chair. Beside her was a bulldog of a man, who stood, too, but slower, disbelief written across his features. "Mr. and Mrs. Greenfield, your son-in-law is here." The smile on Nurse Clemmons's face lit the room. "Congratulations, Sergeant Raymond. I'm sure everything will be fine."

Before Joe could say another word, Nurse Clemmons was gone, and Mrs. Greenfield was crushing him in a bear hug. "Oh, my boy, our Ivy will be ever so glad to see you!"

But Ivy's father stood back, a mixture of disbelief and disapproval with shades of relief flicking across his features. He offered Joe a hand, which Joe took. More than shaking Mr. Greenfield's hand, Joe was shaken.

"I'm sorry, what she said—a mistake," Joe started.

Mrs. Greenfield pulled him to a seat beside them on the far end of the row of chairs. "Well, not so long as you're married," she whispered. "Our Ivy told us but I'm ashamed to say we didn't believe her. And never so much as a letter from you. Were you wounded, then?" She looked at Joe's leg.

He was getting pretty tired of people noticing his leg. He did all he could not to notice it himself. "Normandy." It was all he needed to say, and most people didn't ask more.

"A shame. It was bad there, wasn't it?" She seemed to be trying to make inroads, so Joe, for Marshall and Ivy's sake, tried to warm up.

"The worst."

"Still, seems you could have written in all this time," the father growled, but softly, clearly not wanting to get on Joe's bad side or garner more attention from others waiting for news of loved ones.

"Just after I got Ivy's letter I came down with influenza. I was released from the hospital yesterday. I wrote her—she didn't get my letter?"

"So, you didn't know she was in the family way till then? Ivy said you didn't—that she didn't find out herself until after you'd been shipped over to France. And then, what with the war and all, and no news—nothing, for ever so long. Oh, she will be glad to see you!" Mrs. Greenfield gushed.

Joe hated to burst this bubble, but it had to be done. "Mrs. Greenfield, you need to understand, I'm not Marshall."

"Of course you're not. I'm sorry she ever told you about him. Don't know what got into her, seeing that colored."

"You'll not hold that against her, then, will you?" The father seemed a mite nervous on that account.

Joe had had enough. "Marshall's the finest man I know, of any color or any nation. He's my best friend and I'll not—"

"Hear, now, lad," the mother cut in. "He wasn't meanin' anything unkind. Just that we're glad it's you that's come for our Ivy."

"I haven't seen Ivy since the wedding."

"Well, before or after, it's all right now. But, please, keep your voice down. We've had enough talk from the neighbors; we don't want it here."

Joe felt sorry for the woman. He felt sorry for her husband. Most of all he felt sorry for Ivy and Marshall, especially when this should be the happiest day of all their lives. A baby—a new generation of family— a family that would go on and not be cut off at the knees. But Joe was tired. He needed to sit down, to stop his head from swimming and his knees from shaking. Weakness and dehydration. He'd known it was too soon for him to be making this trek, but he'd meant to say something, to do something. What was it? How to put it into words?

"Are you all right, son?" Now the man seemed concerned. "You look pale as a ghost on Guy Fawkes. Here, take a seat." He pulled Joe to a chair and Joe was grateful.

"A cup of tea. Get him a cup of tea, Bert, and a biscuit."

Mr. Greenfield was gone in a flash to the end of the hallway and through the door leading to the stairs Joe had walked up. Joe was glad the conversation had stopped. When he finally got his point across, things could get ugly, by the look of it. Might as well not rush it. He wanted to see Ivy, after all, to know she and the baby were all right. That might not happen until the drama and mess of birth were done and the grandparents laid eyes on their grandchild. Male or female, son or daughter of their daughter—they had to love that.

After a cup of lukewarm tea laced with milk but no sugar and a stale, nearly sugarless cookie, Joe felt a little life coming back into his veins. Maybe he should go ahead and lay his cards on the table.

"It was a small wedding, was it?" Ivy's mother began, a little tentatively, a little sadly. Joe didn't wonder. What mother wouldn't have wanted to be at her only daughter's wedding?

Joe nodded. "Just Ivy and Marshall and me—and the vicar and his wife, of course."

"Of course." She nodded solemnly. "Marshall was there?"

"The thing is, Mrs. Greenfield, Mr. Greenfield, Ivy loves you both very much. She wasn't sure you'd approve of her decision."

"Well, she could have given us a chance to know you, but all's well in the end. You've turned up now. Suppose you'll be taking her and the baby back to America with you, then, when the war's over." Mr. Greenfield spoke gruffly, but Joe sensed relief tinged with maybe a little sadness.

"That's their plan—the last I knew, that's what Ivy and M—"

But he was cut off when a doctor came into the hallway and addressed Ivy's parents. "You'll be glad to know your daughter made it through. It was a difficult birth, but she'll be all right."

"And the baby?" Ivy's mother looked as if she held her breath. Joe held his.

The doctor hesitated, kneaded the back of his neck. "Not exactly what I expected, but she's doing fine."

"A girl, then." Ivy's mother seemed pleased.

"Yes, a strong baby girl. You'll be able to see mother and daughter in a few minutes. I wish you all well."

"She'll be off to America soon," bragged the father, "her and the baby."

"Not too soon, I hope." Ivy's mother softened.

The doctor had already turned to go when he noticed Joe standing there. Ivy's mother jumped to make introductions.

"This is our Ivy's young man, Doctor. Wounded in the war, just back from the influenza." As if explanations for Joe's tardiness were needed.

Joe wondered if there was any point in correcting the woman now, but the doctor gave Joe a penetrating stare, nodding to his insignia. "Medical Corps, I see."

"Yes, sir, stationed north. I just came down for the day to see about Ivy."

He nodded. "You come see me if you have any questions. I'll make time for you before you go back."

Before Joe or Ivy's parents could respond, the doctor walked crisply away, as if some emergency awaited him beyond the doors he passed through.

Joe figured he knew what the doctor meant. He wasn't Ivy's young man at all, and the baby couldn't look like him. He needed to set this straight before it went any further.

"Mr. and Mrs. Greenfield," Joe tried once more, but was again interrupted.

"Mother and baby are ready to see you now." It was Nurse Clemmons, but this time she wasn't smiling. She glanced at Joe in pity, at Ivy's parents with apprehension, then looked away, stiffening to an all-business stride.

They all followed her down the hallway, Joe hoping for the best.

"You should go in first, love." Ivy's mother pushed Joe ahead of her.

"No, ma'am. You're Ivy's parents."

"That's not the pecking order, son, not no more." The bulldog in Ivy's father returned, if a little subdued.

They passed a ward of women and a nursery full of baby cribs, but Nurse Clemmons walked on. Several doors down, at the end of a long hallway, the nurse stopped and stepped aside.

"A private room?" Ivy's father frowned.

"Doctor thought you'd all be more . . . more comfortable here."

"What's that gonna cost us?"

"Nothing more, I'm sure." Nurse Clemmons didn't look him in the eye. "Doctor thought you'd want a little privacy, that's all."

"Well, I reckon the US Army can pay for that," Ivy's father grumbled.

But it felt like holy ground to Joe, walking into Ivy's room. He'd expected to see her back in a ward—wards were all he'd known. But there was Ivy, lying on a hospital bed in a room of her own, with a little bassinet beside her. Ivy held the baby close to her chest, as if she'd been nursing, and quickly covered herself and the baby. Both looked too small in the high-ceilinged room.

"Joe! Joe, you came!" Ivy looked older, peaked, the worse for wear, like maybe she'd been to Omaha Beach and back, but glad beyond words to see him.

"Good to see you, Ivy. Never thought I'd get to see two of you." Joe meant it.

"We just met your Joe in the waiting room. Rushed here straight out of the hospital to reach you, Ivy," her mother quipped. "Go on, Joe, give your wife a kiss."

Ivy looked blank and Joe squirmed. "Joe's not my husband, Mum."

"What?" Her mother paled.

"You said you'd married the bloke," her father accused.

"I did. Joe was there. He stood with us, but—"

"Then you're not the father?" Ivy's mother looked as if all her hopes had been dashed.

"That's what I've been trying to tell you both." Joe felt helpless.

Ivy's father looked wary. "So where is he?"

"America," Joe said. "He was at Omaha Beach, then sent back to the States. I don't know where yet, but I'm trying to find out." No point in saying why. If they assumed Marshall'd been wounded, that might be better for now.

Ivy's father took that in. His face lost any softness it had held, and he grunted. "Let's see the little nipper, then."

Joe saw Ivy tense, draw in a breath. "She's sleeping, but when she wakes, you'll see she has the most beautiful eyes." Ivy drew back the blanket.

Her mother gasped. "But, she's b—"

"Brown!" Ivy's father spat the word as if he were issuing a death sentence.

Ivy paled even more, if that was possible, but spoke bravely. "Yes, she is. My beautiful chestnut-brown baby, my daughter."

"Marshall will be so prou—" But Joe was cut off.

"Marshall? You mean that—"

Joe was ready to give Ivy's father a right hook, but he did his best to keep his voice steady. "Like I told you, Mr. Greenfield, Marshall's the finest man I've ever known, black or white or green. He'd be here right now if he could. He was here in the first place to help defend your country. You should be proud to know he's your son-in-law, father of—"

"Proud?" The man grunted. "I'm not proud. We're through here, Myra. Come on."

"I thought you gave him up," Ivy's mother pleaded. "Your da told you to send him packing."

"I love Marshall, Mum. I was the one you sent packing. That's when we married. In the church."

"And where is he now? Not here. Joe's here. Joe could—"

"No, Mum. Marshall's my husband. Joe's our friend."

"The only one you're likely to have now the cake's out of the oven." Her father pushed stubby fingers through slightly graying hair. "Don't think you'll be bringing that thing home with you, Ivy. You get rid of it—you should have gotten rid of it from the start!"

None of this was Joe's business, but he couldn't listen to that, and Ivy didn't deserve it. "She's your daughter, and this baby's your granddaughter, Mr. Greenfield. Your family."

"No family of mine. Not now. Not ever. You make your own way, girl. You made your bed, now you've got to lie in it. Don't come knockin' round lookin' for handouts from me." He was halfway to the door. "Myra, I told you to come on. We're through here."

Ivy's mother's eyes filled, and Joe saw the heartbreak, the ripping of her soul as she left her daughter and followed her husband.

"Mum!" Ivy choked the word, reaching out for her mother with one hand.

Her mother glanced back once and shook her head, disappointment dripping in every word. "Oh, Ivy. Ivy."

And then they were gone. It seemed to Joe that a tornado had swept through the place, sucking every breath of air with it. Ivy and her still-sleeping baby looked even smaller, more waiflike than before. Tears trickled down Ivy's cheeks, though she didn't utter a sound.

"I'm sorry," Joe said, still standing by her bed.

"This was supposed to be the happiest day of my life, next to my wedding day."

Joe wanted to say, *Don't let them spoil it. They don't know what they're saying, what they're missing.* But he didn't think it would help. Some wounds were too deep to be healed by words.

"Where is he, Joe? Where's Marshall?" Ivy pleaded but didn't look up.

Joe pulled up a chair, as close to Ivy and the baby as he dared. "I'm not sure yet. But I'm working on finding out. The surgeon that tracked down his transport papers said he was shipped to the States." Joe didn't know how much to tell Ivy, especially when he didn't know what had caused the charges. "I'll let you know the minute I learn where he is."

"I went to the Army base twice, trying to find out what happened after—after Normandy. But nobody'd tell me anything. I couldn't tell them I was Marshall's wife. I was afraid that would get him into trouble, but I've been so afraid for him, afraid of what happened to him."

"All I've learned so far is that he was charged with disorderly conduct. I don't know why or what for, but I can't believe—"

Ivy gasped and, as she did, tightened her grip on the baby, who let out a yowl.

"There's got to be an explanation. Marshall wouldn't jeopardize his Army record like that. I swear I'll find him for you."

"It's my fault, because of me, isn't it? Somebody found out. He was worried that his CO was suspicious."

"We don't know that." Joe tried to reassure Ivy, though it was the first thing that had entered his mind. Marshall was not a violent man, but if somebody insulted Ivy, Joe wasn't sure how he'd react.

"I think my parents kept letters from me, letters from Marshall."

"How do you know?"

"I can't be sure. A few months ago, after I'd moved back in with them, Mum became very possessive of the mail. A couple of times I saw her burning envelopes in the can, out in the back garden, where my dad usually burns the trash on Saturday mornings. It was odd that she didn't just wait for him to do it. I asked her about it, but she said what she did was her business and I was to never mind. I think she may have suspected that the letters were from Marshall. Maybe she thought he was still pursuing me."

"If it was Marshall, that means he's able to write. That's good news, Ivy, the best."

"But I can't be certain the letters were from him, can I?"

"I swear I'll find him, and when I do, I'll tell him about . . . What's her name?"

Ivy snuggled the baby closer and stroked her cheek. "Violet. Her name's Violet. The first gift Marshall ever gave me was a little bouquet of violets he bought off a street urchin. His first gift to me, and maybe she's my last."

"Not your last, Ivy. We'll find Marshall." Joe smiled and spoke to the baby. "Violet." That made him think of Celia, and how she'd once written that she wished she had a flower name. Celia would approve the name of Marshall's baby. "A beautiful name for a beautiful baby."

"Do you want to hold her?" Ivy asked tentatively.

Joe had never held a newborn baby. "Will I hurt her?"

"Not a bit of it, Joe. Just wrap your arm down her spine to her bottom and support her neck in the crook of your elbow. There, like that."

Joe held Violet as if she might break, which set the baby crying.

"Hold her close, so she feels secure."

Joe snuggled baby Violet against his chest, which he figured wasn't as soft as Ivy's, but if it was security the baby needed, he'd offer her that. Something swelled inside him, something Joe hadn't felt since Nonni had wrapped her arms around him to say goodbye the day before he was shipped out. Joe heaved a sigh he didn't realize he'd been holding, ready to take on any man or woman who threatened this child. He'd do what he could for Ivy and Violet, until Marshall came to take over.

Chapter Twenty-Four

SEPTEMBER 1864

We buried Emma in the Shady Grove churchyard, next to her lost babies, not far from Mother. There was still time to dig lily of the valley rhizomes and cover her grave as I knew she would have wanted—like the graves of her babies, like Mother's and her babies, but I had no heart for it. I had no heart for anything save the little girl Emma left behind.

What does it mean to adore and resent a life at the same time? To see a tiny child as the cause of joy and hope and wretched despair all in one breath?

I did not write Elliott. I did not, in truth, know where to write him. He'd not given us the location of his regiment's winter quarters in his letter, if indeed they'd settled in. It was enough to know that he was alive and that I could be relieved of the burden, at least for a time, of telling him that the love of his life had died birthing the child they both had longed for.

Mother Sally, an older mother among the slaves who nursed her own baby of six months, served as wet nurse for Emma's baby. The baby. I wanted to call her by name, but it didn't seem right, didn't seem my place to name her. And yet it wasn't right to forever call her "the baby." It felt so cold, so impersonal, as if she wasn't even a member of the family.

If I could have traded her for Emma, I would have a thousand times within those first few days. But afterward, after we'd buried Emma and said our goodbyes, as I held the little girl, as she wrapped her tiny palm and fingers around my baby finger and I saw her blue eyes focus on mine, I knew I would have fought both armies to protect her, to keep her.

With Elliott gone and Emma having left no instruction for the naming of a daughter, the weeks passed, and I didn't know what to do.

"Aren't you just a little Ellie," Alma cooed one November morning after breakfast as she brought the baby to my arms, fresh from her feeding with Mother Sally.

"Ellie? You think she looks like someone named Ellie?"

Alma smiled. "Oh, don't mind me. I was just thinking this morning how Miz Emma wanted her baby named after Mr. Elliott, and how Ellie might be a fittin' way to do that."

"Ellie," I repeated.

"Short for Eleanor," Father said from the head of the table, which surprised us all, for he'd barely spoken since Emma's death and had never held—had in fact refused to hold—the baby.

"Yes," I said, more because I was astonished than anything. "Eleanor. Ellie—for Elliott. That's good, isn't it, Father?" But he didn't answer.

"I reckon Miz Emma'd be mighty pleased." Alma tucked the blanket around Ellie's feet and patted her back.

I held Ellie against me and breathed another *thank You* to the Father for Alma. She and Martha had walked with me through each and every dark day since Emma's passing, often gently guiding me without so much as a say-so. They were sisters I'd never had, never even imagined beyond Emma.

. . .

It didn't occur to me that I was now mistress of Belvidere Hall, not until one December morning, very near Christmas, a holiday we'd no heart to celebrate. I'd just stepped from the nursery—the room beside mine that had once belonged to Elliott and Emma—and gently closed the door as Ellie slept. Grayson stood in the upstairs hallway, having cornered Alma against his bedchamber door. Grayson had grown two inches and gained shoulder width in the last year. He towered over tiny Alma, who even I could see was far more woman than teen now, and beautiful at that.

"Grayson!" I called brightly, as if I didn't notice or ascertain his intentions. "Your niece is begging for Uncle Grayson. She's got the loveliest smile today—come, see her!" I motioned to him.

Caught, he removed his arm from the door above Alma's head. She darted away and down the stairs. He knew precisely what I was doing but allowed me to take his arm and lead him to the nursery, where, of course, Ellie was sleeping soundly.

"Nicely done, sneaky sister." Grayson pulled his arm away.

"I've no desire to embarrass you, Grayson. Father's already warned you. Stay away from Alma."

"I do live here. I have every right to—"

"You have every right to ask me if you need something. I remind you that Father has placed me in charge of the household."

"That won't always be the case, dear sister. In fact, that will not be the case much longer."

"Whatever do you mean?" I could have ignored him if I didn't know that Grayson had grown as devious and plotting as he had grown handsome.

But he did not answer. And that worried me.

That night I wrote Elliott. I'd put it off as long as possible, but I feared I could not control Grayson and that things would come to a head before long. Elliott did not know our people were still enslaved. He did not know that his beloved Emma had died, or that he had a daughter. He did not know how far Father had deteriorated. I needed him, needed someone, so I poured it all out in writing to my dear brother.

Still, I had no idea where to send my plea, and we'd received no word from Elliott since September. I sealed my letter and tucked it with the others addressed to Elliott, inside the first book of *Les Misérables* that he'd given me, hoping, praying we would hear from him soon and that I might place each one in his hands.

Chapter Twenty-Five

DECEMBER 1944

It had been a busy and exhausting weekend for Joe. He was ready to go back to the base, to get to work on things less emotional than the birth of a baby, loved more than life by the mother, rejected by grandparents who couldn't see beyond their noses. He was only sorry he hadn't been able to hold baby Violet again. He'd liked doing that; it made him feel strong and brave and humble all at once.

But he'd secured new digs for Ivy and the baby. He'd spent all of Sunday morning going from boardinghouse to boardinghouse, asking for a place for them, assuring landladies and proprietors that he'd send the weekly rent, a month in advance, until Ivy could find a job. But he didn't want any trouble for Ivy, so he told them straight up that she was bringing home a brown baby, that she was married to a fine man, but the soldier had been shipped back to the States.

He'd hoped the long lease and the guarantee of pay and his US Army uniform would help, and they did, until he stated that the baby was the child of a colored American serviceman. Most said their other tenants wouldn't have it, it would be too hard for business, or they were sorry, they'd momentarily forgotten that they'd already promised the room to someone else.

It wasn't until the fifth establishment that Joe struck gold. The older landlady had only two rooms to rent. One was already taken by a young lady who worked in a secretarial pool downtown. The other was available if he paid right away, and she didn't seem to mind, or said she didn't mind, that there was a brown baby, "as long as the mother doesn't flout it among my neighbors. They'll see, soon enough, but I've a gated back garden where the baby can sun and play. I wouldn't mind having a little one about. I miss mine—long grown, of course."

It seemed the perfect setup. If Ivy was lucky, maybe she could pay the woman to watch Violet when she was up to getting a job.

He didn't have time to see Ivy and Violet again—he'd have missed his train and couldn't afford to be declared AWOL—but he'd left a note for her at the hospital desk. Nurse Clemmons had walked on duty then and promised she'd deliver it. Joe believed her. She seemed on the up-and-up, and sympathetic, or at least intrigued.

By the time Joe returned to his barracks, he was spent and hoped he wasn't facing a relapse of the influenza.

• • •

Joe hadn't been able to get another weekend pass to see Ivy and baby Violet, but he exchanged letters with Ivy. Both were doing well, recovering from Violet's birth. A week after delivery Ivy had moved into her new room, and if the letters were honest, she and baby were settling in.

It seemed the landlady was not quite as grandmotherly as she'd given Joe to believe, once Violet kept the whole house up at night. He guessed a squalling baby could do that. "False advertising" is what he'd call it—innocent little baby sound asleep against your chest one minute, awake and screaming for hours the next. He'd liked holding the baby but was just as glad to be stationed far away.

Three weeks into the new year Joe answered mail call, figuring it would be from Ivy, but it wasn't.

Dear Joe,

> *It's really good to hear from you. No letters had come for so long I didn't know what to think, especially after the reports we'd heard on the radio and read in the paper about the Normandy invasion. Thank God you're okay, or that you'll be okay.*

Joe wondered if Celia'd still see him as okay when she saw his limp. He knew, from things she'd written before, that she loved to dance, fox-trot and jitterbug and even something called clogging, which Marshall had done his best to demonstrate and teach him. Joe had promised to teach Celia the Lindy Hop when they finally met. He didn't figure he'd be much of a dancer now.

> *No, I haven't heard a word from M, but his uncle, Olney Tate, said he'd received a letter and M is stationed back in the US. That's all I know. Olney didn't say where, didn't seem to want to.*
>
> *Whenever he returns to No Creek, we'll be mighty glad to see him, have him back.*
>
> *Olney said M's discouraged and needs prayer, that things are tough for him now. He's been trying to reach Ivy in England, but she doesn't answer his letters. I finally told Olney and Doc Vishy about the wedding—probably should have told them sooner, but I didn't want to worry them. They're relieved he's back in the country, even though they know there are going to be lots of complications. I'll give Olney your address to send M. I know he'll want to write you. Maybe you can help him find Ivy.*
>
> *There's something else I need to tell M, something I hope will make a difference for him, if we can prove it. I don't think I should say more about that now, not till I know how things can play out.*
>
> *I turned fifteen last month. Did you remember?*

Fifteen. She'd turned fifteen in December and he hadn't even remembered her birthday. What kind of friend was he?

Daddy's recovered and doing so much better—back working at the shipyard over in Norfolk. Mama's home again, and I'm glad she's here. You never know how much you'll miss family till you don't have them.

Joe swallowed hard, setting down the letter. Truer words were never spoken.

• • •

Right away Joe wrote Ivy all he'd learned about Marshall. She'd be over-the-moon happy to know he was okay, that he'd been trying to reach her. Maybe Ivy was right—maybe her parents had destroyed Marshall's letters. That would fit with what Celia'd said.

After meeting them, Joe wouldn't put it past either parent.

He wrote Celia, asking her to give Ivy's new address to Marshall's uncle to forward to Marshall. He'd let Ivy tell Marshall about baby Violet, as it should be.

The war was turning in the Allies' favor, despite Germany's nasty V-2s to the south of England in retaliation for D-Day. It was those unforeseen "gifts" that worried Joe for Ivy and Violet. No way to know if they'd come again, despite German guns being taken out across the Channel.

He wished there was a way to send the two of them on to America. Joe knew it wasn't safe to travel the Atlantic, what with German submarines still on the prowl. But their arrival would give Marshall the boost he needed for whatever was going on. Family was everything to Joe, and he knew that Ivy was everything to Marshall.

• • •

A week later Joe felt pretty hopeful when he was able to negotiate a two-day pass. He'd take the train to London and check on Ivy and Violet. The three of them could celebrate the news about Marshall together, maybe get dinner in a café. He'd like that and he believed Ivy would.

The night before his pass began, Joe went off duty late. There'd been more emergencies than usual at the hospital, and he'd been needed. Never glad to see injuries, Joe was glad to help, to stitch men up and get them on the road to healing—the thing he'd been trained to do, what he hoped to do for the rest of his life.

It was a surprise to find his letter to Ivy on his bunk, marked "Return to Sender."

Joe turned the envelope over, as if he might see an explanation on the back. *Makes no sense. Ivy's there, with baby Violet. Without this letter she doesn't even know that Marshall's been trying to reach her. Lousy mail service!*

Joe tucked the letter in his uniform pocket. He'd deliver the good news in person.

Chapter Twenty-Six

Mrs. Chatsworth's March 1 note came as a thunderbolt from heaven. I'd been up half the night walking baby Ellie. Mother Sally and I had both done all we could to settle our colicky treasure, but to no avail. It was nearly nine o'clock and I wasn't even dressed, hadn't run a brush through my hair or a stick across my teeth. I wouldn't have answered a social call, but this note did not indicate anything of the sort.

> *Please, my dearest Minnie, come quickly.*
>
> *Adeline Chatsworth*

Tom. All I could think of was Tom. I'd not written him since receiving his note about Elliott's trial, nor had he written me again, a thing I did not understand. Surely his mother had written him of Emma's passing. Surely he would know how we craved news of Elliott. When he'd learned of Elliott's sentencing and that it had been reversed, why did he not write me through his mother? I wondered afresh if it was because he could not.

Delay or wonderment would not help me know. I changed into a day dress as quickly as I could, taking time only to brush my hair and sweep it into a loose bun.

Obadiah was not in the stable, so I saddled Tammer myself, a thing I'd learned to do as a girl but had rarely done as a young woman.

It felt good to ride hard and fast, to take the reins with horseflesh beneath me, hammering the road in rhythm with my heart. Tears coursed down my cheeks as I rode. I didn't know why I was crying. I had no information yet—only anxiety, guilt, anger, sadness, and frustration. Whatever more there was to face now I didn't want, yet desperately needed, to know.

The front yard sat deserted, but no black wreaths adorned the door or windows. That gave me space to breathe. I tied Tammer to the hitching post and ran up the steps. The door opened and Shelby, her face unreadable, motioned for me to go upstairs.

The door to Tom's room remained closed, but his mother's door stood open. I hesitated in the hallway. "Mrs. Chatsworth?" I spoke softly, uncertain.

"Minnie." Her voice came in a moment, and I followed it into the room.

There, in her bed, lay Tom. Sleeping peacefully, I prayed. But his mother's tears and the redness of her eyes told me otherwise. She reached out her hand for mine and I went to her. Kneeling down, I cradled her head against my heart, attempting to find words that would not come.

He looked so peaceful, so still. I thought—but no, his chest rose and fell. I nearly fainted in relief.

When some minutes had passed and her new wave of tears subsided, I whispered, "Is he wounded?"

"Grapeshot in the arm and chest. They took his arm. My beautiful, beautiful son, and they took his arm." She wept afresh.

For the first time I noticed that I'd only seen Tom's arm nearest us, resting atop the quilt—the quilt that lay flat on the other side of his chest.

"But he's alive. He's alive." I wanted to shake her, to make her understand how wonderful that was.

She only shook her head. "Dr. Hendrix has been here, and he holds little hope. He's lost so much blood, and the doctor in Richmond took more of his arm—up to his shoulder—when gangrene set in. They've sent him home to die. My son."

"Is he sleeping or—?"

"Unconscious—a coma, the doctor said. We don't know if he'll waken, if he'll ever even know he's home." She sniffed and gasped in her attempt to control hiccups that would come despite her best efforts.

"I'm sorry, so very sorry." My voice caught, thick, but there were no words to follow. Loss after loss in this horrid, cruel war, and now Tom— our friend and playmate from youth, the boy who'd walked me home from church, the man who wanted my heart. A heart I could not give.

"I knew you'd want to see him." She squeezed my hand and it brought me back to the moment.

"Of course. Of course."

"Dr. Hendrix said that some believe those in comas can hear—that hearing may be the last sense to be lost. I thought . . . I thought, if you talked to him, Minnie, if you told him how you love him and want him to return to us, that he might . . . he might want to live."

"Oh, Mrs. Chatsworth—"

"You must call me Mother now, my darling girl. If Tom lives, you will be my daughter. I know you were only waiting until the war is over. He told me in his last letter. He could hardly wait to come home to you."

I wanted to pull away and I wanted to embrace her. I wanted to comfort her in any way I could, but I had not agreed to—what had Tom told her? Why had he?

"Talk to him, take his hand, let him feel you, let him know how you love him. He's not responded to me, but I know he will to you. He has to. Please, please, my darling girl!"

I held her close until she stood and gently but firmly placed my hand over Tom's. I sat beside him, conscious of his shallow breathing, of his dark and unruly beard—a thing I'd never seen on Tom's clean-shaven face—and more than conscious of his mother standing beside us. She must have sensed my discomfort.

"I'll leave you two alone. I'll be just outside the door. You'll call me if there is any change—any change at all."

"I promise."

She squeezed my shoulder. I felt the weight of her worry. And then Tom and I were alone.

I sat and stared for a time . . . Tom's hair had gone gray at the temples. He couldn't be more than twenty-eight . . . too young for gray hair. And then I remembered that Elliott had gone almost entirely gray after his imprisonment. I touched the quilt with my other hand and smoothed it across Tom's chest. There was nothing on the other side and though I knew this and saw this, still, my breath caught, and I pulled my hand back.

"Tom," I finally whispered. "I'm here, Tom. It's me, Minnie." I took his one hand in both of mine. "You mustn't leave us, Tom. Your mother couldn't bear it . . . and neither could I. I don't know what to say, my dear, dear friend. Your mother is convinced we're going to marry. Did we agree to that? If you don't wake up, we can't prove her right or wrong. Please, Tom, dear Tom, open your eyes."

But he didn't, and the minutes passed. His mother peeked back in the door, her eyes both hopeful and resigned. *How does a person capture both in a moment?* I shook my head sadly.

She nodded. "I'll have Shelby bring us tea. You'll stay with me, won't you, Minnie? Please don't leave me alone."

"Of course I'll stay, as long as you want. Let me go for the tea. You stay here with Tom."

"No, my dear. He needs you now. If anyone can bring him back—" But she couldn't finish and turned quickly away. I heard her footsteps echo down the hallway.

I smoothed the curls of dark hair from Tom's forehead, traced the lines of his face, trying to remember the young man who'd gone to war. I couldn't whisper sweet nothings and endearments I did not mean, but I loved this man for the boy he'd been, for the friend he'd been to Elliott and to me even though he was first to arrest my brother, even though we stood on opposite sides of this cursed war, even though we disagreed on the dignity of life for every man, woman, and child, regardless of color. Still, he was my friend.

I did not want him to die, but I could never marry him and I could never bring myself to tell his mother this. She would not understand.

"Minnie." My name came as a breath and caught me unawares. I couldn't be certain I'd even heard it.

"Tom?" I pressed his hand anew between my own.

His fingers moved, ever so lightly, within my grasp. "Tom!" But there was nothing more. A minute passed. "Tom? Tom? It's me, Minnie. I'm here, dear friend. Come, wake up and go walking with me. We'll tramp through the woods. Snow's coming—maybe our last till spring. I feel it in the air. You love snow—swirling off the mountain. Remember how we caught it on our tongues—how we laughed?" Now that he'd stirred, I felt much greater the need to pull him back to life. I rambled just so he could hear my voice—if he could hear my voice. As long as there was hope and possibility. "Tom! Oh, Tom, please open your eyes."

They flickered for a moment. He didn't look my way but, eyes closed, he whispered . . . something. I leaned over his chest, my ear to his mouth, and listened, hoping he'd speak again.

"Elliott."

"Elliott? What about him?" My heart pounded afresh.

"Elliott. Didn't help him. Didn't speak for him. Forgive . . ."

I didn't know exactly what he meant, but clearly it troubled him. "Whatever it is, all is forgiven, Tom. Elliott is alive and well." Perhaps he didn't know of Elliott's reprieve. I hoped those words would bring him peace, but he grimaced in pain.

"Bring him home before . . ."

"Before what, Tom? Bring Elliott home before what?" I massaged his arm, hoping to rouse him, but there was nothing more.

His mother walked in, Shelby behind her with a tea tray.

"He stirred, only for a moment. I think—I think he said my name and he moved his fingers, just a little, a very little." I couldn't tell her he'd asked forgiveness—that he'd not spoken for Elliott. What could that mean for her now?

His mother knelt beside the bed, taking his hand from mine. "Tom! My boy, my son."

And then Tom opened his eyes. He took moments to focus, and I was sure a fleeting smile passed his lips as he saw us, truly saw us—his mother who loved and bore him and the woman he loved, the one he was so certain he could make love him. And then, in a blink of my eye, he was gone—his eyes still open.

It took moments before I comprehended the change, the loss of breath, the stillness and utter serenity that only death brings.

"Tom? No, no—Tom. Tom!" His mother grasped his shoulders with both hands and shook him. "Tom, please—oh, no, Tom!"

I sat back as she laid her head across his chest, weeping as if the world had fallen off its axis. I knew that for her it had, and I was sorry—so very sorry for everything. And fearfully I wondered what Tom had meant, what he'd known of Elliott that I did not.

• • •

We buried Tom two days later, and though his mother insisted that I sit with her in church and stand with her by the graveside, I saw that I was not welcomed by other members of the community. Though Southern, I was not Confederate and not deemed worthy to be considered a member or close friend of the Chatsworth family.

When we left the graveside, I heard one of the Mae girls whisper to her mother, "Parading about as if she's his widow. Shameful! He'd never have married her—a Confederate officer and a hero. That Yankee traitor's not fit to wipe his boots."

• • •

The day after the funeral I needed to return home. Tom's mother begged me to stay, but I needed to see Ellie, to make certain she was safe and well . . . and simply to hold her young life in my arms. I promised Mrs. Chatsworth that I'd return soon, the next day if possible.

Shadrach, the half-Cherokee, half-Negro groomsman for Chatsworth Lodge, led Tammer round to the front of the house.

"Thank you, Shadrach, for caring for Tammer. She looks wonderful. You've kept her in fine fettle for me."

"You know you're welcome as can be, Miz Belvidere."

"You must call me Minnie—everyone does. Miz Belvidere was my mother." I hoped my smile conveyed the kindness I intended.

Shadrach smiled. I knew he'd do no such thing as I'd suggested. Miz Minnie was the best I could hope for. "I sure was sorry about Massa Tom."

"I hardly know what his mother will do without him."

"He worried about that most of the time—from the moment he got that load of grapeshot in his arm."

It had never occurred to me ask if Tom had taken a manservant to war with him. Of course, Tom took Shadrach. They were raised together as Elliott and Obadiah had been—best friends until age and society's perceptions of race separated them. "Were you there? Were you with Tom?"

"Yes, ma'am, these four years. Four long years."

Tom's words came back to me in a flood. "Before Tom passed, he spoke of my brother Elliott."

"A fine man. I sorry 'bout what happened to him, too. Mighty sorry."

Carolina clay lodged in my throat and I reached for Shadrach's hand, uncertain I could stand. "What happened? What do you know?"

Shadrach's eyes widened, as if he didn't want to be the bearer of bad news, and as if my touch burned him. I pulled back.

"Don't be afraid, Shadrach, only tell me. Please tell me all you know of my brother."

"You best sit down, Miz Minnie. You look a mite faint to me, and I don't want to be caught carryin' a white woman up these steps." He motioned to the front verandah steps and I stumbled there, sitting down as quickly as I could, desperate for whatever news he might share.

"Same battle as got Massa Tom, up by Hatcher's Run. It was a bad day for the Confederates. Massa Tom's regiment tried to turn to their right, but bluecoats outflanked them, runnin' over the breastworks and—" He stopped. I was sure it was because of all he saw in my face. "Mr. Elliott, he was drivin' ambulance, headed for the plank road."

"Ambulance? I thought he was a cook!"

"General Lee ordered all the Confederate personnel to join ranks and take up arms—except for ambulance drivers. Major Slone got Mr. Elliott assigned to General Cook as his ambulance driver."

"Go on."

"Minié balls flying left and right like hailstones, and then his mules stopped . . . just stopped in the middle of the battle."

My hand went to my throat.

"He not dead—no, ma'am—least not then. They brought him back, into the field hospital, wounded in the thigh. Pretty bad, but he still talkin'—talkin' to Massa Tom, who ended up in the same tent."

A sob escaped my throat.

"Mr. Elliott, he talked Massa Tom through till he was under the chloroform . . . when they took his arm. They in cots side by side for all that time."

Thank You, Father. Thank You that Elliott was there for his friend, that—

"Only two days and already Massa Tom's arm showed signs of gangrene. Doc wanted to take more, up to the shoulder. Said it was the only way to save him."

I shook my head, imagining how awful that was for Tom, wishing with all my heart that Shadrach would tell me about Elliott, yet knowing I could not, should not rush him through his memory.

"He didn't want that, feared he'd be nothing of a—" Shadrach hesitated, searching my eyes, a thing I knew slaves never did.

"Nothing of what?"

"Of a husband for you, ma'am. He loved you, Miz Minnie, intended to marry you. Before he'd agree to lettin' them take more of his arm, he asked Mr. Elliott if he thought you'd still have him—if they took it all."

"Elliott couldn't have known—"

"That's right, ma'am, he didn't know nothin' about you two courtin'. Caught him by surprise, sure enough. Told Massa Tom that he did not believe takin' his arm or his shoulder or his leg, if it come to that, would make a whit of difference to his sister, but slave holdin' could not be yoked with abolition. Said if Massa Tom saw his slaves' lives as equal to his own, he believed his sister could love him and be proud to be his wife." Shadrach's eyes took on a light, a light I understood. He looked away.

Elliott understands. "What did Tom say?"

"Not one more word to Mr. Elliott. Lay beside him and never spoke another word. Before Massa Tom went under the saw again Mr. Elliott asked could he pray for him, pray with him. Massa Tom wouldn't answer, so Mr. Elliott prayed anyway, and I believe those prayers were answered."

"Tom died."

"Yes, ma'am." Shadrach broke convention again and looked into my eyes. "But he got home to his mother and she got to see him, and he got to see you."

"Yes."

"That's what he wanted. All he could hope for, a man cut up bad as him. They couldn't get all that gangrene. Doc said it woulda taken over no matter what more they did. Said send the man home. He might make it that long."

"And Elliott? Please, Shadrach, what happened to my brother?"

Shadrach sat back. "That the hard thing, Miz Minnie. There be so many wounded, so many shot up beyond any recognizin', and there be so few doctors—two, for all that battle. They had to choose who to work on, who the highest rank, who might live if they helped and who might die anyway."

I swallowed. My throat felt like fire.

"They operated on Mr. Elliott, saved his leg, at least to begin with. That why he in a cot beside Massa Tom those two days. But when they come round again, they suspected gangrene might be settin' in for him, too."

"They took his leg?"

"I don't know, ma'am. I think they would have, but there was a lieutenant from Massa Tom's regiment, one that knew Mr. Elliott from No Creek, spoke up and said he was nothin' but a traitor, that he was a bluecoat at heart only saved from fightin' by his daddy's money."

"That's not true."

Shadrach shook his head. "There's a lot ain't true in this world, Miz Minnie."

"I don't understand. They didn't operate?"

"Left him. Moved him out to the field where they'd get to men in time if they could."

"Tom . . . didn't speak for him . . . did he?"

"No, ma'am. Reckon it's wrong to speak ill of the dead, but you have a right to know."

It was a relief to know the truth. "Is there a chance—any chance that Elliott might still be—"

"While there's breath there's hope, Miz Minnie."

Tears spilled from my eyes and I half laughed, perhaps as much from hysteria as hope. "That's what Elliott always says."

"Mr. Elliott a good man. Best send somebody after him. War's near done, Miz Minnie. I could see that. Even Massa Tom, much as he not want to face it, could see it comin'. If Mr. Elliott still alive, he'll not make it back on his own."

Hope. That's what I had, all I had. "I will. Thank you. Thank you, Shadrach, for everything. Hatcher's Run, you said?"

"Yes, ma'am."

Shadrach helped me mount.

"Miz Minnie?" Shadrach turned awkward. What could he possibly feel awkward about after all he'd told me? "Miss Alma still at Belvidere Hall?"

"Yes, she's my right arm. You know Alma?"

"Met her at a corn huskin' before the war. Right taken with her. I believe she thought somethin' of me. You reckon I might call on her, should I get a pass to come by?"

And then the pieces fell into place . . . why Alma had never taken to any of the men working Belvidere Hall land . . . why she was always eager to run errands for me to Chatsworth Lodge. How had I been so blind? So self-centered? "Of course, Shadrach. We'd be proud to have you come by—if Alma agrees."

"Yes, ma'am." He stepped back, and the grin that lit his face shamed the sun.

Chapter Twenty-Seven

FEBRUARY 1945

By the time Joe reached the boardinghouse it was midafternoon. He didn't like dropping in on Ivy unexpected, but there'd been no time to write, and if he had, would his letter have been returned to sender again?

Joe knocked at the door. Several moments passed. He knocked again. Finally, he heard shuffling steps and the turning of a lock. The landlady, who'd looked so kindly and grandmotherly when he'd rented the room for Ivy, looked haggard and worn, a good five years older and a little unkempt.

"Oh," she nearly moaned, looking at Joe.

"Mrs. Waverly?" Joe had never elicited that kind of response from anybody.

"I should have written you. I just couldn't do it." Tears welled in her eyes.

"What's wrong?" A dozen tragic scenarios ran through Joe's mind. He didn't want to hear any of them.

"Such a good girl. Such a kind, sweet mother."

"Ma'am, you're scaring me, and I don't scare easily."

"Come in."

Joe followed her into the sitting room.

"I'd offer you tea, but I just can't seem to—"

"Mrs. Waverly, I don't want tea. I want to know what's wrong. Is Ivy here?"

She sat down heavily in the armchair nearest the fire, which had all but gone out. The room was cold—too cold for a woman her age or for a tenant with a baby.

"I didn't know what to do, did I? All this time through the war, and here we are surely nearing the end . . ."

Joe thought he might tear his hair out, but he knew patience was the only way to get to the bottom of whatever it was. "What's wrong, Mrs. Waverly? Let me help you." It was what Joe did, what he knew how to do.

"It was the garden, you see."

Joe nodded but didn't see at all.

"The meadow near that house out Tockingham way. She'd left Violet with me—trusted me with her little one, she did." Now the tears came in earnest.

But Joe heard no baby sounds. "Violet? Where is she?"

"That's just it. I don't know, do I?"

"Please, Mrs. Waverly. Start at the beginning."

"Mrs. Raymond—Ivy—had gone to interview for a position—a good position it seemed, as a typist, for someone writing a memoir or some such thing. The pay was decent, she said, and there'd be a place for her and the baby. I didn't want to see them go. I should have stopped her."

Joe's nerves stretched taut.

"Well, she took the bus, didn't she—out Tockingham way. The letter said the place was still a half mile beyond the main road. She was worried she'd be late for the interview, that's what she told me, but that she'd just walk on, follow the lane when she got there. She must have thought she'd save a bit of time, cutting through that meadow." The older woman gasped, trying to catch her breath.

Joe knelt down beside her, gently rubbing her back, urging her to continue. "So, she crossed the meadow . . ."

"And there it was. A bomb that had never exploded. No telling how long it had been there. The constable said the field lay fallow for a year or more."

Joe sat back on his heels. *Ivy.* He'd seen plenty of death, plenty of casualties . . . but *Ivy.*

"I got worried, you see, when she didn't come home, so I rang the station. I was afraid some bloke had waylaid her or . . . I didn't know what. The constable came round and talked with me, took down what information she'd left me. I kept baby Violet best I could. She cried terrible for her mother." Mrs. Waverly shook her head at the memory. "The man came round again the next day and told me what happened. He said it was surely quick, that he was sorry."

Joe thought he might be sick, but he had to be sure. He couldn't trust a rumor. "You're sure it was Ivy. The policeman—the constable—was sure."

"Her shoe was blown clear across the meadow into the man's garden. He gave it to the constable. It was hers. I know it was hers."

Joe couldn't move. *Distance. Maintain distance.* That was the only way to cope with trauma, to do his job. But it had never been this personal.

Mrs. Waverly trembled, and Joe saw that the shock of reliving it all through the telling was wearing. He forced himself to stand and wrapped an afghan from the settee around her. He shoveled a bit of coal on the nearly quenched fire to warm the room.

"Wait here, Mrs. Waverly. I'm going to make us both a cup of tea."

She didn't respond.

At the door he stopped. "Is Violet upstairs? Is she sleeping?"

But Mrs. Waverly burst into fresh tears. Joe didn't ask more, couldn't take more. He'd make the tea, sweeten it with sugar no matter the rationing. If he could find brandy, he'd give them both a heavy dose. He just needed to do something physical to move the situation forward, a kind of triage to the next station, the next level.

He lit the stove and set the kettle to boil. He found the teapot, the canister of loose tea, the ration of sugar. No brandy. It had been the perfect place for Ivy, for Violet. *Dear God, where is Violet now? Mrs. Waverly kept her, so she's got to be here. Why isn't she crying?*

Marshall. How will I tell Marshall? Everything in Joe sank to the floor.

The kettle whistled. He poured the boiling water, stirred the tea, wrapped the pot in a tea cozy from the counter to keep it steaming hot. He spooned sugar cubes into cups, poured milk, gritted his teeth. *Is this how You take care of those who trust You?* Age-old bitterness, the bitterness of a six-year-old boy, flared in his heart.

I didn't drop the bomb.

The thought came to Joe as if someone had spoken aloud, and he knew, even in his anger and grief, that it was so. *But You didn't stop it— You didn't keep Ivy from walking over it!* Joe was ready to fight, wanted a fight, whether or not it was a fair fight, or one he could win.

Mrs. Waverly stood in the kitchen doorway. "She loved him, you know. She loved her soldier husband and couldn't wait to go to him. She didn't know if he still loved her, why he hadn't written, even if he was still alive."

Joe groaned inside. *War. How can I blame God for all the insanity of war? Mankind—what a misnomer—humans do this, create this hate, spread this hate, leave the consequences of hate in all our paths, in Ivy's path.* He spread his hands on the table, trying to get hold of himself.

Mrs. Waverly walked over and laid a hand on Joe's shoulder. That was all it took. Joe broke down, sat down in the nearest chair and cried. She wrapped her arms around him just like Nonni would have, like she had when his parents died, and held him until he stopped.

She poured the tea, still warm, and spooned an extra lump of sugar into his cup. They sat and drank in silence.

Still nursing the warm cup in his hands, Joe asked, "Violet? Where is she?"

A ragged sigh escaped Mrs. Waverly's lips. "They took her away."

Joe looked up.

"I didn't want them to. I'd have kept her if they'd let me. I telephoned Ivy's parents. She'd told me about them, you see, how they'd turned her out when Vi was born. Still, I thought surely they'd want to know what happened to their daughter. I thought they'd be ever so sorry and want to take their granddaughter, to raise her now, the only family they have."

Family. The only family. Joe swallowed the bile that threatened to come up his throat.

"But they're cold, those people. The father said 'just as well, what'd she expect' when I told him about Ivy. I nearly dropped the telephone. I told him his granddaughter needed him now, that he and his wife ought to raise her, that she was a lovely child and a good baby, that she needed her mother."

Joe could well envision the bulldog's mouth turning down.

"He said they'd send someone round."

"They didn't come for her?"

"Not at all. They sent some man and woman from a home, along with a constable, to take the baby. I tried to stop them, to tell them I'd look after her till you or her father came, but they'd have none of it. Said it was none of my affair. I tell you, 'none of my affair'? I loved that baby. I'd have given her a good home."

"I know you would, Mrs. Waverly. You're a good woman. Where did they take her?"

"That's just it, they wouldn't say. Just that they took her where 'all the colored Yanks' refuse goes.' It was awful, just awful. I should have stopped them, but I didn't know how."

"It's not your fault. You did everything you could."

"They wouldn't even take baby's blanket, just her nappies and clothes. How they'll get her to sleep without her blanket, I don't know."

Joe didn't know either. He didn't know what he could do, but he could find Violet; he was sure of it. He could do that much for Marshall, and then Marshall could take up the fight.

"Ivy's things. I asked her father if they wanted her things and he said no, she was dead to them before now. Such a hateful man. But I wonder, what about her husband? Have you heard anything of him?"

"I did; that's what I came to tell Ivy. He was sent back to the States. Been writing to Ivy ever since but I don't think Ivy ever got the letters. The only address he had was her parents' home."

"Oh, they'd never have given them over to her. I'm sure of it."

"I agree."

"I don't imagine he'd want her clothes. It would cost ever so much to mail a box like that. I could give them to the jumble sale for those bombed out."

"I think Ivy would like that."

"But there's a couple of things—a baby rattle and blanket of Violet's. She should have those someday. And there's a little snapshot of Ivy and her soldier. I don't know if it's their wedding day or not, but it's a nice one and the only one Ivy had. I imagine her husband would like that, or that someday little Violet would."

"I'm sure he would. Thank you, Mrs. Waverly. I'll see that he gets them, that Violet gets what belongs to her."

"That's it then; I knew you would. I'll just wrap them up." She stood with a renewed purpose and walked to the door before turning again. "You'll find her, won't you? Baby Violet? You'll make sure she's well looked after?"

"I swear it."

. . .

Joe had planned to ask Mrs. Waverly if he could sleep in her front parlor, but he didn't need to ask. She made up the bed in Ivy's room for him and insisted he stay.

"You'll be doing me a favor, lad. I couldn't bear to change a thing in her room. It just didn't seem right. But I've got to let the room. These two rooms to let are my only income besides my old-age pension. You stayin' here sort of breaks the spell, and I'm grateful."

Joe was glad to help the woman, but he sure didn't relish spending the night in Ivy's bed.

For two hours that night he tossed and turned, then lay awake, staring at the ceiling. It gave him the creeps to sleep in a dead person's bed—a person he knew and had cared about—and that made him sadder yet. But he needed to stay in London overnight. He needed to see Ivy's parents before returning to Cheltenham, to find out where they'd sent Violet.

He needed to write Marshall—how he dreaded that—but couldn't write him that his wife was killed without telling him where his daughter was.

He heard the downstairs clock chime three before he finally drifted off.

. . .

By eight the next morning Joe was on his way to Ivy's parents. He hadn't rung them first. He didn't want to be put off as they'd done to Mrs. Waverly. He'd stand outside their door until they let him in or told him where they'd sent Violet. Exactly what he'd do then, he wasn't sure, but something . . . He'd do something.

Joe rang the bell twice before the curtain by the doorway moved. He turned aside so they couldn't see his face. He didn't want to give them any excuse not to open the door. He waited. Nothing. He rang again and determined he'd stand there and ring all day till the door opened. Finally, it did. Ivy's mother stood in her housecoat, her hair still mussed from sleeping.

"You've got to stop that ringin'. The noise goes right through to the neighbors in these row houses."

"I'm sorry about Ivy, Mrs. Greenfield, truly sorry." Joe wanted information, but he wanted to get off on the right foot. He felt sure that despite all that had happened, the woman must be heartbroken. The sudden tears in her eyes confirmed it.

"It's you. Joe, is it?"

"Yes, ma'am."

"You've got to leave before my Bert gets back. He's just nipped down to the corner for some cigarettes. He won't like—"

"I won't stay. I've come to say I'm sorry about Ivy and to find out where you sent Violet, Ivy's baby."

Her shoulders rounded. "Bert said she had it comin', that it was no wonder, what with—that it was God's judgment against her for . . . for . . . but . . ."

"God's not like that, Mrs. Greenfield, and their marriage was no sin. They loved each other and God gave them Violet. Most people never get to experience a love like that. They did, for a little while." Joe didn't know where he got the idea for any of that, but he believed it was true, knew it in the marrow of his bones, and despite this woman's abandonment of her own daughter, he wanted to comfort her.

Mrs. Greenfield shook her head, pulling a handkerchief from her pocket to swipe at her tears.

"I'm not trying to upset you more. I just need to find Violet. Her father will want to take care of her."

"And how's he supposed to do that, young man? You tell me." Joe hadn't heard Mr. Greenfield come up behind him. "Him, off to see the world and a girl in every port, leaving his black seed strewn across—"

It was all Joe could do not to hit the man right there. "Violet's your granddaughter, the only part of Ivy left to you."

"She's no part of me, nothin' to do with me."

Mrs. Greenfield gasped her tears behind Joe.

"She has a father who will want her. Just tell me where she is, and I'll leave you be."

"What affair is it of yours? What you gonna do about any of it? She's gone. We've washed our hands of the n—"

Joe stepped up to the bulldog's face.

The man backed down but said, "That's the end of it. Now get on out of here before I call the police."

"Just tell me—where has she gone?"

"Myra, ring the coppers. I've had enough of this Mussolini Yank. Now get on with you!" He pushed Joe aside, deliberately bumping his lame leg until Joe lost his balance and fell from the stoop into the garden bed. The door slammed behind him.

Chapter Twenty-Eight

MARCH 1865

Plans made and discarded and made again whirled through my brain as Tammer pounded the road home to Belvidere Hall. If there was a chance, one chance in a million, that Elliott was alive, I would find him. I had no idea where Hatcher's Run was, but surely maps in our library would give that information. How I'd travel was beyond me. Railroads throughout the state had been destroyed, and a woman alone on a horse or in a buggy . . . I'd need a wagon to bring Elliott home.

If only I could trust Grayson, I would send him after our brother. But I dared not. I held no proof that he'd played a role in Elliott's early second arrest, but instinct told me he was not innocent.

By the time I reached home it was nearly noon. The yard sat eerily quiet. Not even Obadiah came out to meet me, so I tied Tammer to the hitching post by the water trough and patted her. "I'll see to you soon, dear girl."

The winter kitchen was deserted, and dirty dishes piled high on the table—unlike Martha. I took the steps two at a time and was through the gathering room before I heard Grayson, intense and bullying.

"You must face it, Father. I'm all you have left. Elliott's gone and now Minnie has left you. It's time you put Belvidere Hall into my hands before it's too late, before we lose everything. You—"

Martha and Alma, who stood listening in the hallway, didn't hear me come up behind them, and for once I didn't even speak but pushed past them into the library.

"Grayson! What is the meaning of this?" I raised every inch I could muster.

"Minnie!" The relief on Father's face was palpable. "You're here."

Grayson's face reddened, but I saw no embarrassment there, only fury.

"Of course, I'm here, Father." I went to him right away and knelt before him. "I would never leave you."

But his lip trembled. "Where were you? Where have you been, Daughter?"

"With Mrs. Chatsworth. Her son, Tom, died, you know. The funeral was two days ago, and I've been with her, just as Mother would have done."

"Oh, that's right." Grayson smirked. "You remember Tom, don't you, Father? He's the one that came and arrested Elliott, the one that dragged him away in the dead of night."

Father's face clouded and I saw that he was confused.

"Isn't it interesting that now your darling Minnie has taken up with Elliott's enemies?"

"Grayson, stop it!"

"Tom Chatsworth," Father remembered. "He took Elliott away."

"He did, Father, but he is dead now, and I've learned where Elliott is."

"Elliott?"

Grayson blinked and the red of his face paled.

"Elliott's alive, Father—or at least I think he is, but he's been wounded, and we must go to him, bring him home."

"In the middle of a war, certainly. You've lost your mind, Sister."

"I need you here." Father's voice came feeble, and I knew he was right.

"If he's alive and fit for the journey, the army will send him home, like they did Tom." Grayson ground a cigarette, a new habit he'd taken up, into the dish on Father's desk. "Little good that did him."

"He didn't come on his own. His manservant, Shadrach—"

"His slave, Minnie—they're called slaves!"

"Shadrach brought him home. I think we should send Obadiah. Obadiah is strong and able to be trusted." Much more than I could say for Grayson.

"Obadiah is needed here," Grayson insisted.

"We can manage a few days, a few weeks without the work Obadiah does. We cannot manage without Elliott." I challenged Grayson, staring him down.

"Obadiah. Yes, send Obadiah," Father spoke, his voice still quiet and breathless, but with certainty.

"Father, you know that's—"

"Enough, Grayson. Minnie, tell Obadiah to bring my son home."

"Yes, Father. Right away." By the time I stood, Grayson had gone. By the time I looked up to see the fabric of Martha's and Alma's dresses move beyond the library door, I heard the front door slam and Grayson's boots on the steps. Never was I so glad to hear him go.

• • •

March had all but ended when a worn and thinner Obadiah returned with Elliott stretched out in the back of our wagon, wound in quilts for warmth and as little jostling as possible. Even before Obadiah lifted my brother to carry him into the house, I knew that his left leg must be gone. The quilt collapsed below his pelvis.

I'd set up a bed for him in the front parlor. Alma helped me sew draperies from bed linens to seal off a part of the room to give him more privacy. I hadn't known what to expect and now I was glad he would not need to navigate steps.

For two solid days Elliott slept, waking only to take in broth I spoon-fed him, broth Martha had made from the last of our chickens. After that he was awake but weak and did not speak.

Each day Father sat next to his son's bed, watching him sleep until he, too, dozed in the chair beside.

Alma shook her head. "It be a beautiful and pitiful sight all at once."

I had to agree, but I was thankful beyond measure that these two men I'd loved and looked up to all my life were here, under the same roof, with me.

• • •

Obadiah had told me the night they returned that the first words Elliott had spoken were a plea for Emma. Obadiah had broken the news of her death as gently as he could.

"He just shut down after that, no matter that I told him he has a baby daughter waitin' at home for her daddy. Never spoke one word more."

"You did all you could, Obadiah, and I can't thank you enough for going to get him. I'm sure it wasn't easy."

"No, Miss Minnie. Those Confederates were glad to see him go—one less mouth to feed. They weren't payin' him much mind. Too many wounded and dying to care for, too many dead and in need of buryin'. If I hadn't been the only one to bring Mr. Elliott home, they'd have pressed me into service for burial detail."

"Obadiah." I didn't know what else to say.

"We made it through by the grace of God Almighty. No other way around that. Through skirmishes and past ragtag home guard lookin' for money and whiskey. We had nothin' left to steal but our wagon and mule. I wasn't sure we'd get past, but the Lord led us through that wilderness and brought us home."

Home. Home for Elliott. Please, God. Let Elliott live long enough to see his daughter and to free our people, to make this land a real home for them, too.

• • •

March winds subsided and the snow never came. The greening of the mountain and hills surrounding us began with the bursting of forsythia—sunshine on the ground, Alma called it.

It felt like the dawning of the world that morning Alma ran to the nursery where I rocked Ellie, telling me that Elliott had sat up by himself for the first time.

Hope sprang in my chest. I carried Ellie downstairs and into the front parlor, praying all the while that she would bring some amount of health and healing to my brother. I pulled back the curtain and saw him awake, resting in the bed, propped up on feather pillows. Alma had shaved his unruly and matted beard, and Obadiah had washed his hair and scrubbed his skin till it no longer looked brown. I nearly cried out, he looked so much like the brother I'd feared lost.

When Elliott lifted his eyes to the bundle I carried, they widened. He drew a sharp breath and held it, and I prayed he would release it, would welcome his daughter. A moment passed and he looked away, his eyes glassed over with unshed tears.

I stopped midway across the room, uncertain whether or not to continue, and let the clock swing its pendulum back and forth, back and forth, back and forth.

I stepped forward and a floorboard creaked. Elliott looked my way, his eyes sad and full of love. "Bring her to me," he whispered.

With a lighter heart and fragile smile, I laid his beautiful daughter in his outstretched arms. "Ellie. We named her Ellie after you. Eleanor."

He didn't speak, simply looked in wonder at the babe in his arms.

"Is that all right? Emma believed she'd bear a son and wanted him named after you. So we thought—"

"You did well, Sister." He looked at me. "You've done well, and I can see you've kept Belvidere Hall going in my absence. I know Father . . ."

"Can't. He can't anymore, Elliott. We've needed you so badly."

"Why? Why have our slaves not been freed? I thought Obadiah was a free man, but every military man we came to demanded to see his papers and he showed them a pass."

It was the moment I'd dreaded and yet the moment I'd prayed would come. "Grayson burned all the freedom papers, all the deeds you prepared for land division."

"What?" Color drained from Elliott's face and I stepped forward to catch Ellie as he nearly dropped her. "When?"

"The night you were arrested. I came down just before dawn and found him in Father's library. By the time I realized what he was doing, they were gone—every one in ashes."

Elliott's breath came hard and fast.

"Emma and I rewrote the manumission papers, even made copies. We had Father sign them, but Grayson said that Father had made you his power of attorney, that the papers are worthless unless you sign them, too. He vowed that if we tried to set one slave free, he would take Father to court and prove him unstable."

"Grayson?" Elliott spoke as if in disbelief. "He'd take Father to court?"

"He swore he'd not see one acre of Belvidere land go to a slave, free or not."

"Where are the papers now?"

"I hid them, until we could find you and have you sign them. I don't even know if what Grayson said was true, but there was no one else we could ask, no one to trust, and Father wasn't able." If I sounded like I was pleading, begging, I could not help it any more than I could help the tears that streamed down my face.

"Bring them to me. I'll sign them now."

"Are you strong enough?"

He was not; he was breathless, pale, and fading fast. "Bring them to me. If I cannot sign them all now, you will hold my hand and guide it until we're finished. Not another minute, Minnie. Bring them to me."

• • •

I almost ran through the hallway, the gathering room, and winter kitchen, calling for Alma, Martha, or whoever would come. "Take Ellie. Take her now." I all but thrust the baby into Martha's arms. "Find Alma. Tell her to take Ellie. Nothing else matters now."

"What's wrong? Is Mr. Elliott—"

But I didn't stop to speak. Time and again circumstances had intervened—Father's reluctance to make the change until his death, the war, Elliott's arrest, Grayson's threats and his burning of the papers, the lack of mail in these horrendous days—but I would not be thwarted, not again. Elliott may or may not live, but while he had breath in his body, I knew we were of one mind.

I raced upstairs to the attic, to the safe room where slaves had hidden on their journey to freedom over the years, and indentured servants and patriots before them. I felt for the nook below the windowsill, pulled out the key hidden there, and unlocked the trunk that had belonged to the first Belvidere to settle No Creek. I pulled out knee breeches and vests—moth-eaten and nearly threadbare—a tricorn that I'd only seen worn in a daguerreotype of men posing for photos of bygone eras, a Bible brought to the New World by our first ancestor, a British subject of Italian descent who'd remade his life in the hills of North Carolina.

When all lay on the floor and the trunk was bare, I stuck my finger in the small hole in the back corner of the bottom panel and lifted. The pile of manumission papers rested there, twenty-five declarations of freedom and twenty-five copies of the same, as neat and pristine as the day Emma and I had penned them, as legal as the day Father had signed them. All they lacked was Elliott's signature, and today they would have it.

Thank You, Father! Thank You, Almighty God, sovereign and holy!

I prayed as I rushed them down the stairs, grabbing pen and inkwell from my room. But when I reached the parlor on the first floor, the door was shut. I tried to open it, but it didn't budge. Locked. I knocked and called softly, in case he was sleeping. "Elliott? Elliott, are you awake?" I knew he couldn't have locked the door. He couldn't have walked to the door. Through the front door glass I saw Grayson's horse tied to the hitching post and panic flooded through me. "Elliott! Elliott!" I pounded on the door. "Grayson, I know you're in there. Open this door at once. I demand you open this door at once!"

Muffled voices came from the other side of the door. I could not understand them, but I clearly perceived the intensity in Elliott's faint baritone.

"Martha! Martha!" I screamed, making no effort to erase the fear from my voice. "Get Obadiah! Get him now!" I heard a dish drop in the dining room and steps run out the back door.

Not a minute could have passed before the lock turned on the parlor door and Grayson stepped out, closing the door behind him.

"What were you doing in there, Grayson? Tell me." Trembling, I challenged my brother. If he wanted war, he would have it. "What have you done to Elliott?"

"My, my, Sister. Nothing, of course. Just having a little talk with my elder brother." But his eyes were cold. "You do have a suspicious mind. If you must know, I'm going to war." He brushed past me, doing his best to knock the legal papers from my arms, papers I was certain he recognized. But I would not be deterred. Not this time.

Elliott lay pale and wasted on the bed beside the window. "Elliott, are you all right? Did Grayson—"

But he shook his head. "I can't talk about Grayson now. Give me the papers."

Elliott shook so, from weakness and perhaps anger, that I had to hold his hand.

"Help me, Minnie. God, help me!" He trembled.

"Finish later, Elliott. I'll keep them safe."

"Now. Guide my hand, Minnie. Not one more minute will these people be enslaved, not to us, not to anyone."

I guided Elliott's hand, and though by the time we reached the last set of manumission papers his signature was almost illegible, they were legal, and our friends were free.

Chapter Twenty-Nine

FEBRUARY 1945

Celia was thrilled when she picked up the mail from the post office. Two letters from Joe in as many weeks. She didn't even see Olney Tate as she flew down the store steps on eagle's wings.

"Whoeee! Celia Percy, you look like you're ready to fly to the moon."

Celia stopped in her tracks but couldn't take the grin from her face. "Mornin', Olney! I just got a letter I've been lookin' forward to, that's all." She felt her face warm.

"Wouldn't be from that soldier boy, would it? Friend of Marshall's?"

"Might be." Celia wasn't wanting to say but couldn't keep from smiling.

"Well, when you write him back, you tell him things are lookin' up and our Marshall's likely comin' home."

"Coming home? For real? For good?"

"We hope. He wrote that the Army's near finished its trial. He thinks it may take some time yet, but they'll discharge him, honorably. I reckon he'll get back to England soon as he can or bring his Ivy here after the war. We'll just take all that one day at a time and help how we can. The Lord knows what we don't."

"That's good news, Olney—the best. Joe will be so glad. He's been worried sick about Marshall. Couldn't learn what happened to him for the longest time."

"I know the feelin'. It will sure be good to have our boy home again. And you tell Joe that when he gets sent back to the States, he's got a home with us anytime he wants it. Marshall tells me he's been a brother to him."

"I will." Celia's grin liked to split her face. "I surely will."

Marshall's coming home! Thank You, God! Celia could hardly take it in. She realized from what Olney said that there was some kind of trial going on. She didn't know what that meant, but hard as it was, she knew better than to pry. Olney was proud that Marshall was being vindicated, that was clear, and it was good enough for her. She knew a thing or two about the shame trials could carry after all her family had been through when her daddy was incarcerated, and every story, she knew very well, held many sides.

She'd read Joe's letter and respond right away. *He'll be so glad, so relieved, for himself and for Ivy. Soon, maybe, Marshall can send for Ivy and enroll in medical school. That's been his plan—his and Joe's.*

Celia almost laughed out loud for the happiness of it all.

She was nearly to the top of the hill when, unable to wait a moment longer, she ripped open Joe's letter.

Dear Celia,

I'm writing you now because I don't know where to turn, what else I can do.

What I'm about to say sounds like a bad dream—a nightmare I can't wake up from. I've got to write our friend all that I'll tell you here, but he's going to need help, someone to help him through this, and I don't know anyone to ask but you.

A couple months before D-Day, when our friend married, I'd never seen him so happy, and Ivy was, too. What he didn't know before that day we stormed Normandy, and what he doesn't know yet, is that she was pregnant. She tried to find him, but just like me, she couldn't. The baby came after Christmas. A girl. Her name is Violet.

When I got word about where our friend was, I wrote Ivy right away, but the letter was returned. I got leave this past weekend and went to tell her in person, but she'd been killed—an undetonated bomb exploded in a field she walked through. She's gone, Celia, and before I got there, before I knew anything about it, the baby was taken away—somewhere. I've tried my best to find out where. Ivy's parents won't tell me, but I think they know. I've gone to the police and either they don't know or won't tell me.

Violet's a beautiful baby girl. I know our friend will want his daughter, but I don't know how to find her, and I don't know what to do, how to tell M that Ivy's gone.

Help him, Celia. This is going to rip his heart out. He loved her and they were good together.

Through all this I've started praying, something I haven't done much since my parents were killed in that fire when I was a kid. I can't say I have answers, or that I'm even sure God hears me. None of this makes sense, but I don't blame God for it like I used to. I blame the ugliness and hatred of people. How God can stand to look at us, I don't know, but I need Him. I sure need somebody.

Pray for our friend. Pray for me, Celia.

Joe

Celia had started reading in the middle of the road and hadn't moved. She didn't even realize she was holding her breath until she went a little light-headed and drew a long one.

Marshall has a baby. Bomb exploded. Ivy dead. Celia couldn't take it in. The early February wind blew down the mountain and stole the breath from her pipes.

What to do? Where to turn?

Joe was right. This would kill Marshall. The idea that he'd married, that he'd given his heart to someone, had been astonishment enough for Celia. Now Ivy was dead . . . and their baby . . . gone.

Celia reached Garden's Gate and plunked onto the front porch step. It was a mess, surely. She'd ask her mama what to do, but Joe had made it clear that this was private, a secret between the two of them so that she could help Marshall when he learned of Ivy's death. She wondered if Marshall had received Joe's letter yet, if he'd get it before he was discharged and reached No Creek.

She'd be able to tell by Marshall's face the moment she saw him. Marshall had never been good about concealing his feelings from his eyes, unlike a lot of their friends down at Saints Delight who practiced no expression before white people . . . for good reason, she knew.

She couldn't tell Olney and Mercy; that was up to Marshall. She could only wait to be there, be a friend for Marshall when he got home. *But what about the baby? Baby Violet? What a pretty name, a flower name. She'll be so welcome, if Marshall can get her home.*

Joe said he'd tried everything he knew to do. Celia believed that. Even she knew that a medic couldn't move mountains. But she knew someone who might, who championed the underdog with every bit as much grit as Celia herself. Only this person possessed more clout.

Ten minutes later Celia sat in her room, pulled a sheet of notebook paper from her school binder, and wrote to Joe.

Chapter Thirty

APRIL 1865

Grayson's vow to go to war was short-lived. I came upon him in the parlor the next morning discussing with Elliott, in much calmer tones, his talk with Sam Newton from up the mountain. I joined them, lifting Elliott's stump to tuck a pillow beneath, a help that gave him some relief from the night's pain.

"Sam's agreed to go in my place . . . for four hundred dollars. I believe he'll take Confederate money. It doesn't need to be gold." Grayson sounded like a banker, making a transaction.

"I thought three hundred was the going rate." I could not help my sarcasm. They both ignored me.

"The war will be over soon, Grayson. There's no need for you to go or send someone in your stead." Elliott spoke calmly but I sensed a growing weakness in him.

"There wasn't a need until you freed our slaves. In case you didn't know—or maybe you did and that's why—as long as we owned twenty slaves a man's not got to go."

"The Confederacy assumes a farm or plantation that size will produce enough to supply the war effort, but that applies—"

"Yes, well, that was true of Belvidere Hall until you and Minnie—"

"You can't think we freed the slaves so you would have to go to war! That's ludicrous!" I fumed.

"Why else free them now? This minute? Especially if you both believe the war's all but lost and that good old Abe will send each and every slave on their merry way any day now." Was that fury in Grayson's eyes . . . or hurt?

"Grayson, you're not eighteen yet. You won't be conscripted. Our slaves would have been freed long before if you hadn't interfered."

I was astonished at Elliott's phrasing. *Interfered* was a tame word for Grayson's theft and destruction.

"So does that mean you won't pay Newton's fee?"

"If you turn eighteen and are conscripted and that's what you want, it will be up to you."

"Why not give me the money now?"

And then there was silence in the room. We both stared at Grayson and I couldn't help but wonder if none of this was about the war, but about the money, and Grayson's mounting gambling debts. "Grayson." I spoke with pity and insight.

"Is there something you need to tell us, Brother?" Elliott asked quietly, respectfully.

But Grayson did not answer. His jaw set, he knocked a vase from the table, sending it crashing to the floor and across the room, and strode from the parlor.

"Grayson," Elliott called after him, but he was gone.

• • •

There was no freedom party as we'd once planned, but there was much rejoicing in the house and quarters that night as we handed out the manumission papers with their copies, and for days to come. Freedom lifted the darkness of Belvidere Hall for the first time since Emma had died. Grayson was gone for several days, and I'm sorry to say we all felt relief.

Father's mind cleared somewhat with the joy of seeing the culmination of his and Mother's lifelong plans, and with the belief that his eldest son was home to set things right.

But the confrontation with Grayson and the signing of papers had taken their toll on Elliott. He slept for three days straight.

Throughout those days some of our new freed men and women came to me, asking what now. Were they to leave? To stay? Where could they go and what must they do? Some left right away, headed for Union lines where they believed they would be safe and protected. I had no information about that.

I urged others to stay, to wait until Elliott recovered more, telling them that I knew—at least I believed—that he and Father would settle land upon them, land they'd own free and clear and could work for their own good. But most refused, determined to move as far from the South as they could, as quickly as possible, before North Carolina's soldiers returned to the foothills. I gave them what I could in gold and goods. Elliott had warned me that soon Confederate scrip would amount to nothing. I was certain that if they'd only wait a day or two more, Elliott would rouse—at least I prayed he would—and would know of more we could do for them.

Despite all the news of the waning Confederacy, everyone feared to speculate what might happen once the war was over. They dared not trust that pattyrollers or even Home Guard wouldn't capture and sell them south again—somewhere far worse than Belvidere Hall. I couldn't blame them.

By the time Elliott was able to sit up again and we began drawing maps for the allocation of property, three-quarters of our freed people had gone. It cut Elliott's heart to the quick. "If only Father'd freed them years ago. If only we'd settled this land for them then." He saw it as the death of friendships and family and bemoaned that he hadn't done more for them.

But Obadiah stayed, as did Martha and Alma and a few of our field hands and their families. I was so very grateful. I didn't know what I'd have done without any one of them.

Martha and Obadiah married two days later in our parlor, with Elliott, Father, and me looking on. Elliott was proud to serve as Obadiah's best man, and Alma stood as her sister's maid of honor. Every freed man and woman came, as well as Shadrach, who'd received a pass from Mrs. Chatsworth for the day. Only Grayson was absent, but he wasn't missed.

It wasn't a legal wedding. Even among freed Negroes the law did not recognize marriage. But God did and we did, and we were ever so glad for this union that should have taken place years before.

"Nobody ever gonna take you from me now, Martha Tate—not you nor our children."

"Tate?" asked Father.

"Tate was my daddy's name, and we take it for our last name."

Elliott nodded. "A good name, after a godly man."

"Yes, sir, Mr. Elliott."

"Elliott. No more *massas* or *misters* here, Obadiah."

"One Master of us all," Martha whispered.

"Amen," we said in chorus.

Obadiah and Martha had waited longer than any couple we knew to say their vows and tie their knot. They hadn't wanted to wait to plan a celebration, but it took so little to hire a fiddler and a mouth organ player. I hadn't played the piano in a long while, hadn't had the heart, but I did my best for the two I loved so dearly.

Alma and I, both fairly green when it came to baking, had created a wedding cake to remember from what we could scrounge. It tasted fine, I suppose, but it drooped something like a snowdrop in January. The punch was mild, at least to begin with.

"A toast to the bride and groom," Father spoke up, raising his glass.

"Hear! Hear!" we all echoed . . . as Grayson stumbled through the front door and into the party.

I nodded for Edwin Earl, the fiddler from the other side of No Creek, to continue and left my piano, hoping to nudge Grayson toward the kitchen. I looped my arm in his. "Come, Grayson, I saved the most delicious plate of ham and potatoes for you. We even opened the last jar of peaches. You must be star—"

But he wrenched away from me. "Get your hands off me, Minnie. I know what you're doing, and I won't have it." The timbre of his voice rose with each word.

"Please, Grayson, calm down. I'm only trying to save your dignity and mine. This is Obadiah and Martha's wedding day."

"Well, excuse me. I beg your pardon for intruding on the great Obadiah's wedding day—the darky slave who's ascended to the ranks of son—second born at the very least." He mocked a bow and nearly fell over.

"You're drunk. You're drunk and you're rude, Grayson," I whispered. "I won't have you ruining—"

"You won't have me ruining what? Your day? Another day you and Elliott live vicariously through our slaves? Look at yourself, Minnie. You're inching past your prime. You don't even have a beau. Elliott's crowding thirty. He's crippled and his wife is dead—dead!"

"Grayson, please, lower your voice!" I hissed with all the frustration I possessed.

"Lower my voice?" he nearly shouted. "Because Father has killed the fatted calf when the prodigal returned with his brother slave? Tell me, what did Father and Elliott give them as a wedding gift? Prime tobacco land? Water rights for the best of Belvidere Hall's pastureland? Don't you think it odd that's he's never given you anything? Or me, his true son that's been here all along, not so much as an acre of land?"

"Grayson, we're his children. We have no lack. There's so much land to divide among—"

"Among slaves?"

"Among free men and women who've served us all our lives, who've worked alongside us to help others become free while they were not. You know that we will be provided for, that Father will be generous with us."

"Oh, yes. Yes, Sister, he will." Grayson leaned forward, his finger and whiskey breath in my face. "I told you once that if I'm heir—when I'm heir—I will see to it that we don't lose everything, and I mean to keep that vow."

The kitchen door opened and there stood Elliott, leaning precariously on crutches. "Grayson. You go too far." The steel in Elliott's voice sent shivers up my spine and seemed to sober Grayson, at least a little.

But then he straightened, took the punch glass I'd brought him, and downed the drink in one long gulp. He slammed the glass to the table so hard that I jumped. "And what, dear crippled widower brother, are you going to do about it?"

"Grayson!" His name escaped my mouth in a horrified whisper and plea, but he didn't answer, simply pushed roughly past Elliott, nearly knocking him to the floor as he stormed through the hallway and up the stairs.

I rushed to Elliott and caught him just enough to steady him. "You shouldn't be up. It's too soon."

His breath came in gasps and I could feel his heart slamming against his thin chest.

"Help me to a chair. I'll be all right. We'll be all right."

But it was a lie, so many lies, and I recorded each one in my diary that night, in a prayer, a plea to the Lord.

Chapter Thirty-One

Mail call was the highlight of every man's day and the hope each one went to sleep with at night. Hardest of all was when guy after guy got called up for letters and you didn't. It was so hard that Joe had long ago stopped going. Letters would end up on his bunk if he'd received any, which was rare as an English day without rain.

So when Celia's letter came it felt like a gift. Maybe a gift from God.

He waited until everybody else had gone to the mess hall and slit the letter carefully.

He scanned the page—just one sheet this time, and brief. But Celia had poured out her heart and her heartache for Marshall and his wife and their baby, and she'd poured it out for Joe. The lump Joe'd been carrying in his throat for weeks grew tenfold. He'd not been able to talk the losses over with anybody but had carried the burden alone. Now, to know it was shared and understood meant everything.

It was near the end of the letter that Celia provided a path forward, or what might be a path forward, that gave Joe hope.

You remember I've talked and talked about Miss Lill, about how she owns Garden's Gate and invited us to stay with her here? You remember she married Reverend Willard, who's a chaplain in the US Army now? He was wounded early on and she went to him, right there in England. He's recovered, from what Miss Lill writes, and stationed in Weymouth. Miss Lill says it's one of the places wounded soldiers are shipped first.

I think if anybody can help you find baby Violet, they can. Reverend Willard's a good man, one who helped to save our friend's life the night the Klan tried to hang him. And Miss Lill—well, she'll fight to the death for anybody who needs help she can give. They'll help find Violet, I know they will.

Miss Lill's staying in a boardinghouse near the base. I'll write her address below. Write her, Joe, or go see her if you can. You can trust them to keep a secret.

There's something else. Reverend Willard's parents were killed in a house fire when he was a boy. He'll understand more than you can imagine. I just thought you should know.

I'm praying about what to do about our friend when he gets home. I met Olney Tate at the store today and he said M's hoping he'll be honorably discharged. I don't know if he'll get your letter before he comes home or not. I'll let you know whatever I learn, but I'll be on the lookout for him.

My heart is heavy for all of them and my heart goes out to you. I wish I could help you. You're the best of friends for M and the best of friends for me. Keep praying, Joe. It helps and I know God hears you. I know He loves you. He's your Father and mine—that makes us family.

Do you have a Bible, Joe? If you do, look up Zephaniah 3:17. Read it. Know it's meant for you.

> *Your friend,*
> *Celia*

Joe set the letter down, doing his best not to choke up. He wasn't alone, not with Celia, and maybe, with what she'd said about the

Willards, more besides. Maybe God did watch over him. What other explanation could there be that Joe even made it off Omaha Beach alive? But why him? Why not a hundred other guys?

He did have a steel-covered Heart Shield Bible, a Protestant version that fit in his breast pocket, at least a New Testament, issued by the Army. He looked, but that didn't have any Zephaniah in it. He guessed it must be a book from the older part, what they called the Old Testament. He'd have to ask the chaplain about that.

Skipping dinner was a little thing compared to writing to Chaplain Willard and his wife, and Joe did that right away.

• • •

Two days later the major called him into his office.

"I'm concerned about that foot, Rossetti. I've noticed you're limping more. Giving you pain, is it?"

"No more than usual," Joe lied. He didn't want to be taken off duty. What little medical treatment he was able to give the wounded kept his hands and mind busy. It was downtime, office chairs, and letting his mind worry that brought him low.

"Right." The major leaned back in his chair, observing Joe, a thing that would have made Joe squirm if he wasn't determined to stand at attention. "Sit down. Take a load off."

Joe sat, but that didn't make him more comfortable.

"I'm sending you home."

"Home?" It was the thing most guys longed to hear, the moment throughout this long and stinking war they lived for, but there was nothing at home for Joe, and his work here wasn't done . . . not his work on the base and not his search for Violet.

"War's nearly over. You're not going back into combat. We're going to be all right here, and you're limping worse than you did six weeks out of surgery—especially since you came back from that weekend pass. I don't know what happened there, but it set you back."

Joe wanted to argue, but he knew the doctor was right. His foot was worse, ached all the time, and the compensation he'd been giving it had distorted his hip and leg. The pain was constant. He'd thought he'd hidden it well.

"Before you go, there's a surgeon I want you to see. I don't know what help you'll get back in the States, but we've got the best orthopedic surgeon in the Army right here in England. I want him to take a look at that foot and see what he can do. It may not be too late to correct—"

"Sir, another surgery—"

"Don't argue with me, soldier. You said you want to go to medical school, become a doctor?"

"Yes, sir." It was what Joe wanted more than anything else.

"How many patients do you think are going to come to you if you can't walk to them? Consider this an investment in your future. Besides, it's an order."

"Yes, sir." It was all Joe could say.

"I'll prepare the paperwork. You'll leave within the week."

"Leave?"

"For Weymouth. I'll call the surgeon myself. He's a friend of mine." The major leaned back in his chair. "A number of men are going home to their families because of what you did on Omaha Beach, and they're going home in better shape because of what you've done here. I wish you the best. That's all."

"Yes, sir. Thank you, sir." Joe saluted and closed the major's door behind him. *Weymouth. Weymouth! Chaplain and Mrs. Willard are in Weymouth.* Joe's heart beat faster as he limped back to his barracks. *This can only be You, God. Violet's going home. I know it.*

Chapter Thirty-Two

APRIL 1865

I did not think the gift extravagant for the many years, let alone the generations, that Obadiah's family had served the Belvideres. It was more than earned. But I hoped that Grayson would not know, would not get wind that Father and Elliott had given Obadiah and Martha one hundred acres of prime land and one hundred dollars in gold as their wedding gift.

"The war will be over soon, Minnie," Elliott explained one morning when we were the only ones at breakfast. "The South has all but lost and slaves everywhere will be free before long. Thanks to you and Mother, those who've served us know how to read and write, how to count their money, but they've had little opportunity to use those skills. Now they will, and we must do all in our power to help those that remain not be taken advantage of. There will be many opportunists. I saw it in the war—men eager to clean the unsuspecting soldier or the ignorant worker out of his coin with promises for something better that doesn't exist."

"I'm not sure how we can do that. We've no right to interfere in their lives—that's what freedom is, what it means. The few who've stayed won't be living here, not anymore."

"I'm thinking there may be some who'll want to stay on. Maybe have their own home or cabin, own a stretch of land but still work our land or in our home for wages."

"Can we afford that?"

"Not as much land as we gave Obadiah and Martha, and I don't know yet about the amount in wages. But if we sell some of our land, we surely can settle thirty or forty acres on those few who are left, and a wage that will enable them to live. It must be a fair wage. That's what I'm recommending to Father. If they don't want the land or want to sell it, I'll offer a fair price so our property lines are not divided, not split up by folks trying to take advantage."

"Why are you telling me this now? Why, when you've never included me before in any of our family's business dealings?"

Elliott leaned forward. "Because I don't trust our brother. If left to him he would still own every man, woman, child, and acre of land. I'm not sure that even the war's end will end the war of greed in him."

"It's more than greed. He's hurt and angry and in debt. He's not the man that you or Obadiah are, and he can't abide that. He can't abide that Father doesn't respect him."

"He's worked hard to earn Father's disrespect. I cannot change that for him. But I'm worried for the rest of you. He's bullied Father. He's bullied you. I'm worried for Alma, for the way he treats her, speaks to her, looks at her."

"As am I. I will hate to see her leave us, but I think it would be best, before . . ." I didn't want to finish.

"I spoke with Obadiah this morning. He's going to build a cabin on the edge of the acreage Father gave them. We'll deed land to Alma, but I wonder if he and Martha would make room for her to live with them—for safety. She's Martha's sister, after all."

"Mmm. If I don't miss my guess she won't be wanting to live with her sister." I smiled.

"Meaning?"

"You didn't notice the attentions Shadrach of Chatsworth Lodge paid her at the party?"

Elliott cocked his head, considering. "You think—"

"I do, as soon as Shadrach is free. Alma told me he's been saving to buy his freedom, hoping Mrs. Chatsworth will agree, but he's loath to leave her so soon after Tom's death. They grew up together, you know, as you and Obadiah did."

Elliott raised his brows. "Apparently not exactly as we did."

"No," I sighed. "It was the ownership of others they considered as less than themselves that Tom and his mother could never get beyond, that Tom and I could never agree on."

"That day of reckoning is coming. The war is going to end, and soon."

"I pray you're right, but I wonder—will it make people change their ways? The moment I saw Grayson burning those freedom papers and land deeds, I realized that the strong, the politically powerful rule this world, even if it means they flaunt the law. And our people are free now, but I worry that—"

Elliott leaned back in his chair. "I'm tired, Minnie."

"Let me help you to the parlor. You can rest awhile before Mother Sally brings Ellie in to play." I stood to go round the table to him.

"Yes, but that's not all I meant. I wish you were settled."

I stopped. It was the thing I could not think about.

"Is there no one?" He looked so tired, yet genuinely concerned.

"When has there been time for courting?" I tried to laugh it off as I handed him his crutches, helped him stand. We walked together, my arm about his waist to steady him, into the parlor, where he sank into the overstuffed chair. I propped pillows round him.

"In the field hospital, when we were wounded, Tom spoke to me about you. He wanted—"

"What Tom wanted I could not give him." I turned away, biting my lip. "He gave me a set of *Les Misérables*—did I ever tell you that?"

"Tom?"

"He said the books were so popular in the Confederate ranks that men called themselves Lee's Miserables." The memory and hope of Tom and my disappointment that he'd taken such different meaning from the book had burned a sharp dagger in my soul.

"I heard men say that. There were copies of the books, ragtag and spines broken, passed from man to man. They talked about it around the fires at night. But what they read was a different edition. Pirated, changed."

"Yes. Every reference to the freeing of slaves omitted. Without that, it was not what Victor Hugo wrote—a compromise and more, a lie. You can't take what's real and bend it to suit a notion. That's what that Richmond edition did. And that's what Tom and his mother believed about slavery—that it was not really slavery in the sense that the people they enslaved lost anything. They believed—Mrs. Chatsworth still believes—that they need to care for the people they've enslaved, as if they can't navigate the world on their own. How would they know? They never gave them the chance. Bending a notion to suit—well, it didn't suit me and never will."

"People do it all the time, Minnie. They do it with law, with politics, with Scripture. They take a truth and bend it to mean what they want." He paused. "I'm sorry about Tom."

"Sorry? It sounded to me as if he left you to die. He didn't speak for you—he told me so, though I didn't understand what that meant until Shadrach told me what happened."

"Don't hold that against him. I'd told him a hard truth he didn't want to hear."

"But it was truth, Elliott. I wouldn't have married him, couldn't have, knowing his beliefs, his actions."

A knock came at the door. "Miss Minnie? Mr. Elliott? I've got little Miss Ellie here."

"Alma, come in, please. And remember what I told you? No more *mister* and *miss*." Elliott smiled, reaching for his daughter.

"Old habits die hard, Mr.—they just die hard, Elliott."

"For all of us." He smiled again, but I saw the dark circles beneath his eyes and the way his arms still trembled in weakness as he took Ellie. Though she weighed little she was sitting up now, squirming and wriggling, determined to stand and jump, all the while needing to be held. She was a handful, even for me.

"I'll be in the kitchen with Martha. Just call when you want me to come get her."

"We will," I assured her.

When she'd gone, Elliott whispered, "Minnie, can you take her?"

"Come to Aunt Minnie, sweet girl." I scooped Ellie into my arms just before Elliott dropped her. "Elliott?"

"I'm sorry. I'm not myself. I don't seem to be getting any stronger."

"You just need more time. So much has happened, Elliott. You—"

"Listen to me, Minnie. We need to get the deeds signed and registered at the courthouse."

"I thought you believed it would be safest to wait till the war's over. You said it won't be long."

He shook his head. "We need to do it right away. I'd like to think I have all the time in the world, but I know that's not true. You know that's not true."

Looking into his eyes, his Belvidere eyes as blue as the Blue Ridge at dusk, I gripped Ellie too hard, trying in my heart to hang on to all we had, what we were together. It was too much for Ellie. She sent up a wail, a wail I wanted to echo.

To have my brother home at last, to share a like mind on so many things, to not stand alone against Grayson . . . I could not bear to lose him now. "Hush, now, Ellie. I'm sorry, lovie, I'm so sorry." I cuddled the little girl closer, already mourning all she would miss in her dear father.

. . .

Elliott used every ounce of energy he had to speak with those freed men and women who'd remained working at Belvidere Hall after receiving their papers. Together they selected and he allocated plots of land. I wrote out the deeds. Elliott signed them, and to make certain there would never be a question, I helped Father sign as well and press his seal.

Elliott wanted to register the deeds himself, but he'd grown too weak to manage even the short ride into town, so I went, and Obadiah went with me.

"You sure your brother knows what he's doin'?" the clerk in the courthouse office asked. "Registerin' land to slaves ain't legal, Miss Belvidere."

"These are all deeds for land awarded to free persons, Mr. Bass."

Mr. Bass's eyebrows rose high in his forehead.

"Each and every one possesses free papers. Each and every one is now our employee."

Mr. Bass's face reddened. "I don't know as I can—how do I know these ain't forged? It's not likely for a woman to come in here—"

"You may know that my brother, who served in this war, was wounded at Hatcher's Run and is now at home, resting and recovering from a lost limb."

"Then how do I know he's in his right mind? This hardly leaves Mr. Belvidere with enough acreage to—"

Obadiah stepped forward—six feet and well-muscled, towering over Mr. Bass, who couldn't have been more than five feet three and balding. "I believe you'll see both signatures there, Mr. Bass . . . that of Mr. Elliott Belvidere and that of Mr. Horace Belvidere, owner of Belvidere Hall."

I saw the Adam's apple in Mr. Bass's neck ride up and down. "Well, I don't know . . ."

"The deeds are legal and binding, Mr. Bass. It's your job to register deeds, isn't it? Or do I need to take them to your superior?" I had no idea who that might be but stood as straight as I could and rose up on my toes, giving the impression of every inch I could muster. Obadiah stepped closer to the counter.

"Well, all right then, if you're sure these people he's signing over land to are free."

"Legally free," I affirmed.

"Well, all right then. I'll take care of it."

"We're happy to wait." I smiled. "I've never seen deeds registered. I'd like to see exactly how it's done." I pasted the most innocent, possibly flirtatious smile across my face I could conjure. Obadiah shifted beside me, and I sensed he was trying not to smile.

Mixed emotions swept across Mr. Bass's face—annoyance, anger, a bit of humiliation lined with intimidation, and then an inclination to the feminine interest being shown him. But he did his duty, at least I hoped he did. Obadiah and I both witnessed his actions.

When we walked down the courthouse steps I felt as if the world had been righted, as if there was hope for a new day, possibly a new era. Until I saw Grayson standing outside the saloon, leaning against a post, arms crossed, watching us.

Chapter Thirty-Three

FEBRUARY 1945

Mail service overseas could take a week or weeks or sometimes a month or maybe never arrive at all, but mail service in England was exceptional, even during wartime. Joe heard from the Willards within the week. They were fully on board to help find Marshall's baby. Even with all the abbreviations and clandestine phrases, which they used in return, they seemed to have a pretty good picture of the situation and to comprehend the danger for Marshall and Violet.

He hoped the Willards were miracle workers.

They wanted the address of Ivy's parents. Grimly, Joe wrote it out for them. *Little good it will do.*

. . .

A week later Joe found himself in the surgeon's office in Weymouth for the second time. The doctor posted X-rays before a light board.

"These are the X-rays taken at the time of your first surgery, and I have here what we took this morning."

Joe swallowed. He knew what he saw wasn't good. One brief twist or snap and he'd be lucky to be on crutches the rest of his life.

"You have enough medical training to see why a second surgery is required. It's a wonder you're able to walk at all, Rossetti. It appears you've sustained some further injury."

The doctor waited, but Joe didn't fill the space. He didn't want to explain that an irate father had knocked him off a front stoop, or why.

"Monday. We'll operate Monday."

Monday was so soon, less than a week away. He needed to meet with the Willards, needed to . . .

"Rossetti? Are you with me?"

"Yes, sir. I'll be ready, sir."

"Stay off that foot as much as you can till then—my orders. Any further damage or swelling will make the surgery all the more difficult, and your prognosis more grim."

Joe understood. He walked back to the barracks, mindful for the first time of how and where he stepped. He'd been given a reprieve. Could he get a pass for the weekend? He didn't know.

He walked out of the mess hall that afternoon and was nearly across the grounds when he heard his name called.

"Sergeant Rossetti!"

Joe turned. Nobody knew him here, at least he didn't think so. A man with a limp worse than his own walked toward him. "Joe Rossetti?"

"Yes, sir." Joe recognized the chaplain's insignia on the man's uniform.

"Chaplain Jesse Willard." The man reached his hand to Joe, forgoing salutes.

The wind was stolen from Joe's pipes for a moment. "Chaplain Willard? Celia's Reverend Willard?"

The man laughed. "That's right. Celia's Reverend Willard. I understand you know our girl from home."

"She's a pistol."

Jesse Willard laughed again, the light of home and memory in his eyes. "My wife received your letter. Is there somewhere we can talk?"

"Looks like we might be dealing with some similar injuries, sir." Joe eyed the man's bum leg. What he really wanted to say was that he knew the chaplain's parents had died in a fire, as had his, and he was sorry. At the same time, he was glad to talk to a real person who'd been through something so similar, so painful. Somebody who'd get where he'd come from. But it was too much, too personal. Maybe it was enough to know they shared that long-ago wicked loss.

Chaplain Willard lifted his pants leg to reveal a prosthesis. "Lost my leg in France. I've been stationed here ever since recovery, visiting the boys coming in from the Continent." He pointed to a bench in the open square and they headed that way.

Joe tried to remember. He was sure he'd seen this man with the artificial leg before. "It was you. You spoke to me, prayed with me—in Cheltenham—after my no—after my grandmother died. I'm sure it was you."

"That's right. I'm glad you remember. How have you been since then?"

Joe sighed. Where to begin? How he was didn't matter. What mattered was getting baby Violet home to Marshall. And that's what he talked about, in detail, giving the entire picture he hadn't been able to divulge through a letter that had to pass through his staff sergeant's hands and eyes for censorship—or discipline.

Chaplain Willard waited until he was finished, nodding in all the places Joe needed to know he understood. "My wife and I read some of this between the lines of Celia's and your letters, but not all. I'm so sorry for Ivy, for Marshall, for the baby."

"We've got to find her, Chaplain. They're operating on me Monday. I know how this works. I won't be convalescing here. They'll send me home on the first troop ship out to a military hospital in the US. I can't go without knowing what to tell Marshall. He'll be on the first ship over here unless there's another path forward. I know him."

"I agree. Let me tell you what we've done."

Done? He's already done something? Joe was all ears.

"Mrs. Willard—Lilliana, my wife—and I followed up on the address you sent for Ivy's parents."

Joe sucked in his breath. He hoped the bulldog hadn't knocked the chaplain off the stoop like he had Joe. "You met her father?"

"No." The chaplain smiled. "After all you wrote we thought it best to visit during the work week, when he'd likely be out. We met with Mrs. Greenfield. I think having my wife along helped. Lilliana has a way about her."

Joe hadn't thought of that. He could see that having a woman—a gentlewoman with nerves of steel, from all Celia had said about her—might help. A chaplain showing up on your doorstep was a lot like a vicar or a priest. That could help, too. "What happened?"

"She was reluctant to give us any information at first, but Lilliana spent some time with her, helped her open up to her own grief for the loss of her daughter . . . something I don't think she's felt free to do in the presence of her husband."

Joe could believe that. "Does she even know where they took Violet?"

"Somerset County. A couple of hours by car from here, I think, based on the map. There's a National Trust house near Minehead that's been set up by the Somerset County Council, requisitioned in 1943 for evacuees. Now it's being used as a nursery for 'brown babies'—mixed-race children born of English women and colored American GIs."

"Orphanage for kids nobody wants." Joe's blood simmered. If it hadn't been for Nonni, he would have ended up in an orphanage.

"Sometimes. Or sometimes the mothers can't keep them . . . We can't know all the reasons people give up their children, Joe, and we've no right to judge that. But maybe we can help get Violet and make sure she has a home and a family."

"Marshall's her father. He's her family." Joe didn't want anybody losing sight of that.

"Yes, I understand. Now he's a single father, a widower, but as the result of a marriage that the US Army didn't sanction, and his own state of North Carolina won't recognize. I don't know how that will play out for him. If we can get Violet delivered into Marshall's care, that's the best, the first choice, as long as he wants her."

"He'll want her. I know he will."

"I believe that, too. I feel sure that his aunt and uncle, back home in No Creek, will help, would gladly take her in. But we don't know that the British will release Violet to Marshall or to them."

Joe sighed. Such a mess. Such a sticky mess. "And if they don't, what then?"

The chaplain settled against the bench back. "Lilliana and I have talked about it. If they won't allow Marshall to take his child, or the Tates, we'll apply to adopt her."

Take Marshall and Ivy's child? Over my dead body.

"We'll be going back to No Creek after the war, once my duty's done here. We could take Violet with us, care for her, give her every opportunity to see Marshall and get to know him as her father."

Joe drew a deep breath. He nodded. It wasn't the perfect outcome, but perfect outcomes didn't seem to be falling into place. It was the best the chaplain and his wife could offer, and it was a generous offer, he knew.

"We're going to Holnicote day after tomorrow. I've already called and talked with the matron there. Would you like to come? Like to see Violet before you go back home?"

Would I! "Yes, sir, I would—very much. I'm off duty till my surgery Monday. But I'll need to get a pass."

"I think I can help with that. We're renting a car. Lilliana drives now—even though it's on the left side of the road. I can just about manage the clutch but am glad to let her drive until we get home." He smiled. "We'll pick you up at the front gate Friday morning, say eight o'clock."

"You secure the pass, Chaplain. I'll be ready."

• • •

Two days later Joe waited by the gate, fifteen minutes before the hour. He didn't want to delay the trip one minute. It was the last good thing he'd be able to do this side of the Atlantic and the only thing that mattered to him at the moment. It was helping the friend who was like a brother to him. It was fulfilling a promise to a young woman who'd trusted him to do the best for her daughter. Even more, it was finding a future for a kid, a little baby, who had no one to help her—a lot like the kid he'd been after his parents' death.

And then there was another truth, the one that hit Joe in the heart. When he'd held baby Violet for the first time, he'd imagined what it would be like to have a family, to be a father. It was something he hoped for in the future with a woman he could love as much as Marshall loved Ivy. But for now, it was Violet who'd drawn those feelings from somewhere deep inside him and all he wanted to do was hold her again, protect her, secure a hope and a future for her.

By the time the Willards pulled up to the gate Joe was an emotional wreck. Everything he'd put off thinking about, feeling, for the longest time crept very near the surface. But he choked it down, determined to keep a level head.

"Call me Lilliana, Joe. It is all right that I call you Joe, isn't it?" The chaplain's wife smiled briefly into the rearview mirror.

"Yes, ma'am. Sure thing—Lilliana. Celia likes your flower name, likes the flower names of all your family—Hyacinth, Rose, Camellia." It was a stupid thing to say but the one that sprang to mind. Joe hadn't been in the presence of many beautiful women, but Lilliana Willard was a knockout.

Lilliana laughed. "Celia's the finest young lady I know, Joe. I'm glad you're writing her. I'm sure she gives you all the news of No Creek."

"I feel like I know the town already, like it's a second home—kind of." He hoped that didn't sound too presumptuous.

"I hope you'll make it so. I know Celia does, and from what you both say, Marshall will hope the same."

Joe studied the two in front as Lilliana drove. Her husband was a good-looking guy, but Joe wondered what she thought of his wooden leg. She didn't seem to mind, the way the two of them looked at one another, the little playful nudges shared between them. Maybe if she didn't mind, there was hope for Joe, too. Maybe there were women who could see beyond war injuries.

By the time they reached Holnicote House it was nearly noon. They'd eaten early in the car from a boxed lunch Lilliana had packed—savory meat pies and Empire biscuits that melted in Joe's mouth—so felt ready to face whatever lay ahead.

"Rather imposing, isn't it?" Lilliana remarked as they stepped from the car.

"Used as a hunting lodge for a wealthy family at one time, I heard—one of those rambling old country mansions," her husband answered.

Joe could only think of the labor to keep such a place going. The stucco work alone would require constant upkeep. "Take a look at all those chimneys! I'd hate to be the one to keep that many fires going."

The three stood on the doorstep of the gigantic house and rang the bell.

"Think what it must cost to heat this place," Lilliana whispered. "I wonder if they're able to do that—keep all the children adequately warm throughout the winter."

Moments later the door was opened by a cheery girl in nurse's uniform, a teen who looked like she should still be in school and knee socks.

"May I help you?" the young nurse inquired, more curious than businesslike.

Chaplain Willard stepped up. "We're here to see Matron Foyle and . . . a certain baby girl."

The nurse stepped back, allowing all three to enter. "Your name, sir?"

"I'm Chaplain Willard with the US Armed Forces, and this is my wife, Mrs. Willard. Sergeant Rossetti is here to represent the father of the child."

"Very good, sir. Right this way, if you please."

The small troop followed the nurse down the long hallway to a closed door on the left, where she knocked softly.

"Yes?" came a voice from the other side.

The nurse opened the heavy carved wooden door and repeated word for word the introduction that Chaplain Willard had made.

The matron rose from her desk to greet the group. "We were expecting you, Chaplain Willard, Mrs. Willard, Sergeant Rossetti. Nurse Milford, please see that Violet is dressed and ready for visitors."

"Yes, Matron."

Joe thought the nurse might curtsey before she slipped from the room. It would be in keeping with the surroundings.

The matron motioned to chairs before her desk. "Please be seated."

"Thank you for seeing us, Matron Foyle."

The matron clasped her hands, resting them on her desk. "I've looked into your case, Chaplain Willard, and I'm sorry to say that we may be at something of a standstill."

"I don't understand. We're ready to take the child today. My wife can care for her and we will personally see she that she reaches her father once we return to the US."

"I'm very willing. I'd love to care for baby Violet," Lilliana spoke up.

"It's not that simple," the matron expounded. "Under British law, our 1939 Adoption Act, children are only allowed to be sent abroad to live with British subjects or their own relatives."

"Marshall—her father—is her relative." Joe couldn't see the problem.

"Be that as it may," the matron continued, "British law sees American servicemen as putative fathers and therefore does not count them as relatives. I'm sorry."

"What's *putative*?" Joe wanted to know.

"Roundabout, I'd say." Lilliana tensed.

"That's the craziest thing I ever heard of," Joe fumed. "Marshall and Ivy were married. He's the baby's father!" Joe felt his blood pressure rising. Lilliana laid a hand on his arm, surely to calm him down, but Joe didn't feel calm. He was sick of the rules and regulations and prejudices and denigration that had kept Marshall and Ivy and now baby Violet apart.

"It's the way it is now, but I'm hoping things will change, and soon. Celia Bangham is Somerset's superintendent health visitor. She's doing everything she can to acquire special dispensation to allow adoptions by putative fathers or other near relatives, even other colored families in the States. She's petitioned Mr. Ede, the home secretary, and is hoping for a meeting in the near future. We're very hopeful, but until the act changes or is amended, there's nothing we can do."

"What if we stay in England?" Lilliana proposed. "Could we adopt her here, now?"

"Darling," Chaplain Willard cautioned, "we don't know how long I'll be stationed here, and Joe's being shipped back within the month."

"My coming and going isn't necessarily tied to yours," Lilliana spoke softly.

"I'm sorry, Mrs. Willard, but you're not a British citizen, are you?"

Lilliana looked from her husband to the matron and sighed. "No, I am not."

"Well, then . . ." The matron raised her hands in surrender.

"What can we do?" Chaplain Willard stayed on point.

"Pray that Celia Bangham is convincing in her appeal and is truly heard. Pray for those in power to have a change of heart, for them to see that what is best for these dear children is best for all, and act quickly. And, please, Chaplain, Mrs. Willard, Sergeant Rossetti, pray for these children and their future. That weighs most heavily on our minds. Our facility is set up as a nursery and we're only able to keep the children until they turn age five. After that they'll be taken into other homes for either adoption or fostering. I worry what these children's lives will become in British society. We gamely say there is no 'color bar' here, but . . ."

"We understand," Chaplain Willard agreed, "better than you know."

"That is another thing. There is the concern that these mixed-race children will not be accepted in America. We've seen how your own colored soldiers are treated by white American soldiers, and the laws in so many of your states prohibit the unions that created these little ones."

Joe couldn't deny that. He was worried, too. Where would Marshall live? Where could he safely raise Violet? Based on all he'd heard from Celia and Marshall both, No Creek was not a likely place, and yet that's where Marshall had family. *Every kid needs family.*

Joe didn't have the answer, but he knew Violet should be with her father. Making that happen seemed much harder now than it had before they'd found her. *The most hopeful thing about all this is that this woman going to bat is named Celia. If anybody can fight for the underdog, it's somebody with a name like that.*

"Would you like to see her?" the matron kindly offered.

"Yes!" Lilliana spoke first.

The matron really was not a battle-ax, Joe knew. If left to her, he figured she'd send Violet home with them today. But it wasn't up to her. She was in her own kind of army with superiors and rules and regs.

"I brought my camera," Lilliana whispered to Joe. "We'll get pictures of baby Violet for Marshall. You hold her first, so I can snap one."

Joe thought his heart might flow out his eyes, so he blinked hard. He wasn't going to cry, not in front of anybody, not in front of Violet or for the picture, for sure. He couldn't let the baby think he was without hope. There'd be a way to get her home; he was sure of it.

Chapter Thirty-Four

APRIL 1865

Was it premonition that prompted me to make a second copy of Obadiah's deed to the land the moment he and I returned home? Or was it the Holy Spirit speaking to me?

Whatever it was, I woke Elliott to sign the copy as soon as it was ready and again guided Father's hand across the page and set his seal. I hid the deed copy beneath the false bottom of our ancestor's trunk in the attic, just as I'd hidden the freedom papers and later, their copies that Obadiah, Martha, and Alma had asked me to safekeep. I intended to write copies of the other deeds as soon as I could. I didn't trust Mr. Bass, even though I'd seen him at work on our deeds. I didn't know if there was anything Grayson could legally do to stop the transactions, but I didn't trust my brother, either, and I wanted proof of the land allocations in my own hands.

I trusted Grayson even less when he stormed into the house that afternoon, demanding Elliott explain to him why he was partitioning off Belvidere land to slaves.

I would have locked Grayson from the parlor if I'd gotten there first.

But Elliott said, "Let him stay. Grayson must be told; he deserves to know."

I propped another pillow beneath Elliott's neck and back and refused to be sent from the room. Elliott was too weak to sit in a chair and I feared that Grayson's tirade would do him in, or that, God forgive me for such a thought, Grayson might.

"You're not lord of the manor, Elliott!" Grayson stormed. "You had no right!"

"You know that was always Mother and Father's intention." Elliott spoke calmly.

"To free them after Father's death—not before. That was bad enough. But to give them our land!"

"They've earned that land, many times over, and those that wish can stay on as our employees, selling back that acreage if they wish. Mother wanted our people to have a start in life, a way to begin on their own."

"Nobody does that."

"That's what people do in a free society, Grayson."

"You had no right," Grayson said again and again.

"I had every right, and it was Father's wish. I shouldn't need to remind you that he is still owner of Belvidere Hall."

"You should have waited till he died and divided Belvidere between us, let me decide what to do with what's mine."

"Is that what this is about?"

"It's my land! It should be mine as much as yours, and I'm the one going to live long enough to be saddled with its debts and with Minnie. You should have at least waited till Father dies—that was the plan, as you say. If it happened after the war, at least we'd know what the land is worth."

"That plan was made before there was a war, a war that will determine the legal status and rights of the people heretofore enslaved."

Grayson blinked and walked slowly toward Elliott, who lay helpless. Grayson's brawn, his strength and anger frightened me. I tried to slip between them, but Grayson pushed me away. He stuck his finger in Elliott's face. "If you think this is over, you are sadly mistaken. I swear to you that not one of those darkies will ever get an acre of Belvidere land!"

He accentuated his words with a stab to Elliott's shoulder and turned on his heel, slamming the door behind him.

"It's done, Grayson!" I called after him. "It's already done!"

"Let him go, Minnie."

But all our voices were drowned out by Alma's and Martha's screams from the hallway. I didn't make it to the parlor door before they threw it open.

"News from town—General Lee has surrendered the Army of Northern Virginia. It means it's over, doesn't it? The war is finally over!"

Alma clasped her hands together and Martha raised her arms toward heaven.

Elliott closed his eyes. "Thank You, Father!"

. . .

April is still chilly in the foothills of North Carolina, but occasionally warm enough to leave windows open at night. I'd done that each spring, hoping to hear the year's first whip-poor-will call. I did that the night we learned of General Lee's surrender.

I lay awake, thinking through the day's events—Grayson and his tirade and threats. The miracle of General Lee's surrender and the hope that it meant the war was truly over, that the husbands and sons and brothers of our neighbors would come home and not one more name would be typed in the post office's window listing of Confederate dead.

Through all those musings and half prayers, I smelled woodsmoke. It could have been a fire in one of our own fireplaces or even one of the cabins in the quarters, but that seemed odd, for the temperature was unusually mild.

Memories of the night I found Grayson burning freedom papers and deeds came to mind. I turned over, grateful beyond words that those deeds were filed at the courthouse and no longer in my possession. I closed my eyes, determined to shut out unruly thoughts. That's when I heard the church bells—church bells frantically ringing in the middle of the night, our town's call to arms. Someone in need. *Fire!*

I pulled on my shoes and threw a wrapper over my gown. I ran down the stairs and heard Obadiah's footsteps on the porch just as I opened the door.

"I'm going into town, Miss Minnie. See what I can do."

"Obadiah, I don't think you should. You don't know what—"

"I'm a free man, Miss—Minnie. This is my town now, too. Our people—somebody needs help. I smell fire—no tellin' how bad it is, how far it's traveled."

"Wait for me. I'm going with you."

"There's no need."

"I'll go alone if you don't wait for me. If there's a fire, there's bound to be something I can do to help."

"I'll get the buggy, load it up with buckets and rakes, rugs from the barn."

"I'll bring our medical kit and bandages. There's bound to be burns."

Martha was already in the kitchen, gathering supplies. "I heard what y'all said. You be careful now, Minnie. I can't be bandagin' you up and takin' care of Mr. Elliott all at the same time."

I wrapped my arms around her and felt her trembling.

"I told Obadiah don't be a hero. I don't need a hero; I need my husband back in one piece."

"We'll be careful, I promise, and we'll be back." I prayed that was a promise we could keep.

Obadiah helped me into the buggy and took the reins. We lost no time. No Creek proper was not far from Belvidere Hall. Before we reached the church, we could see flames leaping into the night sky from the center of town. We reached the general store, but a crowd stood between us and the fire—a crowd that didn't seem to be doing anything to put out the fire. Mrs. Mae and her grown children stood on the porch.

Beyond the crowd of bystanders, townsfolk who'd turned out with fire buckets and rakes and rugs, stood the silhouettes of men on horseback, prancing before the fire, creating a shield against those who would help.

"What is it? Why aren't they putting out the fire?" I leaned from the buggy and called to Mrs. Mae.

She covered her mouth with her hand. It was too dark, and I could not read her eyes, not until she saw Obadiah driving our buggy, and then the whites of her eyes widened. "You value your man, you get him out of here, Minerva Belvidere. You get him out of here right now." It was a rash statement and one that made no sense. But I knew Cordova Mae would not have said it without cause.

From near the fire there was a chorus of whoops and then that terrible screeching rebel yell I'd read about and heard discussed around the stove in the store but had never heard with my own ears. It sent chills over my body and terror through my heart. Riders in front of the burning courthouse reared their horses, and hats flew into the air, lurid specters against the flames. The crowd of spectators stepped back. I recognized one neighbor and another, but no one did a thing, the terror on their faces as clear as my own.

"Obadiah . . . I think we'd best turn around."

"The courthouse—it's the courthouse on fire." He said the obvious, as if he disbelieved. "They not puttin' out that fire, Minnie. They—"

"Turn around, Obadiah. We've got to get out of here." But Obadiah seemed frozen in the moment. I shook his arm. "Obadiah! Please! Take me home!"

"I'll get you home, Miss Minnie. Sure enough, I'll get you home."

He turned our already frightened horses and snapped the reins. With no words between us he drove me straight to the front of the house. "I'll let you out here."

But I wouldn't budge. "You can't go back. You can't be part of that, whatever it is."

"You know that's where our deeds be—every one of Belvidere Hall's freedmen's deeds."

"I know. I know, but they're gone now. They're surely burned. You saw that fire. The deeds are already registered, Obadiah. Don't worry. You mustn't worry, but you cannot risk that crowd—they're drunk and bent on destruction. You have everything to live for. Please, put the buggy away. Don't go, I beg you, for Martha's sake." I didn't want to believe that the fire had anything to do with those deeds, those hopes and dreams and livelihoods for so many.

Obadiah helped me down and walked me to the house. He returned the buggy and horse to the barn and I walked through the door of my home believing that he'd gone back to Martha.

I looked in on Elliott, who'd apparently slept through it all. "Thank You, God!" My prayer was whispered but sounded loud in the still house. Elliott roused then but did not wake. Father's and Grayson's doors were closed, and I wondered how it was that neither had smelled the smoke or heard the church bells, neither had been drawn outside. The night had turned chillier by then and their windows were closed. It was the only explanation.

I checked on Ellie and stroked her baby cheek, thanking God that she knew nothing of these days. For hours I lay awake, praying for the people of my hometown, praying for the outcome for all whose deeds we'd registered the day before.

Shortly before daylight I heard the clopping of horse's hooves on the drive and waited for someone to pound the front door. I sat up, ready to shove my feet into slippers and meet whatever new tragedy awaited. But no pounding came.

I cracked open my door, heard the downstairs back door open and close. Moments later I heard another door open. I grabbed my wrapper and had just cinched the waist when I heard footsteps on the stairs. I opened my door in time to see Grayson taking the stairs in his stocking feet. Reeking of woodsmoke, he slipped through his bedroom door.

I wanted to believe my brother had been part of the crowd who'd gathered to help put out the fire, prevented from that good task though they were. But in my heart, I knew it was not so.

. . .

When I came downstairs next morning, I found that Elliott's window had been opened wide and the fire had gone out. The parlor was freezing. Elliott lay wheezing, nearly unconscious. He couldn't catch a deep breath. I sent Alma for Dr. Hendrix before breakfast. It was midafternoon before he arrived, looking as if he'd not slept for days. By then I was frantic. I stood outside the room while he examined my brother. It was several minutes before he met me in the hallway.

"Afraid there's not much I can do for Elliott now, Minnie. I'm sorry."

"What do you mean?" I knew perfectly well my brother was dying, but surely a miracle stood at hand.

He shook his head sadly. "Pneumonia's set in. Best thing is to make him comfortable as you can."

"We can't manage without Elliott." I sounded like a child. I felt like one, as young as Ellie.

Dr. Hendrix placed his hand on my shoulder. That simple sign of sympathy was my undoing. Tears I couldn't stop coursed over my cheeks, and the old doctor, formal as he was, as much a Confederate as I was loyal to the Union, took me in his arms and let me cry on his shoulder.

He patted my back as I would pat Ellie's, finally pulling away. "Are your people all right? I don't usually treat Negroes, but after last night . . . Mrs. Mae said she saw you there with that big buck Obadiah."

My heart constricted. "We only went to see if we could help put out the fire. He was with me the whole time."

"Well, thought I'd ask."

"What happened last night? What started the fire?"

Dr. Hendrix hefted his black bag. "Hard to say how it started. A bunch of hotheads on horses is what I saw, but the blame was cast on a group of coloreds standing by. I don't see how—"

"What happened to them?" My skin crawled.

Dr. Hendrix's gaze leveled on mine, as if taking my measure, uncertain what more bad news I could stand. "Lynched three of them before it was over. Right there in town."

I gasped and might have fallen backward if the doctor hadn't steadied me.

"Looked to me like they'd come to help put out the fire, but . . ." He shook his head. "I swear I don't know what we've come to. Best that your people stayed away. Best keep clear of town for now."

That's when I realized I hadn't seen Obadiah, or Martha for that matter, all morning. Alma had served breakfast and lunch, quieter than usual. Ellie'd been with Mother Sally all the morning. Obadiah hadn't directly said he wouldn't return . . . *Dear God, please . . . please, not Obadiah.*

The doctor had been saying something else, but I hadn't heard. Now I made myself focus.

"I've no more quinine, and no sense bleeding him. He's too weak now. It would finish him. Have Alma fix up mustard plasters. I'll write down what's to go in them. Keep him comfortable. I won't lie to you, Minnie. I know you wouldn't want that."

I nodded, my heart too burdened to speak.

"I'm sorry."

I stepped aside to show him out.

"Never mind that. I know my way. You take care of yourself, Minnie, and your father. How is Horace?"

"The same." It was true. Father sat in a chair and stared into space unless Elliott or I spoke to him, and for several days it had only been me, and only when I'd thought of him. There was so much to do, so many to care for, so many to worry over, or so it seemed to me.

Dr. Hendrix's hand was on the door handle when he turned. "Minnie."

I looked up from my daze.

"Be careful. Mind how you go."

"What do you mean?" I needed him to speak plainly. My head was too thick for innuendos.

"This war's come to its end. Folks around here are not happy about the way things are headed, the way they're bound to go. I'm not happy we've lost this war, but I'll pick up my boots and go on doing the work I've always done. There's them that won't, that will do what they can to wreak their revenge on those they blame."

He meant me. Father. Elliott. And now every freed man and woman at Belvidere Hall. "I understand." But I didn't. Not in my core. I'd never understood how a person could think it right to own another person or beat them as I'd seen Rosalee beaten before this cursed war started, or think they had the right to accuse innocent bystanders and lynch them—all the while knowing the law would do nothing to prosecute them even when half the town witnessed the truth. Why did politicians think it worth destroying a country to have their way? How could wealth and power over others matter more than human life and integrity? No, I didn't understand all I knew.

Chapter Thirty-Five

FEBRUARY 1945

Monday morning the anesthesiologist pulled the needle from Joe's arm. It wouldn't take long until he was out cold, and Joe was glad of that. It had been a draining weekend. Finding baby Violet, holding her, having to leave her there at Holnicote House, not knowing if they'd be able to get her home to the US or how Marshall would take it all was more than he could manage. It didn't look like the Brits were going to let her go, at least not anytime soon. Lilliana had promised to visit Violet regularly, as long as they were in England, to hold her and tell her about her father and mother, to show her the picture Mrs. Waverly had given Joe of her mummy and daddy and the one Lilliana had taken of Joe holding her. She'd promised to send pictures of Violet to Marshall and to Joe . . . She'd promised . . .

. . .

Joe woke hours later to find a nurse standing over him, taking his vital signs.

"Wake up, soldier. Open those pretty brown eyes for me, let me see a twinkle."

249

"Pretty brown eyes." Nobody ever told me I have pretty brown eyes. Joe didn't think he did, didn't think he'd said that aloud, but the nurse laughed as if he had.

"Doc's finished?" Joe tried to keep his eyes open, make his mouth work.

"Hours ago. Said you did just fine and should make a great recovery. Going home soon, I hear."

"Right."

"You have to stay off that leg for a while. Anywhere you need to go, you call me. No trips to the john or anywhere else, understood?"

"Aye, aye, Captain." Joe was waking up now and didn't mind the scolding from a pretty nurse. It even helped drive back the pain. He winced.

"Starting to feel that, are you? Let me get you something. The pain's likely to be a killer for a bit."

Joe didn't think much of her choice of words, but he was grateful the surgery was over. He hadn't wanted to think how that would go, let alone about the end result. He closed his eyes. *Going home.*

Two hours later Chaplain Willard stopped by.

"I spoke with your surgeon. All good news, Joe. Said you'll be on the next transport ship—possibly within the week."

Joe nodded, a little feeling of déjà vu creeping through him. "I feel like I've been here before."

"Must be the anesthesia. It'll wear off."

"No, I mean really. When I came in from D-Day, all busted up."

"I'm surprised you can remember anything from that day. Most of the men who came through in those days were in pretty bad shape."

"I was one."

"You've done a tremendous job over here, Joe. You deserve a break. I hope you get into medical school as soon as possible. You'll make a fine doctor."

"Thanks. I hope so. I hope Marshall can join me. That was our plan all along, even before—before—" But Joe couldn't finish. He couldn't believe he was going to leave the country without securing Violet's future.

"We'll do all we can for Marshall and for Violet. We'll keep the fight going until we leave here and if we're not successful, we'll continue from home—as long as Marshall wants us to. You're an amazing friend to him, Joe. God bless you for that."

Joe wondered. He wondered what God thought of him, but he knew it had to be God who'd pulled him through this far, who'd led him to the Willards, who'd helped them find Violet. The timing was too amazing to be his own doing. "Say, Chaplain, do you happen to have a Bible on you?"

Chaplain Willard grinned. "Always."

"Somebody wrote me a Scripture to look up, from some book called Zeph—Zeph something."

"Zephaniah?"

"Yeah, that's it. I can't remember the verse. Is it a long book?"

"Not too long. Was it Celia? Celia Percy?"

"How'd you know?"

"Because Celia and my wife end all their letters to each other with a particular Scripture. Zephaniah 3:17."

"Can you tell me what it says?"

"Without looking. 'The Lord thy God in the midst of thee is mighty; he will save, he will rejoice over thee with joy; he will rest in his love, he will joy over thee with singing.' It's the perfect Scripture for you, Joe."

Joe closed his eyes, letting the words sink in. *He is mighty. He does save. Does it mean God rests in His love or that I do? I can. I think I can. Does He love me? Does He really take joy in me—like singing?* It was hard to imagine.

"You know what this means, don't you?"

Joe opened his eyes.

"You're part of the family now. The Lord's got you, Celia's adopted you, so that means Lilliana and I have, too. You're already a brother to Marshall. Sounds like a lot of family to me."

Joe swallowed the sudden lump in his throat. *Family. Part of the family.* "I can't turn that down."

"Best not. Those two women will be after you no end." Chaplain Willard tilted his head, considering Joe. "Have you thought where you'll go after you're discharged? I mean, besides medical school? Where you'll call home?"

"I've been trying not to. Nonni—my grandmother—was the only family I had."

Chaplain Willard nodded. "Think about No Creek. I don't know if Marshall's planning to stay there, but it's home for us and for Celia and her family. We'd be mighty proud to have you. I know Dr. Vishnevsky would be glad of the help. He's getting on in years and run off his feet with patients to care for. It's a small town and country community. You and Marshall would likely face challenges and it would take time, but if you're game, I believe you both could set up full practices."

Joe's eyes widened. *Does he mean it?*

"Think about it. You can stay at Garden's Gate with Lilliana and me in between your medical studies, and as long as you need till you settle. The Percy family's there now but I'm sure they won't mind. Sounds like you and Celia are good friends already."

Good friends. We are. "That's the best offer I've ever had, Chaplain. I just might take you up on that."

"Good, then you'd best get ready to call me Jesse, soon as we're out of uniform." The chaplain reached for Joe's hand and they shook, a lifeline for Joe.

"Now, let me pray for you before I go."

Joe couldn't think of anything he wanted more.

"Father God, holy is Your Name. We come before You with thanksgiving for the successful surgery on Joe's foot. We pray for his rapid healing, for Your care as he travels home, for the homecoming he'll surely receive. We thank You for sparing Joe's life in battle and for the lives he was able to rescue, the hearts and minds of men he's been able to encourage during his service. Bless him, Lord, we pray. Let him know the fullness of Your love and the oneness of Your family. Watch over Violet, Lord, and show us both the way forward for her. Help Marshall through these hard days and give us all wisdom and courage to keep going. Through Jesus Christ our Lord and Savior, amen."

"Amen," Joe said, and he meant it.

"See you at home, Joe." Chaplain Willard squeezed Joe's shoulder.

"See you at home, Jesse." Joe couldn't check the smile spreading across his face.

Chapter Thirty-Six

Late April showers fell gently as we buried Elliott beside Emma in our family's section of the churchyard, the graves of their lost children at their feet. I held Ellie, fractious, in my arms as Reverend Snow spoke the final prayer. She'd remember nothing now, but one day I wanted to tell her that she'd been there, at her father's burial—the man who'd loved her and her mother more than life, the man who'd nearly died for his principles and a vow he'd made to God, who did die in the end because of them.

Father was too weak and too distraught to attend. Grayson stood beside me, hat in hand, as the first clods of dirt fell onto our brother's coffin, as they pierced my heart like daggers. His presence, though expected, felt a sacrilege.

A thousand times I'd wanted to confront Grayson, to ask him if he'd doused the fire in Elliott's room that night of the fire in town, if he was the one to open the window, ushering in cold air and death. But I knew it would do no good. Elliott had already been dying. There was nothing I could prove, and Grayson would find a way out of it, just as he and all the other young men responsible for the burning of the courthouse had cast blame elsewhere, taking the lives of innocent men. I could not deal with more of Grayson.

We were home less than an hour when Grayson packed to leave. Of all things, I'd not expected that.

"Where are you going?"

"Raleigh, Sister. I'll be gone a few days. I imagine you can manage without me that long."

Grayson's leaving was a relief, but I'd come to distrust his sudden movements. "We'll manage." It was all that was safe to say, and I wasn't up to guessing games.

"When I return, we'll go over the household accounts. I'll be taking charge of those, of course."

I blinked. But there were more important matters to discuss. "We need to go together to the registrar, Grayson. We need to clear the matter of the deeds."

"I don't see why."

"Because they were burned. We need to make certain everything is legal and binding for Obadiah and Martha and all the others."

"Oh, yes, Obadiah." Grayson all but smirked. "We must certainly see to Obadiah."

My stomach turned over. Obadiah had been beaten to unconsciousness the night of the courthouse fire, so badly that he hadn't been able to attend Elliott's funeral. "Tell me the truth, Grayson, did you have anything to do with—"

"Truth is relative, dear sister, and I have a long ride ahead of me. I'll see you when I return." He hefted his case.

"Grayson!"

"Goodbye, Minnie." And he was gone.

. . .

Martha nursed Obadiah herself. She didn't trust a soul outside Belvidere Hall and not all those within. Each of my visits to their cabin had been when Grayson was out of the house. With him gone a few days, I wanted to move Obadiah into the main house.

"No, Miss Minnie." Martha was adamant. "We don't know when your brother will return and my husband's doin' fine right here."

But he didn't look fine. The discoloration below his eyes and the swelling there looked painful, even though the better part of a week had passed. I didn't know the extent of his injuries I could not see, but he could not sit up and around his chest and rib cage Martha had bound wide linen strips.

"It's just gonna take some time. Alma's best with herbs and poultices I've ever seen. Even our mama couldn't do better. My Obadiah just need to lay low for a time."

With a shudder Dr. Hendrix's warning came back to me, and Grayson's near threat concerning Obadiah.

• • •

Alma came to me later that morning as I rocked Ellie in the nursery, fresh from her time with Mother Sally. "I'd like to speak with you, Miss Minnie."

"Minnie, remember? Of course, Alma. I'd love your company." With all my attention given to Elliott these last weeks, I'd hardly noticed or spent time with Alma, my closest friend.

"Martha say Mr. Grayson be gone a few days."

"That's right." I sighed. "Just as well."

"That what I'm thinking, too." But Alma looked as if she was thinking more.

"What is it?"

Alma drew a deep breath. "I want to speak freely, ma'am."

"Speak freely, Alma—always—and please stop *ma'am*-ing me. You're a free woman now."

"Inside these walls, with you, I'm a free woman. Outside, in town, or with Mr. Grayson, I ain't nowhere near free, no matter the South done lost this war. Not one of us is . . . not even you."

I stopped rocking Ellie, the truth of Alma's words hitting hard.

"I don't know what Mr. Grayson gonna do next, but I'm scared. I'm scared for Obadiah and Martha. I'm scared for you and little Ellie, but most of all I'm scared for me. I hate the way he looks at me. Makes my skin crawl, and I got no protection against him that won't bring a fist or a knife or a rope to those I love."

The stark truth of Alma's words struck me dumb. "I got to do somethin', Minnie. I can't let him take me."

"Are you leaving?" I wanted Alma safe above all things, but the thought of her going away was like being cast adrift in the sea.

"Where would I go? I've no place to go and Martha and Obadiah be my only family."

"Then what? What can we do? What can I do? You know I'll do anything in this world to help you. Neither of us can trust Grayson, and I can't control him."

"You got that right. I want to marry—while he's away. I'm a free woman now, and if I marry, he won't touch me. At least, I hope he won't. And I've got to get out of this house before he comes back."

"Shadrach."

"Yes, ma'am. Shadrach. He's taken the name of Chree, Shadrach Chree. My name soon be Alma Chree." Alma lifted her head in pride. "Miz Chatsworth's begged him not to go and he feels loyal to her, but we got to somehow make our own way. She's not offered, but we hope she'll hire him on, hope we can get some little place of our own, maybe in between here and Chatsworth Lodge."

Alma's leaving felt like the last thin straw of my world breaking apart. I loved Mrs. Chatsworth. She'd been nothing but good to me and I had sorely neglected her since Elliott returned. She was Tom's mother, after all, and for all that Tom had not spoken for Elliott when he needed him to, Elliott had forgiven him . . . and so must I. Still, I knew Alma must not depend on Mrs. Chatsworth's ability to see beyond slavery with so much at stake.

"The war's over, Alma. She can't make him stay. I can talk with her if you want—"

"That not what I'm askin' and you ought to know that, Minnie."

I felt justly reprimanded.

"I'm askin' if you'll stand by us if we marry, in case Mr. Grayson come after me."

"You know I will. But do you love Shadrach? Is it safety you're seeking or do you—"

"I have loved him since before he went off to war with Mr. Tom. If he'd known how to read, I'd have written him the whole war through, but he never learned. We been waitin' only till he be free and now Shadrach's waitin' till Miz Chatsworth get it in her head she need to hire his help. He lived there all his life and don't want to leave her high and dry. But we need to marry now, even if we can't live together every day. Since Mr. Elliott passed, I'm afraid to wait. Massa Horace can't protect me, and neither can you."

Everything she said was true. "Can Shadrach come here? We can have the wedding right here in Belvidere Hall. I'll get Father to attend, to sit, and see that he gives his blessing. I know he would bless your union if he was able now that Shadrach is free. And whether or not Mrs. Chatsworth accepts his offer to work for hire, he is a free man. North Carolina will have to recognize that soon. It might be best if he just leaves, Alma. We can hire him on here. You both need—"

"No, ma'am. I won't ask Shadrach to do what he don't think right. Before God Almighty I won't."

I stared at Alma. Principles. As strong as Elliott's. I admired her more than I could say and feared for her just as much.

"I'll ask Brother Rollins to come officiate, then, when Shadrach can get away. All right if I don't know exactly when yet?"

"Day or night, you come, and we'll make ready."

"It got to stay secret just till Shadrach gets things worked out with Miz Chatsworth, but we be married and we—we need to use one of the cabins in the quarters for our wedding night, if he can get leave. There's plenty empty."

"You can have a room in the house."

"No, ma'am. Not this house."

I wished I didn't understand all she meant. But I did, and I vowed then and there that I would do whatever was needed to help my dear friend, no matter the repercussions. I was learning at every turn that I could not control life—not mine and not the fate of those around me.

Almighty God, we are in Thy hands, surrendered to Thy will.

Chapter Thirty-Seven

Joe couldn't complain about the hospital care or physical therapy he'd received Stateside, but by the time they were ready to let him out, honorable discharge papers in hand, he was champing at the bit to take advantage of the new GI Bill President Roosevelt had signed the year before. By getting out of the service before the glut of returning GIs, Joe figured he stood a pretty good chance of getting into medical school somewhere. He was just sorry it wasn't that easy for Marshall.

Once Marshall was released, Joe, the Willards, and Celia had all urged him to grit his teeth, stuff his anger at the military's unfair treatment and his terrible grief for Ivy, and forge ahead. Now he was determined to build a future stable enough to convince the British government to let him have his daughter. It needed to be done, but not taking the time to mourn the love of his life was something Joe knew would come back to bite his friend in earnest. Still, Joe wanted to encourage Marshall. Looking forward was the thing he needed now.

"Medical school," Joe told his friend over the telephone, two days after Victory in Europe—VE Day—had been declared. "With all we took before we enlisted there's enough summer courses for us to finish out and graduate college, then enroll in medical school in the fall. Who knows? Maybe they'll count some of our Army time as medics. Can't hurt to ask."

"You know I looked into medical schools before I enlisted. The best ones only take whites or some token number of coloreds. My service record's not stellar, thanks to my CO's lies. I know he thought he was saving my life, but I lost that time with Ivy. I lost Ivy." He choked up. "I don't see how—"

Joe knew they both had to push past Marshall's unfair treatment and his grief to keep going. "Then go where you can and get what you can. That's what I'm going to do. You always said you planned to practice in No Creek—that's where your family is, where you know you're needed. You won't need a degree from Harvard."

"That was before Violet—before Ivy."

Joe heard what that cost Marshall, just saying her name. He spoke lower, quieter. "Ivy's not here now, Marshall. There's nothing to stop you bringing Violet back to No Creek once the Brits cut their red tape. You have family in No Creek, friends. That'll be good for Violet. And your Doc Vishnevsky's counting on you to take over in No Creek—that's what Celia wrote."

"That won't happen, not with the white folks. But my people need a doctor. There's not even a hospital for coloreds less than sixty miles away."

"There's your reason to get going. Get your medical degree, set up a practice, become the doctor in your community. How are those Brits gonna turn you down then? Violet's daddy'll be the best doctor in No Creek."

Marshall gave a grunt, the first time Joe'd heard anything akin to mirth in his friend's voice. "The *only* colored doctor in No Creek. Maybe you can take on the white folks along with the doc. There's more of them."

"Maybe I can," Joe wished with every breath. "Maybe I can."

• • •

Joe knew he'd probably painted No Creek in rosy strokes. He figured it couldn't be as idyllic as in his imagination, but he wasn't prepared for the reception at the general store the June day he showed up in uniform, still relying on a cane.

"Well, well, well, how can we help you, soldier?" The woman behind the counter, hand on hip, maybe on the far side of middle age, flirted a little.

"Good afternoon, ma'am. I'm hoping you can tell me the way to a place called Garden's Gate or the Tate home, whichever comes first on the road."

The woman straightened, the curve of her lips turning into a straight line. "Those are two different places entirely, soldier."

"Yes, ma'am." Joe knew from Celia's letters that it was best to agree with Ida Mae—for that was surely who the woman was—whenever possible.

"Home from the war, are you? Looks like you found your fight all right."

"The foot came courtesy of Normandy. Medic, 101st." Joe figured that was what she wanted to know. That, and about Marshall and the Willards. He knew better than to mention Celia and create fodder for gossip. "You must be Mrs. Mae. Chaplain and Mrs. Willard told me you're the center of town—the store, the post office. I'm Joe, Joe Rossetti. Pleased to meet you, ma'am."

The "ma'am" and the "center of town" seemed to smooth the woman's ruffled feathers.

"Call me Ida Mae, everybody does. Well, we appreciate your service, soldier."

"Thank you, ma'am."

"So, you know the Willards?"

"Fine people. I met them in England."

"How is it you know the Tates?"

If Joe hadn't been forewarned about Ida Mae, he'd have felt insulted by the woman's prying. As it was, he felt annoyed. "Marshall's a good friend. I'm looking forward to meeting the rest of the family." From what Joe knew of the Willards and Marshall and Celia Percy, he figured it one big family. Ida Mae apparently didn't agree.

"You staying up to Garden's Gate, then?"

"Yes, ma'am, for a while. The Willards invited me."

"That's mighty neighborly of them, not being here. Gladys Percy know you're coming? She was just in here this morning and never said a word."

"I believe the Percys are expecting me." Lilliana Willard had written that everything was arranged. He hoped that was true, but he didn't know what business it was of Ida Mae's or why he gave her so much information. "How far?"

"How far?"

"To Garden's Gate or the Tates'?" Joe figured he'd spent enough time chewing the fat with Ida Mae.

"Just up the hill to Garden's Gate, the other side of the church cemetery. The Tates are a bit farther on, but you might need help finding it—off the road, don't you know."

"Thank you, ma'am." Joe touched his cap and hefted his duffel, glad to have come and seen, glad to be on his way.

"You tell Gladys Percy I can send up some extra groceries if she's not prepared for company," Ida Mae called to the accompaniment of the bell jingling over her store's door.

Joe didn't turn or reply but raised a hand in acknowledgment. He snorted as he limped up the hill. *Celia wasn't kidding about Ida Mae.* She'd described the nosy woman and the store to a T.

Now he couldn't wait to meet Celia, her brother, and her parents, though truth be told, he was a little nervous. It was one thing to write letters as friends, another to meet a real girl—a girl who, though smart and full of big ideas, was only fifteen. He imagined braids, bobby socks, and saddle oxfords. Still, her letters had revealed a heart of gold and a love for family that Joe needed more than anything else.

He paused when he reached the church, the ache in his leg pronounced, and took a seat on the steps. Given a breeze off the mountain it wasn't hot, but Joe wiped the sweat from his brow. He'd done well in physical therapy, but the residual pain from the surgery and walking more than the hospital grounds was effort he wasn't used to. He could have stayed another two weeks before being discharged, but he'd assured the doctor he'd keep up the exercises, could work through the routines and get enough rest on his own. Besides, hospital beds for returning injured veterans were in demand. So he'd pushed it—something that had seemed a good idea at the time. Now that he was on the cusp of meeting Celia and her family in person, he wasn't so sure.

Working up his courage to finish the last leg of the journey, Joe prayed he hadn't made a mistake, hadn't been too presumptuous in taking up the Willards' offer of hospitality, especially since they were still in England.

Joe struggled to his feet as a man appeared around the corner of the church, carrying a basket of peaches. Except for being shorter, he could be the spitting image of Marshall in fifteen or twenty years. For two seconds Joe actually thought the man might be an angel.

"Joe? Sergeant Joe Rossetti?" The man seemed just as surprised to see Joe, but not tongue-tied in the same way.

"Mr. Tate—Olney Tate—Marshall's uncle?" It had to be. No two people could look that much alike otherwise. "Glad to meet you. I've heard everything about you and your family."

"Marshall said you'd show up here this week, just didn't know which day." Olney set down the basket and grabbed Joe's hand. "You shore are a sight for sore eyes. Marshall's been mighty worried about you. He'll be glad to know you're here."

"Is he home already? I thought he wouldn't be discharged for another week or two."

"On his way. Ought to get here by tomorrow evening. I just came up to pick these peaches off the far end of the church property before they go to spoil. Nothing Marshall likes better than his Aunt Mercy's peach pie."

"I've heard all about her blackberry cake and her pies—peach, blackberry, apple, sweet potato—"

"Ha! You gonna have to stay awhile to get through all those seasons. And I hope you do."

"As long as No Creek will have me, at least for now."

"I understand. You and Marshall got big plans. He told me all about it—about Ivy, everything. It's a sad and sorry business for our boy, that and the way the Army treated him. You been a mighty good friend to him, and we won't forget it."

"Marshall's been a mighty good friend to me, Mr. Tate."

"You call me Olney."

"Joe." They shook hands again.

"You're welcome in our home, you know that?" Olney seemed a little cautious.

"I'd be honored to stay with you and your family, but I figured you'd be busting at the seams with Marshall coming home. Chaplain and Mrs. Willard invited me to stay at Garden's Gate." Joe hesitated. He knew from Marshall he could be straight with his uncle. "Marshall told me how it is here in No Creek. I don't want to cause any trouble."

Olney sighed. "Yes, oh, yes. That's how it is here, I'm sorry to say."

"Me, too." Joe meant it.

"But you come on down to the house for supper soon as Marshall gets here. You fellas will have a lot to catch up on. We'll fix up a mess o' greens, some country ham, a little spoon bread, top it off with Mercy's peach pie. Won't take no for an answer."

Joe grinned from ear to ear. "I'll come hungry."

"Best way, Joe, best way." Olney hefted the basket of peaches. "Come on with me. Garden's Gate's on my way home. I reckon Celia'll be mighty glad to set eyes on you. Your letters mean the world to that girl, and it's been good of you to be the go-between for her and Marshall to write. I know that's meant a lot to Marshall, letters from home. Celia's a good girl."

Joe tried to keep his grin in place. He just wasn't sure what to say, wasn't sure if Olney was giving him a gentle warning or making conversation.

The house on the other side of the cemetery took Joe by surprise. Three stories with white columns rising from a front porch. He could see why it was called Garden's Gate—flowers and shrubs and trees and things he didn't know the names of ran rampant to create a storybook-cottage garden in the front yard, surrounded by a white picket fence. If this was where Celia lived, she'd be expecting much more from life than

Joe had any idea of. He didn't realize he'd stopped in the middle of the road till Olney spoke.

"More'n you expected?"

Joe nodded, not quite able to take it all in. "It's a lot more than I grew up with in Philadelphia. Wrong side of the tracks, I guess."

"Don't you mind that. Percy family's quality but didn't come by any of this on their own. All of it belongs to Miss Lilliana—Mrs. Willard now. Miss Lilliana and her great-aunt, Miz Hyacinth, God rest her soul, took the Percy family in when things got too bad for them. They've never forgotten who they are or where they came from. Best of all, they've never forgotten whose they are."

"Whose they are?" Joe didn't understand.

Olney looked up to the sky and nodded. "Who we all belong to, if we got the sense we were born with."

Joe nodded in return. He was beginning to understand that.

"You go on in now, make your acquaintance. You'll be all right. They'll look after you." Olney chuckled. "Celia's a handful, but she won't bite."

Joe drew a deep breath. He'd faced life and death and Omaha Beach. He'd set broken bones and amputated arms and stuffed the insides back in men's chests and abdomens. Why was he so afraid of a big house and a teenage girl in bobby socks?

He made it up to the door, set down his duffel, and knocked, though the sign on the door said, "Come Right In During Library Hours." *How's a person to know what library hours are when they're not posted?* Joe waited, not sure what to do. After a minute he knocked again and tried the latch. Just as he pushed the door open and a bell over the top jingled, a woman pulled it wide.

"Hello!" The woman stepped back. "You must be Joe—Sergeant Rossetti."

"Yes, ma'am." Joe removed his cap.

The woman laughed. "Don't look so surprised. Ida Mae telephoned from the store that you were on your way. We're expecting you. Do come in. I'm Gladys Percy." The woman barely caught her breath.

Celia's mom, younger than I thought. Joe was more used to his *nonna's* generation.

"Joe Rossetti—Joe—oh, you said that, knew that already." Joe felt heat creep up his neck as he stepped into the wide foyer. He didn't know why he was fumbling but couldn't seem to stop.

"Welcome to Garden's Gate. Reverend Willard and Lilliana wrote fine things about you. We're glad to have you."

"Thank you, ma'am. I'm glad to be here, and I appreciate you taking me in, a stranger and all."

She laughed again. "Well, you're no stranger to Marshall or Celia or even the Willards, so you're no stranger at all. I'm sure we'll get to know one another. Let me show you to your room and you can get settled." She looked at his leg, a shadow of concern crossing her face. "Are you all right with stairs? If not—"

"Stairs are no problem, ma'am, best therapy in the world just now. Just takes me a little longer than some."

She smiled. "Well, then, let's get you settled and with a bite to eat before the children get home. Celia and Chester will talk your ear off."

Joe followed her up the stairs. Leaving his cane against the banister, he refused to let Gladys Percy carry his duffel. *A guy has some pride.*

She was like a mother hen, showing him his room and the lavatory and telling him the whereabouts of the downstairs phone. "Anything you need, anything at all, you just ask. Chester's room is next to yours so even in the night he'll be handy if you need him."

Joe nodded. All the attention and potential worry over his bum leg and foot was overwhelming, stifling. He'd planned to stay two weeks. Two weeks sounded longer now than it had before he'd stepped off the train.

"I'll see you downstairs, Sergeant."

"Joe, please."

"Joe, then. I'll whip you up a little lunch."

"Please, Mrs. Percy, don't go to any tro—"

"It's no trouble at all, and you can call me Gladys." She smiled again and was gone.

Joe sat on the quilted bed—a quilt too hot for summer nights, surely, made up in an intricate pattern Joe had never seen. A sudden weariness came over him, as if he'd just run the first leg of a marathon. Trouble was, there were more legs of that marathon to come.

Chapter Thirty-Eight

JUNE 1945

Celia had been counting the hours as she and Chester weeded garden and cleaned house for the Widow Cramer, a job they'd been doing each week all summer and for several summers before. It wasn't for the money—the elderly widow still paid in nickels meant to be spent on candy at the general store no matter how old they got or how much work they did—but because she was alone and in need of help.

Today her cow, Buttercup, was about to calve and the widow, though long experienced in midwifing livestock, was no longer strong enough to help Buttercup through what appeared to be a breech birth. So she coached Celia and Chester through all the messy, bloody, slimy birthing that in the end, after five hours, produced the smallest, most perfect miracle of a calf Celia or Chester had ever seen.

"He's a wonder!" Chester marveled.

"She's a wonder," the widow corrected. "You can tell by—"

"She's a wonder!" Celia repeated, not anxious to hear the widow's anatomical explanation in front of her thirteen-year-old brother.

They waited until the calf struggled to her feet and on wobbly legs found her mother's teats.

"Want us to see you back to the house, Widow?" Celia asked, loath to leave the newborn calf but anxious to get going.

"Believe I'll stay right here and enjoy the bonding 'twixt Buttercup and Daisy." The widow smiled her toothless smile. It was the happiest Celia had seen her in a month of Sundays. "You children go on and get your nickels by the counter. Don't eat all that candy in one swallow. It'll rot your teeth."

"Yes, ma'am," Celia and Chester spoke respectfully. They loved the widow, even if she did consume days they wished she didn't. *Today of all days.*

Joe was due to arrive, and Celia wanted to get home early to wash up and comb out her hair. She didn't want to meet him with blood-soaked arms and shirt, or garden sweat streaking her face or her hair sticking out in frizzy braids. There was no way to know which train he'd catch, but she hoped with all her heart it would be the last one of the day. She fairly ran home. Chester easily kept pace.

"Where's the fire, Celia?" Chester taunted, knowing full well why his sister was in such a hurry. "Off to meet the prince at the ball?"

She wanted to swat him but couldn't afford the loss of energy.

"Don't you know he's gotta be a good five years older than you? He's gonna think you're a moonstruck kid, you keep acting this way. Oh, scuse me, I forgot—you *are* a moonstruck kid!" Chester laughed as if his observation were the most hilarious thing on earth.

Celia ignored him, or tried to. Past the church, past the cemetery, through the garden gate and around the back of the house, sweating profusely and stirring up clouds of dust with her dung-streaked shoes, she rushed through the back kitchen door only to stop on a dime when Joe looked up from his late lunch, coffee cup in hand.

Mortification. It was an amazing word Celia loved but had not, until this moment, found a way to legitimately use.

Chester, who'd been on her heels, stopped on a dime, too, but lost his balance and fell against his sister, who then sprawled across the floor and into Joe's shoulder, spilling coffee all over his uniform.

"Celia Percy!" Gladys exclaimed, no matter that it wasn't Celia's fault, not altogether.

"Oh," Celia groaned, humiliation in every breath. "Joe," she summoned weakly.

Joe didn't drop the cup, which Celia thought extraordinarily dexterous of him.

"Celia," he said, setting the empty cup in its saucer. "Celia Percy. I'm pleased to meet you." He held out a hand, seemed to realize it was still dripping coffee, and quickly wiped it on his shirt.

Celia caught her mother's jerk of her head, indicating she needed to get out of the kitchen and clean up. She was pretty sure Joe caught it, too. At least that could account for the grin that spread across his face, or maybe it was just that Celia had made the most astounding and messy entrance into his life of any creature yet.

"Sorry about that," Chester had the good sense to say. That helped Celia gather her wits.

"I'm sorry—so sorry." Celia couldn't think what else to do or say, so she fled through the kitchen door and up the main staircase, two stairs at a time, until she reached her room and slammed the door. She sank to the floor, covering her face with her hands.

This is not the impression I wanted to make! She groaned again, this time more softly. If she could crawl beneath her covers, even on this hot day, and disappear for the century, she would.

She'd nurtured such dreams of making the perfect entrance, shining hair flowing about her shoulders—never mind that her hair rarely flowed—and wearing an actual summer dress, something reserved for Sunday church, and presenting Joe with a plate of her home-baked cookies—something she hadn't burned while reading.

Celia shook her head. *Ruined. You only get one chance at making an entrance or first impression and I blew it—right out of the water.*

Celia allowed herself a silent tear before crawling across the floor and onto her bed. She couldn't imagine going downstairs again, clean or dirty.

Five minutes later she heard a gentle knock at her door. She figured it was her mother, come to read her the riot act. *Well, I won't answer. It wasn't my fault and I know what you're going to say. If I don't answer, you'll go away.*

But the door opened quietly. Celia closed her eyes, pretending sleep, which even she knew would never fly.

"Celia." It was Chester who sat down quietly on the bedside. "Come on, get yourself together, Sis. He barely got a look at you, it was all so quick. Mama said to give you the bathroom first and we should come on back downstairs and visit with Joe."

Celia rolled over, facing the wall.

"He's a nice guy. I told him what we'd been doing, and he was impressed that you'd helped deliver a calf. He's a medic—gonna be a doctor one day. To him, that stuff is great."

Celia considered that. *Mollification.* Amazing new words flowed through Celia's mind like water over brook stones.

"Besides, Janice Richards is downstairs, talking to him now."

"Janice Richards?" Celia sat up, the blood in her veins suddenly rising.

"Says she came by to check out a book from the library. But she's not dressed like she came for a book. Better get down there. Just sayin'."

Chester might be a pain-in-the-neck younger brother sometimes, but Celia knew he was also her greatest ally when the fat hit the fire, and Janice on the prowl was like lard on a cast iron skillet. All sizzle, no substance, but liable to smoke.

Celia couldn't bring herself to look in her brother's eyes, but she squeezed his forearm and got herself off the bed in record time. "I'll be quick in the bathroom."

"Ha! Believe it when I see it." Chester stretched out on the vacated bed. "Wake me up when you're done."

"Get your boots off my bed. Mama'll have a fit."

"You had your shoes on the bed!"

But Celia had regained her spirit and with it some semblance of order. She knocked her brother's feet from her quilt.

Chester grinned, stretching his arms behind his head. "That's the sister I know."

Celia tossed her dung-coated shoes out the window, landing them on top of the woodpile below. She'd deal with them later. It would take a good amount of scrubbing to get the smell of blood and calf from her hair and skin. The dirt- and blood-streaked clothes would have to wait. Her mama would understand that.

Celia scrubbed her arms until her skin shone pink. She washed her hair until her scalp tingled.

By the time she was dressed and had found the tube of pale rose lipstick her mother had given her on her last birthday—the lipstick she'd never bothered to use—and brushed her still-wet brown hair back behind her ears, nearly an hour had passed.

She hoped that was enough time for Janice to come, do her flirting, and leave. She didn't want to be compared to Janice Richards with her store-bought dress and kitten heels and the upswept chignon her mother had started doing in her sixteen-year-old daughter's hair. It all made Janice look three to five years older, what with her blooming figure and all. Celia knew she couldn't match up to any of that. It wasn't that Celia was ugly, more that she was not noticeable and a late bloomer—at least that was Celia's estimation of herself, and she thought it fair.

Celia left the bathroom in decent order for her brother and walked quietly down the stairs. It wasn't until she'd reached the bottom that she heard Janice's simpering.

"I just can't tell you how much I admire the work you do, Sergeant Joe. GI Joe—I bet they all called you that, didn't they?"

Celia was turning to creep back up the stairs when her mother called her name.

"Celia, there you are. Come on in, dear, and help Janice with a book. She needs to check it out and be on her way, and I need to get back to the kitchen."

"Oh, I'm in no hurry, Mrs. Percy. Joe is just so fascinating. Not many of our men have returned home yet, so it's a pleasure to talk to a real man of the world."

Celia thought she might throw up but knew that wouldn't be lady-like. She wished with all her heart that she didn't need to make an entrance at that moment, but her mama stood in the library doorway and she'd brook no disobedience no matter how old a person got to be.

"Janice!" Celia put on her game face. "Ready with that book?"

Janice, turned out for more than a Sunday church picnic, took Celia in from head to toe and back again. "Why, Celia Percy, I don't believe I've seen you in that dress except for church on Sunday, or in any dress since . . . well, since school let out. Don't you look sweet?"

Celia felt her face flame. "You look nice, too, Janice." She'd meant to point out that this was unusual for a weekday but couldn't bring herself to do it.

"You really ought to let your mama put your hair up. You're nearly as old as me and it wouldn't be such flyaway—especially helpful for mucking stalls and birthing calves." Janice flicked at Celia's hair, not half dry. She kept smiling with her mouth but laughing with her eyes.

Joe, on the other hand, looked impressed, and Celia didn't know what to do with that, either.

How the next two hours passed Celia could never remember, but she was glad to set the table for supper. Joe wanted to help and didn't seem to mind whatever her mother asked him to do, even peeling vegetables.

"We all got to peel potatoes from time to time—KP—for the smallest infraction. The guys all figured they were just short of kitchen help. But I used to help Nonni—my grandmother—in the kitchen. It was nice, working with her. I miss it, so ask me anytime."

Celia's mama was duly impressed with that. "I wish you'd pass that on to my children, Joe. We could use a little more cheerfulness in the kitchen."

Celia groaned inside. Chester groaned audibly. But it was all good-natured and Joe seemed to fit right into the family.

By the time the dishes were done and the table set again for breakfast, Celia's mama was worn. "I've got to get off my feet. Don't you kids keep Joe up talking too late. He's had a long day."

"Good night, Mrs. Percy." Joe stood, though Celia saw it pained him. "Thank you again for having me. That was the best meal I've eaten since I enlisted."

Celia's mama smiled. "You're most welcome, Joe. We're glad to have you. You need anything in the night, just ask Chester."

"Yes, ma'am. I can't think of another thing."

"Well, then. Good night, you all."

"Good night, Mama," Celia called, and Chester echoed.

The silence in the parlor lengthened, awkward in Celia's estimation. There'd been so much she wanted to ask, to say to Joe, so much that had connected them through letters. Now, with him sitting there in the living, breathing flesh, she couldn't think of a thing.

"So, Joe," Chester began, "Celia says you're Italian."

"My grandparents came from Italy—Naples. My parents and I were born here—well, in Philadelphia."

Celia had told Chester about the death of Joe's parents. She hoped he wouldn't forget and ask again.

"What was it you called your grandmother?"

Joe half-smiled. "Nonni. It's Italian for little grandma—*nonna*."

"I was sorry she passed." Celia needed to say that. There was nothing worse than losing someone you loved and people not saying anything, never mind if it was awkward.

Joe looked fully in Celia's eyes and she did not look away. She wanted him to know she meant it. How long that lasted, Celia wasn't sure, but Chester stood up from the rug he'd been stretched out on.

"Think I'll check on the hens and then turn in. Some critter's come off the mountain to worry them at night."

Celia could have hugged Chester, but once he'd gone, she still didn't know what to say to Joe, this first time alone. Thankfully, Joe took up the mantle.

"Your letters meant a lot to me, all those months. Years. Helped me get through the war. Helped me get through losing Nonni. Thank you, Celia."

Celia's breath almost caught. It was his letters that had helped *her*, changed *her*. Didn't he know? "That's mutual, then. I'm glad."

Joe smiled and, after a time, looked away. "Marshall's anxious to get home. I'm looking forward to seeing him."

"Me, too." Celia meant it. "But I think it will be hard for him."

"Without Ivy, you mean. Without Violet."

"That, and just how things are here. He wrote several times how much better the colored troops were treated in England."

"Not by our own Army."

"No, but I think he expects, at least hopes, things will be better here than they were before the war."

"Double V for Double Victory—it's the hope of every colored soldier. 'Victory abroad and victory at home'—victory against fascism overseas, and race equality at home. They've more than earned those rights."

"I agree, but I don't reckon No Creek's got the message . . . any more than anyplace else in the South." Celia saw Joe's jaw tighten. She didn't make or shape the community's attitude. It was better Joe understood what Marshall was bound to face.

"Marshall's hoping to set up practice here after medical school. I convinced him he needs to be around family for his sake, for Violet's."

"Family's one thing; the Klan's another."

"He told me everything." Joe sounded impatient, and tired. A minute passed.

"What happened? Why did they bring him up on charges, put him on trial?"

Joe didn't answer.

"Maybe it's none of my business." Celia hesitated. But Marshall was her friend, too. "You don't have to tell me."

Joe sighed, the weight of whatever it was pressing down his shoulders. "Evidently somebody in his battalion caught wind of his relationship with Ivy. Somebody who thought well of Marshall, ironically."

"Call that a friend?" Celia figured with friends like that Marshall didn't need enemies.

"If Marshall had been caught, if his and Ivy's marriage or Ivy's pregnancy had been made public, the Army would have brought him up on charges of rape. That's an offense for capital punishment."

"Death?" Celia couldn't believe it. "But they were married!"

"Not in the Army's eyes. He'd already applied for permission to marry and been denied. Best Marshall can figure is that his CO thought he was saving his life by picking a fight, then charging him with disorderly conduct and getting him shipped Stateside for trial. The trial was minor in comparison, and the officer who picked the fight dropped the charges once Marshall was shipped back. They both suffered a demotion. That's why Marshall exited the Army a private. He'd been promoted to corporal after D-Day. He saved a lot of lives."

"So, the guy saved Marshall's life but destroyed his marriage."

Joe looked up but only shrugged.

"Wow." It was all Celia knew to say. "It's all so unbelievable, so unfair. But if Marshall thinks things have changed here in No Creek, he's going to be disappointed."

"Then why should he come back here? Why not go north—to Philadelphia, New York, or maybe even Canada? Maybe we both should."

Celia's heart caught in her throat. She stood. This wasn't how she'd meant the conversation to go. "Best I turn in, Joe. I'll see you in the mornin'. Just flick off the lights when you go up, please."

Joe pushed to his feet, getting his cane beneath his hand. "Celia, I'm sorry. I don't know why I said that. I didn't mean to take it out on you. It's just . . . so hard, is all, and I'm sick of life being unfair. You're the last person I want to hurt."

That warmed Celia through. "You don't need to apologize. I get it. It is absolutely unfair."

"If there's really nothing for Marshall here, then—"

"But there is. There's so much, more than he knows, and there are so many possibilities." She wanted to reach out, to catch his hand, to tell him all she'd discovered. But it wasn't Celia's place to tell Joe—certainly not before she talked with Marshall, before she showed him the diary, the deed. If she followed Olney's directive, she'd never tell Marshall anything, but that wasn't fair, either. If she stayed another minute, she'd spill the beans, every last one of them. "I best go up. I'll see you in the morning. Sleep well."

Joe caught her hand, taking her by surprise. "Good night, Celia Percy. You sleep well."

Celia felt her face flame, but she didn't pull back, not right away. When she did, she walked out of the room without looking back, thinking she might never wash that hand.

Chapter Thirty-Nine

Two weeks after we buried Elliott, I was in the kitchen with Martha, snapping beans, as baby Ellie played with cookie cutters on the floor between us, when we heard a buggy creak to a stop. I scooped up Ellie and the three of us made it to the verandah just as Grayson guided a beautiful auburn-haired woman up the steps and a wagon loaded with furnishings entered the drive.

"And here is our welcoming committee to your new home, my love." Grayson smiled as if he were lord of the manor. "Minnie, Martha, allow me to introduce to you my wife and the new mistress of Belvidere Hall, Mrs. Rose MacLaren Belvidere. Rose, my darling, this is my sister, Minerva—we call her Minnie—and our kitchen slave, Martha."

"I'm so pleased to meet you." Rose smiled with what I hoped was kindness and grace but must have been perplexed at our silence and ashen faces.

"Where are your manners, Minnie? Step aside." Grayson took Rose's arm and ushered her through the door while Martha and I followed with our mouths agape.

"And who is this little one?" Rose asked, lifting Ellie's finger from my collar.

"Elliott's orphan." Grayson spoke as if our treasure were a throwaway. "She's well looked after. You won't need to bother."

"What bother could such a lovely little girl be?" Rose smiled. I didn't like the proprietary glimmer in her eyes.

"Martha, get Obadiah and have him bring in the trunks. Might take a couple of bucks to handle the furnishings. They can go into the parlor until Rose has a chance to decide where she'd like things placed. I suppose we can sleep in my room tonight. Tomorrow Rose can choose our room. We've had a long drive. How long until dinner?"

"Dinner was served two hours ago," I said, conflicted between disbelief and the habit of hospitality.

"I'm sure I can find something." Martha took Ellie from my arms.

"See that you do," Grayson ordered, "and bring it to my room."

"More than food I'd love a hot bath. So much dust from the drive." Rose smiled again. "Is that possible?" She'd directed her request to Martha, but Grayson addressed me.

"See to it, Minnie. Have Alma bring up hot water." He started toward the stairs.

Fury that I'd been able to quell so far rose within me. "Alma is not here."

He stopped midstair and turned. "Where is she?"

"Alma, Mrs. Chree, is married and no longer lives here." I wasn't about to tell him where she was. "She'll be in tomorrow to help with housework. She's not paid to work round the clock." It was satisfying to say that.

The ice in Grayson's eyes chilled me. The confusion in Rose's unnerved me.

What is to be the end of all of this?

• • •

I didn't see Rose again until the next morning at breakfast. She insisted on coming down, though Martha would have been happy to take up a tray. It would have been so much easier for all of us. But it helped that Grayson lay abed.

"It doesn't seem you were expecting me. Is that true?" Rose asked, and it appeared she asked innocently.

"We were surprised. We didn't . . . I didn't know that you and Grayson . . ." I didn't know what to say. *Didn't know that you were courting? That he was going away to marry you? That you existed?*

Rose stirred her tea, staring into the cup, and finally set down her spoon. "I take it Grayson didn't tell you about me."

"If we'd had any idea, we would have prepared a room." So many questions I wanted to ask but couldn't find the words.

"It was all rather sudden, the wedding, and our courtship wasn't long."

"I'm sorry, Rose. I didn't know there was a courtship. Grayson's young." There. I'd said it. I thought Rose was young, too, but perhaps not as young as Grayson. What had he told her? Had it mattered?

"I do understand he seems so to you; he told me that. Grayson told me that you've been grieving your older brother's death for some time. Perhaps he mentioned me, and you didn't realize—"

"Elliott died just over two weeks ago. The day he was buried, Grayson left, never saying where he was going or why. He's never mentioned you to me."

Rose stopped, staring at me as if she was trying to gauge whether or not I was telling the truth.

"I'm sorry if that sounds rude, Rose. I don't want to get us off on the wrong foot. I'd like us to be friends, but I had no idea. None of us did."

Minutes passed. We ate in silence. At length Rose stood and excused herself from the table.

"Rose, if you like, I can introduce you to Father. He'll want to meet you."

"I want to see him, too. I'm glad we were able to get back before he passed."

I felt my eyes go wide. "Before he passed?"

"I understand he's near the end and not able to communicate."

"He's weak and sometimes confused. He's grieving Elliott's death and the state of our family, but he's fully able to speak, if that's what you mean."

Rose's forehead furrowed.

"Rose, what has Grayson told you?"

"I think . . . I think it best I speak with my husband before I say more." She started toward the door.

"Yes, perhaps you're right."

"Oh, could you have one of the slaves bring up some hot water? Grayson will want a shave."

"We no longer have slaves, Rose," I spoke quietly, hoping I sounded respectful. "The war is over, and even before it was, we freed all our slaves. Did Grayson not make that clear?"

Rose stopped, her hand on the doorframe. "I'm afraid very little is clear to me."

Chapter Forty

JUNE 1945

If only Marshall had telephoned ahead, Joe could have met him at the train platform or Olney and his kids would have been there. Maybe, if there'd been enough people around, those guys wouldn't have jumped him.

The news came because Chester had run down a half hour after the first train to check for passengers and found Marshall beaten and prostrate in the bushes by the side of the road. Joe was already racing out the door, Celia close on his heels, by the time Gladys Percy had picked up the telephone to call the town doctor.

Joe was at Marshall's side, dressing wounds and swearing in Italian words that he knew would have made a sailor blush, when a car pulled up.

An older man carrying a black bag got out and knelt beside Joe, who was struggling to remain steady on one knee. "A fine job. May I take over?"

"Doc," Marshall moaned. His eyes, despite their beating and swelling, tried to focus.

"Rest easy, my son."

Joe straightened. "Dr. Vishnevsky?"

Doc Vishy nodded. "And you must be Joe. Marshall wrote me about you. I'm glad you were here, Joe." The doctor spoke while deftly running his hands over Marshall, who moaned only when the doc reached his ankle. "Nothing broken, I think, but a bad sprain."

Joe allowed Chester to help him to his feet as Doc Vishy braced Marshall's leg.

"Followed me off the train and jumped me before I knew what was happening." Marshall's breathing came hard. "Shoulda known better than to get off with nobody around. I thought they'd leave me alone, my uniform and all."

"Who were they?" Chester demanded.

"Don't know." Marshall had a hard time talking through swollen lips. "Nobody I recognized."

"But why?" Joe pleaded. *Why, God? Why now?*

"To control through fear, to make certain that nothing changes here." Dr. Vishnevsky spoke through clenched teeth. "Still, even after this war, they are ignorant of the equality of men."

Chapter Forty-One

MAY 1865

Soldiers, returning from the war half starved, many of them barefoot or their feet wrapped in rags, stopped by Belvidere Hall, hoping for a plate of beans, a biscuit, a slab of corn pone, or anything we might spare. They were men on their long treks home to the bosom of families they hoped still lived and breathed. Most came with all their limbs, but some with empty sleeves or glass eyes or no eye at all where they'd been shot.

Martha and I gave them what we could and even Rose came downstairs to help when Grayson was away. He kept her close when home, as if afraid she might be contaminated by Martha or me, the only ones in the house full-time now besides Father and Ellie.

Rose took to Ellie like a duck to water, laughing, playing, cooing with the little girl, and Ellie responded, glad for a new playmate. Martha and I had but little time between the cooking and laundry. I looked forward each day to the hours that Alma came, not only for her help but for her friendship. I could see that friendship was a mystery to Rose, whose family, I learned, had owned a dozen slaves for house and garden, though they lived in a mansion in Raleigh. Her father was a man of old money, much of which he lost in the war, having invested heavily in Confederate bonds.

"Papa could never afford to pay slaves—freed people—as you do here. I don't know what Mother will do without them when their hand is forced, how she'll manage," Rose lamented, watching from the window as Alma hung the wash.

"Just as we do. Just as anyone does. Women who've never owned slaves know how to take care of themselves and their families. We'll learn what we don't know." I smiled. "Things we never imagined."

Rose smiled, tenuously, for the first time since the day she'd stepped through the door of Belvidere Hall. I could only imagine the bill of goods Grayson had sold her to get her to marry him, including the lie that he was five years older than he looked, than he was, and that he was indeed master of Belvidere Hall. Rose was caught in a trap not much better than the rest of us.

None of the freed men and women of Belvidere Hall trusted that I'd be able to get their deeds rewritten, filed, and made legal after the burning of the courthouse. "No matter what you do, Miss Minnie," Mother Sally had confided, "they not gonna let us have that land. Mr. Grayson see to that—and if he don't, there's others will."

I hadn't wanted to believe her, but I knew it was true. The war didn't end all of slavery. In the end, none stayed on the land except Obadiah and Martha, Alma and Shadrach. Even Mother Sally went away with her oldest daughter and her husband. When I asked where they were going, most didn't know. "West. Just west, or north, or anywhere that Confederate flag don't fly."

I had no means to help them beyond sending what food we could. At least they had the gold Father and Elliott had given them to make a new start.

Chapter Forty-Two

JUNE 1945

Celia fought back the tears that filled her eyes—tears of anger and frustration as much as sadness—as the men lifted Marshall into the back of Doc Vishy's car.

"Chester, I will drop you off at the turn to the Tates'. Tell Olney that Marshall has come and that he's going to stay with me. He's had a concussion. I want to keep watch and it will be safer, just for now, until we know those hoodlums won't return."

The doc offered to drop Celia and Joe at Garden's Gate, but Joe declined. "Let Marshall stretch out on the seat. The walk's good for me, Doc. You take care of him. You'll let us know how he's doing?"

"Better than that. Marshall can telephone once he's up and around—tomorrow, perhaps. Celia? You want to ride?"

"No thanks, Doc. I need to pick up the mail. I'll walk with Joe."

The doc drove off slowly, raising only a slight plume of red clay dust.

Joe and Celia walked silently up the hill.

When they neared the general store, Celia climbed the steps. Joe followed, the bell over the door jingling their arrival.

Ida Mae wasted no time on greetings. "Celia, was that Chester in the car with the doc I just saw go by here?"

"Yes, it was."

"Is he all right?"

"Fine. Chester's fine."

Joe looked at her as if he didn't understand why she didn't tell Ida Mae about Marshall. She gave him a small warning shake of her head but either he didn't notice or still needed to vent his fury.

"He was carrying Marshall Raymond. Some thugs beat him as he got off the train, left him there in the weeds by the platform. A veteran in uniform!"

"Oh, my land. What are we comin' to?" Ida Mae shook her head. "Is he gonna be all right?"

"Doc thinks he'll be fine," Celia intervened, trying to brush it off.

Joe shot her a disgusted look. She couldn't help that. He wasn't from No Creek. He didn't understand.

"Well, that's a relief. It's a terrible thing, I grant, but what did he expect? Flaunting a United States Army uniform like that!" Ida Mae tsked and handed Celia the mail for Garden's Gate.

Celia saw Joe's eyes go wide and his mouth open to speak as she shoved him toward the door. "Thanks for the mail, Ida Mae. Be seeing you!"

Joe swore under his breath in that language Celia didn't recognize as she pushed him down the outside steps. "Why did you do that? Why do the Tates stay here? Why does anybody stay here?"

"Because this is our home. It's been home to the Tate family ever since they came to this country as slaves."

"Slaves?"

"I know that sounds crazy to you, but there's so much you don't know, Joe, so much I need to explain."

"If you think of Marshall and the Tate family as slaves, if that's how you see them connected to this community, I don't see as we have anything to—"

Celia's dander was rising. "You can push all that past aside if you want to, but until you understand where people around here came from and why they think the way they do, you won't be able to help them get beyond it. You can't just whisk a magic wand and make the past disappear or rewrite it because you don't like it. You'll never change the present if you do that. You have to learn from what's gone on and work hard if you want to make the future better."

Joe stopped. He stared at Celia, but she couldn't tell what he was thinking. He looked like he might bust a gusset. He started to speak, stopped, and walked on. They trudged up the hill in silence. Celia could feel the heat coming off each of them. Marshall had been beaten by no-account thugs. Why was Joe so angry at her?

Just past the church Joe slowed, his foot clearly aching him. "Look, I'm not mad at you, Celia. I'm just mad—at those guys, at that woman, Ida Mae, at the way things are here, the way they're holding up Violet back in England—everything. This place is like stepping back a hundred years."

"I know what happened to Marshall is dead wrong. I know what Ida Mae said is stupid," Celia spoke softly. "I know that keeping Violet from her daddy is terrible, but it's not enough to be mad. We have to help change things."

Joe looked incredulous. "How? Just how we gonna do that? How can anybody change another person—a whole society? We don't know who those morons were that jumped Marshall. Trying to change Ida Mae would be like changing Ivy's father. He just couldn't see beyond the color of Marshall's skin, and neither can she."

Celia held her breath. If she told Joe, asked for his help, she'd be breaking a promise to Olney. But she needed someone who believed things could change, somebody who'd help her. Was Joe that person? Could she make him see?

She started speaking softly, as if to herself as much as to Joe, but she knew he heard. "How can people think of themselves as equals—how can others think of them that way—when the whole race stays uneducated and dirt-poor? How can *that* change when the state gives them lousy textbooks and won't pay for teachers and schoolhouses of the quality they do for us? How can things change when they can't own their own *land*, when banks won't give them loans to *buy* houses or land, when they can't reap a crop to benefit themselves but have to pay landowners so much to sharecrop or tenant-farm?

"That's how the Belvideres got rich. That's how the Wishons got rich—well, besides moonshine. They owned land. The colored families—slaves long ago and tenant farmers and sharecroppers now—did all that work for them but never owned land of their own."

"They provided the labor that got white men rich, the backbreaking labor," Joe agreed.

"Yes." Maybe he did see.

"It's a vicious cycle. Slavery's been gone more than eighty years, but do you have any idea how hard it was for Marshall to get into college? How hard it's going to be for him to get into medical school—any of the few that will accept coloreds?"

"Exactly." Celia stopped and set a hand on Joe's arm. "It's a vicious cycle until somebody breaks it. Till somebody maybe shines a light on a wrong from the past that, when it's righted, might change the future for some. At least might change it for Marshall."

Joe grunted and walked on. "Miracles are God's business."

"But He uses us, when we're willing."

"Miracle workers? I'm not seeing volunteers."

"How about you," Celia ventured, "and me?"

Joe stopped dead in the street, staring at Celia. "Right a wrong from the past? Nothing I'd like better than to rattle some skeletons around here. I'm in if you've got any bright ideas."

Celia grinned. "Like a light bulb."

• • •

For the next three hours, while Celia's mother canned tomatoes with Mercy Tate at the Tates' cabin and Chester spent the afternoon playing stickball, Celia and Joe huddled in the library at Garden's Gate, bent over the old Belvidere ledgers, documents, and deeds that Doc Vishy had returned to her, insisting she let Miss Lill handle everything. Only when they'd gone through everything word for word did she show him Minnie's diary.

"I haven't even shown these to Mama or Chester. I mean, Chester knows there were papers in the attic, and Olney knows some. He and Doc Vishy are the only ones I've shown any of it."

"What did they say? Does Olney want to—"

Celia snorted, sitting back. "He doesn't want any part of it. He says that the land deeded to his grandfather is now owned by Rhoan Wishon, and it was Rhoan's father who led the Klan to kill his daddy over it. For him that's the end of it."

Joe shook his head. "But if they owned the land, how could—"

"Olney's daddy held no proof at the time Old Man Belvidere—that was Miss Lill's great-grandfather—sold it to Rhoan's daddy at auction. The only proof left after the courthouse fire during the War between the States was hidden in the attic, here at Garden's Gate, and nobody knew about this copy of the deed—only Minnie Belvidere, and I guess she never told, or maybe never told where she'd left it. My guess is that she didn't know her brother had the attic room sealed off. I think she must have left before that happened. The room itself became a legend nobody'd believe. Even Olney said he thought the whole story of the safe room and the deed was the ravings of an old man, a wish of his granddaddy's gone sour."

"He's afraid what might happen if this comes to light."

"Yes, he is," Celia agreed. "He's scared for himself and his family and he's scared for Marshall. Rhoan Wishon's a big part of the Klan here. Olney doesn't want to raise a tussle he'd lose, one he fears he or Marshall might hang for."

"Unless it came out in the open—legally and publicly enough that they couldn't do anything to stop it."

Celia sighed. "Olney said if it was up to him, he'd burn all these. I told him that I can't; they rightfully belong to Miss Lill. She's the last of the Belvideres, far as I know, and I can't help but think she'd want to make this right. It was her family that granted the land, her family that hid these documents away, and a member of her family that wrongfully sold the land."

"Have you told her?"

"No, Olney made me swear not to bother her while Reverend Willard was injured. We were all so worried he might not make it."

"Well, seems to me she'd want to know now. She's a strong woman; I could see that."

"She is." Celia knew how hard it had been for Miss Lill to put her past and the oppressors from that past behind her and move forward.

"If she knew that Marshall had better prospects here, it might help in her fight to get Violet released to his care. She'd have to own that her great-grandfather was a rat—a cheat. Would she be willing to do that?"

"To help Olney or Marshall? In a heartbeat—I know it. She's faced up to things that bad and worse in her growing-up family, even when they were made public and folks shamed her."

"Then write her." Joe sat back. "Lay it out before her without telling her what to do. Trust her."

"But I promised Olney . . ."

"You said that was because her husband was in danger."

"Reverend Willard's not in danger now, so my promise is fulfilled." Celia wished she'd thought of it that way before. It was a relief to have a friend to talk this over with, someone outside the family, someone from outside of No Creek.

"I wouldn't send the originals across the Atlantic."

"No, I'll just tell her the gist. She'd not want me to risk losing anything." Celia hesitated. "I know you're close to Marshall, but I don't think you should tell him about this until we know what Miss Lill wants to do. Getting his hopes up if things should go wrong—"

"It's not my business to tell anybody anything. I appreciate that you showed me all this. I know it's in confidence. I won't betray that. I won't betray you. You can trust me, Celia."

Joe's openness warmed Celia through. "I know. I'm glad you're here, Joe."

Joe covered Celia's hand with his own and squeezed. "So am I."

Chapter Forty-Three

JUNE 1865

Obadiah kept our horses and barn and put in as much spring planting as one man could manage. I paid him what I could from the accounts, until Grayson realized what I was doing. Things came to a head between us in the foyer one June evening, just before a dusk thunderstorm.

"You keep your hand out of the till, Minnie. It's not yours to squander."

"And it's not yours, Grayson, not while Father lives. He placed me in charge of funds for the house and—"

"That's right, he did—for the house. And it's time we took care of that."

"Exactly what is that supposed to—" But I was cut off by the sound of a stampede of horses down the drive and another rendition of the rebel yell. Images of the burning courthouse and the vile lynchings and beatings that followed sprang through my mind. Even Grayson looked alarmed.

Father had been in the library, quiet with his pipe all evening, but the unholy howl roused him.

Rose appeared at the top of the stairs, alarm in her eyes. "Grayson? Grayson! What is it? What—"

"Get in the bedroom, Rose. Lock the door—now!" Grayson called, heading for the gun cabinet.

A wail from Ellie's room sent chills down my spine as the howling came closer and closer. Three shots fired and the oil lamp in the parlor shattered, sending flames across the floor. I grabbed the rug beside Mother's best chair and beat the flames. Next thing I knew, Rose was behind me, beating flames from my skirt and shirtwaist, throwing a pitcher of water over my back. It took what felt like an eternity to douse the flames, and it wasn't until the fire had gone out and the room was dark that I realized the pain in my back and thighs or that my hair had singed. I fell into her arms.

"Come, come with me. We have to get upstairs to Ellie's room." Rose took charge and I was grateful, petrified, and in terrific pain.

We passed Grayson in the hallway, loading a hunting rifle. He hissed at Rose, "I told you to get inside and lock the door!"

"I won't leave her!" Rose was firm.

Father rushed past us in the hallway, brandishing a pistol. I couldn't move my arm to stop him. "Grayson! Get Father!" Surely Grayson would try. But Rose and I had only made the first stair when the front door flew open and Father ran out, firing his pistol and screaming words I'd never heard him say, swearing to avenge his son's death at the hands of warmongering devils. Grayson crouched by the window, his gun aimed through the curtain.

And then the night exploded with gunfire. "Father!" It came as a scream from my soul but with no sound.

Rose pulled me up the stairs, half carrying, half dragging me into Ellie's room. She locked the door, laid me down on my stomach across the daybed, and ran to scoop up Ellie. "Hush, hush, sweet baby. It will be all right. Everything's going to be all right."

As the gunfire blasted to a conclusion, I wondered why people say such things, why we tell each other lies in such terrifying moments. Just before I blacked out, I knew. We lie to comfort ourselves, not others, hoping, praying we can believe.

• • •

They buried Father beside Mother the next day. My burns were too severe to attend the funeral, and truthfully, I'd already buried too many of my loved ones. I couldn't bear to throw another clod of dirt on a coffin.

For two weeks Rose and Alma tended my burns. The fire in my skin slowly subsided, but the ache and ugliness remained. Dr. Hendrix said I was lucky. If Rose hadn't been so quick-thinking, the flames would have consumed me in all my long skirts in moments.

We learned soon enough that the raid had been conducted by men from town, men known to Grayson—men he'd been accustomed to drink and play cards with. Grayson threw it off. "Jed Wishon's cousin was one of Johnston's men who surrendered in Durham a couple months back. Family got word today that he couldn't stomach surrendering to that brute Sherman. Jed and Johnston's men coming home are still spitting fire. They were drunk, out for a night of pillaging. It didn't matter where—wasn't directed at us. Belvidere Hall was just the first big house on the road from town."

"Jed Wishon? Your drinking brother? You recognized them, yet you said nothing at the time." I couldn't fathom it, and from the look in Rose's eyes, neither could she. "They killed Father. They murdered our father."

"He was shooting at them, Minnie. What did you expect?"

"But you weren't shooting. You crouched by the window, hiding, until they left. I saw you." Rose was brave to say that.

"I realized who they were and that they were just blowing off steam. Better not to antagonize them so they'd go away. It was the right thing to do." Grayson sounded irritated, defensive.

"Why didn't you stop Father?" I wanted to know this more than anything. "I called for you to stop him. There was time. You were right there—you could have stopped him."

"How did I know he'd run out there, firing like a madman? You can't blame me for that."

But I did, and I blamed him for so much more. In that moment I remembered the thought I'd borne before Tom died, when I wondered if it was possible that everyone in my family might die but Grayson, leaving me to his mercy. I shuddered, it felt so like a death knell.

"Grayson," Rose spoke softly, "tell me truthfully. Did you know they were coming?"

"Did I—? Of course not! What a question! How dare you—oh, wait. I see now. Minnie's been filling your head with—"

"Minnie's said nothing of this to me. But I have eyes and ears, Husband."

I felt the tension crackle between them. It was as if I'd stepped into their private bedroom.

"Then you'd best keep them focused on your responsibilities, *Wife*, and leave your wonderings to yourself and Belvidere Hall to me." Grayson's boots echoed sharply in the hallway. It wasn't long before we heard his horse's hooves pounding the drive. He did not return home that night.

Chapter Forty-Four

LATE SUMMER 1945

Celia waited on pins and needles, but the mails were slow and August passed before Miss Lill's response finally came.

Dearest Celia,

Your letter and startling revelation have only increased my desire to go home. Jesse's extended term of service will be complete this autumn. I'll sail in mid-November—passage already booked—and Jesse will be returned to the US via troop ship, both home in time for Thanksgiving, surely. I can hardly wait!

In the meantime, I'd like you to do something for me. I've written to my legal counsel, Rudolph Bellmont, and apprised him of the documents you found. I've asked him to arrange a meeting with you or with you and Joe, if you prefer. I'm sure Mr. Bellmont can come to No Creek. Please turn over the documents you've found to him so he can begin researching their validity and how we might best proceed to help the Tates. His telephone number is in the right-hand drawer of my desk in the library.

I appreciate that you've kept faith with Olney and not mentioned this to anyone, although I understand why you've shared the documents with Joe. He's a wise young man and certainly has Marshall's best interests at heart.

I think it best not to mention Mr. Bellmont's involvement to Olney or anyone else just now. I don't want to put you in an awkward position with your mother, so if you feel the need to ask her permission to convey the documents to Mr. Bellmont, I certainly understand. I just don't want to raise hopes or expectations that might be dashed for the Tates or create unnecessary drama among locals. I know you will understand this, things being as they are there.

As for news of Violet . . . She is a darling baby. I will miss being with her more than I can say. I'm even sorrier to write there is no grounded hope I can give Marshall. Jesse and I have forged a strong relationship with the matron of the home, but she is helpless in the face of British regulations. Nothing in those laws has changed, though there are those still working to that end. For now, we visit, help in every way we can, and continue to pray. You pray, too, Celia.

With all my love, dear friend, and with hopes to see you soon. Remember, above all, that you are never alone—Zephaniah 3:17.

Lilliana

Celia folded the letter and sighed. Miss Lill's letters filled her soul. She never spoke or wrote to Celia as if she was a child, but as an equal, a friend. She trusted her with the documents and to deliver them to her lawyer. Celia took that charge to heart.

She didn't want to keep things from her mama or from Chester. Goodness knows, they were her rock. But this was a secret mission, and Celia still had enough of the love of mystery and detective work in her that she wanted to keep it secret—except from Joe. Unfortunately, he'd left for school before the calendar had turned to September—he and Marshall both.

Celia wouldn't write the discouraging news about Violet to Marshall. She'd let Miss Lill do that. He didn't need to hear it twice. She'd write only encouragement for his studies and the good he was doing. She knew that was what he needed most.

Celia waited until the end of the month, until her mother was scheduled to take the train to Norfolk to visit her daddy, who was, thankfully, well and working overtime. Chester was glad to be let off chores to play ball with his friend, Red, from the hollow. When the house emptied, she lifted the telephone receiver and waited for the operator. She hoped Ophelia Mae, Miss "tele-Mama," wasn't on the switchboard, or Ida Mae and all of No Creek would know. A woman's voice came on, but it wasn't Ophelia. Celia breathed in relief and asked to be connected to the number she'd found in Miss Lill's desk.

Before the person at the other end could speak, Celia blurted, "Hello, this is Celia Percy. I've been asked to give you something. Can you meet me?" She thought that sounded clandestine enough.

"Yes," the man's voice answered. "Where? When?"

Celia hadn't thought that through clearly. "The library. Soon as you can come."

She hoped he knew where she meant.

"Yes," and the man hung up.

Celia, startled, held the receiver a moment longer. When the operator started to speak, Celia hung up. It was all much more cloak-and-dagger than even she'd imagined.

Celia didn't know whether to close the library and draw the curtain, peeking through the corner, or not. *That might be too suspicious. Best leave things as they are.*

Waiting was not Celia's strong suit and she knew it. She spent the next half hour assembling the portfolio and all its documents and placing them and the diary in a box. It would be best if Mr. Bellmont carried everything out in a box, so nobody'd see what he took.

Another hour passed before the bell over the front door—the library door—jingled. Celia did her best to put on a grown-up face.

"Miss Celia?" the man asked. She nodded.

"Mr. Bellmont?" she asked, though she knew it was him. She'd seen him come to visit Miss Lill on rare occasions.

"You were very discreet on the phone."

"Had to be. You know what it is around here."

"I do, and I must say, well done. Now, I understand you have some intriguing documents for me. Mrs. Willard wrote."

Celia was certain the corners of his mouth resisted smiling. Still, she nodded, proud to be the bearer, yet suddenly loath to let them go. Until now, except for Joe and Doc Vishy, not another soul had perused these documents in eighty years. Once she turned them over, it couldn't be undone. Still, it might bring good for the Tates, for Marshall, and she'd give anything for that. She handed him the box.

His brows rose. "So many?"

"I didn't have a smaller box—didn't want to squash anything."

He nodded, taking her measure. "Mrs. Willard wrote very highly of you, Miss Celia. I can see she was justified."

Celia felt herself blush. "Thank you, sir."

He took the box and turned to go.

"Mr. Bellmont?"

"Yes?" He turned to face her.

"When will you know? When will you know what can be done?"

"That's hard to say until I read what you've found. I'll be in touch with Mrs. Willard as soon as she returns. I believe she expects to be back in a month or two."

"By Thanksgiving."

He nodded, studying Celia. "I do urge you not to get your hopes up, Miss Celia. Documents so old, once the land is sold . . . Well, I'm not sure what can be done."

Celia's heart sank. "But the land was deeded. It should go to them."

"I understand." But he looked away.

"You'll try, won't you?" Celia felt desperate on Marshall's behalf.

"I promise you that I'll do my best for all involved." He tipped his hat and walked through the door, the bell jingling.

Celia had to be satisfied with that. She watched him drive away and prayed like she'd rarely prayed before.

• • •

Days turned into weeks and Celia heard nothing from Mr. Bellmont. Her skin prickled waiting for Miss Lill's return from England, knowing she'd get things rolling as soon as she arrived home. But passage for both the Willards was delayed in favor of returning troops. It looked as if it would be the new year before they could get back to the States, though it was not clear when.

Knowing that Mr. Bellmont would need to read Minnie's full account, Celia had copied some of the entries from Minnie's diary into her own, especially those near the end, just in case anything happened to the original diary. Given old fires and whatnot, Celia figured you could never be too sure.

Still, giving up the diary had been hard. Celia had anticipated that, but she wasn't prepared for the emptiness it left inside her. Minnie had become a friend with Celia's own heart. With Minnie's handwritten words gone, Miss Lill's return to Garden's Gate uncertain, and Joe and Marshall both far away, Celia felt a peculiar sense of loneliness, one she couldn't seem to get past.

Besides schoolwork, chores, the library, and helping Widow Cramer now and again, Celia threw herself into letter writing—Joe, Marshall, Miss Lill—and to keeping her own diary . . . one in which she wrote stories and prayers for Marshall, baby Violet, and Joe, one in which she occasionally gave way to romantic dreams she hoped and prayed no one would ever see.

Chapter Forty-Five

I looked back on Father's death as a turning point in the sisterhood that grew between Rose and me. Rose was devoted to Grayson but, I believed, lonely in their marriage and no longer blind to his character, which he'd evidently concealed from her throughout their brief courtship. My handsome brother could be charming once he set his mind to it but could never carry that on for long. I was sorry for Grayson. He could not believe that he could be loved or forgiven once his sins were revealed, and thus he had no peace. He never surrendered, not to the Lord, not to anyone who might hold a mirror to his face.

All that summer, Rose and I breakfasted together as Grayson slept late, nursing headaches from his late-night drinking in town. I took midday dinner in the nursery with our beloved Ellie, who had begun walking and talking, and who was my joy and delight.

Suppers were miserable and stilted affairs when Grayson was home, though frequently he went out shortly after. Rose and I spent most evenings in the parlor with our needlework or sharing a book. She liked me to read aloud and do the voices, just as I'd done for Elliott and Grayson when we were young, and I enjoyed that. It reminded me, too, of the years I'd spent teaching our former slaves to read. I prayed those lessons had stood the freed men and women who left Belvidere Hall in good stead, and I vowed to teach Ellie to read as soon as she was old enough.

My burns had taken weeks to begin healing and would take longer still to heal completely, leaving me unable to yet face a battle with Grayson over the land that should be settled for Alma and her new husband, Shadrach, and that land already belonging to Obadiah and Martha—land on which they had, with the help of friends, built their cabin.

In the meantime, I had given Alma and Shadrach my cabin up the mountain—the small cabin Papa built for me when I was a girl of ten. It was his indulgence after I learned that only his sons would inherit our land and demanded a house of my own. Father assured me that I would one day marry and have no need of Belvidere land. Little did he know! So he had a small cabin built for me partway up the mountain for the time I was at home, a place to order to my heart's content.

I was glad now to offer that cabin to Alma and Shadrach. It felt as if the Lord had gone ahead of us, all those years ago, using even my selfish demands to provide a home for them, humble though it was.

Finally, as August's heat faded into September's crisp mornings, Obadiah, Martha, Alma, Shadrach, and I began considering how best to proceed with securing new deeds for their land and inquiring about taxes. Even though the original deeds had been burned, we knew they must do everything they could to establish ownership. Paying taxes seemed a proprietary step, and they could not afford to lose land for nonpayment. Unfortunately, none of us knew anything about that—not when the taxes were due or how much they might be.

Grayson had taken over Father's library and desk as well as all the account books and legal papers belonging to the family. I hoped there were papers outlining the plot awarded to Obadiah and that an adjoining plot could be settled upon Alma.

The night before Ellie's first birthday, I prayed with her and tucked her into bed, promising a wonderful surprise the following morning if she went right to sleep. When I heard her soft whiffling breath a few minutes later, I stole away to Obadiah and Martha's cabin. Shadrach and Alma would join us there. We needed to settle our plans.

Martha poured cups of coffee all around and served slices of her warmed corn bread, smothered in butter and honey from their own bees. Their cabin felt like home and haven.

"This is the best ever, Martha." I savored a bite.

"It's just corn bread, Minnie—most humble of fare." Martha smiled, setting the coffeepot back on the stove. "You're used to much finer."

"Still Martha's cookin'." Alma winked.

"There is no finer," Obadiah affirmed, wrapping his arm around his wife's waist and pulling her close to him. Martha laughed and playfully pushed him away, joining the rest of us at the table.

It was in such moments that I felt like an intruder and sensed keenly not having a husband or anyone with whom to share such intimacy. I wondered if there would ever be a time or place for that. I couldn't imagine it, certainly not in No Creek. Grudges over the war ran deep. And truth be told, the war had created its own shortage of husbands and prospective husbands.

"Miss Ellie's birthday tomorrow." Martha smiled.

"Yes, a very happy day, as well as sad." Tears came, unbidden. "I'm sorry. I miss Emma."

"And Elliott," Alma was quick to add.

"Yes, oh, yes, I do." I swiped the tears away with the back of my hand and squeezed the outstretched hand of my friend.

Obadiah remained silent, but the sadness in his eyes told me he missed them, too. Shadrach looked down at his hands. I knew he'd respected Elliott, but he'd served Tom, and surely there was still conflict for him.

"The best thing we can do to honor their memory is to get all this about the land settled. I think we should go together into No Creek and see the regis—"

"Won't be that easy, Minnie." Obadiah shook his head.

"What do you mean?"

"I stopped over to the jailhouse this mornin'—that's where that fella we met in the courthouse does his work since the fire. He said he don't have record of any deeds for freed colored men."

"Everything was destroyed in the fire. That's why we need to—"

"Said he don't recollect our comin' in to register any deeds."

"What?"

"Said he don't remember you comin' in and as far as he knows, no colored man has ever owned an acre of land in No Creek and, if he can help it, never will." Obadiah sat back in his chair.

"Was that a threat?" But I knew it was.

"I'm afraid, Minnie," Martha said. "No land is worth what they did to those three poor souls they lynched right there in town. No land is worth what they did to Obadiah."

I felt the fury rise inside me, but with the anger I also felt a wave of helplessness washed over by fear. It was one thing for me, a white woman—even one they considered on the wrong side of the war—to go storming into town and demand restitution, but I knew that neither Obadiah nor Shadrach dared do that. I'd already heard and seen what men drunk with power and liquor could do. "Then we have to get Grayson involved. That's the only way."

"I don't believe he's gonna agree." Shadrach spoke now.

It was a sore point with Grayson that I'd given Alma and Shadrach my cabin. But here was a way to rectify that—give them their own land where they could build their own cabin, just as Obadiah and Martha had done. "He'll have to agree. It was Father's and Elliott's wish. Everything was perfectly legal, and if there is any question, we have the signed copy of Obadiah's de—"

"Think you best hang on to it till we see the lay of the land, Minnie." Obadiah leaned forward, clasping his hands on the table. "I don't mean disrespect, but I don't trust your brother, not now. Let's just see what he say when we talk to him. You and me."

Obadiah was right; we all hung in the balance of Grayson's whim. Only God could change a heart as hard as my brother's. So I walked home that night, praying all the way for wisdom, discernment, and an open door.

Dear Father, this war, this cursed war, may well be over, but it has taken its dreadful toll in lives, in families torn apart and lands ruined. What the future may hold for any of us, I do not know. I only know You are wiser and more merciful than men on earth. So I trust You, come what may.

. . .

We waited until after the noon meal. My experience with Grayson was that he was likely to be in a better frame of mind with meat and potatoes under his belt.

Obadiah met me in the kitchen, and we walked together to the library, where Grayson sat at Father's desk—a sight that always tightened my chest. I knocked on the open door and my brother looked up from a ledger he'd been perusing. "Grayson, Obadiah and I would like to have a word."

"Ah, timely. I was just thinking the same." Grayson sat back from the ledger and considered us but did not invite us to sit.

"When the courthouse burned," I began, "all the deeds registered, the ones Father and Elliott had signed, were burned along with the other town records. Sadly, most of our freed people have moved on and I don't know what to do about their land. But Obadiah and Martha and Alma are here, and we need to make certain their deeds are again properly registered. The registrar claims to have forgotten that we brought them in . . . before the fire."

Grayson leaned back in his chair. "I don't see what I can do about that."

"We can register them again. You can remind the registrar that our deeds were submitted and recorded. We waited and saw him do it. I think a little reminder from you might help his memory."

"I wasn't there, Sister. I cannot vouch for what I didn't see."

"But you know that Father and Elliott allocated land and signed the deeds."

"They're not here."

"Surely the plot plans are still in Father's desk."

"Well, if they were, if they existed, they're not here now." He all but smiled and I remembered the night he'd burned the original deeds and maps.

"Grayson." It was all I could say.

"Mr. Elliott and Mr. Horace awarded me one hundred acres, Mr. Grayson. I believe you know that." Obadiah's fists clenched beside me, but he kept his voice even.

Grayson stood. I didn't think he liked Obadiah towering over him. "What I do know is that you've been receiving wages from Belvidere Hall since you got your freedom papers. You've been living in a house built on Belvidere land. If you'd like to keep that house and continue living there, you'll need to begin paying rent on, say, ten acres."

"Grayson! That's his land—and more than ten acres—one hundred acres! It's no longer ours."

"*My* land, Sister, in case you've forgotten the terms of our Father's will. And I'm not about to hand over one hundred acres of prime land to a slave—oh, excuse me, former slave." He turned to Obadiah. "You can take those terms, or you can get out, you and your brood."

"Grayson!" Horrified, ashamed, incensed—there were not enough words to describe my anger and fury. "Those were not the only—"

But Obadiah stepped between me and Grayson and mouthed *"No"* to me. "Let it go."

He turned and walked from the room. "Obadiah!" I called after him, but he was gone. "Grayson, you've gone too far! You can't take back their land!"

Grayson was around the desk and standing over me in a moment, grabbing me by the arm.

"Let go! You're hurting me."

"You'll remember that I once told you never to speak to me that way in front of a slave again."

"Obadiah is not a slave."

"He'll never be more in my eyes. Father and Elliott are not here to coddle and protect him now—or you. I advise you to keep your place, Sister, and mind your own business."

"They are my business—and yours, until we do right by them."

"Keep it up and I'll raise their rent." He let go of my arm and returned to his desk.

"Grayson! How can you—"

"Do you understand, Minnie, that the only reason you're still here is because Rose wishes it so?"

"What?"

"Bear that in mind." He pushed my arm away.

"You want me to pay rent in my own home now?" I was being sarcastic.

"Belvidere Hall is my home, and I don't want you here at all. You've become a thorn in my side, always niggling away about the rights of this one and that one. I'm sick of it. You're still here because I indulge my wife, and you make a fitting nursery maid for Elliott's orphan."

A weight fell onto my heart. I opened my mouth to speak but no words came out, no words formed in my brain.

There came a knock at the door and Rose entered. "Minnie, Grayson, you're just the two I was looking for. Ellie's birthday party is ready. Can you come?"

"Go ahead without me, Rose," Grayson ordered. "I've things to attend to. Minnie will join you."

But all notions of parties had gone from my mind.

• • •

Once Ellie was asleep in her bed for the night, I stole away to Obadiah and Martha's cabin again, though how I would look them in the face I didn't know. Alma and Shadrach were there, as if they knew we'd all reconvene.

"I'm sorry, so very sorry, and so ashamed." I couldn't bring myself to look any one of them in the eye.

"It's not your fault, Minnie." Alma laid her hand on my shoulder. "You done all you could."

"It's not enough. I know it's not enough, and now I'm afraid I've made things worse for you all." I turned to Obadiah. "Did you tell them everything? They've a right to know."

He nodded. The weariness in his eyes undid me.

"Grayson's meanness gonna catch up with him someday." Martha pulled off her apron and folded it, laying it on the table.

"The only thing I can think of is to take the copy of your deed to Grayson and to—"

"No, Minnie. No." Obadiah was firm. "Whoever burned that courthouse down, whoever lynched those men, won't hesitate to do it again."

Images of Grayson sneaking in late that night, smelling of woodsmoke, flooded my mind.

"He's done torn up and burned those deeds once, like as not helped to burn that courthouse. He said plain as day he's not about to turn over these hundred acres. No, now is not the time to bring that copy out. You keep it safe, keep it hidden with those copies of our freedom papers. They'll come in by and by."

"When? This is your land, Obadiah. You've earned it in every way. You've paid for it many times over."

"I don't want my man paying for it again with his life, Minnie." Now Martha was firm. "Let it go. I say let it all go."

"I'm not saying that," Obadiah warned. "I'm sayin' that now is not the time. But there will come a day, even if we have to wait till after Grayson has passed. He gonna grow old like his father before him."

Alma snorted. "You think you gonna outlive him? You gonna wait that long?"

"If I have to," Obadiah said. "Maybe in years to come he'll let me buy that land."

"When pigs fly," Shadrach said.

"Or when my son is old enough to farm, maybe he'll buy it. I may not get that land in my lifetime, but God will make it right one day. Just look: he gonna be born free, and that's a far cry from when I was born. Yes, indeed. God will make it right."

"Your son?" We all looked from Obadiah to Martha, who smiled shyly.

"Or daughter," she corrected. "'Bout six months from now, I reckon. Obadiah, you just best remember what happened with Miss

Emma—so sure that baby be a boy and now look at little Miss Ellie, pretty as you please."

"Congratulations. I'm thrilled for you both!" I said and meant it. But my heart still broke that this dear and growing family would not own the land and home Father and Elliott had intended, the land and home that belonged to them.

Chapter Forty-Six

MARCH 1947

Two years passed with no move forward on the land belonging to the Tates and very little hope for change offered by Mr. Bellmont. It hurt Celia's heart so much that sometimes she wished she'd never discovered the hidden deed.

Two years of battling British red tape on behalf of baby Violet had also worn down each of the crusaders, even Celia, who'd never set eyes on the child except through the photographs Miss Lill had sent and the dozen more she'd brought back with her to Garden's Gate that winter.

Still, Marshall was determined to unite with his daughter. Celia knew that he wired every spare penny toward her care, so much so that he hadn't the money to come home for Thanksgiving or Christmas. He worked and took classes through summers, determined to finish school as soon as possible, convinced that his industry and a medical degree might help persuade the British powers that be. Even so, not once did he receive an encouraging word from Britain.

Finally, thanks to the help of a compassionate British minister that the matron of Holnicote had connected Miss Lill with—a Dr. Wingate, who'd opened his parish to some of the brown babies—Marshall and the Willards were able to form a new ally just before the Willards had left England. It seemed the minister had more pull than any of the Americans, no matter how they'd pleaded.

Even so, it wasn't until the spring of 1947 that the wheels began to turn and a call came from a local chapter of the North Carolina Welfare Department. A visit to the Willards and the Tates was arranged.

Celia was just carrying over a jar of honey from the bees at Garden's Gate when she met Marshall on the road. "You're here!" Celia hadn't expected him. "Great to see you!"

"Took off soon as I heard they were coming out to meet me. I skipped three days of school to hitchhike a ride home."

"They've already been to talk with the Willards. I reckon they're over with your Aunt Mercy and Uncle Olney now."

"Don't mind if I hurry on then, Celia. I'll see you later. I need to plead my case for my baby girl. She's more than two years old now and never set eyes on her daddy. Wish me luck." And with that, he was gone.

"All the luck in the world, Marshall!" Celia called after him. By listening from the kitchen at Garden's Gate, she'd already heard news Marshall wouldn't like. More than luck, she prayed for him, for all he was about to hear.

Celia reached the woods by the Tate cabin less than twenty steps behind. At the same time a black car rolled off in a red clay plume of dust. Celia saw the cords in Marshall's neck tighten. He reached the porch as the screen door slammed. "Aunt Mercy!"

Mercy Tate turned. "Marshall? What you doin' here?"

"I came to plead for my baby."

"They just left, son."

"That's them? I didn't even get a chance to meet them! How do I reach them? Can we call them back?"

"They're gone, boy." Olney stepped out of the house behind his wife.

Marshall looked as if he couldn't take that in. "Well, what'd they say? They gonna let her come?" Hope fled and panic filled his eyes.

"Come on in, Marshall. Set down. Let me get you some tea."

"I don't want tea. I want my baby, my Violet. Now tell me what they said."

Celia stopped dead, not knowing what to say, whether to go or stay. Mercy seemed to see her for the first time.

"Celia, come on in with that honey. Your mama told me you'd be comin' by and we're glad to have it. I want to send some of my gladiolus bulbs home with you."

"Aunt Mercy!" Marshall looked as if he might explode.

Olney took him by the arm and pulled him into the house. "Now, come on in and set down. We'll tell you everything they said, everything that can be done. Celia, you come on, too. I reckon you know all there is to know about this already, so you might have something to add."

Celia didn't need a second invitation and Marshall couldn't wait a moment longer.

"They gonna let me have my baby or not?"

Olney and Mercy Tate looked at one another. Mercy motioned for Olney to take over.

"No, son, they are not, and yes, son, they are."

"What does that mean?" Marshall looked sick.

"It means they won't let babies come to single men."

"But I'm her father! We were married. I can't help it that Ivy—" He couldn't bring himself to say it.

Olney shook his head. "That's right. I know what they're doin' is wrong, but the fact that the two of you married doesn't help you under North Carolina law, a fact you need to remember. But it doesn't mean you can't have her."

"Uncle, you'd best explain because I'm not following you."

Olney drew a deep breath. Celia knew what was coming. She'd heard it up to Garden's Gate and she knew Marshall would not be pleased. "It means they'll let her come be adopted by a couple, but not by you, not long as you're single."

Marshall sat still. Celia couldn't see the rise and fall of his chest, as if all the breath had been sucked straight out of him. Finally, he said, "You said they'd let her come. They'll let the Willards adopt her?"

"No, I didn't say that. They won't allow a white couple to take colored children. No matter that Violet's half white, they still call her colored. Only a colored couple can adopt her."

"Strangers? They'll send her to strangers?" Marshall's breath came visible now, like the filling of a bull's nostrils.

Mercy reached for Marshall's hands. "They'll let us take her, Marshall—Olney and me. It's the best they can do. They'll let us adopt her, and you can be right here, or someday when you're able, you can have her. It's just that she'll be a Tate for now."

"If we can raise the money," Olney cautioned.

Celia drew in her breath, knowing money would be a bone of contention.

"What money?"

"They want two hundred dollars for her transportation over here, and they want it soon—a sign of good faith to get the ball rolling."

"Two hundred dollars. That's more than—"

But Celia cut Marshall off. "The Willards want to pay that. I heard Miss Lill say so . . . if this is what you want, Marshall."

"I don't want the Willards or anybody else payin' for my daughter. I'll pay it—every penny. I'll find more work. I'll find a way." Marshall sat still as stone. A minute or more must have passed before he said, "What I want is to have my daughter—Ivy's and my daughter, Violet Raymond, with me. What I want is for all these people to stop dictatin' my life and keeping my baby from me."

Olney nodded agreement but didn't speak.

"Think about this, Marshall." Mercy squeezed her nephew's hand. "You've got to finish school. We don't know how long it will take for them to send her, and we can look after her until you can. You know that even when you're done with school and working in a hospital somewhere, you'll need somebody to look after her. We're good as anybody, aren't we? Better than strangers, and by gettin' her here we'll get her close to you, close as we can."

Marshall looked away, frustration, defeat, and resignation passing across his features. "You're better than any mother she has left on this earth, Aunt Mercy. It's just—"

"I know. I wish with all my heart it was Ivy and Violet both comin' across that ocean."

Marshall nodded, his eyes and heart too full to speak.

"I expect you've thought about this, Marshall . . ." Olney hesitated. "But if you were married now, if you found someone to—"

"Ivy was all I've ever wanted. I'm not looking for another." Marshall buried his head in his hands. "I can't go marrying some woman because I need a mother for Violet. That's not right. I can't pretend I don't still love my Ivy."

Mercy kneaded Marshall's shoulder. "We know that, son."

Celia set the honey on the table and stepped back. "I'll see y'all later. I know you've got a lot to work through. It sure is good seein' you, Marshall, and I'm glad as anything that Violet's comin' home."

Mercy smiled, nodding. That was enough for Celia.

All the way home she wished some good word would come from Mr. Bellmont about the land. Even if the land wasn't returned to Olney, even if he wanted no part of it, wouldn't that still leave Marshall to inherit? Marshall's mother had been Olney's sister. Surely the inheritance would have gone to her, too.

If Marshall had that, he wouldn't have to worry about working harder and longer for two hundred dollars. He could sell the land and go get Violet himself, couldn't he? Or he could keep it and build a home for him and Violet. He could open up a practice right there for him and Joe and Doc Vishy. The idea opened a world of possibilities. With their prayers for Violet being answered, even if not in the way they'd hoped or expected, wasn't it time to start planning, to prod Mr. Bellmont into action?

Miss Lill had said they needed to wait until Mr. Bellmont exhausted all possibilities, until he was sure he could find a way forward—if he could find a way forward for the Tates. It was turning into years since Celia had discovered the documents in the attic. It was nearly time for her to graduate, to go off to college, and still nothing had been decided. It sure seemed to Celia that they'd all waited long enough.

. . .

The next morning Celia was out early, battling the March wind, raking winter leaves from the flower beds at Garden's Gate, when Marshall stopped by, bag in hand.

"Miss Lill keeping you busy, then," Marshall approved.

Celia pushed the hair that had already fallen from her ponytail out of her eyes. "Just tryin' to keep up with your old job, Mr. Raymond," she quipped, then sobered. "You're going back to school, I reckon."

"Gonna see if I can catch a bus this time. No point in missing more classes now."

"I'm sorry how things are working out about Violet. It's not right, them not letting you have your own daughter."

"No, it's not. But I guess I can see their point. I have no stable home, no real job yet. But I will."

"I know you will." Celia chewed her lower lip. She wanted to tell him all she knew, to give him a shred of hope. What could it hurt? Wouldn't it help? "Marshall, the thing is—"

But just then Miss Lill stepped out onto the porch, pushing her arms through coat sleeves. "Marshall, it's so good to see you."

"Miss Lill." Marshall tipped his hat. "Good to see you, too. You and Reverend Willard doing all right?"

"We're so happy to welcome spring to the mountain. Been a long winter."

"Best time of year here, no doubt."

"Marshall . . ." Miss Lill's brow creased. "Celia told you that the people from Social Services stopped by here to talk with us."

"Yes, ma'am, she did." Marshall straightened.

"I just want to say that I'm sorry for all the restrictions about Violet coming to America, but I'm so glad they're going to let her come—at least it certainly looks that way."

Marshall nodded, and Celia saw he was trying to get hold of himself before he spoke. "I appreciate more than I can say what you and Reverend Willard did for my Violet while y'all were over there. None of this could have happened if you hadn't located my daughter."

"It was a privilege, and she's such a precious little girl." Miss Lill smiled warmly at the memory, but it seemed to go to Marshall's heart.

Celia knew that though Miss Lill had been a godsend for Violet, Marshall had never laid eyes on his own daughter, never held her in his arms, as Miss Lill had. That had to hurt.

"I aim to do all I can to make a home for my daughter and I'll pay our way. It's just gonna take some time."

"I know that, and you will. Getting your medical degree will open doors that none of us have ever imagined, Marshall."

"I owe you and Reverend Willard and Doc Vishnevsky that, too."

"You don't owe us anything. Granny Chree and Dr. Vishnevsky got you started in ways I never thought to do. You've more than earned all you've received, and I feel sure the future is going to look a whole lot brighter." Miss Lill looked as if she believed that, but Marshall didn't look at all certain.

Celia felt her insides might burst. "Marshall, the thing is, there's a strong possibility—"

But Miss Lill had walked down the steps and taken hold of Celia's arm. "Celia, we mustn't keep Marshall."

Celia pulled her arm away. "But Miss Lill—"

Miss Lill gave a silent shake of her head and Celia knew she meant it, which didn't seem fair at all.

"Will we see you this summer, Marshall?" Miss Lill picked up the conversation as if nothing ran amiss.

"Reckon I'll stay over in Nashville, see if I can get more working hours to pay for . . . to pay for things I need to."

"But—" Celia started to speak again. Miss Lill grabbed Celia's arm tighter.

"We look forward to seeing you whenever you get back. God bless and keep you, Marshall." Miss Lill spoke warmly, and Celia knew she meant that, too. She also figured she was likely to have a black-and-blue band of fingerprints around her upper arm.

Marshall tipped his hat again, hefted his bag, and walked on by.

He was barely out of earshot when Celia turned to Miss Lill, who was already on her way back inside. "Why won't you tell him? You know it could turn his world right side up." Never had Celia been angry with

Miss Lill. She was her friend and confidante and had been their family's rescuer more than once. But she was angry now.

Celia saw Miss Lill's shoulders drop in a sigh before she turned back. "Because we don't know anything yet. Because I won't give him false hope or build anger against other people until we know something can be done."

"But that deed—it's a real land deed, and signed, and—"

"And Mr. Bellmont is taking it as far as he can to see if anything can be done, but he doesn't believe it can. It was all so long ago, and all the original parties are dead and gone. As soon as there is anything concrete, anything that can make a difference for Marshall or any of the Tates, you know I'll do it. You do know that, don't you?"

"Yes, ma'am. I do. I just want what's best for Marshall and Violet, and he looks so sad."

"The best thing for Marshall now is to keep marching forward. He's doing a wonderful thing, earning his medical degree and working to bring Violet here. It could still be a long time before she actually comes, and the better prepared he is to earn a good living, the more likely he'll be able to be with her, take care of her, build a life for both of them. There's still a lot of praying needed. That's something we can both do."

Celia bit her lip and turned back to her leaf raking. She knew all that was true. But waiting was so hard, and if it was hard for her, what must it be for Marshall?

Chapter Forty-Seven

NOVEMBER 1947

Spring turned to summer and summer to fall. Joe hadn't heard from Marshall at all since the new school year began, and very little since he'd learned last spring that Violet might, finally, be coming to America.

By doubling up on classes year-round, they were both on schedule to complete their four-year program next spring. This last year would be a real push, and Joe, for one, was already drained. But it meant they'd be ready to begin their internship by summer.

One day at a time. One foot in front of the other. It was Joe's motto, and he dared not lose sight of it. But life was lonely. Between work and school and study, there was no time for friends or walks in the park, and certainly no time for girls. The only female companionship Joe had found was through Celia's letters—funny, heartwarming, insightful, thoughtful as they were. Joe had always considered Celia the kid sister he'd never had, but through their years of letter writing she'd grown into a friend and confidante. He counted her letters as visits and gifts. Now that she stood on the cusp of turning eighteen, he found he could no longer think of her as a kid, much less as a sister. She'd blossomed into a beautiful young woman—a young woman who sometimes made his heart race and his mouth go dry when he saw her, when he thought about her.

But it was a letter with the return address of Meharry Medical College in Nashville, Tennessee, that set Joe's heart ablaze that early November. He ripped open the envelope.

Dear Joe,

> *The best of news—approval just came down from the dean and head of school of medicine. I can do my residency in No Creek, working with Dr. Vishnevsky, next summer. There aren't enough patients in the Hubbard Hospital for the number of medical students. The student-to-teacher ratio is too high. They're siphoning some of us off to Fort Campbell and some of the veterans' hospitals, but I made the case for the desperate need for a medical doctor of color in No Creek, and they've corresponded with Dr. Vishnevsky. Turns out he ranks higher in the medical world than I knew, than he ever let any of us know, and he's agreed.*

> *You understand what this means to me when Violet comes home. There's no sure word on just when they'll let her travel, but it has to be soon. It just has to. Maybe it will coincide with when I'm able to plant my feet there. I feel God moving in this and I know He sees His purposes through.*

> *I'm hoping to see you home for Christmas, friend. We're nearly through—almost there—one more semester.*

> *God bless,*
> *Marshall*

Joe shook his head as he finished Marshall's letter and laid it on the desk in his room. *He's sure come a long way since the war and Ivy's death, despite how he was treated. He's kept his eye on the prize through all of that—sees God's hand in the good that comes . . . How does he do that?*

It was something Joe almost felt inside but couldn't quite grasp. *Maybe there's more reason behind the timing of all this than I can see. If that's true for Marshall . . . Lord, can You hear me?*

Joe waited; he didn't know what for. Maybe it was up to him to take the first step. *I know I haven't lived a life of faith like Marshall or Celia or the Willards or Tates. I blamed You for the death of my parents . . . and when You took Nonni—well, You know. But I'm not making it on my own, Lord. I see You working in Marshall's life, like he said, and I know he has a reason to keep going—motivation. He has Violet to get home to.* Joe drew a deep breath. *What do I have? Where will You lead me if I give You the reins of my life?*

Joe picked up the graduation photograph Celia had sent him in the spring. *Breathtaking. Eighteen in another month. Old enough to marry, but she's just started college. I can't cut that short. It's as fair for her to achieve her dreams as it is for me. But another four years—three and a half? It seems like a lifetime, Lord. What if she falls in love with some guy there? There are no guarantees that won't happen. And in the meantime . . .*

Joe didn't sleep much that night. He lay awake, wrestling with the idea of all he wanted, all he hoped for, and what it would mean if life didn't go that way. Whether or not Celia cared about him in the way he hoped might yet come, he couldn't do this life alone. Finally, toward morning, he pulled back the curtain of his window, checking for the first crimson streaks of dawn. The gray light came first, and finally a pale pink on the horizon that turned to gold streaked with rose.

Lord, I know You're there. I know I'm not much and haven't given You much thought. I'm sorry. You've kept me from all kinds of harm and I'm not sure why. But You've done a lot better with my life than I have on my own. So I give You the rest. I see my need, just can't see the way to go from here. Forgive me for blaming You for the bad things people do, for what they've done, for what I've done. Please, Lord, work in my life. Whatever that means, whatever I gain or lose, I leave to You. In Jesus' name, amen.

Nothing changed in Joe's circumstances in the weeks that followed, at least nothing that he could see. There was no way he could make it back to No Creek for Christmas, not with the work and study schedule he needed to keep, not if he hoped to graduate on time.

But he did write Dr. Vishnevsky, asking about an internship with him, figuring it couldn't hurt. The worst he could say was no, and even then, getting the dean to agree was another step. If that didn't work out,

Joe wasn't sure it would matter where he did his residency. Could he finagle a spot in a hospital near Celia's college? Would the dean agree?

The thought gave him pause, until he remembered he'd given his life to Someone else to lead. *So I'd best let Him do it.*

Chapter Forty-Eight

SEPTEMBER 1873

Dear Diary,

The years fly with the winter winds. Rose and Grayson have long hoped for a child and finally, last month, Rose delivered their firstborn, a beautiful baby girl Rose has named Hyacinth. She's a lovely combination of her mother and father, and Rose is over-the-moon in love with her daughter. But Grayson had expected a boy, fairly demanded a boy to become heir of Belvidere Hall. He never saw Ellie as a threat to his kingdom, but now all has changed, if only in his mind.

Darling Ellie is nine years old today. She's grown as beautiful and graceful as Emma and looks so much like her. But she still has eyes as blue as Elliott's—eyes the color of the Blue Ridge at dusk— and she possesses all the childhood mischief of Elliott and Obadiah combined. Sometimes, when she looks at me and laughs, the years fall away and I see my brother before me, as we once were. In those times I sorely miss him.

*Ellie can read now as well as any girl twelve years old. She
devours every book I give her from our family's library and when
reading aloud, does all the voices, without so much as a hint
beforehand as to how they should be read. Rose says she's a natural
for the stage—though only between us. I imagine Ellie will have
read every book we own by the time she's grown.*

I was interrupted in my writing by a summons to the library.

"You wanted to see me?" I asked Grayson as I stepped inside, surprised he'd not yet left for town and his usual drinking.

"Let me come to the point, Minnie." He was so reserved I didn't
know what to think.

"Please do."

"I've received a letter from Mother's younger sister, Aunt Maud."

"She's well, isn't she?" I hadn't seen Aunt Maud since I was a girl not
much older than Ellie, but I'd always thought of her fondly.

"She's widowed, you'll remember, with no children, and wants you
to come provide companionship for her."

"Companionship? That is a surprise. She hardly knows me. For how
long does she want me to stay?"

"She's offered you a home with her . . . indefinitely."

"That's very generous of her," I spoke slowly, trying to understand
what meaning might be read between Grayson's words, "but I have no
desire to move to Dare County. That's clear the other side of the state."

"I'm afraid it's settled. I've accepted for you."

"What? Grayson, you can't do that."

"I can and I have."

"What about Ellie? I'm working as her teacher, as much a governess
as her aunt, and Rose is depending on me to help with baby Hyacinth."

"Alma is here to wet-nurse Hyacinth now that she's nursing her son.
She'll take over any duties Rose can't handle as the girl grows. Rose can
certainly teach our daughter to read."

"But Ellie—"

"Ellie is going away, to boarding school for now. Possibly some kind
of finishing school when she's older. She no longer requires a nursemaid."

"You can't do that." I felt my world crumbling beneath my feet. "Ellie is my niece as much as yours, and I've cared for her since her birth. I'm the most mother she's ever known."

"I assure you, Minnie, I can."

"Why? Why are you doing this?"

"Because you're a thorn in my side I can no longer abide. I warned you."

"What are you talking about?"

"Rose told me you needled her into begging for a deed to my land—the land you and Obadiah have gone on about over the years. And land for Alma and Shadrach—who never even slaved for us! I never want to hear of this again. I'll sell it at auction before I'd give it to him."

"Then sell it to him. He's willing to pay for it, even though it rightfully belongs to him."

"Never. And this is exactly what I mean. I won't have discord in my house. I won't have Rose beleaguered—"

"Beleaguered? She didn't tell you that, surely. She agrees with me!"

"Which is why I'm sick and tired of your influence over my wife, Minnie. Belvidere Hall doesn't need two mistresses."

"I've never tried to take anything away from Rose."

"Only her allegiance to me."

"You've done that yourself, Grayson. You didn't need me." And then I was certain it took every ounce of what little self-control Grayson possessed not to hit me.

"You're going to leave Belvidere Hall within the week. You'd best pack whatever belongings are yours, settle your affairs, and say your goodbyes. You won't be back."

"Your quarrel is with me. Why send Ellie away? Rose loves her. Ellie already loves Hyacinth. They can grow up as sisters."

"And have my daughter forever living in the shadow of Elliott's orphan, as I did in the shadow of Elliott and that slave? Never. If she'd been a boy, I wouldn't have worried. My son would always come first. But a girl? I won't risk it."

"Then let me take Ellie with me."

"Ha! You're not even married. Aunt Maud did not agree to taking in a child."

"I'll write to her. I'll go without a scene if you let me take Ellie, give me complete guardianship for her, and if you promise to give Alma and Shadrach my cabin."

Grayson returned to his desk, not answering.

"If you don't, I swear I will make things known at the church and in the general store that will turn your hair white, that will ruin you in every way a 'gentleman' can be ruined."

I'd never made such an ungodly threat toward anyone, but the thought of Ellie being sent to strangers, the thought that I could never see her again, was too much. I didn't even know what I would do or say to make good on my threat. It came out in the heat of the moment. But whatever it was that Grayson wanted to hide, whatever he thought I might know, must have carried weight.

Grayson spent moments taking my measure. In my fury I stared him down.

"If I agree, you will both leave here and neither of you will make any attempt to return—ever. If you do, I will put Elliott's orphan up for adoption as far from you as the east is from the west. Do you understand?"

I could not absorb his venom. The room reeked of it. Never to return to Belvidere Hall? Never again to see Rose or Alma or Martha or Obadiah? Never again to visit Mother's and Father's graves . . . or Elliott's and Emma's? Could I agree to that?

"I said, do I make myself clear?" he demanded.

"Perfectly." I could barely speak.

"A train leaves for the east on Thursday. I'll procure two tickets. That will be less of a financial drain than boarding school. I'll send an allowance for Ellie's upkeep until she turns eighteen. See that your trunks are packed. Obadiah can see you both to the station." And then he returned to his papers, as if we'd just been discussing the weather or crop rotation.

I left the library in a daze and spent the evening sitting by the window in my room, listening for the whip-poor-will. There are owls that call in the night, and some say they portend death. But the whip-poor-will had always brought me comfort and hope that whatever rivers raged in my life, things might be better in the morning. This night, I did not hear him sing.

Early the next morning, I made one last entry in my diary, intending to leave it with the copies of manumission papers for Alma, Martha, and Obadiah, as well as the copy of the deed for Obadiah and Martha's land. I'd hide everything beneath the false bottom of our ancestor's trunk in the safe room in the attic. Only Martha and Obadiah knew of the trunk's secret compartment. I trusted they would keep the secret until it was safe for them.

One day, when Grayson's heart changed or he was gone, when Hyacinth was older or Rose left in charge of Belvidere Hall, I would write them and tell them where to find the deed and map, and I would urge them to make all things right.

I ended my diary with these words:

This is not what I'd hoped, what we worked so hard to achieve for our friends, but if I have learned anything these many years, it is that I cannot control another soul, least of all my younger brother. I can work and wait and hope, but I must surrender Grayson and all my dear ones to the Lord. Only He can change a human heart. Even then, I know that heart must be willing.

May God forgive me where I have failed, and may He give His angels charge over our friends, and over Ellie and me now.

Chapter Forty-Nine

Summer brought Marshall and Joe to No Creek, both ready for internships with Dr. Vishnevsky. It also brought Celia, home from her first year of college.

She couldn't stop the grin that spread over her face the minute she stepped from the train. After high school she'd been champing at the bit to get away, to go to college, to learn new things and set the world on fire, though it was a dream she'd never imagined could be realized. If not for Miss Lill paying the first semester of tuition it would not have.

By working weekends and after school three nights a week, Celia had saved nearly enough for the second semester's tuition, plus room and board. But she'd not made it home for Christmas. Besides waitressing at the diner, overtime work at the five-and-dime during the Christmas rush was too important to miss.

By the time the school year ended, Celia was weary, bone weary. It was hard to know if that was all, or if she was truly unhappy, or if perhaps she needed to redirect her goals. She'd taken her mama's advice and Miss Lill's encouragement to pursue a teaching degree, like Ruby

Lynne Wishon had, but Celia wasn't sure she wanted that. She hadn't the courage to tell them what she really wanted. It seemed a dream too grand. She missed her mama and daddy, Chester, Miss Lill, Reverend Willard—everyone in No Creek. Most of all, she missed Joe.

She hadn't seen him in over a year, nearly two, though they wrote regularly, and lately his letters had taken on a more romantic tone. It was plain as day he no longer thought of her as a girl, and that he carried hopes for a future together.

She wondered sometimes if her dreams of Joe were more from imagination and homesickness than reality. Was she infatuated? Was it only a schoolgirl crush? She didn't think so, but without spending more time with him she didn't see how she could know. His internship this summer would give them that chance.

Her stomach full of butterflies at the very thought, Celia made her way into town and stopped at the general store to pick up mail for Garden's Gate. She all but hugged Marshall, glad as she was to see him, when she spotted him outside, but knew enough to keep her distance. Still, she felt her smile nearly split her face when Marshall told her that Violet was set to come in the fall.

"Way longer than we expected everything to take, but the British don't move fast. And the best part is that I'll be here when she comes. God is good. His timing is perfect."

"That's the best news ever, Marshall. I'm so glad for you and for Violet."

"What about you? Ready to take over the school superintendent's job by the time you graduate?" His eyes held teasing, but it was a reminder for Celia of how far her path wandered from her dreams. He must have seen the light fall from her eyes. "Celia? What is it?"

Celia had not confided in anyone, but she needed to confide in someone or she'd burst. "Have you ever wondered if the path you've set your feet on is the right one?"

Marshall's eyes told her that he had. "Teaching's not what you want, is it?"

Celia looked away. It seemed ungrateful to say that. Teaching's what Miz Hyacinth had done that changed the lives of most in No Creek.

It's all Ruby Lynne Wishon ever dreamed of and had finally achieved. It's what her mama and even Miss Lill wanted for her. "It's just . . ." But she couldn't say.

"I always figured you for a writer—you know, like that Louisa May Alcott or one of those Brontë sisters. You, with your 'amazing new words.' Like to drove me crazy keeping up with you when we were kids. And the letters you wrote while I was away. I could see everything in No Creek, just as if I was here, the way you made it all come alive on the page."

Celia's breath caught. "You really figured me for a writer? An author of books?"

Before she could ask more, Rhoan Wishon, stepping from his pickup truck, interrupted.

"Never thought I'd see you back here, boy." Rhoan spat in the dirt by his shoes, not three feet from Marshall's.

Celia was ready with a comeback, but Marshall raised a steadying hand. "I'm working out my residency here in No Creek with Dr. Vishnevsky. I'll see anybody needs a doctor. You come on by if you're in need of help, Mr. Wishon."

Celia liked to choke and did all she could to keep from it.

Rhoan's color deepened to crimson and if there'd been any more room between him and Marshall, Celia knew he'd have filled the space. "You listen here, you uppity—"

"That's right, Mr. Wishon." Doc Vishy stepped from the store at that moment, the bell near jingling off its hook, and made his way down the steps to stand as near Rhoan as a man could. "Dr. Raymond is one of our new doctors and he's doing a fine job. Perhaps now we'll be able to treat more of our local citizens without them having to take the train when they're sick or hide their ailments, hoping they'll go away. It's absolutely wonderful, wouldn't you agree?" Doc Vishy gave Rhoan a stare over the rims of his spectacles. Celia knew the doc had Rhoan's number from days gone by. If it hadn't been for Doc Vishy, Reverend Willard, Miss Lill, and Celia, Rhoan's brother would have gone on abusing Ruby Lynne and Rhoan would have never known, Ruby Lynne being terrified her daddy'd side with his baby brother.

Rhoan didn't answer but shoved past and stomped up the steps to the store. At the door he turned. "You said *one* of our new doctors."

"That's right," Doc said. "Dr. Rossetti is joining my practice, also working out his internship. I'm sure you'll see him in time. We're looking for a convenient location to expand our practice, but until then we've set up in my cabin. Come by if you're in need."

Rhoan unleashed his typical slurs against both Marshall's and Joe's ancestry.

Ignoring Rhoan's profanity and bluster, Doc set his hand on Marshall's shoulder and began, "Marshall, I've been meaning to discuss with you an article I read in one of our medical journals last week. It has to do with . . ."

Celia couldn't hear more as they walked off, but she saw the glare in Rhoan's eyes. The doc meant well, she knew, and had stopped what could have turned into a nasty confrontation, but she didn't like to see that smolder. Smolders sooner or later erupted into fires, and the last thing she wanted was to see a blaze between Rhoan and Marshall.

What she didn't know was what had happened about the land, if anything, but it had occurred to her that it was located nearly central between the colored and white sections of No Creek and could make a great place for all three doctors.

Miss Lill had not answered one of her questions about the progress Mr. Bellmont was making but said she would tell her everything once Celia returned home for the summer.

Celia had written that to Joe, and he couldn't comprehend reasons for the delay, either. Celia was ready for the worst, because it certainly didn't appear there was any love lost between Rhoan and Marshall, but she couldn't tell from either of them that they'd discussed the old deed, and to Celia that was most concerning of all.

• • •

"What do you mean you haven't told them?" Celia faced Miss Lill and Reverend Willard in the Garden's Gate library after her mother and

Chester had gone out for the afternoon. "You haven't talked to Mr. Wishon or to Marshall—not even the Tates? I don't understand."

"Mr. Bellmont said he's researched every possible lead. He even went to Dare County trying to trace the lineage of Minerva and Eleanor Belvidere. There was a small memorial plaque in a former freedmen's school where Minerva—Minnie—evidently taught for a time, but there was nothing about Eleanor—or Ellie."

"Nothing he could find," Celia insisted. "But they went there, lived there. The diary says so."

"Yes, but—" Miss Lill lifted her hands. "There is no other record. I remember Aunt Hyacinth saying once that her father and his older brother and sister were raised in this house. I remember, too, that when she and her father went to Dare County, he left her alone, saying he had personal business there. It was just after that he suffered his first stroke. I wonder now if he went to see his sister or his niece, but I can't know. Aunt Hyacinth never mentioned that Elliott had a daughter. I don't think she knew, or she would have told me. It's like they disappeared, or never existed."

"They did exist! Why didn't the Tates tell Miz Hyacinth about Ellie?"

"I don't know, unless they thought it safest to keep that past buried." Miss Lill looked sick.

Celia thought her heart might break. Minnie and Ellie couldn't have dropped off the face of the earth. They just couldn't. But why hadn't Minnie contacted Rose or Hyacinth and told them about the papers in the attic? What happened? Minnie's diary had ended with them leaving Belvidere Hall, saying they were going to Dare County. There was nothing more.

"Because it was all so long ago that the deeds were drawn up and there is no proof that the land ever passed into Obadiah Tate's possession, there is nothing that can legally be done." Miss Lill twisted her hands together and Celia knew the truth pained her. "I don't think it would help Marshall or Olney and Mercy to know that at this point. It would just seem like . . ."

"Salt in a wound," Reverend Willard finished.

"What do you mean, 'legally'?" Celia wouldn't be put off. She'd waited too long. Surely something could be done. Minnie wouldn't have backed down, and neither would she.

Reverend Willard laid a gentle hand on his wife's back. She looked at him but shook her head, as if it was too much. "She means," Reverend Willard continued, "that the only way this wrong could be righted now is if Rhoan Wishon signs the land over to Marshall. Olney's made it clear that he wants no part of it for himself or his children. It's already caused too much pain in his family. His father was murdered when he tried to gain control of the land—to buy it outright."

"But that was years ago, and—"

"And based on the activities of the Klan in recent years," Miss Lill broke in, "there is every reason to believe that old grudges don't die easily."

Celia's heart beat faster. She could feel the tightness in her jaw.

Reverend Willard leaned forward. "Celia, we know you care about Marshall. We know you want to see this set right and so do we, but now is not the time. Marshall and Joe are here as interns, right here in No Creek, where there has never been a doctor who isn't white. It's a big step for this community—one that should have happened a long time ago, but at least it's happening now, and that's progress."

"It's the dark ages here." It didn't matter that Celia knew Reverend Willard was right about the new steps in the community. It was still wrong, all wrong, and Marshall and the Tates were the ones suffering because Rhoan's daddy and Miss Lill's great-grandfather had done Obadiah Tate out of his land. "Obadiah Tate earned that land. Besides the work, he saved Elliott Belvidere's life."

"Yes, he did. And Elliott's father and Elliott granted Obadiah the land. But there is no public record of the deed, and as Lilliana said, the land never actually changed hands."

"But we have a copy! The deed was filed, and the land should have changed hands! It would have if Grayson Belvidere and his buddies hadn't burned the courthouse!" Celia felt her voice rising and couldn't seem to stop it.

At that moment the bell over the library door jingled, making them all look up to see Joe standing in the foyer—Joe, who took Celia's breath away. "The window's open. I can hear you yelling, Celia, way out in the street."

It crossed Celia's mind that not once in all the time she'd known Joe had she made the entrance with him that she'd hoped for. Each time she'd put her very worst foot forward. Still, her heart beat faster, and it wasn't from humiliation.

Reverend Willard stood. "Joe! Glad to see you."

Miss Lill reached for Celia's hand and whispered, "We'll talk later."

"We need to talk now, before Mama and Chester come back. Joe knows everything. He's seen the deeds, read nearly half Minnie's diary." She turned to Joe. "They said nothing can be done."

"So I surmised." Joe stepped closer to Celia, so close their arms touched. "I'm sorry. That land would mean a home for Marshall and Violet, or something worth selling—a fresh start for all the Tates. Can I ask . . . ?"

"Ask anything," Miss Lill said.

"Have you asked this Rhoan fellow? Have you shown him the deed? Given him the chance to do the right thing?"

Celia knew in that moment that she loved Joe. *Cut to the chase. Do the right thing. So simple. Please, please listen to him.*

"I know that sounds right. But you don't know Rhoan as we do. He'd never—"

"Why not give him a chance?" Celia demanded, though she knew the likes of Rhoan Wishon as well as anybody.

"I heard about his daughter down at the store this afternoon." Joe seemed to ignore them all.

"Ruby Lynne," Miss Lill said.

"She's coming home."

"To No Creek?" Miss Lill sounded as if she couldn't believe it.

"I guess Ida Mae gave you all the ugly history," Celia quipped.

"Every bit. But she said Rhoan's been real sorry all this time. Said they've made some sort of peace, and Ruby Lynne and her son are coming home for the summer." Joe looked from one to the other and Celia knew he was taking their measure. "I'm just thinking that if he's changed enough that his daughter's willing to come back, maybe he's changed enough to consider doing the right thing by the Tates."

Celia snorted. After what she'd just witnessed at the store, she couldn't imagine it.

"You don't think that's possible?" Joe looked crestfallen.

"Unlikely," Reverend Willard answered in Celia's stead. "We may as well tell you both that Lilliana offered to buy the land back from Rhoan. We didn't tell him why or what we planned to do with it, but he's not willing to sell, even at an inflated price, so he's sure not likely to do it out of the goodness of his heart."

"Not likely, but not impossible," Joe insisted.

Reverend Willard turned, looking for his wife's eyes. Miss Lill shrugged, helpless—a thing unlike her, Celia knew.

"We won't know for sure unless we lay it out before him," Celia spoke softly, knowing she had an ally in Joe. "Give him a chance to do right. Maybe Ruby Lynne being here will soften him, Ruby Lynne and her little boy."

"But what if we do harm?" Miss Lill asked. "What if Rhoan takes it out on the Tates, like his father did? I couldn't live with further injury to them."

"We need to help bring people together here, get them to see beyond their prejudices," Joe pushed. "Give them a chance and a reason to know each other and pull together."

Celia sighed. "Good luck with that." She cringed at the hurt in Joe's eyes. "I mean, it's a good idea, but even I can't see as we'll make that happen here. We had to keep separate days at the library for coloreds and whites just to keep Rhoan and his Klan buddies from burning the whole place down."

"That was before he owned up to everything his brother did—at least that's what Ida Mae said. People can change. They can." Joe sounded as if he was pleading, and Celia wondered if he was still talking about Rhoan.

"What are you thinking, Joe?" Miss Lill asked, and Celia could just about see the wheels turning in his brain.

"I'm thinking we recently fought a war where the best of men died to stop this kind of thing. If we can't do better after that, what good are we? And I'm thinking food. Food brings people together. Food is what we all have in common—food and the need for laughter."

"The breaking of bread together is healing, yes. But I'm still not following you." Reverend Willard frowned.

"I have an idea—something the grandmothers did back in Philadelphia to get their warring grown kids together."

"Warring kids sounds about right," Celia muttered.

Reverend Willard's eyebrows rose. He sat back down, beside Miss Lill, and motioned Joe to a chair. "We're all ears, Joe."

Chapter Fifty

Celia had never eaten pasta, let alone made it. She was pretty sure that was true for nearly every citizen in No Creek, but Joe was convinced that every mouth watered for Nonni's recipe and that a party would bring them all together.

Celia remembered the party Miss Lill and her grandaunt, Hyacinth Belvidere, had hosted to celebrate the opening of the library at Garden's Gate. When they'd said the library was for everybody, Celia had taken them at their word and invited the entire colored congregation from Saints Delight. Miz Hyacinth had made everyone welcome and a part of the day, but half the white congregation from Shady Grove church had up and left, and the "coming together" had set the tone for tensions that erupted in cross burnings and a barn burning down the road. Still, Celia understood Joe's heart, and she loved that heart.

With Miss Lill's blessing, Joe spent every free evening in the barn at Garden's Gate, building things that looked like tiny clothes-drying racks, each about twelve inches tall. When he'd made ten, he set to work on something he called *la chitarra*: a strange rectangular box with wires strung in small groups across the length—very close together on one side, a little farther apart on the other—and tied to screws on each end.

"Like a guitar—it has strings, but they're used to cut the pasta. Very thin, like spaghetti or angel hair, or wider, like fettuccini."

"Whoever thought of such a thing?" Celia had meant it rhetorically, but Joe loved the question.

"These were first made in the Abruzzo region—east of Rome, sort of in the middle of the country—but caught on very quickly. Nonni had one she'd brought from Italy and used nearly every day."

"You ate noodles every day?"

Joe straightened. "They're not noodles."

Celia could tell she'd offended him but wasn't sure why. She knew she wouldn't want to eat noodles every day, and as near as she could tell, even if they were different widths or different shapes, they were made from the same ingredients.

The next week Joe took the train to Winston-Salem and returned with half a case of red wine, three huge bottles of olive oil—which Celia had never heard of outside the Bible—and a roll of white fabric intended to be used as tablecloths.

Friday night, Joe toted a twenty-pound bag of flour from the general store along with two dozen taper candles, the purchase of which appeased Ida Mae just a little, then carried up twenty jars of canned tomatoes from the root cellar. Joe and Celia spent hours fashioning meatballs, browning them, then layering them on platters in the icebox.

It was dawn on Saturday morning when Celia set the coffeepot on the stove and scrubbed every counter and table space in Garden's Gate's kitchen.

The first thing Joe did was mix dough for Italian bread, the recipe memorized from years of helping his grandmother in the kitchen. Celia was no stranger to dealing with yeast and rising loaves of bread, so that felt pretty normal. She volunteered to collect and wash greens and make the salad when it was time. There was no shortage of lettuce or spinach, radishes, spring peas and things early from the garden to pull that together.

Once the bread began to rise, Joe browned even more meat—Celia hadn't seen so much pork and beef in one place since before the war began. Onions, garlic, half a dozen chopped herbs, tomato paste, red wine, and olive oil simmered and reduced until the meats rejoined the pot.

"You sure you know what you're doing? I mean, have you ever made a meal this size?" Celia knew she hadn't. "We don't even know if they'll come."

"Faith." Joe grinned. "We've got to have faith—isn't that what you're always telling me? Sharing a good time and good food always helps. It sets the stage for harmony. You'll see."

What Celia had never seen was Joe so happy. A kitchen towel wrapped around his waist, his sleeves rolled up, and humming to beat the band. She was glad of that, but how it would all lead to Rhoan Wishon giving up his land, she couldn't see.

Joe's numerous big pots of simmering sauce—the ones he kept tossing herbs into and tasting, until he was satisfied—were Celia's main concern until he dumped a dozen piles of flour, three and a half cups each, on the kitchen table and counters.

"See, we make a well with high sides here. Hand me the eggs, will you?"

Celia nearly choked as Joe cracked egg after egg into the wells of flour—three whole eggs plus two yolks into each well. She'd have enough whites left over to make meringue for a year, and there'd be no eggs to sell to the general store.

He broke up the yolks with a fork, then worked one well at a time in assembly-line fashion, pouring into the center olive oil, salt, and water, the measurements all "in the eye."

"See, you work in the flour, a little at a time, pulling it in with the fork until you form a dough, then work it with your hands. Fold it over and over, just so." He looked up. Celia did her best to smile confidently, while mostly catching running eggs from her well before they spilled across the table and onto the floor. Joe, she saw, did his best not to smile.

"How long do we do this?"

"Maybe fifteen minutes—until there are no creases in the dough."

The muscles in Celia's arms began to feel it after the first ten. The sight of five more wells on the table and more on the counter didn't help.

By the time they'd each finished two more batches and set them beneath bowls to rest, Joe was ready to return to the first batch.

"We flour this, cut it into cubes, let it rest a bit, then roll it out, nice and flat, very thin." He dumped another mound of flour onto the table's surface and patted it out, covering at least two feet, nearly three, and half as wide. "You have a rolling pin? A short one is best."

Celia dug one out. Ancient, long used, well loved. There was something about a seasoned rolling pin that made Celia feel at home, though she'd only ever used one to roll pie shells or dough for cookie cutouts. Celia floured the pin and handed it to Joe.

"The key is to roll quickly and very thin. You don't want to break the dough, but it needs to be as thin as possible to make a nice pasta."

Celia rolled.

"Thinner," Joe warned.

She rolled again. "Okay?"

Joe tilted his head, considering. "Let me show you." He came around the table and stood behind her, taking the pin she held in his hands, his breath on the back of her neck. He rolled the dough until it was nearly three feet by eight or ten inches, so long and thin she could see through it, then stood back. Celia was no longer thinking about pasta or community or anything she could rationally put into words. All she could think about was how near he was, how thick the hair on his forearms was, and how large and strong his hands looked. She tried to breathe as if she didn't notice any of those things, and knew she failed.

"I see," she croaked, then tried again. "Yes, I see what you mean."

"Good." He stood behind her, so close she was sure she heard his heart beating . . . or was it her own?

The kitchen door opened, and Marshall and Miss Lill stopped, frozen to the spot. "My goodness, this is quite the operation." Miss Lill visibly swallowed.

Celia closed her eyes, mortified—a word she understood full well.

Joe stepped back, flustered. Marshall grinned from ear to ear.

"We were just wondering if you needed an extra hand," Miss Lill asked, keeping her smile mild, as if the scene before her were nothing out of the ordinary. For that, Celia was grateful.

"The more the merrier," Joe said, but Celia didn't hear truth in his voice, and that made her smile. Knowing he wanted to be alone with her was nearly as good as being alone.

. . .

By midafternoon all the dough had been worked, rested, rolled, laid out to dry, then each long piece folded back and forth like a fan. The party was set for six o'clock. It didn't look to Celia as if they'd be nearly ready, but Joe remained confident.

"Now comes the fun part."

Miss Lill, weary around the eyes, looked up. "More fun?"

Joe grinned. "I'll show you ladies how to use the *chitarra*. Marshall, maybe you and Reverend Willard can set up the tables."

"Will do." Marshall tipped his fingers to his forehead and went in search of Reverend Willard.

Joe spread flour across the wires of the *chitarra*, letting more fall into the box beneath.

"See, we open the dough fan we rolled and lay it the length of the *chitarra*. Then we take the rolling pin, also floured, and roll it evenly across the wires."

Celia's eyes widened. "Look! It cuts the dough into long strings." She'd never seen anything like it.

"Well, I never!" Miss Lill smiled.

"You've never seen capellini or spaghetti?" Joe looked incredulous.

"I have—in Philadelphia. I've eaten it there, but never saw it made. I wondered how the noodles could be cut so thin and uniformly."

Celia spoke with authority. "They're not noodles, they're pasta—macaroni, in Italy."

Joe smiled his approval, and Celia, retrieving the long strings of pasta from the belly of the *chitarra*, hung them over Joe's racks to dry, all the while basking in the glory of knowing.

. . .

In the late afternoon, Celia watched through the kitchen window as Miss Lill rolled out yards and yards of the white fabric Joe had purchased as tablecloths over the long tables the men had fashioned from wooden sawhorses and boards. Celia's mama, who'd made every effort to stay out of the kitchen that day, set out mason jars half full of mixed garden blooms and wildflowers with candles peeking out the top and all the china, good and everyday, they could find, beg, or borrow. The tables looked grand.

Daylight in the second half of June ran long. Evenings in the foothills cooled just enough to run pleasantly warm. As long rays of sun spread across the tables, Celia set out trays of sliced Italian bread and fresh butter. Joe nixed the butter and replaced it with little saucers of fragrant dried and chopped herbs, swimming in pools of olive oil.

"Dipping sauce for the bread," Joe instructed.

Celia wasn't sure anybody'd know what to do with that, but she wasn't about to say so.

Celia's mama poured glass after glass of sweet tea and set pitchers on the tables. Joe's tomato and meat sauce—what he called red gravy—had simmered for hours. At six o'clock, he ladled the first batches of spaghetti into boiling, salted water.

"Joe," Celia whispered, as if whispering made it not sound so bad, "nobody's come."

Joe winked at her. "They will." He drew a deep, satisfying breath. "Smell that."

"It does smell great. It's just—I don't want you to be disappointed if—"

"Set that colander in the sink, will you? We'll need it soon. Mustn't cook long. We want it *al dente*."

"*Al dente.* Right." *Whatever that is.* Celia did as she was told, praying and doubting all the while. *How is it those two so often go together?*

Just then the strains of a fiddle entered by the front gate and danced round the side of the house. Celia looked out the kitchen window again. Joe Earl and his fiddle waltzed into sight. Children and couples and little groups of two or three and families followed Joe Earl through the garden and to the tables, oohing and aahing.

"I don't believe it!" Celia whispered. "Joe, do you see?"

"I don't have time to see. I told you they'd come. I asked Joe Earl to fiddle folks here. Most folks can't let go of the promise of music, dance, good food, and natural curiosity."

Celia looked at him. How he knew that after spending so little time in No Creek flabbergasted her. But that was Joe, through and through. He studied people and helped them. Maybe this would work out after all—not, she imagined, with Rhoan Wishon, but maybe a start as a community get-together.

Less than a minute later she heard humming, the singular harmony of the Saints Delight choir, announcing their arrival. She stepped out onto the porch to welcome Reverend Pierce and lead the group around back to join the others. But Reverend Willard and Miss Lill had gotten there first, which was all the better, and walked with the group. The moment the back garden was filled, voices died down and Joe Earl stopped fiddling. Celia could feel the tension in the air.

"Play, Joe Earl, play for all you're worth!" Joleen, his wife, urged, and Joe took up "Turkey in the Straw," a local favorite. Celia had to give the woman credit: she sprouted hair a vibrant orange color that could only have come out of a bottle, but she could keep a party going.

"Take your seats, friends, and let's thank the Lord for this fine meal prepared by our new doctors and their helpers!" Reverend Willard, smiling, bellowed above the music. Before anybody could speak, Joleen laid a steadying hand on her husband's bowing arm and Reverend Willard prayed, "Lord, we come to You this evening as a community of friends and neighbors, hungry for Your blessing and the delicious food that will be spread before us. We thank You for this bounty lovingly prepared and for the new doctors brought to No Creek to train with Doctor Vishnevsky for all our benefit and blessing. Guide their work, Lord. Open our hearts and minds to one another and to You. Through Jesus Christ our Lord and Savior, amen."

Joe, with Marshall and Celia behind him, made his entrance from the back kitchen porch, raising high the first bowls of spaghetti and red gravy. *"Buon appetito!"* Joe cried and Celia echoed, "That means good appetite, everybody—eat up!"

Gladys and Miss Lill followed with bowls of fresh salad, chatting and welcoming folks as they divided the bowls among the tables. Smiles and thanks abounded until the food was set before them, and then a deafening silence.

Six-year-old Cecilly McHone broke the spell. "Mama, how do I eat this? It's so slippery." Charlene McHone opened her mouth to speak, but closed it again, looking to Dr. Vishnevsky to answer.

Doc Vishy stood, fork in hand. "Dr. Rossetti, you've introduced us to your grandmother's fragrant cooking, for which we give you many thanks. Now give us a lesson in how to eat this fine meal!"

Everybody laughed, looking to Joe, who looked around, stunned, then quickly joined the laughter. "My pleasure, Doctor!" Celia handed him a plate of pasta. With a flair Celia didn't know he possessed, Joe spooned meatballs onto the pasta and poured red gravy over all of it. Then he stepped up on a chair to be seen by all. "Hold the plate for me, Celia," he whispered, then proceeded to capture a few strands of the slippery food with his fork and, holding it high, twirled it against the bowl of his spoon, making what looked to Celia like thick thread run round and round a spool, before popping it in his mouth and moaning in pleasure.

Folks looked on in awe until little Cecilly piped up, "Let me try!"

Her mama laughed and said, "We'll give it a go, Joe!"

The rhyme and Cecilly set everybody off, and one after another, Celia witnessed what she'd never imagined. The staid and frivolous, the young and old, the colored and white of No Creek all struggled together to learn something new. Laughter abounded as noodles slipped and slid, as meatballs rolled off plates, and the pristine white tablecloths took on splotches and spills of red gravy. Still racially divided at tables, at least they met in the same backyard to share a meal, and it looked to Celia as if they were having a really good time.

Joe Earl lamented that a little 'shine would go a long way. Reverend Willard gave a warning shake of his head.

"Back home we'd share a bottle of red wine with this meal," Joe acknowledged.

"Sweet tea goes just fine." Gladys Percy gave a warning glare, and Celia caught the start in Joe's eyes.

Just as quickly he agreed, "I'm sure you're right, Mrs. Percy. I'll refill the pitchers."

But Joe Earl grabbed the two from his table and insisted on carrying them to the kitchen. "You go on and meet the folks, Joe. They're here to get to know you. Joleen and I'll take care of the tea."

Celia thought that uncommonly good of Joe Earl. He wasn't one to offer to help outside of fiddling.

Dusk fell, the air cooled, and candles glowed, casting soft reflections into more mellow faces. Joe Earl took up his fiddle again, this time less lively, thanks to Joleen's eyes mooning up at him. Pitcher after pitcher of tea was passed up and down the tables, as folks seemed thirstier than ever.

Ida Mae and her daughters helped pass out strawberry shortcake with bowls of whipped cream—a concession Joe had made to No Creek's seasonal favorite and because the cannoli and biscotti or gelati he raved about would take too long to make. Coffeepots came out by twos. Still, the men preferred tea—so much so that Celia began to wonder if Joe Earl hadn't slipped something forbidden into those pitchers when he'd generously filled them.

Gradually, as the meal ended, Joe Earl picked up the pace, playing old favorites. A few started singing, and once the folks from Saints Delight joined in, the night seemed to swell into something bigger, grander. A couple waltzed in the garden's moonlight. Celia couldn't put her finger on exactly what made the difference, but her heart expanded, and it seemed in that moment that different as they all were, things might work out in No Creek.

Everything seemed to be going pretty smoothly when Reverend Willard tapped Rhoan Wishon on the shoulder. "Rhoan, do you have a minute?"

Celia knew that anytime the preacher asked that, he had something particular in mind. It even made her nervous, much as she loved Reverend Willard and Miss Lill.

Rhoan looked from Reverend Willard to Miss Lill, standing beside her husband. "I reckon." He wiped his mouth and said to his grandson, Kenny, seated between him and Ruby Lynne, "I won't be long.

You finish your supper and we'll get Joe Earl to play some clogging music. Time you learned." He winked, and Celia thought there might be hope. Rhoan was a different man around Ruby Lynne and his grandson. Maybe that "different man" would see things in a new light, once presented with the facts.

Reverend Willard motioned for Celia to follow and the four of them walked inside, to the library desk.

"What's she doing here?" Rhoan lifted his chin to Celia.

"It was Celia's discovery we wanted to talk with you about." Reverend Willard took the lead and Celia knew that was best. Rhoan wasn't likely to give her or Miss Lill the time of day, let alone the benefit of the doubt. "Lilliana and I were in England the spring of '44 when a big windstorm tore through here. You recollect that?"

Rhoan nodded. "Middle of March. Near ripped off my barn roof."

"Well, it brought that old oak down on the house here."

"Crashed right through the roof into the attic!" Celia was into the story now, but Reverend Willard gave her a warning eye.

"When that happened, it opened up a room in the attic that had been sealed off for some long time. I don't believe even Miz Hyacinth knew about it."

Rhoan was listening, but wary. "What's that got to do with me?"

"Celia, I see you're aching to tell and you're the one that was here, so why don't you tell Rhoan what you found."

Celia licked her lips. "It was a narrow room—a hidey-hole, near as we could tell. There were trunks full of old clothes and books."

Rhoan looked as if he was growing impatient. Laughter from outside, a little more raucous, drew his eyes and attention.

"Inside one of the trunks there was a false bottom, and beneath that was a portfolio of documents—manumission papers for slaves the Belvideres freed and a deed for land they'd awarded, and a diary belonging to Minnie Belvidere—the older sister of Grayson Belvidere, Miz Hyacinth's father."

Now Rhoan stepped back, a knowing look in his eye. Reverend Willard jumped in.

"The man who sold your father that plot of tobacco land."

"I know who Grayson Belvidere was—a Confederate patriot, blood brother to my daddy. But all that was years ago. Got nothing to do with me."

Celia could barely contain herself, but it was Miss Lill who spoke up. "It does, because that land already belonged to the Tate family. Grayson Belvidere, my great-grandfather, had no right to sell it."

"The Tate family? They never owned more'n that cabin and the few acres it sits on. They wouldn't own that if your aunt hadn't taken pity on 'em before she died and signed it—"

"I can't be certain if Aunt Hyacinth knew about the original deed or not, but we can show you. It was a perfectly legal deed."

"If it was perfectly legal, how is it old Grayson Belvidere sold that land to my daddy at auction?"

"We can't and shouldn't speculate on his motives," Reverend Willard began, "but we can—"

"Right about that. We can't." Rhoan shoved his hat on his head.

"Celia, pull out the deed." Miss Lill unrolled a group of papers held together by a leather string. "Just take a look at it, Mr. Wishon, that's all I'm asking for now."

Celia pulled the document from the others. "You can see here, there's the date, and the signatures of Horace and Elliott Belvidere."

"Never heard of them."

"Horace was the father of Minnie—Minerva—and Elliott and Grayson. Grayson was the youngest, the only one left when he sold that land, but Elliott was the heir at the time they signed. The deed was filed at the courthouse." Celia tried to make eye contact with Rhoan, but he refused, simply staring at the document.

"Can't be."

"I'm afraid it's so, Rhoan." Reverend Willard sounded sympathetic.

"Then how'd he sell it to my daddy?"

"The courthouse was burned—probably by Grayson himself, and his friends, from what the diary said. All the files were destroyed." Celia held her breath, hoping, praying Rhoan would see.

"Daddy?" Ruby Lynne stood in the library doorway. "What's going on?"

"Nothin' you need worry about, Ruby Lynne. You go back out and enjoy yourself. We're goin' home soon. I'm thinkin' this 'party' is more a plot than good will."

"That's not true, Mr. Wishon. It's a true celebration. We wanted to welcome our doctors and introduce them to the community, and we're so glad Ruby Lynne is home." Miss Lill was never one to back down from Rhoan Wishon. "Ruby Lynne, you look wonderful. We're all so proud of you."

Ruby Lynne blushed but smiled. Celia wondered how a person could so change from the frightened, beaten, pregnant girl who'd left No Creek years before.

Rhoan eased off but didn't back down. "If the papers burned, then this is just a copy. Don't mean nothin'."

"Yes, it is a copy in that it was not registered," Miss Lill agreed. "But it shows intent, and it's signed by the Belvideres, who owned the land at the time."

"You show this to a lawyer?"

Miss Lill hesitated, but Reverend Willard spoke up. "We did."

"What did he say?"

"He said that it was so long ago and that your family's held the land for so long that there can't be a legal claim for the Tates now—more a moral obligation for you to do the right thing, let the truth come out."

"Well, the truth is my daddy paid good money for that land."

"We understand," Miss Lill took up the cause again. "That's why I'd like to buy it back from you, so you and your family don't stand out of that money."

Rhoan looked at Miss Lill as if she was crazy. "You gonna give that land to Olney Tate—who never did a thing to earn it?"

"I'm going to right a wrong committed by a member of my family."

Rhoan huffed. "Not with my land, you're not!" He shoved his hat back on his head, took his daughter by the arm, and turned to go.

"Wait a minute, Daddy. That's the land that belonged to Uncle Troy. If it was really sold to the Tates—"

"Not sold—they're sayin' given, near as I can tell. And like the lawyer said, they don't have a legal leg to stand on. Come on, now, it's time we went home. Where's Kenny?"

"He's out with the Chatham kids, playing somewhere. But, Daddy, that land—"

"Billy Chatham? That boy's trouble. You ought not—"

"They're boys, just playing in the barn. What harm can—"

But then came the alarm. "Fire! Fire in the barn!"

Chapter Fifty-One

JUNE 1948

Joe could never remember which came first—the whiff of smoke or the screamed alarm from someone sitting at a table nearest the barn. He dropped the bowl he'd stood to refill.

Once the cry went up, a riot broke loose. Women screamed, running over the yard and gardens, rounding up youngsters, counting heads. Men rolled out the garden hose, hunted madly for rugs and rakes— some on unsteady feet—pulled tablecloths off the sawhorse tables, and charged the barn. The first one there flung open the big double doors to a wall of flames.

"Get back! Get back!" Reverend Pierce opened his arms to herd the women and children toward the house.

Marshall was at his side in a moment. "Anybody in the barn?"

"No idea," Reverend Pierce answered. "None that I know of, but—"

"I saw two boys go in, maybe twenty minutes ago. Don't know where they are now," a woman called out.

"It was Ruby Lynne's little boy and Billy Chatham!" Gladys Percy called. "Did anybody see them come out?"

"Billy? My Billy?" Mrs. Chatham pushed to breach the barrier.

Ruby Lynne ran out the kitchen door. "Kenny! Where's Kenny?"

"Oh my—they're in the barn!" Mrs. Chatham screamed. "Help! Help them!"

Rhoan Wishon headed straight for the flames, but Marshall was ahead of him. Joe hung back, fighting images he'd long pushed from his mind of his father and mother, burning in the apartment explosion. Images, more recent, of the rain of fire on Omaha Beach—men cut down in machine-gun fire, men engulfed in flames—flashed through his mind in rapid succession.

"Kenny! Billy! You in here?" Marshall called out.

"Kenny, answer me, son! Where are you?" Rhoan choked against the smoke.

"Up here, Mr. Wishon! We're up here! There's somethin' the matter with Kenny. I can't get him to wake up."

"Billy! Get down here, now!"

"I'm afraid. There's fire!"

Joe's chest tight, he forced himself to follow Marshall into the barn, one foot in front of the other. He saw what Billy saw, fire already creeping up the ladder. Threat to human life spurred Joe into action. "Jump, Billy! I'll catch you."

"Roll Kenny out first, to the edge—I'll catch him!" Rhoan called, but it was too late. Billy had already jumped into Joe's arms.

"Kenny! Kenny!" Rhoan beat against the flames shooting up the ladder, stepped above them. But his weight was too great for the half-burned ladder and it broke, sending Rhoan to the floor of the barn in a scream of agony.

"Get Billy out of here, then come help me get Rhoan," Marshall ordered.

Joe did as he was told, rushing Billy back to the barn entrance. Reverends Willard and Pierce grabbed the boy between them, carrying him toward his mother. Joe pushed back into the flames, covering his face as best he could.

Marshall had dragged Rhoan halfway to the barn door, while Rhoan, coughing and crying for Kenny, beat against his chest, shouting to let him go back for his grandson, though he couldn't stand.

"Broken leg—gotta get him out," Marshall choked.

They made it out just as the front beam of the barn collapsed.

"Daddy—Daddy, where's Kenny? Kenny!" Ruby Lynne cradled her daddy's head, screaming all the while for her son.

Marshall headed back in, but Joe pulled him from the flames and they both ended up in the dirt together. "You can't go back in there—it's an inferno!" Joe wasn't about to lose his friend. "There's no way in!"

But Marshall pushed Joe off him, pulled himself up and ran behind the barn.

Joe struggled to his knees and followed. "Where—" He stopped, not believing what he saw. Marshall had hoisted himself up a tree nearly strangled in honeysuckle vines—strong ones, old ones—and was jerking them free, pulling hard, blood running from his hands as the vines cut into flesh. "Marshall, what—"

"Stand back!" Marshall yelled and, pulling back as far as he dared, swung toward the open door of the barn's second story. He came short of reaching the upper floor but kicked hard against the barn's side, swung back, and repeated the attempt. Three times he tried and failed.

Marshall gritted his teeth and set his jaw, pumping his legs for one strong push, and just made the upper floor's edge. Hooking one elbow over the floor, he pulled himself up, hanging on to the vine as best he could, then crawled into the smoke.

"Marshall!" Joe yelled again and again as flames shot into the upper story. Olney and Chester appeared, Reverend Willard limping just behind them. They could still hear Ruby Lynne screaming for her son on the other side of the barn.

A minute passed. Three. Men, dead sober now if they weren't before, and frantic women beat the flames outside the barn, but it was a lost cause.

"The place is tinder with all that hay," Reverend Willard lamented. "Dear God, help! Please help Marshall and Kenny!"

Joe felt the sickness come up from his stomach at the image of his friend burning. The faces of his parents and the shores of France shot through his mind again.

And in that moment when nothing could walk out of that fire alive, Marshall appeared at the top of the barn, his shirt in flames, struggling to stand, but holding a limp child in his arms. "Joe," he barely whispered.

Joe and Chester locked arms and stood beneath the burning building, as close as they dared. "Let him go!"

Marshall did, and Kenny, dishrag limp, fell into the human basket they'd made.

"Marshall! Son—get outta there!" Olney called to his nephew, tears streaming down his face. "Dear God, please help him—help him, Lord!"

But Marshall was too far gone to hear. He stood unsteadily, leaning, nodded as if to some unseen force, and fell, as the barn's upper floor collapsed beneath him.

Joe shoved Kenny into Chester's arms. He and Olney rushed into the burning shreds of the barn and dragged Marshall from the flames. Once clear, Joe pounded the fire from Marshall's shirt as Celia, who'd appeared from he didn't know where, pounded flames from his.

"Is he—"

But Joe couldn't answer Celia. He ripped Marshall's shirt open at the neck to get his fingers against his carotid artery, searching for a pulse. At first, he didn't feel a thing, but he closed his eyes to concentrate, pressing a little harder until he felt a faint beat against his fingers. "He's alive, but it's weak."

"His leg." Celia pointed.

Marshall's right leg was twisted at an odd angle. Worse, Joe knew, Marshall needed help for the amount of smoke he'd surely taken into his lungs and the third-degree burns over his face and upper torso. No telling what internal injuries there might be from the fall.

"Where's Doc Vishnevsky?"

"With Kenny and Mr. Wishon."

"What do you need, son?" Reverend Pierce was at Joe's side.

"We've got to get him to a hospital. He's going to need oxygen—and treatment for these burns."

"Doc Vishy's car," Celia offered.

"We need a truck bed—for Marshall and Kenny both."

"Rhoan will let us use his," Reverend Willard said. "I'll get a pallet made up in the back. We'll drive it around back here. Hold on."

Reverend Willard disappeared. Joe prayed like he'd never prayed before. *Dear God, save him. He's come all this way, all this time, and now this—because he risked his life to save somebody else's child. His own little girl needs him alive and well.*

It wasn't five minutes till Rhoan's engine roared to life and Reverend Willard drove around the still-burning barn. Kenny already lay on the truck bed's pallet, his head in his mother's lap. Joe nodded. Good. Good to keep the boy's head elevated. Reverend Willard limped out of the truck. "Doc's setting Rhoan's leg and treating burns some of the men got battling the fire. He said to get Kenny to the hospital as fast as we can. I told him about Marshall, and he said to take him in first . . . and hurry."

Joe nodded. "Help me lift him. It's going to hurt worse than bullets, but he's out so cold he'll never know."

Reverend Willard, Reverend Pierce, and Olney helped Joe lift Marshall as gently as they could, but even so, skin peeled off in their hands. "Dear God, please help," Reverend Willard prayed aloud, his voice cracking.

Chester and Celia had jumped into the back of the truck, lifting a quilt to Marshall's back so when the men set him in, they could pull him into the truck bed.

"Careful! Gentle!" Joe admonished, though he saw they were. Marshall groaned. *A good sign.*

"I'll drive, Joe. I know the way." Reverend Willard grabbed the wheel and pulled himself up into the cab. "You stay with Marshall and Kenny."

Joe didn't need a second invitation. He hopped up in the truck bed beside Ruby Lynne, carefully lifting Marshall's head to his knee. Celia and Lilliana filled the cab.

"Should I come?" Chester asked, uncertainty in his eyes.

"I could use your help getting them out," Joe spoke up, though there was clearly no room in the truck bed.

In a heartbeat Lilliana and Celia vacated the cab. Chester climbed in, saying, "Olney, you come, too."

Joe was sorry he hadn't said that, but he could barely think. What more could he do to keep the two alive until they reached the hospital? Where was the doc?

As if he could read minds, Olney said, "Doc said you'll know more about burns than he will, and he's needed here."

Joe wasn't so sure, but there wasn't time to argue. The truck engine sputtered, sounded as if it might flood, then finally roared to life. Reverend Willard drove as fast as Joe knew he dared, spewing gravel and swerving to avoid potholes. Joe held a flashlight above Kenny. The boy was still but breathing a little better than when he and Chester had first caught him. "Good. That's good."

Tears streaked Ruby Lynne's face. "Is he gonna make it?"

"Kenny will be fine. He's inhaled a lot of smoke, but he's going to make it. They'll treat his burns, check that arm. I don't think he has other injuries."

"What about Marshall?"

Joe couldn't see the worry in Ruby Lynne's eyes but heard it in her voice. He shook his head. He was a doctor and he could barely bring himself to look into the burned face of his friend. "I hope it's not far to the hospital."

"Next town over. It won't be long."

"The sooner the better," Joe whispered. Ruby Lynne's familiarity with the area gave him hope, but hope, he knew, was a fragile thing.

Twenty minutes later they pulled into the pitch-dark parking lot of a small hospital, or what looked more like a rural medical clinic to Joe. A single faint light burned through the front door.

"At last," Ruby Lynne sighed.

Olney hopped out of the truck and ran up the steps to the front door. Joe heard him jiggle the door handle, then frantically beat on the door. No one came. Joe leaned around the cab. Olney knocked again, framing his eyes with his palms to better see through the glass.

Who locks a hospital?

"I'm gonna run around back, see who I can find." Joe could hear Olney coming down the steps when the door finally opened.

"Who's there?" A woman in white peered into the dark.

"We've two burn victims, ma'am," Chester called, climbing out of the cab. "They're real bad off—a barn caught fire with them in it."

"Land sakes! I'll get the doctor. Can you carry them in? Do you need a stretcher?"

"A stretcher would be good, ma'am. They hurt real bad." Olney was back in a flash, pulling his hat from his head.

The woman, frowning at Olney, hesitated, but looked back toward Chester. "I'll get the doctor," she repeated.

"What about the—" But Chester was cut off when the woman closed the door.

"Let's get them inside," Joe insisted, frustrated that time was wasting. Marshall's breathing came shallow.

Reverend Willard was out of the cab, pulling down the tailgate, drawing the quilt Kenny rested on toward himself. Ruby Lynne, already on her knees, kept her son's head elevated. Kenny was coming to, moaning but very much alive.

"Let me take him, Reverend Willard." Chester pushed between them. It was just as well. Joe knew that with Reverend Willard's bum leg it would be too easy to stumble in the dark.

By the time Chester made the front stoop, the door opened. The nurse led Chester to a room off the side of the hallway.

"Olney, Reverend Willard," Joe instructed, "help me carry Marshall."

Without a word the men worked together. By the time they'd gingerly pulled Marshall's quilt to the edge of the tailgate, Chester was back. Each man took a corner, holding the quilt's hem at intervals, doing their best not to rub against Marshall's already peeling skin.

They were up the stairs and through the doorway when the nurse gasped. "You can't bring him in here!"

"He's in worse shape than the boy. He needs the doctor right away," Joe ordered.

"Not here. Didn't you see the sign?" She sounded exasperated but Joe didn't know what she was talking about.

Reverend Willard intervened. "He needs help. Joe, here, is a doctor and said he might not live if we don't get more help for him."

"Smoke inhalation." Joe couldn't believe he needed to explain. "His lungs—"

"I'm sorry. I can't help who you are or what he needs; this is a whites-only clinic." She was firm—all the while they held Marshall by the quilt, all the while his breathing labored, shallow and short.

Joe wanted to smash the woman's face. What didn't she understand? "He could die." He said it slowly and deliberately, eyes boring into hers.

She lifted her chin. "Don't take that tone with me. I don't make the rules. If you want that boy to live, you'd best get him to a hospital that treats his kind. We have laws, you know, and rules."

"Where?" Olney begged. "We're losing precious time, Joe. We can't be standin' here arguing."

A man in a white coat stepped out of the room Kenny and Ruby Lynne had disappeared into. He took a look at Marshall's face and winced. "Try Kate Bitting Reynolds Memorial. They take colored."

"Where's that?" Olney was the only one ready to go.

"Winston-Salem."

"Winston-Salem?" Reverend Willard gasped. "That's sixty miles! He won't make it. We're in a truck over back roads."

The doctor shook his head. He walked back into the examining room and shut the door.

Joe stood frozen. "I can't believe—"

"Joe, we're wasting time. Get my boy in the truck. Now." Olney was not to be ignored.

It was all Joe could do to turn, to keep his footing sure and the sting in his eyes from blinding his vision.

They laid Marshall back in the truck bed. Olney and Joe climbed in and pulled the quilt deep into the bed as gently as they could. It hardly mattered. *He's unconscious—a mercy and a curse.* The two settled down on either side of Marshall, watching that he didn't roll, making sure his head was elevated and his airway open.

Reverend Willard drove.

"Do you know where this hospital is?" Joe asked Olney. "Will they take him?"

"Only one that close that will. I should have known, should have thought. But we had to take Kenny first anyway."

"He didn't need to come first," Joe bit back. "He's not as bad off."

Olney was quiet for a moment and Joe couldn't see his face in the dark. "Wouldn't matter."

Joe's heart hammered so hard he feared it might explode in his chest. *It should matter. Marshall's life is just as important as Kenny's. He's a veteran and a doctor and a good man—a human being! What more can they want?*

The minutes and miles piled on, one after another, stretching past the hour, nearing two before they reached the outer city limits of Winston-Salem. Joe prayed Reverend Willard knew the way to the hospital. He kept track of Marshall's vital signs, kept his head elevated, but there was little else he could do.

At last Chester called out, "Kate Bitting Reynolds Memorial Hospital! Just ahead!"

It was smaller than Joe would have expected in a city the size of Winston-Salem. *Please, God, let them have what he needs. Take care of Marshall.*

Olney was out of the truck before it fully stopped, running toward the faintly lit emergency entrance, then through the back door. In two minutes, a man appeared with a gurney. Joe breathed. At last something was happening.

Olney and the colored man dressed in white edged the gurney against the truck's tailgate. Chester clambered up to help Joe lift the quilt, keeping Marshall's head steady. The other three men edged the quilt down, sliding it onto the gurney.

The man who'd brought the gurney hadn't spoken a word, but when he saw Marshall's face, he gave a low whistle. "Mmm, mmm. Doctor's on his way. Y'all stand back now. Let me get him inside. You'll need to fill out paperwork at the desk." Swiftly, expertly, the man maneuvered the gurney up the ramp and through the doors, Olney, Joe, and Chester at his heels.

"I'll park the truck and be right in," Reverend Willard called.

The emergency room was nearly empty, but every eye followed the black and white trio trailing the man with the gurney.

When they came to the No Admittance sign, a nurse bustled through, standing between the gurney and the men from No Creek. "That's as far as you go now, gentlemen. Doctor will see to him." She lifted her chin, a crease between her eyes.

"Marshall's my family," Olney insisted.

"And I suppose this is your family, too." The nurse raised her eyebrows.

"Friends—like brothers," Joe insisted, not about to be turned away.

"Not in this town, young man. This is the colored waiting room. You'll have to go to the white waiting room. By the looks of things, this is gonna take a while. Y'all might want to go on home and come back during visiting hours tomorrow. We'll see how he is."

"I'm staying," Olney said. "I'm not going anywhere till my boy's outta the woods."

"We don't want trouble." She looked directly at Joe, until seeing Reverend Willard rush in. Her eyes went wide. "Another one."

"The reverend drove us here, ma'am. We're all friends of Marshall," Chester's voice soothed.

"Like I said, you need to find the white waiting room." She disappeared, closing the door behind her.

"Y'all best go on back now, Reverend Willard. I appreciate you bringing us all this way, but—"

"I'm not going anywhere until we know Marshall's getting the help and care he needs." Joe stood his ground, though the room had begun to sway just a little.

"Joe, you look like you gonna fall over any minute. Reverend Willard, you know that truck belongs to Rhoan Wishon. He's gonna want it back. And Ruby Lynne . . ."

Reverend Willard pushed his fingers through hair grown a little too long, frustration etched in his face.

"I'm staying," Joe insisted.

"They not gonna let you wait in here. You heard the nurse."

"I saw burns aplenty during the war. I can help him, if I have the right equipment. I'm going to talk to the woman at the desk, see if she'll contact the doctor, ask him to let me help." Joe was on his way before he'd finished speaking and poured out his plea to the woman behind the desk.

No matter how he tried to persuade her, she refused to budge. "I'm sorry, but I can't let you back there. I'll send a message that you're here, that you have medical training, but I can't let you in. Sir, you need to trust the doctors here to treat him. We have the best colored doctors here, and they'll do all they can for your friend." She wasn't without compassion, but she wasn't moved.

Olney pulled him away. "Joe, you've got to let it be. Let them do their jobs."

But Joe couldn't. *It should be me in there. I'm the one who should have gone in that barn for Kenny—not Marshall. And to save Rhoan Wishon's grandson of all people—the family that tried to hang him.* Joe plunked into the nearest chair, dropped his head between his elbows, and covered his face with his hands. He felt so helpless—as helpless as he'd felt in the face of Ivy's death.

"Reverend Willard, you best go on now. We don't need trouble here. I appreciate what you've done, bringing us all this way, but—" Olney nodded toward the two big men standing at the door—"you need to take Chester and Joe and go on home now. Mr. Wishon's gonna want his truck back, gonna need to know what's happened with Ruby Lynne and his grandson."

"Surely she will have phoned home by now. I don't think we need to wo—"

"Just the same. It's time you all went home."

Joe looked up. Olney really wanted them to leave. He looked around the waiting room. The few people who were there eyed them all suspiciously, warily, as if they weren't to be trusted. For the first time Joe sensed something of what Marshall must have felt at every turn in England, every day in the US, and it didn't feel good.

"That's what you want, Olney?" Reverend Willard stepped closer to Olney, spoke low.

"It is. I'll telephone if I need you."

"We can come back at any time. I know Doctor Vishnevsky will let us borrow his car."

"That be fine, real fine. We'll need somebody to come get us when Marshall's ready to go home."

Joe groaned inside. *They don't realize how bad this is, how unlikely it is that Marshall will—*

"Joe, you, too. I want you to go on now."

"No, Mr. Tate, please. I want—"

"I need you to go on, let me do this alone. I need you to go on home and pray like you never prayed before."

Joe stared, trying to weigh every reason why Olney insisted they go. Reverend Willard pulled him to his feet, and Chester took his arm, guiding him away. "I'll be back tomorrow. Tomorrow I'll be here. If Marshall wakes up—" But Joe couldn't finish.

Olney nodded. "I'll tell him. I know what to tell him."

Joe wasn't sure when they got into the truck, or how long the drive toward the mountains took, or if he slept against the cab's door or was awake in a stupor the whole time. His insides ached. His back burned. His heart bore a hole—a family-size hole. *First Nonni, then Ivy, and now Marshall. Do You need them all? What about Violet? She's so close to coming. Dear God, please. Please. Please.* It was all he knew to pray.

Chapter Fifty-Two

JUNE 1948

Sunday morning the remains of the barn still smoldered. Everything outside and inside Garden's Gate smelled of smoke. Ash and a layer of grime blanketed everything. Thankfully, neighbors had cleared the back garden of the sawhorse tables and cleaned up as best they could. All the rest would take time.

Celia and Joe prayed and waited shoulder to shoulder by the phone for Doctor Vishnevsky's call. He'd promised that first thing this morning he would phone the medical center where Kenny was being treated and the hospital where Marshall fought for his life.

It was all Celia could do to keep Joe from walking to Winston-Salem. If the train had been running that day, he'd have been on it.

Just after eight the phone rang. Joe pounced on it. Celia pulled the receiver between them so they could both hear.

"Joe? Marshall is still breathing, so that is good. I feared respiratory failure from what the doctor said last night. Respiratory signs fluctuate, better this morning than last night. There is concern for sepsis. The burns are bad—more than 40 percent of his body . . . but this you know.

They're watching him carefully for risk of infection. His legs—so much scar tissue, and deep, to the bone, in addition to the break. Nerve and muscle damage."

"Will he walk?" Joe's breath caught.

"Surgery will be required . . . There are no promises, no guarantees."

Celia heard the doc's voice catch. She felt the tightening of Joe's jaw beside her cheek. Tears streaming down her face were only half her own.

"There is one more thing."

"What more?" Joe choked the words.

"It is not known if he can see. There are bandages covering his eyes now, but . . . time must tell."

Celia couldn't bring herself to answer. Joe said nothing.

"I will drive to the hospital as soon as I've delivered Mrs. Brown's baby. You may come with me if you wish, but they will not allow you to see him. Only family, and me, because I am his doctor. I am sorry."

Celia wrapped her palm over Joe's death grip on the receiver. She needed to break the horror of the moment. "Kenny?"

"Kenny will be fine. Marshall kept the fire from his face when he pressed the boy against his chest. He could not cover his own eyes and do so. The boy's arm is broken but will heal. One burn on his hand that may scar; that is all. It will not need a skin graft. He's already been released."

"That's something." Celia swallowed.

"It is what our Marshall sacrificed himself for."

Joe turned away without answering, dropped the receiver, walked through the door and onto the front porch.

"Thank you, Doc. You'll let us know whatever more you learn?" Celia needed to take charge.

"Yes, I will telephone tonight."

The phone clicked. Celia replaced the receiver, her heart aching. She feared for Marshall, and she feared for Joe. She loved Marshall as her friend, but Joe loved him as his brother. Celia knew what losing Chester would mean to her—unspeakable, unthinkable.

She stepped through the door, gently closing the screen behind her. She wouldn't startle Joe, wouldn't expect anything from him, but she ached to throw her arms about him, to comfort him, tell him it was all going to be okay, even though it wasn't. "Joe?" She laid her hand on his back.

He didn't turn, just stood, staring out into the garden, his arm wrapped around one of the columns. "He made it through the war and Army bureaucracy. His wife was killed. He made it through medical school, his internship set. At last Violet's coming. He's worked these last years to make that happen. And after all that . . . I don't understand."

Celia didn't understand either. But her attention was diverted when she heard the gate by the road open. *Ruby Lynne Wishon. Kenny's mother is the last person Joe needs to see now.* If she could have steered Joe inside, she would have. But it wasn't Ruby Lynne's fault, or even Kenny's, and Celia had seen how worried Ruby Lynne was last night for her son. "Ruby Lynne," Celia acknowledged.

"Morning, Celia, Dr. Rossetti." Ruby Lynne looked about as tense as a cat strung out on a clothesline.

Joe straightened. "Good morning, Ruby Lynne. How's Kenny this morning?"

"Sleeping now, with Daddy. Kenny's fine—besides the broken arm and a couple of burns, but he'll be fine."

"Thanks to Marshall—to Dr. Raymond." Joe underlined the *doctor* part.

"He saved Kenny's life. I didn't realize until after you'd all left the clinic last night that they wouldn't admit him. How is he? Where is he?"

"Winston-Salem—the closest place that would take him as far as we know. Holding on, barely. We don't know if he'll pull through." Joe's voice broke, though Celia knew he did his best to keep it steady.

Tears sprang into Ruby Lynne's eyes. "I'm sorry. So, so sorry."

"We're all sorry, Ruby Lynne." Celia had to say it. "It wasn't your fault, or Kenny's. It's that stupid refusal to treat coloreds."

"But it was—at least partly." Ruby Lynne bit her lower lip, as if trying to keep the words from spilling out.

"What do you mean?" She had all of Joe's attention now.

"Can I—may I sit down?" The color had drained from Ruby Lynne's face, making each freckle stand out like soot speckles on snow.

Celia pulled a rocker forward and Ruby Lynne mounted the steps.

"Sit down, Joe," Celia ordered. If Ruby Lynne had something important to say, something so hard to get out, she didn't need Joe standing over her, arms crossed, like a tribunal judge.

Ruby Lynne sat on the edge of the rocker, closed her eyes a moment, and drew a deep breath. "I asked Kenny how the fire started. He wouldn't tell me, not at first. But finally, it came out that he and Billy had sneaked a flask of Daddy's moonshine from underneath the seat of the truck. They climbed up into the loft of the barn and took turns drinking, then . . ."

"Then what?" Joe pushed.

"Then decided they wanted to see it light up. Billy'd heard his daddy say that moonshine could light up a room like twenty lanterns—or something like that. So they snuck matches from your kitchen, ran back up to the loft, poured some in a pot they found, and set it afire."

"They set the whole barn on fire!" Celia couldn't believe it. *Moonshine burned the barn!*

"They're kids—they didn't know what they were doing." Ruby Lynne wrung her hands in knots.

"You think that excuses them?" Joe was angry now and Celia couldn't blame him. *Such loss of life and lifelong dreams, whether Marshall survives or not . . . such utter destruction of property! That barn was only rebuilt a few years ago, after the Klan, led by the Wishon brothers, burned it down. The apple must not fall far from the tree.*

"No, I don't—not at all, but it explains what happened, and who's responsible." Ruby Lynne met Joe's glare full on. "I've talked with Daddy about covering Marshall's medical bills, whatever he needs now and whatever he needs to recover."

"That means surgery, surely skin grafts, rehabilitation. He might never see again. This could run not hundreds but thousands of dollars." Joe spared nothing.

"Did he agree to that?" Celia couldn't believe it.

"Not yet, but I hope he will."

Joe's knuckles whitened in his fists. He looked away.

Celia wasn't about to look away. "Maybe he needs some persuasion."

"I'll try, but you know Daddy."

"We all do. Maybe you need to target what matters most to him. Maybe Kenny needs to know just what sort of man his grandfather really is, and the man his father was—who his father was. How would Rhoan like it if we told Kenny that his grandfather and daddy tried to murder the man who saved his life, that they were the ones to burn down Miss Lill's barn the first time?"

"Celia!" Joe's face showed horror.

Ruby Lynne paled. "No, Celia, please. I've only ever told Kenny that his daddy died in the war. He knows nothing about Troy or any of that."

"It's high time Rhoan paid for what his family did. What matters more to him than Kenny idolizing him?"

"That would ruin Kenny's relationship with his granddaddy and make me out to be a liar, Celia. I'm all he has. You can't do that, not ever. Please!"

Celia caught hold of herself. She knew that was true. She didn't want to hurt Ruby Lynne or Kenny, but she wanted to lash out at somebody, make somebody pay for Marshall's troubles and the injustice of it all. But it was the look of disappointment and disbelief from Joe that stopped her in her tracks.

"I came because I want to know more about what you were saying before the fire . . . about the land Miss Lill said properly belongs to the Tates."

Celia blinked. She looked at Joe, who'd uncrossed his arms.

"If you won't tell me, I'll go to Miss Lill. I want to know everything, see every document. Start from the beginning."

So Celia told her, everything, from the beginning—what she'd seen and read on her own, and what she'd gleaned from the diary of Minnie Belvidere.

The story took nearly an hour. By the time Celia had finished answering Ruby Lynne's questions she was drained, depleted, but Ruby Lynne looked inspired.

"What are you going to do about it?" Joe wanted to know. "What can you do?"

"I need to talk to Daddy first."

"Olney Tate's afraid for us to bring this out in the open. He's afraid because of what happened to his daddy when he tried to buy the land, and what nearly happened to him and Marshall when—" Celia stopped. "I can't see how you'll convince your daddy to sell that land back. He was determined."

"I can't promise, but I'll do my best."

Joe cut to the chase. "The land return is important, but it won't make Marshall walk again, see again, become the doctor or father he's worked to be."

"No. If there's one thing I've learned it's that we can't undo what's done. But there might be a way forward." She looked at Celia. "Without hurting anyone."

"Absolutely," Joe agreed, "but—"

"Then that's where we need to start." Ruby Lynne stood, as if everything was settled, which made Celia feel as if she'd missed something. "I've got a lot of thinking to do. I'll see you later." And Ruby Lynne was gone.

Joe stepped off the porch, not looking back.

"Joe?"

"Not now, Celia." He stopped, then turned again. "You know, I thought I knew you inside and out, but you've just proved me wrong. Marshall would never hurt Ruby Lynne, and you just threatened to ruin her life and Kenny's in one fell swoop."

"I'm sorry. I shouldn't have said it. I just—"

"Once you start an avalanche like that there's no going back. No amount of 'I'm sorry' fixes it. And it's none of your business!" The fury and disappointment in Joe's eyes, just before he stormed off, left Celia speechless.

Chapter Fifty-Three

JUNE 1948

Three days later Ruby Lynne returned, saying she wanted to talk with Miss Lill and Reverend Willard alone. Celia didn't much like that. She, after all, had found the documents and the diary. She'd set the thing in motion with Miss Lill and Reverend Willard and Rhoan Wishon. She'd all but ruined her relationship with Joe after shooting off her mouth, and she was the one who'd kept so much from Olney and Marshall, though she still thought that was a terrible idea.

Celia busied herself in the kitchen while the three met in the library, the door closed. She was tempted to listen at the door but credited that she'd outgrown those shenanigans. At least she hoped she had. She also needed to formulate some serious crow to eat in her coming apology to Ruby Lynne. On long reflection she didn't know what had possessed her to say those things to Ruby Lynne, to even think them. No matter if they were true, they weren't kind or necessary. Celia knew it was the type of meanness she'd expect from somebody who'd never known grace, but Celia had received grace—again and again in life.

"Please, Lord," she prayed, her fingers twisted in the kitchen towel, "forgive me. I shot off my mouth without thinking with my head or the better part of my heart, pushing every way I knew to get what I figured was best. Not for the first time, Lord, I need to trust You. Help me, Father. I want to be the person You mean for me to be. And, please, Lord, help me mend fences with Ruby Lynne, and with Joe."

Joe was in Winston-Salem with Doc Vishy and Olney Tate—who'd never left his nephew's side. Dr. Vishnevsky and Joe were both doing their best to convince the medical powers at Kate Bitting Reynolds Memorial Hospital—known to the locals as Katie B—that Joe should be allowed to help care for Marshall. It was just as well. Joe wasn't speaking to Celia since Ruby Lynne's last visit.

When Ruby Lynne walked out of the library, Celia took the plunge. "Can we talk, Ruby Lynne? I have some serious apologizing to do."

And just like that, Celia saw in Ruby Lynne's eyes the very picture of grace that she'd been so desperately needing.

• • •

By the time Celia had eaten a hefty meal of crow and Ruby Lynne and she had cried in each other's arms, the truth about Ruby Lynne's visit to Miss Lill came out.

"Truth is, Daddy doesn't own that land. Before Granddaddy Wishon passed, he divided acreage between his two sons—Daddy and Uncle Troy. Uncle Troy owned that tract y'all are talking about, and in his will, he left it to me."

"He what?" Celia couldn't believe one good thing of Troy Wishon.

"Guess he figured it was something he could do to try to make right, or maybe that I'd keep it for his child, but it's clear to me what ought to be done. Miss Lill says Olney Tate's already said he wants nothing to do with it, so now it's up to Marshall and me."

"Does your daddy understand that?"

"Not yet. Pray for me, Celia. I'm going to stand up to Daddy on this, but he won't like it and isn't likely to take it sitting down."

Celia knew that was true. "What do you think of making the land into something good for everybody? It could be the perfect place for a medical clinic—one that would treat everybody."

"I don't know if No Creek's ready for that or if the law would allow it. Anyway, it will be up to Marshall. I'm not about to suggest that Marshall give up that land, not after all he and his family have been through. I wouldn't blame him if he sold it and turned his back on this town."

"You're right. Still, it's a thought, one I'm going to think on."

"One you need to pray on," Ruby Lynne advised. "Keep that horse and cart in proper order."

• • •

Over the next few days, Celia, Miss Lill, and Ruby Lynne talked through the idea of a medical clinic, whether or not it could be located on Marshall's land. They raised every objection they could think of, then countered them.

"It might work," Miss Lill said, "if we can convince the women."

"That needs to be your part, Miss Lill. Folks are more apt to listen to you, being the preacher's wife and all, especially since Reverend Willard's ready to go along."

"But you should be the one to hold the mirror up to their faces, Celia. Miss Lill's been here for years but folks still think of her as from away. She can't get by with holding up that mirror. Nobody expects anything different from you." Ruby Lynne was adamant.

"What about you? You've lived here all your life, too."

"Ha!" Ruby Lynne all but snorted. "I'm a Wishon. They listen to my daddy, but if I speak up, he'll think he's got the right to hush me. No, I'll back you both, but you and Miss Lill need to lead the way. Besides, the clinic's your idea."

• • •

Celia and Joe smoothed things over once Joe knew she'd apologized to Ruby Lynne and that the two were working together. Celia wished with all her heart that Joe could be with them in church that Sunday, but he was about to leave with Doc Vishnevsky for Winston-Salem and Marshall.

Before going, she laid her head on Joe's chest. It felt so natural. When they finished talking, Joe entwined his fingers in hers. She couldn't have said when either pulled away.

She waved the two doctors off and walked to church with Miss Lill. Reverend Willard had gone early to go over his sermon. Chester and their mama had already gone back to Norfolk to visit their daddy.

Celia had planned to go, too, to breathe different air, to see the ocean, but Marshall's injuries, Joe's presence, and plans for the medical clinic had derailed that plan. Miss Lill and Reverend Willard seemed glad to have her, especially since Miss Lill had taken to feeling a mite poorly. Celia worried that the fire—the second burning of Garden's Gate's barn—had taken the stuffing out of Miss Lill. But the idea of the clinic seemed to perk her up.

It was warm in the sanctuary. Celia was glad Reverend Willard had raised the windows, allowing the cool mountain breeze to flow among the hard wooden pews.

Miss Lill fanned herself with a cardstock-and-wooden-stick fan—the kind with a picture of Jesus holding a little lamb.

Jesus, tender Shepherd, hear me—hear Your little lamb tonight . . . The words came from somewhere in Celia's memory. *How we need You, Jesus. How we need You to heal our town, heal Marshall, heal the hearts of everyone and heal everything that separates us. Please.*

It was only as Reverend Willard wrapped up his sermon that Celia realized she'd not heard a word he'd said. She'd been praying clear through—there was so much to pray about. But when Reverend Willard mentioned her name, Celia's ears perked up.

"Celia Percy has something important she'd like to say to everyone here. She's told me what that is, and I ask that you all give her your full attention."

Celia felt the shift in the room. People sat up straighter, craned their necks around one another to look at her. Celia swallowed. She was aware that Miss Lill sat still, relaxed, looking at her hands. *She must be praying.*

Celia walked to the front of the church, stood beside Reverend

Willard, and cleared her throat. "I reckon you all know there's been a lot of speculation about how the fire at Garden's Gate started last week."

Feet shuffled. Nods and murmurs agreed.

"Well, I'm here to tell you the cause of the fire, what happened afterward, and what I think can be done about it."

She had their full attention now. Several of the men from church had helped to rebuild the barn after the Klan had burned it a few years ago. *Fitting,* Celia thought, *since they were likely the ones dressed up in sheets that helped burn it down.* She doubted they wanted to be called out for something they hadn't done or called in to help rebuild that barn again.

"It was two boys—two young boys that decided to experiment with moonshine, drinking it and setting it to flame. Where they got that moonshine is not so important. We all know they could have gotten it in near any house in No Creek."

That caused a stir. "Now, see here, Celia—" came a voice from the far side of the church.

"Understand that I'm not blaming any one of you because we're all to blame for making and drinking and running 'shine like it's mother's milk. It's in near every house and any kid can get hold of it any day of the week and do just what these boys did. Now we know who started the fire and they've already apologized. That's not why I'm here. But I want to say something else.

"Our new doctors, Dr. Marshall Raymond and Dr. Joe Rossetti, saved Mr. Wishon's and Billy Chatham's lives. Dr. Raymond saved Kenny's life. If he hadn't gone up in that burning barn and taken up Kenny—well, I can't even say the words, but you know what they are.

"Now Dr. Raymond is fighting for his life in a hospital over in Winston-Salem. He's fighting for his life there because the clinic that took Kenny Wishon to set a broken arm refused to take Dr. Raymond to treat near-fatal burns and smoke inhalation. He could have died, might have died. The clinic refused to let his friends bring him in the door—even after he'd helped save three lives! Even though he's a doctor come to help us! And do you know why?"

Celia glanced around. Everybody knew why, but nobody said.

"Because not one of us has ever stood up and said that keeping somebody from treatment because of the color of their skin is wrong. It's wrong! Red blood flows in every human body. The image of God is imprinted on every human soul, and yet some man-made law stops us from doing just what Jesus told us to do—love our neighbor as ourselves. How can we come to church and sing our hymns and pray our prayers and spit on the very creation God made above every other living thing on this earth?"

Feet and bodies shifted. Celia felt the temperature in the room rising.

"Since old Granny Chree died, we have had one doctor in No Creek—Doctor Vishnevsky. He's a good man and a great doctor but he can't treat everybody, and he needs supplies, equipment. We can't be running two towns over to get to a medical clinic, or our neighbors running all the way to Winston-Salem to get help in emergencies. We need help here—now. We need our own medical clinic, right here in No Creek. And we need one that will treat whites and coloreds alike."

"That ain't never gonna happen," Jed Brown piped up. "Not one man here will stand for mixing."

"Maybe not." Miss Lill stood up, the color leaving her face. "But I'm willing to bet your Sunday dinner every woman will."

Celia felt as much as saw the women shift and straighten, their eyes on Miss Lill.

"How many of you women need a doctor when you're pregnant or when you're worried over some sickness in your child but Doctor Vishnevsky's out making house calls, and you can't leave your other children for a trip to the nearest clinic, much less a day's train ride to the hospital in the city? Or can't afford it even if you could go? How many times have you wanted to call Doctor Vishnevsky out in the middle of the night for childbirth or fever or a broken bone but hated to do it? Imagine if there was a medical clinic right here in No Creek—one that would treat you or your children. Now imagine if there had been a clinic here in No Creek equipped to treat Dr. Raymond."

"You can't mix the races—you can't have one clinic treating both. It's not done." Rhoan Wishon stood now, and he was the voice for the men in town.

"It's already been done," Celia piped up. "Separate facilities, but shared equipment. We all know that Ida Mae can't carry every pill and tonic in the store that Dr. Vishnevsky needs to treat us or our families. The doc can't operate safely in your houses or on his kitchen table. We need a real medical facility with real medical equipment. By pulling together we can make this happen. But we've all got to pitch in."

The buzz through the congregation rivaled bees. Reverend Willard stepped in. "What Celia and my wife say is worth considering, worth praying about, worth investigating. We could all benefit from a well-run clinic. I've asked Celia to visit some of you in the next few weeks to talk it over more. I urge you to give her your time and attention, and whatever else the Spirit leads. Let's bow our heads."

The reverend closed with prayer Celia heard, but again her brain ran away with her.

As soon as the last amen was sung, the buzz started, and it wasn't likely to let up anytime soon.

· · ·

True to Reverend Willard's word, Celia set about talking up her clinic idea with the women of No Creek. She reached Ruby Lynne three days later.

"You don't have to convince me, Celia. You know I'm all in. I can't help fund this, but I'm all in."

"That's good, because I want you to help me convince Mercy Tate."

"What? Mercy doesn't have money, and I doubt a Wishon on her porch is a sight she's aching to behold."

"I don't want Mercy's money. I want her backing. We *need* her backing."

"You don't think she'll want a clinic that will treat everybody? I can't think of anything she's like to want more."

"All the money in the world for a clinic won't matter unless there's land to build it on."

"Miss Lill said she'll donate land. There's no need to use Marshall's land."

"But the more I talk to folks about the clinic, the more I see there needs to be an investment from both sides of the community—colored and white. I'm not saying force anybody's hand, but I think it's time the Tates knew more about where things stand."

"Miss Lill said Olney Tate wants nothing to do with that land and that I should wait to tell Marshall till he's out of the hospital."

"Maybe so, but she didn't say anything about Mercy. I have an idea how that land can be used to benefit everybody, including the Tates, but we need to get Mercy on our side before you talk to Marshall." Celia was pretty sure this conversation would not meet with Miss Lill's approval, but Reverend Willard had given his blessing to rally the locals. She sure didn't need a second endorsement.

They made it to Mercy's cabin shortly after noon. Celia knew that not since the creation of the world had a Wishon stepped on Tate property, and she saw the shock and wariness of that in Mercy Tate's eyes.

"Ruby Lynne, Celia. What brings you ladies here?" Mercy didn't invite them in, but her eyes scanned the surrounding woods. Celia hated that Mercy had reason to fear.

"Mrs. Tate, we want to talk with you about something important, something to do with Marshall. Can we come in?"

Mercy Tate blinked. Celia knew she'd probably never spoken directly with Ruby Lynne. Mercy stepped out on the front porch. "It's cooler out here. Can I get you ladies a glass of sweet tea?"

"That would be wonderful." Ruby Lynne smiled.

Celia nearly dropped her teeth. Rhoan Wishon swore he'd never drink or eat with a colored. He'd fall over dead to know his daughter did. Mercy looked like she might, too, but to her credit she just nodded politely, reservedly, and said, "Be right back. Y'all make yourselves comfortable."

Ruby Lynne sank into the porch swing, as if she visited the Tates every day of her life.

Mercy stepped out the door with a tray of three mason-jar glasses of tea. "It's neighborly you all stopped by." Her eyes scanned the woods again. "You know I'm glad to see you both, but I don't want trouble here, Ruby Lynne. Whatever you've got to say, I'll listen. But don't you bring trouble on our heads. Marshall doesn't deserve that, nor my Olney."

Celia saw the color spring to Ruby Lynne's cheeks. "No, you don't deserve any trouble—just the opposite. I can't tell you how grateful I am to Marshall for saving my Kenny."

"He'd've done it for anybody. That's who he is."

"I know. That he did it for my son, a Wishon, after all my family has put your family through . . . Well, I'm humbled. We don't deserve it. And I'm sorry—sick and sorry that Marshall's not been treated as he deserves. I couldn't believe that clinic wouldn't take him, help him."

Mercy sighed. "It's the way things are. There's nothing we can do about that."

"We can't change what's been done," Celia agreed, "but maybe we can help change the future."

"What are you saying?"

Celia poured out every detail from the moment the ancient oak tree had crashed through the roof at Garden's Gate. She stepped back in time, telling about Minnie Belvidere and Obadiah Tate and Grayson's crimes against him. She repeated, sometimes word for word, what she'd memorized from Minnie's diary and then explained in detail about the manumission papers, the land deeds, all of it.

Mercy sat in silence, her eyes growing wide as she listened. She picked at a stray buttonhole thread on her dress, that small bit of anxiety telltale. By the time Celia finished, the late-afternoon sun had crossed the sky. The three sat in silence for a minute, maybe more, letting Celia's words sink in.

Finally, Mercy shook her head. "What you say gives credence to every word Olney's daddy told us—what his father told him. But you both need to understand that when Olney's daddy went to your grand-daddy, Ruby Lynne, with money in hand to buy that land—land that should have rightfully been his—they killed him, and they made Olney watch. Your granddaddy did that. Your daddy and his men, dressed up in sheets and hoods, beat my Olney near to death, and it was only by the grace of God that Reverend Willard and Dr. Vishnevsky kept them from setting fire to Marshall and hanging him, right here in these woods, not but a few years past."

"I swear, Mrs. Tate, if I could turn back the clock, I'd do anything

I could to prevent that from happening. I know that's no excuse and I can't change what happened, but I can do my best to right the wrong of the land."

"I know you both mean well. I see that. But what can either of you do, child? For all you've grown up you're still young women, and the Klan don't listen much to women."

"No, but that land was willed to Uncle Troy and he willed it to me. It belongs to me now. I can see it goes to Marshall free and clear."

"And you think your daddy's gonna let you give it away?'"

"Kenny and I are all he's got now, and I don't believe he wants to lose us. If it comes down to that . . . well, it does. I owe Marshall my son's life. The land is not a high price to pay."

Mercy looked at Ruby Lynne with something Celia figured was akin to affection and pity, as if the girl before her didn't understand real life. Celia wasn't sure she did. Convincing Rhoan Wishon of anything that didn't benefit him or make him feel above others was not likely to happen.

"We hope that Marshall will be willing to sell some of it, maybe two or three acres, back to Miz Lill for a fair price." Celia needed to make things plain.

Mercy shook her head. "And what would Miss Lill want with two or three of Marshall's acres, even if they belonged to him?"

"She wants to donate them for the building of a medical clinic, right here in No Creek—one that will treat both coloreds and whites—so no person living here will ever have to go away for treatment or be denied treatment. She wants to call it the Tate-Belvidere Medical Center."

Mercy's eyes looked like they might pop from her head. "Do you know what you're saying? Treat coloreds and whites in the same building? They'll never do it, never allow it. You'd see a bonfire big enough to—"

"Not if the Wishons and Willards are behind it," Celia said.

Mercy stared at Ruby Lynne. Celia couldn't tell what she was thinking, maybe running every bad scenario through her brain. That's what Celia would be doing with anything concerning Wishons.

"How you gonna convince the people here to desegregate for this clinic?"

"We can't. But we can build two areas, one for whites and one for coloreds, with a building for shared equipment and supplies connecting the two. Miss Lill's been working on a proposal with an architect she and Dr. Vishnevsky found."

"And just who you know that will run this clinic?" Mercy wasn't giving in.

"Dr. Vishnevsky will oversee it. He's already agreed, and we're hoping that Marshall—Dr. Raymond—and Dr. Rossetti will work under him. If they don't want to, we'll need to advertise for doctors. Dr. Vishnevsky's getting too old to keep making house calls all over the area."

"A Jew doctor, a colored doctor, and an Italian doctor . . ." Mercy half smiled. "All three chief targets of the Klan, and more so because they're educated. I just don't see how—"

"We believe, if Ruby Lynne's daddy stands with us and the clinic is on Tate land, and if Miss Lill and Reverend Willard give money and blessing for its building, that people will come. That joining of strongholds in the community—colored and white—will show a path forward."

The crease between Mercy's eyes deepened and Celia knew she was taking it in.

"I just wanted you to know what we're proposing. Reverend Willard and Miss Lill and I've been meeting with women from Shady Grove, one by one. Most support the idea of a medical clinic, even shared. Reverend Pierce is willing to go with me, but I'd like you to go with us to meet with the women from Saints Delight, Mrs. Tate. I know they'll listen to you."

"You haven't even talked to Olney or Marshall!"

"The medical clinic doesn't have to be on Tate land. Nobody outside Garden's Gate knows about what I found in the attic except Ruby Lynne and her daddy, and nobody needs to. Miss Lill will donate some of her land if you and Olney or Marshall don't want to do this. I'm just thinking this might be a way of healing some of the divisions in No Creek and making people more accepting of it.

"All I really want is for you to help me convince the women to support the idea of a shared medical facility right here in No Creek. Women are the necks that turn their husband's heads whether they admit it or not, and if Tates, Belvideres, and Wishons support the idea, most are likely to follow . . . At least that's what we think."

"Olney's not here for me to talk this over with. He's staying in Winston-Salem with Marshall until he's released from the hospital. You know, we have no way of knowing if Marshall will even see again, walk again, let alone be able to doctor."

"I'm sorrier than I can tell you. Marshall has worked hard, he's served our country in wartime, and he deserves every good thing. I just hope . . . We hope this clinic can be one of those good things. And if he's—*when* he's ready for it, it will be ready for him," Ruby Lynne spoke quietly.

Tears pooled in Mercy's eyes. Celia knew they were running down her own face.

"I don't want any of this said to Olney or Marshall now. They can't take one more trial, one more disappointment." Mercy paused, her brow furrowed, as she considered. "If you promise me you won't say one more word to anybody, colored or white, about this land idea until—unless—*until* that deed is signed over to Marshall, registered at the courthouse, and he agrees, I'll go with you—long as we speak only about building a shared medical clinic here in No Creek. I want that medical clinic for everybody; I won't lie. But I will not risk losing one more member of my family over that land. Do you understand me?"

"Perfectly. Thank you, Mrs. Tate." Ruby Lynne reached for Mercy's hands. Celia felt as if she'd just been handed the crown jewels of England.

Chapter Fifty-Four

Admittance to Kate Bitting Reynolds Memorial Hospital to visit Marshall was all Joe had dared hope for. To be allowed to assist in his medical treatment and count it as part of his internship was more than he'd dreamed. He thought he knew quite a bit about burns but learned much more from Dr. Kettering, a visiting burn specialist and surgeon from New York, intent on observing the hospital and its working relationship to the white hospital nearby. While there, Dr. Kettering offered to train surgeons interested in the newest skin-graft methods. Marshall was one of his patients. Joe was allowed to observe.

By the time Dr. Kettering completed his surgeries and left, Joe believed he could oversee the remainder of Marshall's rehabilitation. The hospital was short-staffed enough that he was allowed.

Six weeks after the fire, it was time to remove the bandages from Marshall's eyes. Every hope and prayer that Marshall would be able to see was raised inside and outside both churches in No Creek. Inside the family and hospital, every doubt and fear was wrestled against.

Gently, Joe began unwinding the bandages from Marshall's head.

The skin beneath was healing. Dr. Kettering had warned it would look crusted and discolored, possibly turning red. As long as it wasn't swollen or flaming red, as long as there was no fever marking infection, it was a good sign. His friend would be bald, his face hairless, at least mostly, but that would be a small price to pay for eyesight.

Please, God, let him see.

With only two layers still covering his eyes, Marshall reached for his friend. "Give me a minute, Joe."

"All the time you want." Joe knew he needed to prepare for what might or might not happen next. They both did. Neither man dared voice what blindness would mean to Marshall, to his hopes of doctoring, to his life with his daughter, whom he'd not yet seen with his own eyes.

"Before these bandages come off, I want to say something." Marshall struggled to get hold of his emotions. "Thank you. Thank you for being my friend, for standing by me . . . for all you've done for Violet, for what you did for Ivy."

"You've already thanked me. You know I'd do it again."

"I do know that, but I know that if I can't see, my life is gonna change forever. I won't be able to join you and Doc Vishnevsky in practice. I won't be able to see my daughter. I can hardly walk now."

"But you're walking better every day. Your leg's healing."

"Let me finish." Marshall's voice grew husky.

Joe clamped his mouth closed.

"If I can't see . . . Uncle Olney and I have talked this over. I'll go live with them. Violet will come and be with us. I'll learn to do whatever I can to help earn our keep, but I don't want you hanging around, giving up your life and your dreams because you feel sorry for me. You promise me you'll go on, build your life. Promise me, Joe."

Joe's throat thickened. He couldn't breathe and he couldn't promise. "You're my family, Marshall . . . you and your family. That's all I've got. You can't make me—"

"You're a brilliant doctor. You've got a future with Celia, if you want it, I'm pretty sure. But here or somewhere else, you've got to go meet that future, not be held back. You understand me? You promise me before you take those bandages off."

How could Joe promise such a thing? Marshall's family in No Creek, his daughter, Celia . . . Joe couldn't imagine giving up any one of them. But he knew in Marshall's place he'd be demanding the same from his friend. "I'll do my best. That's all I've got right now."

Marshall hesitated. It clearly wasn't the promise he'd wanted, but at last he nodded.

"I'm gonna close the window blinds, mostly, and turn out the light now. Whatever light you can see will be a shock, so take it in slowly."

"I'm ready."

Gently, oh, so gently, Joe pulled the first layer of bandages from Marshall's eyes. Marshall didn't move, didn't twitch a muscle. The second layer came off. The skin on Marshall's closed eyelids looked frail, thin, and Joe wondered what could possibly be left beneath those damaged lids.

Marshall's eyelids opened a crack and then closed. Joe's heart sank, but still he held his breath. They opened again, a little wider this time. Joe could see Marshall's pupils, but they stared straight ahead, not a muscle in his face moving. Marshall's eyes closed again, this time with a squint and frown, as if trying to conjure vision. At last he opened them, once more staring straight ahead.

Joe resisted the urge to wave his hand in front of his friend's face. Marshall breathed in and out. Was he accepting what couldn't be changed? Joe's jaw set. Marshall swallowed, his Adam's apple visibly going up and down, and turned away.

Joe closed his own eyes, swallowing defeat. When he opened them, Marshall was staring in his face, a half grin showing white teeth. "Ugly as ever. You always operate with your eyes closed, Dr. Rossetti?"

Joe shuddered. "You can see? You can see!" It was all Joe could do not to clap Marshall on the back, a thing that would surely send shots of pain through his friend's body.

"I see. I see every little thing in this room. Now open that blind—a little at a time—and let me see how well I see."

Joe opened the blind gradually, allowing Marshall time to adjust to the light. No one kept track of the time. But before they were through, Marshall demonstrated his ability to see well enough to read. It was the biggest battle either of them anticipated. Walking and regaining the intricate use of his hands would be new ventures and take more time.

"You're beating this, just like you've beaten every other thing that's come your way, Marshall. God be praised!"

"God be praised is right. I'm not done yet. I've got Violet to get ready for. Can't have her seeing me like this. I mean to run to meet my daughter. The way things are going, it's okay that she's not here yet. I don't want her to see her daddy lying in a hospital bed. You get that physical therapy lined up for me, Joe. I'm ready."

"I'm not sure your burns are ready to—"

"I said I'm ready, and I mean to get working."

"Yes, sir, Dr. Raymond. I'll see what I can do." Joe couldn't wipe the grin off his face, nor did he try.

Chapter Fifty-Five

SEPTEMBER 1948

True to her word and determined to meet with everyone before returning to college, Celia had visited every colored household with Mercy Tate, Ruby Lynne Wishon, and Reverend Pierce, and every white household with Reverend Willard or Miss Lill, rallying women to her cause for the medical clinic. Some of the men had proven harder to persuade, especially since Rhoan Wishon had not endorsed the venture. Not a word had been said to anyone about the land needed for the enterprise, except that the Willards were ready to make provision.

Meanwhile, Marshall was doing so well in his rehabilitation that Joe had begun to make the train trip back to Garden's Gate on Friday, then return to Winston-Salem on Monday, so Celia sat beside him in church that Sunday.

Celia could hardly listen to Reverend Willard's sermon interpreting the parable of the Good Samaritan focused on loving and caring for our neighbors, though it was surely meant to hit the target. She knew what Ruby Lynne planned next, and it was all Celia could do to stay seated next to Joe, even with his hand wrapped around hers.

After the last hymn, the last prayer, and benediction, Ruby Lynne walked to the front of the church and sat in the pew beside Miss Lill. She'd been sitting in the back with her daddy, her son in between them. For every peek Celia had stolen through the sermon, she'd seen Rhoan's arm wrapped around his grandson.

Reverend Willard began, "As you all know, Celia Percy and my wife or I have visited your homes these recent weeks, talking over with you the idea of building and supporting a shared medical clinic. Reverend Pierce, Mrs. Tate, Ruby Lynne Wishon, and Celia have visited a number of our colored brethren in the community. Nearly every household has committed to supporting the endeavor however they're able, including members of Saints Delight. Isn't that right, Reverend Pierce?"

Every head turned toward the back of the church. Jaws dropped. No one had heard Reverend Pierce step into the building. No one had ever known the colored preacher to walk into Shady Grove church at all.

Before a word could be said, Reverend Pierce nodded and smiled enthusiastically. "That's right, Reverend Willard. I have the word of half a dozen men ready, willing, and able to help build, soon as we're all ready."

"Excellent!" Reverend Willard clapped, Miss Lill clapped, Ruby Lynne clapped, Celia clapped, and everybody near them clapped in response to the preacher's clapping, which set most of the church to clapping and nervously smiling. "I expect we'll have just as many good men here ready to join in that building. Thank you, Reverend Pierce!" Reverend Willard's smile liked to bust his face.

Ruby Lynne raised her hand. "Reverend Willard, might I say a few words?"

Reverend Willard hesitated but got his smile back on. "Yes, of course, Ruby Lynne."

Ruby Lynne motioned for Kenny to come forward. Celia looked back in time to see Rhoan reluctantly pull his arm from around his grandson's shoulders, confusion crossing his suntanned face. Kenny walked up the center aisle to join his mother.

Ruby Lynne laid a hand on her son's back, drew a deep breath, and looked up at the congregation. "I want to thank you all for the wonderful way you've accepted Kenny and me this summer. We're going to miss you all now that we'll be going back to Tennessee for the school year. I want to say how sorry we are about the fire and how it started. There's no way I can thank Dr. Raymond enough for saving my son's life, at terrible risk to his own. But it goes to show how lucky we are to have him for a doctor here in No Creek, if he chooses to stay."

That didn't go over as well as Celia wished it had. Too many would not let a colored doctor touch them.

"There's not much I can do to make up for the wrongs my family has done or to properly thank Dr. Raymond. The thing I can do is to right one wrong, and I feel I need to do that here, in church, with God and you all as my witness."

Rhoan struggled to his feet in the back pew. Eyes shifted in his direction. Celia would have sworn she could hear a pin drop, but Ruby Lynne ignored him.

"I hope Reverend and Mrs. Willard don't mind me saying this, but we ought to all come clean. Years ago, Mr. Belvidere, Miz Hyacinth's daddy, sold my granddaddy Wishon a piece of land that had already been given to the Tate family for years of service."

Rhoan opened his mouth to speak, but Ruby Lynne kept going. "As I understand it, Mr. Grayson Belvidere, Miz Hyacinth's daddy, sold my granddaddy land at a cooked-up auction—land that both men knew had already been registered and deeded to Obadiah Tate by Horace Belvidere and his firstborn son, Captain Elliott Belvidere. But my granddaddy and others from No Creek helped Grayson Belvidere burn the courthouse where the deed was recorded to keep it from being known."

"Ruby Lynne!" Rhoan bellowed.

A gasp ran through the church, but Celia saw from the eyes of a few old-timers cast to the floor that the story might not have been news to everyone.

"Then Grayson Belvidere sold that land to my granddaddy, and you all know what happened to Olney Tate's daddy when he tried to buy back the land that rightly belonged to his family. Now Mrs. Willard's offered to buy back that land at a fair price, a good price, so she can do right by the Tate family, but—"

"Ruby Lynne!" Rhoan wouldn't be stopped this time. "My daddy made Troy and me swear on a stack of Bibles never to sell that land. I can't go back on that."

"You don't have to. I checked with the courthouse and the land was in Uncle Troy's name. Granddaddy left it to him, and he left it to me."

"For Kenny, because—" Rhoan stopped cold when he saw Kenny looking at him.

"As I said, he left it to me. I've earned every piece of dirt on that land and more. Because Olney Tate declined to accept it, I've signed the deed over to its rightful heir and owner, Dr. Marshall Raymond, who has accepted the deed along with my sincere apologies for all the hurt my family has caused. It's registered. It's done."

Rhoan turned three shades of purple, hefted his crutches under his arm, and hobble-stomped out of the church.

Celia drew a ragged breath and exchanged a tenuous smile with Ruby Lynne, astonished at her courage. Even so, she would not want to be in Ruby Lynne's shoes going home to meet her daddy for Sunday dinner.

Chapter Fifty-Six

NOVEMBER 1948

September turned to October and October to November. The week before Thanksgiving brought Celia, Ruby Lynne, and Kenny home for the holiday. On Monday, the Percys, Willards, Tates, and Doc Vishnevsky along with the McHones all joined forces at Garden's Gate to celebrate Marshall's homecoming and the exchange of the land. Even Rhoan showed up, which proved to Celia that there must be at least a grudging peace between father and daughter.

Celia and Miss Lill had put all the leaves in the dining-room table and covered it with Miz Hyacinth's best damask tablecloth. Celia had joined Joe, who was still living and interning in No Creek, to go out the day before to gather bittersweet, pine cones, split milkweed pods and anything to provide a splash of color for Miss Lill to arrange with small pumpkins and candles atop a cream-colored runner the length of the table.

It was a momentous day, a day to celebrate the righting of a terrible wrong—one of many. Miss Lill said that nothing was too grand for such an occasion. She'd pulled out her Grandaunt Hyacinth's fine crystal and polished the Belvidere silver until she got too peaked and asked Celia to carry on.

Celia's mama and daddy and Chester had come all the way from Norfolk to help cook and celebrate. Mercy Tate insisted on bringing her sweet potato pie and whipped cream, which made any occasion special.

Joe and Olney Tate had left in Dr. Vishnevsky's automobile that morning to fetch Marshall from the hospital in Winston-Salem, where he was being discharged. Everyone had agreed to wait until Marshall could be present for this moment. His mother had been a Tate, after all, so Marshall and Olney represented the two remaining branches of the Tate family.

The Willards' attorney, Mr. Bellmont, was there with all the legal documents.

Celia and Miss Lill had created a display of Minnie Belvidere's diary, the manumission papers, the copy of the original deed, letters from the attic, and all the memorabilia that Chester and Celia had discovered after the storm. Once completed, it became, for Celia, a moment of turning in one direction and seeing all those she loved and lived among. Turning the other direction, she stepped back in time, nearly a century, into the heart and mind of Minnie Belvidere. She only wished that Minnie, Obadiah and Martha Tate, and Granny Chree could be with them to see this day. How Miz Hyacinth would have rejoiced to know the truth of all that had happened, and that her family's promise to the Tate family had finally been kept, Celia could only imagine.

Celia was halfway to the kitchen when something made her turn to see Mercy Tate slip a yellowed paper into the portfolio on display, kiss her fingers, touch the paper, turn the page, and walk away.

Celia knew her mama needed her help finishing up the meal, but curiosity got the better of her. Once everyone had entered the parlor, Celia returned to the memorabilia table and pulled the brittle paper from the portfolio. She gasped. *A letter . . . from Minnie.*

My dearest friends, Obadiah and Martha,

It is with a broken heart that I've received your letter. To imagine Belvidere Hall without Rose and dear Hyacinth without her mother is a world come to its end. I cannot imagine what my brother thinks of his life now or how he will parent two daughters alone.

I pray that baby Camellia thrives and am thankful that Rose survived the birth long enough to name her darling daughter— a beautiful flower name, like her own. I'm thankful that Hyacinth now has a baby sister who will surely grow into the closest of friends—two years is but a little space for sisters. I grieve for the loss of their mother . . . and my dear friend.

How grateful and glad I am that Alma continues as Hyacinth's nanny and surely will care for Camellia. My nieces are in the best of hands and the most loving of arms.

I am so very sorry that their own dear Rodney succumbed to the fever, so very sorry that she and Shadrach have not birthed another child of their own—and now to hear that Shadrach was crushed by that wagon load. I pray he recovers and regains the use of his legs. How cruel and hard this life can be. Please give my love to Alma and let her know of my constant prayers. If only I were there to help her, if only I could return.

Thank you for these years of sharing my letters with Rose and for keeping me abreast of the family's news.

As sad as I am to say it, I agree with you both, based on all you say, that now is not the time to approach Grayson about the land. I had so hoped that Rose would live to see justice done. Now I am afraid that we must hope for Hyacinth to grow with the heart of her mother. Know that if ever the opportunity presents itself, I will champion your cause and press my brother to make this right, if that is more help than hindrance. You and I know where the legal documents lie until then.

Aunt Maud continues to fail. I do not expect her to be with us long and I will grieve her passing. She has been most kind and generous to Ellie and to me. As much as I miss you all, I look back and can see the loving hand of Providence in bringing us here.

Never did I imagine I'd find love in this life. But there is a man, a gentleman in every respect, who has become very dear to me and I to him, someone to whom I've confided all that has gone before, and still, he loves me. You will understand what wonder that is to me. He has asked for my hand in marriage and is willing and glad to adopt Ellie as his own—our own. We plan to marry in the spring. I'm not sure we will stay here in Dare County after Aunt Maud passes, but I will write you of any change of address.

Ellie has basked in the sunshine of Aunt Maud's love and doting, so like the grandmother she's never known. She thrives in the light that sparkles each morning on the sea. We take long walks along the shore together and enjoy lively conversations with local fishermen and their wives. "Salt of the earth" is just the way I'd describe these dear souls.

Our school for freed men and women and their children continues to grow, as does my delight in teaching. I know this is temporary, for marriage will change things for me. I see teachers rising up from among my students—teachers who will soon take my place. I am not sorry, for it is the way it should be—should have been long before now.

The longer I am away from Belvidere Hall, the better I understand what an artificial universe we lived in before the war and even after. I'm thankful that Ellie is growing up in a more real world, that she is able to appreciate those with whom she lives and interacts as equals.

I'm thankful that Mother and Father and even our dear Elliott did not live to see what Belvidere Hall has become. Sometimes I imagine what life would have been like after the war if they had lived, if they'd been able to inaugurate the changes that you and they intended. Is No Creek ready for a better, more just world? Perhaps not yet, but someday, I pray. I pray most of all that you and your children and Alma and Shadrach live to see that change.

Forever your friend and sister in Christ,
Minnie

So, they really had known about the hidden room, the trunk— everything, all along. The Tates had suffered and waited—for generations—trusting, like Minnie, that someday justice would be done. Celia understood the security of owning land, inherited wealth, and the possibility for everything so many took for granted. Denied, delayed. But today, at last, something would change.

Minnie found love. I'm glad. I hope Ellie did. I know what it means.

"Celia! I need you, Daughter!" her mama called from the kitchen.

Celia opened the letter and laid it on top of the portfolio. It should be seen, be read, be known.

"Celia!"

Celia kissed her fingers, laid them on Minnie's signature, then hurried to the kitchen.

She'd just added cider to the stewed apples and pulled her mama's stuffed hens from the oven when she heard the bell over the front door jingle. *It has to be them!* She hadn't seen Marshall since the night of the fire. He'd endured multiple surgeries and physical therapy. She hoped she'd recognize him.

But Celia wasn't first in line. The hallway was crowded with folks welcoming Marshall home, wishing him well, saying one to another, "Step out of the way, let the man through. Right this way, Marshall." Olney, most of all, played the role of protective father to his nephew. Celia caught a glimpse of Marshall, his face scarred from the burns but smiling, looking for all the world as if he might be home at last.

Olney and Joe had ushered Marshall, walking stiffly on his game leg, to the settee in the library, not too near the wood-burning fire. Miss Lill had even wondered if they should forgo a fire that might remind Marshall of that awful night, but it was too cold.

"It's good to have you home, Marshall." Reverend Willard was first to shake his hand.

"It's good to be here, good to be among friends." Marshall's smile and the shine in his eyes liked to split his face.

It was such a thing of beauty Celia ceased to notice the scarring. But Kenny didn't. He ran up to Marshall and it was only because Ruby Lynne grabbed him that the boy didn't leap onto Marshall's lap.

"Let me go, Mama! I just want to see!"

"Kenny, you mustn't touch Dr. Raymond. He might still be sore all over."

"I won't touch him, I promise! I just want to see."

"What is it you want to see, Kenny?" Marshall asked.

"Your war wound. Dr. Joe said you got a bad scarred leg 'cause you got burned saving me. He said it was like a war wound. You were in two wars—over there and here. Nobody I know's been in two wars. I just want to see."

"Marshall, I'm so sorr—"

But Marshall cut Ruby Lynne off. "It's all right. If anybody's got a right to see, it's Kenny." Marshall lifted his pants leg and showed his burn.

Kenny knelt on the floor to see the scarring up close. "Wow." The little boy sat back on his haunches. "That looks like it hurts."

"I don't feel it much now. Most of the nerves are gone."

Kenny stood up and leaned against the settee, looking deeply into Marshall's eyes. "I'm sorry Billy and me started that fire. I'm sorry you got burned."

"I'm sorry, too, Kenny. You won't start any more fires, will you?"

"No, sir."

"You won't play with moonshine or matches anymore?"

Kenny's eyes were round. He looked at his grandpa. "No, sir. I won't."

"That's good," Marshall said. "When we learn something from it, no experience, no matter how hard, is wasted."

"Mama says you're our hero."

Marshall huffed a little, clearly not knowing what to do with that.

"You listen to your mama, Kenny." The gravelly and unexpected voice came from the back of the room, along the wall. Rhoan Wishon stepped up and nodded.

"Mr. Wishon." Marshall's face went deadpan.

Celia held her breath for Marshall's sake. *Who could ever trust a man that tried to hang you? I told Miss Lill we shouldn't have invited him. She's so determined this can all be healed. Well, I don't believe—*

"I thank you for saving my grandson. That was brave."

"I'd have done it for anybody. I might have even done it for you."

The room went silent. Rhoan looked the most sober Celia had ever seen him.

"Don't reckon I'd deserve that."

You could hear the wind in the chimney. Joe wrapped his arm around Celia's waist, pulling her close.

"None of us deserve that kind of grace, Rhoan." Reverend Willard placed a hand on Rhoan's back. "It's a gift."

"Freely given," Marshall added, his face relaxing.

Rhoan heaved a sigh, like he was trying to get hold of himself. "This land return is overdue. I see that now." He looked Marshall in the eye. Rhoan looked about as uncomfortable as a man could look. He nodded toward Marshall's leg. "If there's something I can do for you, you tell me."

Surprise registered in Marshall's eyes, but he held his gaze steady with Rhoan's. "Think you can call me Dr. Raymond?"

Color swept over Rhoan's face and down his neck. Tension in the room ratcheted. Moments passed. A log from the fire dropped, sending cinders onto the hearth. Celia ran for the hearth broom so they wouldn't catch the rug. She nearly missed it when Rhoan stepped closer and extended his hand to Marshall.

Marshall struggled to his feet, refusing Joe's help. He stood, unsteadily at first, taking his time, getting a grip on his cane before he met Rhoan's hand and shook it. Both men nodded.

"Mr. Wishon," Marshall said.

"Dr. Raymond."

• • •

Celia looked back on that day as perhaps the most momentous in No Creek history. At least it was a beginning in the healing of the families and races represented in No Creek.

It was a turning point for Marshall, who'd been as ready to leave No Creek as Ruby Lynne had once been. It was another step in Rhoan Wishon's rehabilitation, which Celia figured would likely take a sight more time and patience than Marshall's physical rehabilitation.

Plans for the clinic were on the tip of everyone's tongue. Because the ground was late in freezing that year, they'd already broken ground and were framing the building. Celia worried that too many men with hammers, all thinking they were king of the mountain and sure their ideas were right, might come to blows.

Mostly, Celia anticipated the day that Doctors Vishnevsky, Raymond, and Rossetti would cut the ribbon across the door together. Celia knew that segregation was still the law of the land, the code of the hills, and the way the medical clinic would operate, but inroads were being made in the community that neither she nor Joe had dreamed possible, and that was a very good thing.

Epilogue

CELIA SPENT THE EARLY DAYS OF her December break in Norfolk with her parents, then took the train back to No Creek after her December 15 birthday. She could hardly wait to see Joe.

Flying through the front door of Garden's Gate, Celia nearly jingled the bell off its hook, expecting a warm welcome. "I'm home! Joe! Miss Lill, I'm home!"

But no answer came. Not a lamp was lit. The house stood cold and empty.

Celia prayed that didn't mean anything ran amiss. Joe was probably still working. Miss Lill had discovered the sickness she was experiencing promised a happy ending, a little bundle of joy come early spring. *Please God, don't let there be a problem with the baby!*

Sunlight had begun to fade when she decided she couldn't wait longer. *If anybody knows where they are, Doc Vishy will.* His phone line rang and rang, but there was no answer. *Where are you, Doc? Where are the McHones? Where's Joe? Surely someone's there!* But no one answered and the Tates had no phone. The roads were beginning to ice up and dusk was falling fast. The best she could do was to build a fire, make some tea, and find something in the larder to cook for dinner.

Celia had just laid a fire in the library when she looked up to see a parade of lights out the front window. Old fears, memories of the night so long ago when the Klan had marched in to burn the barn and frighten them to death, surged through her. Her heart beating against its cage, Celia crept to the window and stood behind the curtain, looking out.

Her eyes narrowed, trying to focus on the bobbing lights. They weren't torches but lanterns and flashlights. There were no men in white sheets and hoods but groups—families—walking, some swinging giggling children between them, some slipping on the icy road, laughing and talking. It was like a party—a winter parade party—and they were all headed down the road.

Celia opened the front door. From farther away came the sounds of singing, a melody sweet and pure, growing stronger as it neared. More lanterns, more flashlights, and soon the choir from Saints Delight. Celia could stand it no longer. "Reverend Pierce!" she called. "What is it? What's going on?"

"Celia Percy—you home, child?"

"Just got in from Norfolk. Nobody's here. I can't get hold of Doc Vishy or Joe or anybody. Do you know where they are?"

"I expect they'll be pulling into the platform any minute. Grab your coat and come join us!"

Celia blinked. *The train? Where would they have gone on the train? Why is everybody going to meet them?* But the parade was marching on and Celia was about to miss it. She grabbed her coat and a flashlight from the kitchen drawer. Wrapping a scarf over her head and pulling on gloves, she closed the door, the bell jingling merrily. Slipping and sliding over frozen paving stones that led to the gate and the road, Celia did her best to catch up.

Last in the parade and just behind the choir, she made it to the train platform as the train slid to a stop. It looked like most of No Creek was there, certainly all the colored community and a few of the white. The choir sang on, filling the night with reverence, with thanksgiving, with awe.

The train door opened, and a conductor jumped to the platform, taking down luggage Reverend Willard handed him. Then Reverend

Willard stepped down, awkward on his artificial leg, turned, and took Miss Lill's hand. In the lantern light Celia could see the little swell beneath her coat. She looked tired, but happy.

Next came Joe, who stopped on the bottom step, turned back to the train, and offered his hand first to Mercy, then to Olney, as they stepped down onto the platform. On the train's top step stood Marshall, holding a little girl in a red coat and hat, nestled tight against his chest, her eyes watching the spectacle on the platform, wide in wonder. The smile on Marshall's face was enough to light a thousand lanterns.

Mercy Tate reached up for the child, but Marshall wasn't about to let her go. Cheers rose from the crowd. Congratulations for Marshall and the Tates followed one upon another, and shouts rang out of *"Welcome home, princess!"* and *"We've been waiting for you, Miss Violet!"*

Celia felt her own heart swell to bursting, felt the tears sting her cheeks in the cold. Marshall—everyone—had waited so long. All she could think was that the Lord had heard their voices, all their pleas here and across the ocean, across the decades as far back as Minnie and Elliott, and had not only answered them, but had worked in changing hearts, turning the many cries into a symphony. No longer was it a hundred crickets screeching, but a choir, a hundred crickets singing a chorus of praise, just like the Scripture that she and Miss Lill had written in their letters for years. "The Lord thy God in the midst of thee is mighty; he will save, he will rejoice over thee with joy; he will rest in his love, he will joy over thee with singing."

Magnificent wasn't a big enough word, not even for Celia. Reverend Willard and Miss Lill waved, and Celia waved back for all she was worth, slipping in for a hug and her own welcome home.

"I'd have written, but there wasn't time," said Miss Lill, breathless. "We got word just day before yesterday that Violet was coming—on her way. We traveled day and night to get to New York to meet her."

"Marshall looks every bit the proud and happy father," Celia marveled. He was only a few years older than she was, and yet he looked as if he'd matured beyond reason.

The next moment an ecstatic Joe was by Celia's side. "You're home!" He swept her up in the air, right off her feet, and twirled her around, hugging her for all he was worth. It was an entrance and welcome Celia had only dreamed of. "She's home, Celia! Violet's finally home."

At last Joe set her down. Celia, her smile stretching inside and out, reached for his face with both hands. *Thank you, Lord! All our voices, all our prayers, come together!*

"Celia Percy, if I've never told you, I need to now. You're my forever home, my always family." He breathed her name again and kissed her hair, her cheek, her lips.

"And always will be," Celia, barely able to breathe, returned, her heart too full for more.

Joe leaned his forehead against hers, brushed her lips with his own once more, and whispered, "And always will be."

• • •

Returning to school was a hard choice for Celia. She doubted that she'd ever use that teaching degree, now that she'd determined to write and had garnered the courage to tell her mama and Miss Lill so . . . and since Joe had proposed marriage on Christmas Eve and championed her dream. Still, education was an important opportunity, and she remembered what Marshall had said to Kenny—*No experience is wasted if we learn something.*

She'd already started submitting short stories to *The Saturday Evening Post*, *The Atlantic*, *Good Housekeeping*, and on a whim, to *The New Yorker*. "Rejection letters make good wallpaper," Celia declared to Joe, "better than the Sears and Roebuck catalogue and issues of the *Journal-Patriot* that papered my cabin walls when I was a kid."

"They're just stepping-stones," Joe had insisted, holding her close. "Battle scars. You'll get there; you know you will. Look what you've already accomplished right here in No Creek—better and more imaginative than fiction."

Celia grinned. She loved that Joe knew her, that he loved her and loved her dreams almost as much as she did.

Late the night before returning to college, as everyone in the house slept, Celia found herself wide-awake. It seemed that life had come full circle since the night of the storm that had ripped open the attic room so many years ago.

She'd be leaving Garden's Gate for good when she and Joe married. It wouldn't be right to take away the treasures she'd discovered in the attic, let alone Minnie Belvidere's diary from the house in which it was penned.

Celia switched on the lamp beside her bed and pulled Minnie's diary, the two collections of *Les Misérables,* and the portfolio of returned documents from her wardrobe. She wrapped herself in the throw from the corner rocker and crept up to the attic, to the secret room, to the chest with the false bottom. She lifted the lid, pulled out the contents, and poked her finger into the hole at the bottom, lifting the panel made to fit securely. She hugged Minnie's diary to her chest, as if saying goodbye to a friend, and tucked the book in the bottom, atop the other books.

One day, perhaps far into the future, another girl would discover these treasures and wonder about them. It would only be fair that she'd find the diary to unravel all the pieces of their mystery.

Celia knew Minnie had hoped that Hyacinth would take up the cause of the Tates and Alma in her time, that one day there would be mercy and justice, when all would be made right. Minnie had considered it the true mission of the Belvidere women.

But that hadn't happened. As far as Celia and Miss Lill knew, Miz Hyacinth had never known about the secret room, or discovered the copies of *Les Miserables*, the legal document copies, or Minnie's diary—never even met her aunt, let alone knew how she'd loved her.

Celia could only guess that Minnie had died with questions unresolved—so many questions she'd written, surrendered to the Lord, trusting He would make things right in His time.

But the truth was, Miz Hyacinth had done what she could. Without knowing anything about her daddy's deception, she'd kept faith with Granny Chree and the Tates, giving and accepting their friendship and love. She'd kept an open door for the members of Saints Delight and taught every child she could for years, sharing her books—who knew how far and wide. She'd willed what she'd believed was a prime plot of Belvidere land to Olney Tate and honored the gift her aunt had made of the cabin to Granny Chree all her days, evidently never knowing the background story.

All her life, Miz Hyacinth had stood against the Klan, doing the best she knew how to shield her friends, even when her own daddy stood at the head of it. And in the end, in her last days, she continued those relationships and that determination through Miss Lill and the library. Without ever knowing, Miz Hyacinth was a Belvidere woman after Minnie's own heart.

Celia marveled that she, a girl who came from not much and not a Belvidere woman at all, had been privileged to make the discovery Minnie had longed for. *Why? Why me?* She didn't know but thanked God for the opportunity—and the gift.

She thought again of some future girl discovering those treasures, her young heart burning for justice and mercy. And then, because she was a lover of tales and amazing new words, Celia couldn't help but think that all that had happened might make a fine story for that imaginative girl and perhaps for other girls to read . . . a long story . . . a full-length book. *Who better to write that book than me?* And with that thought blooming, Celia figured she might never sleep again.

Note to Readers

LONG HAVE I LOVED THE CHARACTERS brought to life in my first No Creek novel, *Night Bird Calling*. They are friends and family, some cohorts and some folks I'll forever hold at bay, the small town we all might have grown up in or imagined from a bygone era.

I was not ready to leave those dear souls behind but felt eager to better understand their past and wanted to imagine their future. In them and their history I saw a microcosm of our world, of our past, and wondered what they might have to say to us, so many decades later.

I felt the same about our national narrative on race. I needed to understand more about the past in order to make sense of the present and garner realistic hope for the future.

In history classes there has long been a gap between the abolition of slavery in the 1860s and the march for Civil Rights in the 1960s, let alone where we are today. What happened during Reconstruction? Why was it cut short? How and why did Jim Crow first appear? Why did we, as Americans, allow the oppression and cruelty of Jim Crow after fighting a bloody civil war meant to end slavery? Why was there still division of race in the US military during WWII, and what was the result of that? Why were black American soldiers treated differently in Europe than they were in America—even after fighting a war to end Nazi supremacy, persecution, and oppression of other races and minorities? Were black American hopes of "double victory"—victory in the war and victory at home—realistic?

News reports such as the blinding of Sergeant Isaac Woodard, a returning black WWII veteran in uniform, just hours after being honorably discharged, by a South Carolina police officer suggest not. Sergeant Woodard's experience inspired the beating that Private Marshall Raymond received in *A Hundred Crickets Singing* when, honorably discharged, he stepped off the train in No Creek.

There were measures written into our laws to help veterans returning from WWII, but did the American GI Bill help all veterans regardless of race? If so, why did comparatively few black GIs benefit? Why the continued disparity in wealth and opportunities? Why does such a divide still exist today? What does it mean to grow up white in our society? What does it mean to grow up as a person of color in our society?

Researching these topics opened a floodgate of new questions, insights, and revelations that I'd never gleaned in history class. More digging was required. In that digging and through personal interviews, I discovered a mine I'd not tapped—historical records; books; firsthand accounts, anecdotes, and stories; film footage, newspaper clippings, and propaganda.

The memories of older people, many now passed, were precious troves. Little did they know what a treasure their records and stories would prove to writers—novelists, attempting to tell the stories of their time.

Though the characters and experiences in *A Hundred Crickets Singing* are fictitious, many are based on compilations of the experiences of real people.

Elliott Belvidere's Civil War experience as a Southern militia captain who remained loyal to the Constitution, was tried and condemned to death for treason by Jefferson Davis, and finally reprieved to serve as a Confederate army cook and later as an ambulance driver through the intervention of a superior officer was inspired by the archives, the stand, and experiences of Samuel Smith Goforth, my great-great-grandfather. His story helped me realize that few issues leading to war are clear-cut to those caught in its reality.

History judges in retrospect, when victors and facts are better known, and the trajectory of paths and their consequences plain to see. Living in the moment and through such times is a different story.

Issues and "sides" expressed through many voices, each one convinced they are right, that God is on their side, determined to carry the day, can create confusion—a hundred crickets screeching—or glimpses into a path forward. As Celia wondered, how can God listen to all that? Does He take sides in war? The Union and Confederate armies were each convinced that God was on their side, as many have been in wars and arguments since.

No matter what we judge to be true, it is clear that wars and the causes they battle in the first place are of our own making. The important question is not whose side is God on, but are we on God's side and will we allow Him to change our hearts to become more like His? In that transformation, our cacophony is more likely to become a hymn of praise, a symphony of very different instruments—lives lived to bring Him glory and praise and to dwell with one another in harmony.

Listening with a determination to understand the why behind rhetoric and actions, even those we deplore, can help us reach across the divide to one another as human beings, discard lies and propaganda, defuse anger, embrace truth on every side, deal straightforwardly with consequences, and build pathways to a better tomorrow.

I'm reminded of a poem that I learned while growing up, "If We Only Understood," attributed to Rudyard Kipling. The final lines capture the heart of its message: *"We would love each other better if we only understood."*

I hope that *A Hundred Crickets Singing* is a step in that direction.

I love hearing from you. Write to me through my website, cathygohlke.com. Let me know what you think and what you see or are doing to help heal the wounds in our world, in our nation, in your community or family. Know that I am praying God's rich blessings for you.

By His amazing grace,
Cathy Gohlke

Readers can subscribe to my newsletter and find me at my website, cathygohlke.com, on Facebook at CathyGohlkeBooks, on Goodreads, and follow me on Bookbub. Through my website I'm glad to schedule virtual visits with book clubs, schools, churches, or reading groups.

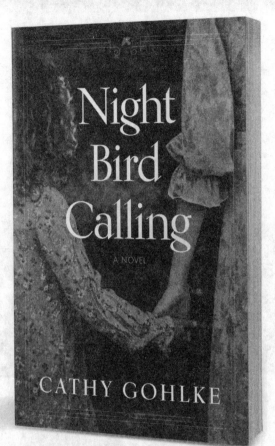

Discussion Questions

1. Elliott Belvidere is a North Carolina native determined to remain loyal to the Constitution even when his state secedes and joins the Confederacy. What do you think of his refusal to bear arms for the Confederacy, even to the point of death? What do you imagine you'd have done in his position?

2. *Les Misérables* was popular with both Union and Confederate troops during the American Civil War, but they identified with the story in different ways. How does Tom's reaction to the book differ from Minnie's? Where have you seen examples of people interpreting the same words through different eyes and hearts?

3. How does Minnie attempt to ensure that her family's wishes regarding the land deeded to Obadiah and Martha Tate will be heeded? In what ways is she held back by the constraints of her time? How does Celia try to help, and what barriers does she encounter, even so many years later?

4. After his parents died when he was only six years old, Joe stopped believing God cared or had the power to stop such things from happening. How does his faith change over the course of this story? Which characters influence him along the way? Who has played a pivotal role in your own journey of faith?

5. Black Americans who served in WWII generally received more respect and better treatment by foreign governments and societies than they were used to at home. Were they right to expect that race relations and treatment would have improved when they returned to the US—Double V for Double Victory? What did they discover upon returning? How do you think that affected them then and in their future?

6. What do you think of Britain's early policy regarding the adoption of "brown babies"—children born of black American soldiers and white British women and placed in orphanages? Why do you think Britain did not want to recognize paternal rights of the biological fathers? Do you think their decisions were based on issues of race, politics, prejudice, or something else?

7. Alma, later called Granny Chree, willed her life savings to Marshall, but neither Granny Chree nor the Tates told Marshall that she was his great-grandaunt. Why do you imagine he was not told? Why do you think Olney didn't want to talk about slavery days or reopen the question of his family's land?

8. The GI Bill, signed by President Franklin Delano Roosevelt on June 22, 1944, provided returning veterans with unique opportunities to procure higher education, housing, low-interest loans to start businesses, and a year of unemployment compensation. Black veterans, while not strictly excluded, were not as able to take advantage of those benefits as white veterans. How did the ability or inability to take advantage of the GI Bill affect different people? Did those advantages or disadvantages affect your family? In what way?

9. Celia knows that "in No Creek, there were things you just didn't ask, opinions you dared not give voice to, unless you were sure of the person." How is this demonstrated in both the Civil War and WWII eras? In what ways does No Creek change in the intervening years?

10. Joe believes that "sharing a good time and good food always helps. It sets the stage for harmony." Is he proven right through the community pasta dinner? Have you experienced a time when food and fellowship broke down barriers?

11. Grayson Belvidere never told his daughter, Hyacinth, about her aunt Minnie or the work she did to transport enslaved people to freedom and to share the family's land with the freed men and women of Belvidere Hall. Why do you think Grayson never revealed this history to his daughter? In what ways is Minnie's legacy still realized in Hyacinth? In Lilliana? In Celia?

12. The title *A Hundred Crickets Singing* calls to mind a line from Minnie's diary where she laments trying to make sense of the conflicting voices all around her. But Celia eventually likens all the voices and prayers across the decades to "a choir, a hundred crickets singing a chorus of praise." Discuss that change in perspective. Where have you seen God work—over many years or even many lifetimes—to bring harmony out of what might at first seem like chaos and discord?

About the Author

Bestselling, Christy Hall of Fame, and Carol and INSPY Award–winning author CATHY GOHLKE writes novels steeped with inspirational lessons, speaking of world and life events through the lens of history. She champions the battle against oppression, celebrating the freedom found only in Christ. Cathy has worked as a school librarian, drama director, and director of children's and education ministries. When not traveling to historic sites for research, she and her husband, Dan, divide their time between northern Virginia and the Jersey Shore, enjoying time with their grown children and grandchildren. Visit her website at cathygohlke. com and find her on Facebook at CathyGohlkeBooks; on Bookbub (@CathyGohlke); and on YouTube, where you can subscribe to Book Gems with Cathy Gohlke for short videos of book recommendations.

TYNDALE HOUSE PUBLISHERS IS CRAZY4FICTION!

Fiction that entertains and inspires

Get to know us! Become a member of the Crazy4Fiction community. Whether you read our blog, like us on Facebook, follow us on Twitter, or receive our e-newsletter, you're sure to get the latest news on the best in Christian fiction. You might even win something along the way!

JOIN IN THE FUN TODAY.

 crazy4fiction.com

 Crazy4Fiction

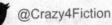 @Crazy4Fiction

CP0021

By purchasing this book from Tyndale, you have
helped us meet the spiritual and physical needs of
people all around the world.

Tyndale | Trusted. For Life.